THE DEVIL AND HER DETAILS

MINA MYLES

Original Cover - Elizianna (@elizianna.the.one)

Chapter Header Art - Sam, Ink and Velvet Designs

Developmental Editing - Sam, Serpent and Sword Author Services

Line & Copy Editing - Cassidy Hudspeth Editing

AUTHOR'S NOTE

Dear lovely reader,

Thank you so much for picking up *The Devil and Her Details*. I've wanted to write a mafia romance for years now, and am so glad it's finally here! Please note that this book contains graphic scenes that involve blood, gore, torture, and gun violence, mentions of human and sex trafficking from rival mafias (off page), domestic abuse (off page) and drug overdose (on page). Moreover the main characters experience loss of their parents, grief, anxiety, panic attacks, and survivor's guilt. This book also contains profanity and explicit sexual acts (all consensual). As much as I would love for you to meet Zahra and Declan, your mental well-being is most important to me.

With Love,
Mina

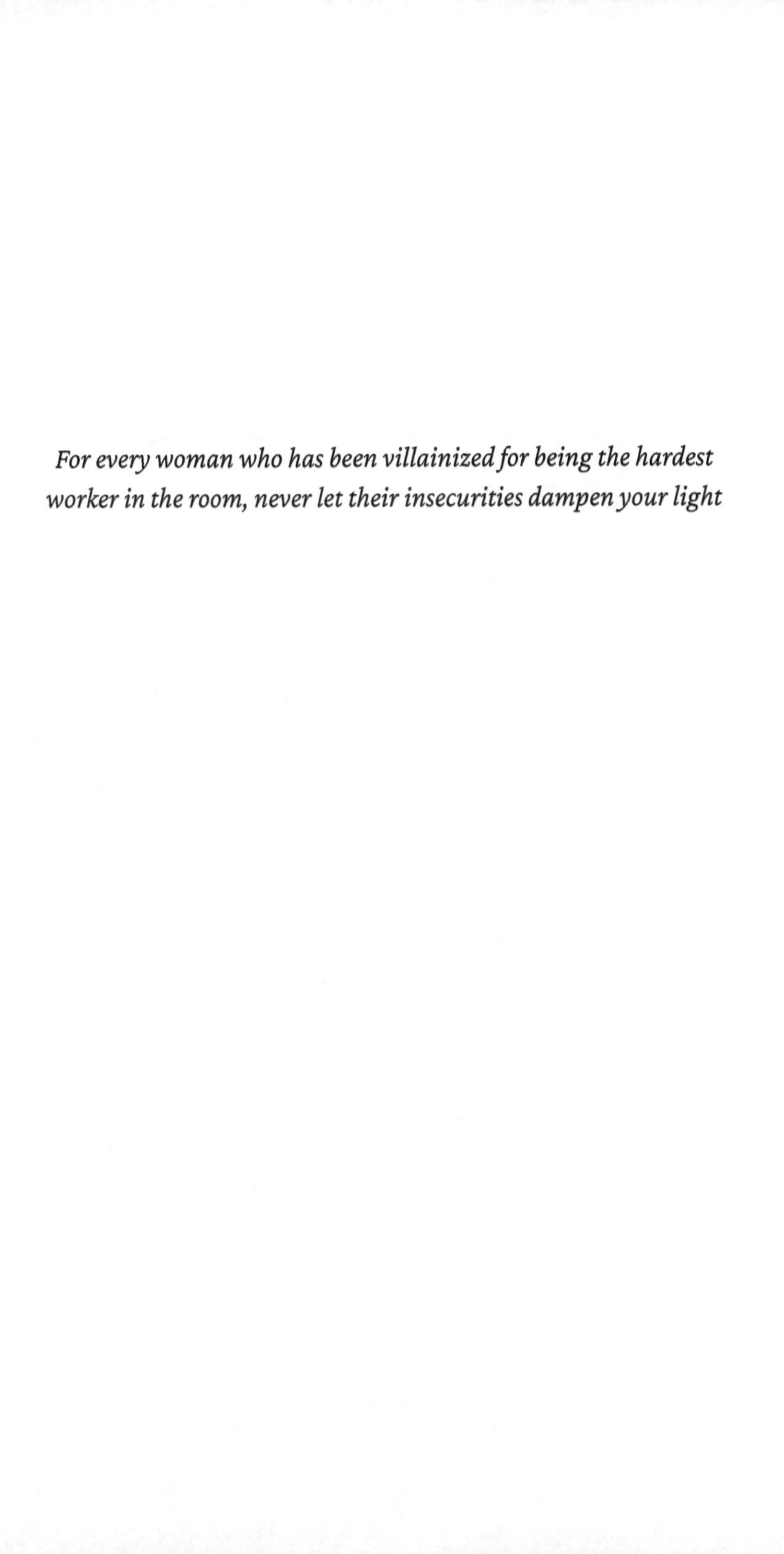

For every woman who has been villainized for being the hardest worker in the room, never let their insecurities dampen your light

PART ONE
TREACHERY

1

DECLAN

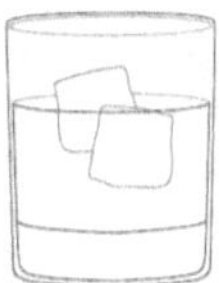

If my uncle opens his mouth again, I'm going to put a bullet through it. I would never understand why my father demanded on his deathbed that his idiot brother serve as my second in command. I was convinced he'd only given Lorkan so much power, even temporarily, to test my patience. That and to push me to find a bride sooner rather than later. Because, naturally, the main thing on my father's mind was chastising me for not finding love yet. My father, the former fucking *mafia boss*, cared more about whose bed I would share for the next few decades than how I would take over the family legacy. I suppose I had spent my entire life working toward the latter, whereas the former had never felt like a priority. The list of women who wanted to be married to a Don was never-ending, so I never considered it a pressing issue. When the time came, I would find someone kind and loyal enough to have an heir with. Until then, my priority would be maintaining the Irish Mob's control over Boston.

My father's rule was responsible for overthrowing the Italians. Though I wasn't around to see it, from the stories I've heard, the war was an absolute blood bath, one that left the city in such disarray that no one dared fuck with us after that. Especially after we rebuilt from the damage and made sure to help support political campaigns that would ensure our control over the city would go unthreatened. It wasn't too hard to get most of the city officials on our side, either, given that the Italian's drug trafficking had started to take its toll on the community.

"God, it's so sterile and dark here. What happened to all the artwork that used to hang on the walls?" my uncle complains.

"They probably took them down given the circumstances."

"Well, it makes this place feel like a hospital basement. Or like someone died," my uncle mutters under his breath in Irish.

My hand twitch, desperate to reach for the Glock tucked in my coat jacket. "Someone *did* die, Uncle," I spit out, "that's the whole reason why we're here."

Loyalty was never something my father would compromise on. The Persians weren't on anyone's radar forty years ago. Still, somehow my father caught wind of the spyware they had been developing and selling to anyone willing to buy it, including your neighborhood housewife who had an inkling that her husband had been cheating on her. My father knew nearly nothing about technology, but he did know that he hated rats. So when Naser Ahzimi approached my father with evidence that his head of security, and second cousin, had been feeding information to the Greeks for months, he felt forever indebted.

In that moment, Naser not only gained my father's trust but also a lifelong friendship. With my father's support, Naser built his own empire in Boston's Little Tehran, and the newly minted Persian Mafia became our strongest ally, which remains to this day.

Their friendship also lasted the length of both of their lives. In their final moments, Naser used his own chest to block the bullet that was meant for my dad. My father made sure I knew it. Made sure his best friend's loyalty would never come into question, as he bled out from a stray bullet that had ricocheted off the banister and into his gut—a message from the Italians for messing with their business.

"Well, it wouldn't have killed them to at least spruce up the place, it bit. Make it feel like a place where we would want to have dinner instead of feeling like we're headed to watch an autopsy," my uncle scoffs, looking at the bodyguards blocking the massive wood-paneled door in front of us with disdain.

While it doesn't surprise me to hear such vile language coming from my uncle, he is a Made Man after all, I can't stop the rage that fills me at how cavalier he is. The last time I stepped foot in the massive mansion that sits alongside the south shore of Massachusetts, it was covered head to toe in traditional Persian adornments and the most elegant paintings and sculptures I'd ever seen. Now the walls and rooms are barren sans for the furniture, as if even the home itself is mourning the death of its owner. I know their mourning all too well, know they are grieving not only the loss of their boss's death, but also the death of my father.

Which is why I refuse to tolerate any disrespect. I turn my head to my uncle so that he can see the rage in my eyes. The jokes he made earlier would be the first and last pass I give him today. He keeps his back straight, attempting to appear unfazed, but I know better. I watch as a bead of sweat trickles down his neck, and I can practically smell the fear coming from him.

"Declan, it's good to see you." Arman, Naser's head of security, is the first to speak. The man next to him is familiar to me as well.

"You too. Though I wish it could be in better circumstances."

I get a nod in response.

"I guess I finally get to meet your new boss. Never understood why Naser was so hellbent on keeping us apart." As close as our fathers were, and the sheer amount Naser used to boast about how incredible his only child was, it always surprised me how he had never introduced us. It was a puzzle that had always bothered me. Our dads were best friends, and Naser viewed me as his own child, yet I never met his son.

Arman gives me a smirk in response. "Probably because he knew the two of you together would unleash hell on earth."

"Incredibly likely. You would think that's what he would want though, no?"

"It can be hard to let go of what you know. And who you love."

The truth behind Arman's words rocks me to my core, freezing me in place. For a second, I see a look of mutual pain flash over his eyes. He breaks the moment by speaking again, "You can bring in one gun. Anything else has to stay behind."

The house rules are second nature to me now. I hand over the gun that was tucked into my sock and the knives that lined my coat jacket. My uncle scoffs at the request but follows through anyway. Arman and his henchmen pat us down before opening the door behind them and standing aside.

My throat goes dry as I take in the familiar dining room table that stretches the length of the room. Any important meeting, and even the non-important dinners, between my father and Naser happened in this room. All of Naser's old commanders have taken their seats, and everything feels so normal that I almost expect my father and Naser to stroll in five minutes late, laughing up a storm about whatever stupid prank they decided to pull. For a moment, the tightness in my chest releases, until my uncle sits in the chair I would normally select, abruptly bringing me back to reality.

As I take my father's seat, *my* seat, everyone's eyes are on me. Well, everyone except for the person to my left, who is feverishly typing endless lines of code on their computer screen. It's all gibberish to me, always has been, yet I can't stop myself from staring at the string of numbers and letters. The rhythmic typing of the keys gives me something to latch onto as my eyes move from the screen to the keyboard, and the delicate manicure is responsible for me practically falling into a trance.

Cyrus, Naser's second in command, is the first to break the silence. "We appreciate you joining us today, Declan. Now more than ever, it's crucial we discuss the terms of our alliance and ensure justice is served to those who dared to threaten our control over the city and stole our family from us." He gestures for the staff to pour our drinks, officially opening our meeting. Naser always insisted that negotiations needed to happen with a clear head while drinking hot tea from Iran, his home country. While my father was always charmed by his musings, my uncle is not.

"You've wasted enough of our time, Cyrus, and I won't have you waste any more. We came here to speak to the new boss. Naser's *heir*. Not his friend who always rode his coattails," my uncle spits, and I do my best not to strangle him then and there. His mouth is about to get him in trouble.

"His heir is present, Lorkan. I would have never started this meeting otherwise. To do so would be an insult to everyone in this room." Cyrus' tone carries a level of lethality that causes several men at the table to grip their weapons—ready to follow through on any command he gives against my uncle. Cyrus waves them down.

As if he didn't have half a dozen men ready to murder him, my uncle continues his disrespectful tirade, "Well, I recognize every man in this room. So, unless you're telling me one of you staged a coup and killed your own boss and my brother so one of you imbeciles could take over—"

Cyrus seethes. "How dare you. I will have you ki—"

"Or perhaps you've been lying to us this entire time. Keeping Naser's heir disguised as a Commander—

"You will *not* question the loyalty or character of our former boss!" Cyrus stands up from his chair and charges at my uncle, who meets him right in the middle.

"I'll do whatever the fuck I want until one of you decides to stop wasting my time and telling me and my nephew the truth."

Everyone stays silent. Unsurprising, given my uncle doesn't have the authority or frankly the respect to be throwing out demands. He huffs at me as if that will bring me to his side. As if he hadn't spent the entire morning testing my limits, pushing me closer and closer to turning him into a target for my shooting practice. I ignore him, no doubt furthering his irritation, and take the time to look at everyone sitting at the table one by one.

Every face is known to me. Every face but the woman sat next to me. Except the more I look at her, the more familiar she becomes. Her eyes are a deep shade of brown I've seen before... The curve of her nose and her high cheekbones...I can't shake the feeling in my gut that I know her somehow. She catches me looking, narrows her eyes, and flares her nostrils.

Holy shit.

I've seen that exact expression a dozen times before. *It can't be, can it?* It has to be. Why else would she be in his seat? My heart starts racing in realization. No wonder Naser wanted to keep his heir's identity hidden.

"Naser's heir is present in the room with us, Uncle. No need to throw a fit." I pick a piece of lint off my suit and flick it off, hoping everyone believes my facade of calm and composed.

"Oh, so this is all one big joke to you all? Trying to push me until I snap. I will not be treated like this!" My uncle slams a fist on the table to assert his dominance. No one is moved.

"There's no need to throw a tantrum, Uncle. If you took a moment to think instead of letting your rage take over, you would come to realize what I have." I give him a pointed look that forces him to sit back in his seat.

"And what, darling nephew, would that be?" he seethes.

"Naser's heir. The new boss of the Persian Empire. His *daughter* has been sitting next to me this whole time." My words fall over the room as I turn my gaze to the stunning woman sitting next to me. She gives me a small nod followed by a smirk that screams *'Took you long enough to figure out.'*

"A woman? You think Naser would let a woman take over his legacy?" my uncle spits vehemently, shaking his head.

"Allow me to make a few things clear, Lorkan. The first is that my father didn't *let* me do anything. I earned my keep. I always do," Naser's daughter finally speaks, her voice so melodic it sends a jolt through my body. "Second, my father never cared about where you come from or who you are. He cared about loyalty, intelligence, and work ethic. All three things I possess in spades. All three things make me an excellent boss."

Well said.

My uncle is less convinced. "You can't be serious? Sweetheart, I appreciate you wanting to step up and take over for your father, but this job is not for the frail or faint of heart."

Her eyes narrow to slits. "I'm aware. I'm neither of those things."

I look at every member of Naser's former cavalry.

Every man looked at Naser's daughter with nothing but respect and care. It was clear she had their unconditional support. And if Naser wanted her at the helm, then so did I. It was that simple.

"Declan, are you going to say something?" My uncle looks to me as if *I'm* the one who's making a fool of himself.

"Naser has made his choice. And I respect that fully."

An unsettling silence comes over the room, the only noise coming from the grandfather clock sitting at the other side of the room. The hands tick as I wait for whatever pending explosion is bound to come. If my uncle were smart, he would know better than to push the Persians. Know better than to push me. But intelligence and self-restraint were never my uncle's forte, which is why I have no doubts my father put me in charge of babysitting his petulant younger brother.

If my uncle had seemed pissed before, he's now reaching a level of outrage and distress that matches that of a hungry, screaming toddler. "You. Cannot. Be. Serious," he snaps. "If you want to ruin your reputation, go ahead, but you are our strongest allies. Your decisions impact *us* as well. And I won't be made a laughing stock because you want to impose your feminist values on us."

The entire room shakes as every man at the table stands up in rage and moves to draw their weapons. On my left, I see Naser's daughter, still seated, raise a hand to stop her soldiers. She turns to me, cocking an eyebrow, her expression screaming, *'Fix this before I have to do it myself.'*

"Uncle, the only one embarrassing us is you. Now sit down before I get an—"

"You can fuck right off, Declan. I was your father's second

hand when you were in diapers. I won't be pushed around by you, and I sure as shit won't work with some bitch who doesn't know what she's doing." He leans over me to yell right in her face. I will have none of that.

A second goes by before I pull out my Glock, aim it at my uncle's knee, and pull the trigger.

2

ZAHRA

en are so dramatic.

Society will spew that it's women who can't be trusted to lead because they're too emotional, and yet my afternoon has been filled by one man freaking out because he may have to work with me, and another man deciding to fix his problems with a bullet. Typical. So damn typical.

"Was shooting him really necessary? He's getting blood all over my rug. It's going to be such a pain to get out." I roll my eyes, finally standing from my chair.

"He's been testing my patience entirely too much today. Maybe now he'll learn not to run his mouth around me." Declan shrugs, running his hand through his light brown hair, like his uncle isn't laid out crying on the floor in front of us. "I'm happy to pay for dry cleaning. Or buy you a new rug. Assuming this is a handwoven Persian rug from Mehraban?"

I blink, trying to maintain my composure. He's not as cold and calculated as I'd predicted, especially with all the blood on his hands. "Are you really talking to me about rugs right now?"

"You're the one who brought it up."

"Along with the fact that your uncle is bleeding on my floor." Which some may consider to be a more pressing issue.

"He'll be fine. I'm sure he's already alerted our medical staff to be ready upon arrival to mend his knee." Another shrug.

"You might want to take him to our medical ward instead, with the rate he's bleeding. Also, I intercepted both of your cellphones, so any calls or texts you send would get routed to me instead. Your staff is definitely unaware of what just happened." I pause, waiting for Declan to shift from calm and collected to irritated and angered. Men hate being undermined. Especially men with as much power as him.

Instead, a smile forms on his face, probably the same one he uses to throw people off his scent before he strikes. "Is that what you were doing at the beginning of our meeting? When you were typing away on your computer?"

"No. That was a separate issue I was dealing with. I fixed your phones when you were in the hallway."

His smile widens as he sticks out his hand. "Declan McAlister."

I shake it, feeling the calluses on his palm and the way his hand engulfs mine. It's strange finally meeting the man I know so much about. The man who has taken so much from me. "Zahra Ahzimi."

"Zahra," he repeats my name as if he's savoring it. As if he's been waiting years for this very moment, and finally, it's arrived.

I suppose for him, there was greater anticipation. Despite keeping my identity a secret from anyone outside the Empire, my father never kept me in the dark about anything that involved his mafia and his allies. He never hesitated to prepare me as his heir. He also just wanted me to live as close to a normal life as possible. My stomach squeezes at the thought of my father. And his death. The squeeze is replaced by a rush of anger as I look Declan in the eyes. Look at the man who murdered my father and his own father in cold blood to gain power.

"Cyrus. Take Lorkan to the medical wing and ensure he receives the best possible care. Everyone else is dismissed. Declan, I would like an extra minute of your time."

I need Declan alone. Need to see if I can make him crack. If there was any bit of remorse in his body, his guilt should be slowly eating away at him. But I wouldn't hold my breath. I've spent my whole life surrounded by monsters who would do anything to gain power. As the new boss, Declan now has a world of power at his fingertips.

While I trust my inner circle, I know I have to keep my plans to uncover the truth about Declan to myself. Either my inner circle would tell me it was the Italians who killed my father, or they would kill Declan themselves. But I can't let them. Seeing the life drain from his eyes is my destiny. My duty to my father.

Declan gives me a small nod, curiously keeping his eyes on me. We both wait for the room to clear. Lorkan's curses and groans continue to fill the room until he's carried out into the hallway. Cyrus being kind enough to cover up the pool of blood beneath our feet with a tablecloth. Not that it bothers me. I was the daughter of a mafia boss. Forget that. I *am* a mafia boss. A little bit of blood is never going to get the best of me. Not with all the things I've seen. All the things I've lived through.

We stand in silence as the room clears. Arman, one of my bodyguards, lingers by the door until I give him a nod to dismiss him. I appreciate his willingness to protect me but I can protect myself. Closed-door meetings are common among families as bonded as ours, though I doubt Declan has any consideration for family and loyalty. No amount of charm or smoldering smiles would convince me that he was anything other than a poisonous snake.

"I have to admit the suspense is killing me," Declan teases, his thick Irish accent coming through. According to my father, Declan had spent most of his childhood and teen years in Dublin. Over a decade in the States has done little to assuage his accent.

My body tenses. Here goes nothing. "I've been working on a...project. Typically, I prefer to work alone, but in this instance, I don't think keeping it from you would be fair."

His eyebrows furrow together. "What kind of project?"

Shoving my hand into the pockets of my pants, I toy with the small pieces of metal inside before placing them on the table. I searched his face for a tell—any tell—that reveals his guilt. Naturally, he, like most who were raised in our line of work, shows no emotion on his face. His entire composure is unshaken. "Is that..."

"The bullets that killed our fathers. I had our surgeon retain them so I could do some further investigation." I pinch the bullets between my fingers. Such a small piece of metal caused so much destruction. So much pain.

He places his palms on the wooden table in front of him. I do my best to subtly check for my gun that's tucked into my waist. I have no doubt that he'd try to kill me if he knew my true intentions. "So what's this project you're proposing? Are you suggesting a different plan of retaliation?"

While this is the first time Declan and I have spoken in person, we've communicated via our respective inner circles on how to best deal with the Italians. Back when I was still naive and assumed it had to be them who murdered my father.

Killing two mob bosses was not something that could be

taken lightly and the last thing we need is for anyone to question our authority. I had spent a week with very few hours of sleep, trying to hack into the Italian's security systems. By day four, I was in, and by day seven, I had transferred every single bit of information to our database. Including the location of the Italian boss, his family, and the security code for all his apartments and mansions.

Declan wanted to immediately kill any major player he could get his hands on, likely because he wanted to move on from the situation as soon as possible. The quicker we got our revenge on our fathers' killers, the quicker it would appease our two families. By holding the Italians accountable, no one would ask questions. No one would wonder if someone else had killed our fathers. No one but me.

While I had already begun collecting small pieces of evidence that proved the Italians had been framed for this assassination, I didn't have enough information to confirm that it was Declan who killed them. At least not for now. In order to buy myself some time to gather the evidence I needed, I played along. With respect to revenge on the Italians, I suggested a more psychological approach. First, we pick off their allies, then the closest members of their circle, ones that would rip their hearts out. And finally, we would come for them. From what Cyrus told me, Declan took some initial convincing, but once he was able to see how much damage my plot would cause, he was on board.

"I still believe the plan is our best path forward, so long as you still agree." I pause, waiting for confirmation, which Declan gives me in the form of a nod. My grip on my gun tightens. "What I'm not sure about is our target. I don't think the Italians were responsible for killing our fathers."

I hold my breath for his response.

Everyone who's involved with mobs has trust issues. My

trust issues are just exacerbated by the fact that I'm constantly scrutinized for simply existing in a space that traditionally hasn't welcomed women, and especially not women of color. I hoped Declan would view my curiosity as justified suspicion, not a direct accusation.

Declan's eyes close, his hands balling into fists.

I wait patiently as Declan takes a series of deep breaths. He manages to regain his composure much quicker than I expected, though I refuse to let my guard down.

"What do you mean it wasn't the Italians?" he asks through gritted teeth.

I've spent the last few days debating how much I should reveal. How much I could say to demonstrate I was suspicious *broadly*, but not necessarily suspicious of him. I need him uneasy enough that he feels drawn to keep me close to him, but not so uneasy that he feels the need to take me out because I threaten his very existence. I need him to think I'm smart enough to be an ally worth saving, but not so smart that he can't control and manipulate me. Should be an easy enough task to accomplish, given that most mafia men would rather eat a bullet than admit a woman could outsmart them.

My eyes are locked with Declan's as I continue, "All of the Italian's best shooters were already in custody by the time our fathers were....targeted. They wouldn't send any amateur to get the job done. It would be too risky. There was no sign of forced entry into the room, indicating my father must have let the killer in. The sigil in the wall had been drawn in a bright red ink instead of the typical maroon the Italians use."

There were more details I had uncovered. Like my father's final words on the hospital bed. Words I never got to hear myself, as I was away on a business trip. Words that Cyrus, my father's second in command, repeated back to me. A name my father said over and over again as he faded.

Declan's name.

The man in front of me finally speaks, "They were killed by lead bullets. That's the Italian's signature." Declan picks up the bullet closest to him and brings it closer to his eyes, inspecting it just like I had when I discovered its secret.

To my annoyance, my heart starts racing with each tick of the clock. Would he lie and claim not to see what I so obviously did? How long can I stand being in a room with him before I finally snap and listen to that voice in the back of my head that tells me to kill him here and be done with it? Sending a bullet to the back of his head would no doubt end with one in mine not too long after. It's too early to seek my revenge on him. I have to be patient. But what if I wasn't able to break Declan? What if I never found any other evidence than what was left? *You can achieve anything you set your mind to.* My father's words replay in my head. He always believed in me. And that's all that matters.

I will avenge him. No matter the cost.

The longer we stand in silence, the more unnerved I become. Silence used to be a solace for me, used to carry a level of peace. But now my thoughts unravel in it. Memories of my father's life fading from his eyes replay over and over in my head, tormenting me. My racing heart serves as a reminder of how much I've been affected by the events of the past few weeks. I pick at the seams of my blouse, desperate for a distraction. Any distraction.

When toying with my sleeves doesn't bring me solace, I shift to staring at Declan's and how they're pushed up to his elbows. His arms are covered in what I assume are traditional, and incredibly intricate, Celtic tattoos. I get lost in the series of intricate knots that start at his wrist, trail up the inside of his arm, and disappear under the rest of his dress shirt. By the time Declan cuts the silence, my heart has come back down to its normal pace. If he noticed my momentary discomfort, he doesn't show it.

"The bullet looks like lead to me," Declan starts, and I feel a twinge of hope leave my body.

So he's going the route of denial. Typical.

Before I can respond, he continues, "But I assume there's something I am missing?"

I blink, not expecting the open curiosity that's in his eyes. As if he genuinely doesn't know the truth. I have to give it to him. His poker face is next level.

"The bullet's *coated* in lead. But the base is copper. Solid lead bullets are heavier than the one in your hand. That was my first giveaway that something was off. I had my lab confirm my suspicions."

Declan tosses the bullet in the air, over and over again. He stops suddenly, his fingers curled into a fist around the metal as if he could disintegrate it with his hand. I bet he wishes he could. Get rid of one of the few remainders of that night. "You're right. Dammit," he snaps with rage.

I wait for more, screaming internally for him to confess and do us both the favor of ending his act, but he stays silent. And so I continue to push, "It's pretty deceiving. Hell, neither of our staff members who combed through the scene of the hit noticed it. But noticing the small details and differences was always a strong suit of mine. It comes in extremely handy with coding computers. One extra space in a line of code can cause it to crash, leaving you going crazy trying to find why it's not working."

Good, Zahra. Give him reasons to keep you as an ally.

"I have no idea how you do all of that. I can't even send a text without making a typo. Or figure out new settings on my phone. You must have the patience of a saint." He gives me a small smile. One I'm sure has led to a long string of broken hearts.

"It's predictable. And controllable. Two things we don't get a lot of in our world. It keeps me centered."

"Well, it's impressive nonetheless. The amount of destruction you can cause just by a few taps of your fingertips."

I can't tell if he means it as a compliment or an acknowledgment of the threat I pose. I bring us back to the task at hand. "The destruction I cause can be reversed. Can't say the same for a bullet."

All I get is a small nod in response. "The British are fans of copper. Lord knows they've hated us for centuries—"

Of course he would just blame it on another one of our rivals. I suppose this could be a good thing. If I can convince him that all my attention is now on the British, he'll be less likely to suspect that he's my true target. "Dammit, you're right. You can never underestimate the colonizers," I spit, which brings a smirk out from Declan.

"...But they're usually more brazen. They like taking credit for the kill. Why would they hide from this one? And why blame the Italians?" He places a hand on his chin, contemplative.

What a bastard. If I didn't know the truth about him, I would assume these were genuine questions, that he truly wanted to get to the bottom of who slaughtered our fathers. But I know better. How could he stand here and act like he was so curious, act like he had no idea who killed his own father, when his hands are drenched with blood? I've gone toe to toe with many monsters in my life, but none of them made me as sick as Declan McAlister does at this very moment. His beautiful face is just a distraction for the vile toxins that keep his cold heart beating.

Don't lose track of your plan, Zahra. Make him think you

believe his lead. "They probably figured if they started a war between us, they could reap the benefits while we kill each other."

"If you're right, it could be any one of our enemies. The British, the Russians, the Greeks…" He trails off. We'd be here all day if he wanted to list all the people who want to take us out. All of these enemies could've aimed their guns at us, and instead, someone on the inside did the job. Someone neither my own father nor his best friend saw coming.

"The list of people who could be guilty is endless. Which is why I need you to help me narrow it down." *I need to get you to trust me enough to let down your guard. And then I'll get justice.*

"Whatever you need. Whenever you need it. I'm yours." The words fall off his lips like they're a promise to me. And whether he realizes it or not, those words have just sealed his fate. Because he's right.

He is mine now.

Mine to deceive, mine to ruin, and mine to kill.

3
DECLAN

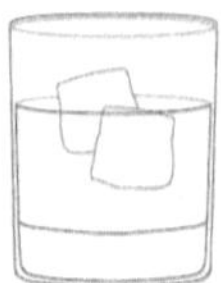

The Italians didn't kill my father.

I've been fixated on that truth since Zahra laid out all the details she had uncovered: the bullet being different than the signature one used by the Italians and the fact that all the assassins the Italians would normally use for these killings were already being interrogated by state police. Nothing made sense anymore. The one thing that's clear to me, and clear to Zahra, is that someone tried to frame the Italians for the murder of our fathers. Someone who knew of the turbulent history between our three mobs, and enough of the Italians' signature marks to frame them. The list of suspects has gone from being clear-cut and defined to never-ending, and now may even include the very men who we break bread with.

How the hell was I supposed to solve my father's murder while keeping business going as normal? The meeting with Zahra was supposed to focus on discussions of trade routes, package drop-offs, and training of new recruits. I had anticipated some tension from my uncle as Naser's heir was revealed, but I never thought he would fully explode like he did. Though I suppose I shouldn't be surprised. Until she passed a few years ago, my father had always allowed my mother to call the shots in their marriage, and when it came to the mafia. She was the voice of reason and logic we needed. My Uncle Lorkan had deeply resented my father for it. Resented my father for not giving him more power within the inner circle.

Maybe that resentment drove him over the edge and led him to killing his brother?

It isn't the first time I've considered it. Frankly, I don't think most people would be that surprised to hear that my uncle tried to usurp my father, but I know better. For as much bark he has, he lacks in bite. My uncle doesn't want all the burdens of being a boss. He just wants the clout. Which is why he felt the need to verbally throw his weight around and cause me additional problems. Me shooting him in the knee was a mercy he should be grateful for. If not for that display of loyalty to Zahra, I have no doubts Cyrus would have killed my uncle then and there.

My eyes flicker between the watch on my wrist and the door of my office, debating if I should wait any longer or pour myself a drink now. After a minute of silence, I throw open the bottom drawer of my desk, open the bottle of whiskey inside, and take a long swig. The liquor burns down my throat, but I'm thankful for the sensation. A reminder that I'm alive and breathing.

Aidan, my secondhand and younger brother, struts into the room a second later. Nothing ever phased him. It was a person-ality trait that both annoyed me and made me grateful for his presence. Even the darkest of moments were recoverable to Aidan.

"Our uncle should be back on his feet in a couple of weeks,

in case you're wondering," Aidan says as he drapes himself on the chair across from mine.

"Happy to hear it."

"You don't sound happy," Aidan presses.

"Well, sorry if I'm not chipper about the fact that our uncle's mouth does him more harm than good, that my father and his best friend were murdered, and that I have no idea who killed them," I snap, my hands balling into fists. I need to punch something, or someone. I need to get all this pent-up rage out before I take it out on the wrong person.

Aidan raises an eyebrow at my atypical loss of control and reaches over for the bottle in front of me. "You couldn't have at least waited for me?"

"It was a rough day." I drag a hand down my face.

"That would be an understatement." He takes a large gulp, wincing. Shaking the bottle of whiskey in front of me, he asks, "Is this a new batch?"

I nod. "Aged in white oak and for twice as long as the other barrels. Makes the flavor richer, although a bit more bitter."

Part of how my family line had managed to maintain our power for this long came from our willingness to branch out into other businesses that were more...legal in nature. Creating our own distillery was my grandfather's idea, and in the past few decades, McAlister whiskey grew from a local Irish brand to one seen in every high-end bar in Boston and cities across the world. The success of our liquor business has also allowed our more questionable lines of business to go under the radar.

"Gets me drunk all the same, but I suppose I was never a whiskey connoisseur like you are." Aidan toys with his fingers before locking eyes with me. "What's this about not knowing who killed Dad and Naser? Do you no longer think it's the Italians?"

Fuck. I had said that out loud, hadn't I? I opened my mouth

to divulge everything Zahra had confided in me, but I couldn't silence the voice in my head questioning whether Aidan could handle the truth. Him and our father had major issues with each other, and as much as he's denying it, I know he regrets that our father was killed before they could truly repair their relationship. So instead of burdening him with my latest discovery, I stay silent and ignore the pit starting to form in my stomach.

Aidan cocks an eyebrow at me, likely knowing I am holding something back, but doesn't probe. Instead, he pushes the bottle in my direction and asks, "Is there anything I can do to help?"

"Tell Marcus I need a date," I state, referencing my personal assistant. "Dinner next week. The Black Rose."

"Well, I'm sure he'll be flattered by the invite. I wasn't aware he was your type." A smirk covers Aidan's face.

"*Not* what I meant—"

"But I have to admit I believe Marcus has a boyfriend, so he'll probably turn down your offer." He snickers.

"It wasn't an offer," I snap.

"No need to deny your true feelings. It's important to learn how to process our emotions."

"Keep talking and I'll put a bullet in your knee next."

"Violence is never the answer, Declan. I thought you knew that already." His snicker turns into a full-fledged laugh as I shoot him my best *'I'm going to strangle you'* look.

"I hate to be the bearer of bad news, but if violence is never the answer, you may want to consider a new line of work," I offer.

"I would, but then I wouldn't get to see your bright shining face every day. And what a disappointment that would be."

"You're a pain in my ass."

"I am. But you love me anyway..." He holds his chin

between his index and thumb, contemplating. "So, who would you like me to tell Marcus you want a date with? Since he's unavailable."

"Zahra."

"Is she ready to publicly stake her claim on the Persian Empire? Or is she still trying to keep her identity a secret?"

I stifle. Of course word about Zahra has gotten out by now. I have no doubts my uncle would have continued to make a fuss while Aidan checked in on him post-surgery.

"I'm not sure," I confess.

Aidan's persona shifts from relaxed to rigid as he switches to work mode as my second. "Well, if she's ready to make an entrance, a very public dinner will do it. And if you two show up together arm in arm...that would send a message to everyone about where our two families stand. How much power our allyship still has."

"Exactly. Now more than ever, we need to show everyone that no one and nothing can break us. Tell Marcus to call Zahra," I order.

"Sounds good, Boss." Aidan gives me a tense smile. "And Declan?"

"What's up?"

"You know you can tell me anything, right? I can handle it."

Under normal circumstances, I would say yes in a heartbeat, but these weren't normal circumstances. So instead, I give him a terse smile and wait for him to leave before finally planning my next steps.

4
ZAHRA

"Say the word and I'll get you out," Arman reassures me as the car pulls up to The Black Rose, an elite members-only restaurant that politicians and mafia dons regularly attend to discuss their business moves. Declan chose the location of our first public encounter wisely. I have no doubts that the second this reservation was booked, every boss in the city was informed that Naser's heir would make their first public appearance.

"She is more than capable of handling herself." Azula rolls her eyes, double-checking that all my guns and knives were secure in the holsters embedded in my blazer. Despite her collected and harsh exterior, the subtle hint of uncertainty in her eyes clued me in to how she was really feeling. I couldn't blame her for being nervous. Once my true identity was revealed, I would also have to announce my new second in command. Azula had been an obvious choice from the beginning. Her financial savvy and ruthlessness in torturing information out of our enemies was unmatched. Plus, I refused to be the only woman sitting at the table during our inner circle meetings.

My father committing to making me his heir of the Empire was a step in the right direction, but I wanted more than a step. If I was going to break boundaries and expectations of what a woman's role in a mafia should be, I was going to do it alongside other strong women who had been kept in the dark for too long. Other women who had been underestimated. My tenure as boss and all I've accomplished reflect on my success and stand as a means for proving the worth of all the women by my side, as well as those who have been discredited for their entire lives. It's an immense amount of weight to bear on my shoulders. And it's one I carry with extreme diligence. I have no illusions about what will be said about me as I rule. And nothing will give me greater joy than proving my doubters wrong.

"I'm well aware she can handle herself. I am still her head of security though, which means it's my job to ensure all threats are removed," Arman huffs as we all exit the car and head toward the entrance.

"You'll never be able to keep me entirely safe, Arman, and you know that. Though I do appreciate your dedication." I give him a terse smile before stepping away and approaching the host.

"I'm here for Mr. McAlister," I announce, not missing the ever-so slight eye roll I get in response.

"While I'm sure Mr. McAlister is dying to see his...beautiful friend, he's awaiting a *very important* business meeting, darling. But I'll be sure to let him know you dropped by." His condescending tone is like nails on a chalkboard to me. I try not to take it too personally. I'm sure this isn't the first time he's had to ward off eager mistresses dying to get a hold of whatever man had used and discarded them. Still, I can't stop the bile building in my stomach at how easy it was for him to dismiss me. How easy it was for someone to assume I wasn't worthy of their time.

"I'm more than aware of Declan's meeting. I am also aware that it has yet to begin, given I'm the guest of honor." I lean over the stand and point to the notepad in front of him. "If you double-check your books, I'm sure you'll see my name listed: Z. Ahzimi. Z for Zahra."

His eyes flash between mine and the notepad, in disbelief. He refuses to relent. "That...can't be..."

Fucking hell. Declan's diligence in keeping my identity hidden was a smart idea in thought, but in execution, it's pissing me off. *That's probably what he wanted anyway.* His respectful demeanor toward me may have my staff fooled, but I refuse to give in. Especially when I know the truth about him. When he had initially proposed this lunch, it took everything in me not to drive over to the McAlister manor and put a bullet in his head. But I know better. I have to keep my temper in check. And so I agreed, intending to use this meal as another chance to obtain more information from him.

Gaining his trust will be imperative, and will make it all the more sweet when I finally get to watch the life drain from his eyes. Revenge is a dream, one that's proving to be harder and harder to achieve, given I can't even get through the damn door of this restaurant.

"I understand you're just doing your job, but I feel it imperative to warn you that I'm beginning to lose my patience. And things get really messy when I lose my patience." The threat to my voice is clear. Unfortunately for me, it has the opposite effect on the host.

"Doll, you're not the first, or frankly, twentieth girl that has come crawling back for more after a night with McAlister. I very much like this job, and if I let in every one-night stand who claimed they were something more to him, I wouldn't be standing here still. You're more than welcome to stand outside until he's done to see if you can catch him. If he doesn't opt to leave through the back to avoid your crazy ass. But beyond that, I'm afraid I can't help y—" He's cut off by the sound of dress shoes clicking on the floor.

"There you are. I was wondering what was taking so long. Aidan informed me your car arrived ten minutes ago." Declan's massive frame takes up nearly the entirety of the door frame. The sleeves of his dress shirt are rolled up to reveal his inked arms as he toys with a ring on his index finger. A ring with his family's sigil, the ring of the Irish boss on his finger.

The bile in my stomach continues to rise, outraged at the audacity he has to wear his father's ring. I shove my hand into my pockets as they curl into fists. "It appears there's been a misunderstanding. Evidently, someone here believes I'm your mistress and not the heir to the Persian Empire," I scoff, shooting daggers at the man in front of me, whose face has turned as pale as a white linen sheet.

The snap of Declan's jaw slamming shut with rage causes the host to visibly cringe. His eyes dart toward mine, filled with terror, as he bows the top half of his body down, as if he's ready to kneel and beg for forgiveness. Declan crosses his arms around his chest, more than happy to see him sweat it out. I have no desire to entertain this.

"Stand up. No need to make an even bigger scene than what has already transpired," I snap.

The host slowly rises, though I can see him shaking. "Ms. Ahzimi, I am so, *so* sorry for my ignorance. Please forgive me. I-I just assumed—"

"No apologies needed. I would recommend that you leave interrogations to the bosses next time. It's clearly not your forte." I don't even wait for a response, entering the restaurant with Declan trailing behind me.

A slow wave of silence comes over the room that had just been filled with chatter. I feel dozens of eyes fall upon me, taking me in, and I hear a few shocked breaths from the patrons who can't contain their shock as they see me enter. As they piece together that *I* am Naser's heir. Though I've imagined this very moment hundreds of times, none of my mental preparation compares to how on display I feel right now. Declan makes a subtle movement to extend his elbow out for me to hold onto. I shake my head. I won't, *can't*, stroll through the restaurant on the arm of a man, even if he is the deadliest man in the city. I have to stand on my own. Even if I can barely feel my legs at that moment.

Declan leads us over to a fairly intimate booth tucked away in the corner of the restaurant, ideal for discussing current affairs without worrying about prying ears. We've barely sat down when a waiter with dark brown hair approaches the table. "Can I get you both something to drink?"

"McAlister Whiskey, on the rocks, for me. The new shipment that we've launched." Declan's eyes are on me, not giving any attention to his surroundings. I can't tell if it's because he's being respectful or trying to size me up like a lion would prey. Probably the latter.

"I'll have the same. Neat," I announce with no hesitation. Declan raises an eyebrow at me as our waiter scurries away. "What? I don't want the ice to dilute the taste."

"Your father hated whiskey." A smile forms on Declan's face, as if he's recalling a fond memory. As if he isn't the monster that took my father away from me.

"I am not my father," I state, as if I need to make that clear.

"Obviously," he teases, though I can tell something has made him uncomfortable by the slight scrunching of his eyebrows and the way he bites his lip. It's then that I notice the slight scar that occupies most of his lower lip and slightly extends down his chin. "Just trying to get to know you a bit better. Though I can understand why talking about your father is a sore subject." He gives me a sympathetic look, and I hate how sincere it looks.

"I certainly miss him, but that's not the only reason why I don't want to discuss my father. It's hard enough making your own legacy as a boss when you're the son of a legend. As his daughter..." I trail off, not needing to elaborate. "Plus, I don't think this is the place to discuss the other concern I have brought to your attention about our fathers," I whisper.

He gives me a small nod. "Understood. About all of it."

"Shall we discuss the new trade routes?" I shift into business mode.

"The shipments are all in place and ready to be dispersed." The McAlister's successful whiskey business makes an excellent cover-up whenever we need to disperse our weapons. Underneath each carton of liquor was enough bullets and guns to support an army. And it did. Our army. "And how did the imports go?" Declan inquires.

The Irish aren't the only ones who have a secondary business. Our barrels of dried saffron and tea had arrived a few nights ago, the hidden security equipment and computer chips alongside it. Between the weapons and the undetectable spyware we would install, thwarting our enemies' plans and winning wars should be easy. We just have to ensure all our supplies make it to our other branches throughout the states. "Everything is as planned. I have my best pilots ready to fly. They take off from New York in a couple of hours and should land in San Francisco by tonight."

Declan nods. "Excellent. My men will meet yours at the runway and move to immediately disperse the goods."

"And you're sure traveling at night is the safest?"

"Aye." His thick accent rings clear. "Our vans are black, with no license plates, of course, and we have confirmation that the sheriff is throwing a big retirement party for one of his buddies. All the police that night will be occupied."

While the Boston police and politicians have been firmly in our back pocket for decades, our influence in other major cities is still in the works. Slowly but surely, we will get enough of them on our side. Everyone has a price, even if they deny it.

Before I can update Declan on how our Chicago branch is faring selling his guns, a different waiter, one with piercing grey eyes, interrupts. "I have two whiskeys for the table." He sets down the glass with ice in front of Declan before quickly dropping off my drink with trembling hands and scurrying away.

If Declan notices how uneasy the waiter is, he says nothing. I watch as Declan swirls the whiskey a few times, letting the ice mix in. I do the same, except my eyes are laser-focused on the liquid inside of my cup, which, when I hold it to the light, is a slightly different hue than the one in Declan's. Bringing the liquor to my nose, I inhale deeply. I probably look like a snobby whiskey drinker, trying to show off that I can scent the hints of cinnamon and citrus in this particular batch, and initially, that *is* all I can scent until a hint of something else starts to come through. I slam my glass on the table, startling Declan, who follows suit.

"It's poisoned," I exclaim.

5

ZAHRA

I whip my head around to find the waiter who served us and catch him wide-eyed, heading toward the back kitchen. Declan reaches over to take my glass and gestures to Aidan sitting at his own table across the room. The restaurant explodes into movement. I shove to my feet as the two brothers and Arman barrel straight for the attacker. Azula is at my side almost immediately.

"Take Declan's whiskey glass and have it sent to our lab," I order. Many mafias use poison, but most have their own signature. Whatever is in that glass could clue us in to who's targeting us.

While Azula takes charge inside, I head in the same direction as where the waiter had left. It doesn't take long before I'm in a back alley, the coppery scent of blood filling the air. From a quick look, both Declan's and Arman's hands are bruised and covered in red liquid. Aidan has his arms wrapped tightly around the waiter's chest, and for a moment, I don't see a man who tried to kill me. Instead, I see a terrified boy who bit off more than he can chew.

Declan's voice echoes on the brick walls as he leads the interrogation. "Did you really think you could use my own whiskey to poison us?" He nods his head toward me before pulling back his fist and landing a punch square in the nose of the man in front of him. The man crumples to the ground as Aidan lets go of him.

"T-There's no poison in the drink...I swear...I'm just a waiter," the man groans, albeit somewhat convincingly. I refuse to believe him. You don't make it far in my line of work if you can't tell a good lie.

Declan grabs at the man's shirt and rips it off, revealing a chest covered in ink—the silhouette of a vulture. I'm not familiar with what mafia this represents, but by the look of terror on the man's face as his secret was revealed, and the fact that he had laced my drink, I have no misconceptions about whether or not he's my enemy.

The adrenaline starts to wear off and the reality that this stranger in front of me nearly killed me sinks in, and I feel my blood boil. I step up beside Declan, pulling out a sheathed knife tucked in my thigh holster, and strike the waiter across the face, leaving a large gash across his cheek that will forever remain as a scar. If I let him live after this. "Just a waiter? Are you sure you want to maintain that story?"

The man refuses to say anything, letting out only a few grunts and moans of pain.

Declan lifts the man from off the ground with ease, pinning him up against a wall with his hand wrapped around his throat. He squeezes. "Who sent you here?"

The man stays silent though his face turns a faint shade of purple.

"He can't answer your questions with your fist wrapped around his neck." I roll my eyes, stating the obvious.

Declan turns his head toward me. "Are you alright?"

The softness in his voice causes me to stumble. From his tone, you would think he was checking in on me after I accidentally spilled a drink on myself or told an embarrassing joke, not that he was covered in blood, beating the man who tried to kill me to a pulp.

"I'm fine. Never took a sip," I reassure him.

"Even if she did, she'd be fin—" The man attempts to console Declan, who just squeezes his fingers even tighter around his neck.

"Why don't we test that theory, shall we?" Declan snarls, signaling to Aidan, who I realize still has my drink in his hand. Declan presses the glass against the man's face and I don't miss how his eyes widen with fear.

"Please...Please don't..." the man begs, but to no avail.

"Why not? You said the drink was fine. Unless you want to confess who sent you," Declan presses. The man shakes his head in defiance. I suppose I couldn't blame him. Either he would die now at Declan's hands or with the reputation of a rat once his boss discovered he had snitched.

"Very well." Before the man can protest again, Declan pries his jaw open and pours some of the poisoned drink down his throat. Taking a step back, Declan lets the man fall to the ground and comes to stand next to me. We both watch as he convulses on the floor for a few minutes before stopping.

Aidan does the honors, checking the man's pulse.

"He's dead."

———

The scalding water falling down my back, mixed with the scent of lavender and orange blossom, is the only thing keeping me grounded at this moment. I'm no stranger to rough days, violence, and death, but this is the first time someone has directly come to take *my* life. And if I hadn't had my wits about me, it would've been the last. Declan had been oddly protective of me once the man had died—insisting he be the one to put me back into the car, and following us back to my home before leaving back to his mansion that was on the complete opposite side of town. I suppose I shouldn't be that surprised. Any true ally would have done the same when their partner was threatened. And regardless of what I know to be true about Declan, he still had a facade to maintain.

Stepping out of the shower, I wrap myself in a robe, rub cream all over my body, and run some leave-in conditioner in my hair to help form the subtle waves nearly identical to my mother's when she was still alive. I'm fully settled in the loveseat in front of the fireplace in my room when Azula walks in.

"Are you sure you want to do this tonight?" Azula checks. "We can always reconvene tomorrow."

"No. I'm fine. The sooner we start to piece together who sent that man to kill me, the better." I gesture for her to take the seat in front of me and pour us both a cup of warm tea from the pot I had ordered to be delivered prior to my shower.

"Arman is running the vulture tattoo through our entire database. Thus far, we have no matches between the largest known mafias in the states or prisons. Arman is going to do an international search soon, but it may take a few days for something to come back."

"If that falls through, I can probably hack into the local traffic cameras and see if we find something there," I offer, refusing to let this be a dead end.

Azula blinks and gives me a rare smile. "You know how to do that?"

"Don't insult me. I've gotten through Ukrainian and Italian cyber walls in a matter of days, less if you account for the naps I took. Cities can't afford extra protections for their security systems. At least not the security systems that would make it harder for me to get in. I can crack their code in a couple hours. Four max, is my prediction." I blow on the steaming tea in front of me before taking a sip from the mug, relishing the warmth that comes over my body.

"I'm surprised the Mayor hasn't asked for suggestions on how to fix that." Azula snickers.

"I offered to help revamp Boston's entire security system, but they were concerned I'd leave some sort of untraceable bug to use for nefarious means." I roll my eyes. "Which, for the record, is exactly what I would have done, *but* I only would've spied on our rivals. I don't have any interest in what civilians are up to."

Azula snorts. "Well, at least you're honest. Plus, it's not like you don't have the Mayor in your back pocket anyway."

"That's what I said! And yet he still turned my idea down. Make it make sense."

"You can't. Men." She rolls her eyes.

"Men," I agree. Nothing more needed to be said. "Did you get the labs back on the whiskey?"

Azula gives me a quick nod, eyes darting to the untouched tea mug in her hand. She toys with the glass long enough for me to know I won't like whatever comes from her mouth. "Declan's glass was clean."

My entire body stills as Azula confirms what I already suspected.

"No traces of poison were found in his glass. We tried to test the remains of what was left in your glass and we *think* the chemical makeup of the poison could be tetrodoxin, a neuro-toxin, but we can't be sure. There wasn't enough left after

Declan, you know..." Azula drags her index finger across her neck.

It all made sense.

Declan had tried to have me killed.

And when one of his foot soldiers failed, he covered up his tracks by killing him. Declan had been the one to chase after the waiter, the one to expose the man's tattoo, and concoct the story that the vulture on the man's chest represented some other mafia were unfamiliar with. The look of fear in the waiter's eyes when he faced off against Declan. He probably realized that he could either drink the poison and have a quick death or be skinned alive later for exposing Declan's duplicity. And by ensuring the waiter consumed as much of the drink as possible, he not only made himself appear as my ally, but he also hindered our ability to determine what he tried to kill me with.

"So I was the target." The only target. Declan is an idiot. He could have at least laced his own drink and dumped it to lessen my suspicion. It was an amateur move that only increases my focus on him as a threat to my life. An amateur move that Declan would never make if he was truly in the right state of mind. Maybe the guilt of killing his father is slowly starting to get to him. Good. He deserves to be haunted by the consequences of his own actions. I would do everything in my power to capitalize on his weakened state of mind. He has taken his first direct shot at me, which I refuse to take lightly. Declan may have missed, but I'll do everything in my power to make sure I don't.

"You seem pretty calm for someone who just lived through an assassination attempt," Azula notes, her hard features softening ever so slightly, dropping her guard the way she only ever does around me.

It's a kind gesture, though not completely necessary. At

least that's what I tell myself. As much as a part of me wants to sit for hours and rehash today's events, I know that doing so will open up the floodgates. Today was a close call....but I've had many close calls in my life. Beyond expanding my shooting and martial arts training, and adding a few extra members of security, I processed any threats to my life by moving on. It was all I could do. My father was always transparent about the risks of our line of work, which had driven him to keep my identity hidden.

"Likely the first assassination attempt of many. Not worth shedding any tears over." I shrug, ignoring the lingering pit in my stomach that had formed hours ago.

I have to appear unfazed and collected. Not only is that what everyone would expect from a mafia boss, but I know any sign of emotion from me would be dramatized. While I know Azula would never speak ill of me, the walls of my mansion have ears. Another lesson my father had instilled in me from a young age. *The only person you can trust in this life is yourself. Everyone else, including the men you think are loyal to you, can turn in the blink of an eye. Especially if they sense weakness. For that reason, you can never, ever let them see you falter.*

Azula leans closer, as if she can read my mind and sense why I'm silent. The words from her lips are barely a whisper. "You know you can talk to me, right? Not just as your second but as your *best friend.*"

"I know. And I will, when I feel the need to. Right now, there is no need. I'm alive. That's all that matters," I assure her.

Her lips turn down, but she carries on. "Given the evidence that we have so far, or lack thereof, there's not much we can do with respect to plotting our retaliation."

If only she knew. "Set up a meeting between myself and Declan. Preferably here, but anywhere private should suffice."

"Is that a smart idea, given how often your meetings have ended with bullets flying and poison?" Azula deadpans.

"So, a normal day for us?" I hedge, causing her to break character with a small snort.

"Fair enough. I'll set up the meeting. It's probably worth you and Declan debriefing today's events anyway. Who knows, maybe he noticed something that will clue us in to who tried to kill you."

"Maybe." Or maybe I'll kill him before he can try something else.

6

DECLAN

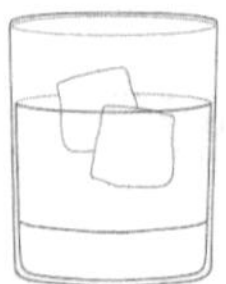

I throw up in my private bathroom the second I arrive back home, and try to ignore the rush of shame that follows. Try and fail. Splashing water on my face, I rub harshly at the skin as if I can simply wash the emotion away. But I know much better than that. Shame follows me around, haunting me like a ghost since my father's and his best friend's deaths. I thought nothing would compare to the guilt of being unable to save the two most important men in my life, but I was wrong. I had nearly lost Zahra as well. And though we are currently nothing more than allies on paper, and strangers in each other's lives...I couldn't stop hearing her father's voice in my head on the drive back home from the restaurant.

All the stories he had told me over the years of how proud he was of his child. Though he never revealed Zahra's name, Naser's love for her was evident in the sheer joy that would overcome him whenever he discussed the latest spyware she had developed, or how well she was doing in school. It was clear that Zahra was Naser's whole world, and I have no doubts she felt the same. And not only had I failed to save Naser, but I had also nearly lost Zahra as well. I need a drink.

Not even bothering to check which bottle of whiskey I have, I throw my desk drawer open and take a long drink. My throat feels like it's on fire and my empty stomach protests at the sensation of the liquor flooding in, but I continue. Right now, I need to quiet my mind, and whiskey always does the trick. The bottle gets ripped from my hands before I can pour more into my mouth, and I glare at my younger brother standing in front of me, looking unimpressed. Great. Another person I've managed to disappoint today. I scowl, both at myself and at Aidan.

"I was drinking that."

"Well aware. Though I don't think alcohol is the cure for an upset stomach." He shrugs, taking a seat on top of my desk, next to me.

"It's not. But it can help an upset mind." I reach over to take the bottle from him like a toddler. He refuses to give in, placing the bottle to his side and out of my reach.

"Maybe at the moment it feels like it's helping, but really it's just drowning out whatever feelings you're trying to avoid. Again, not a solution to the problem," Aidan presses.

"Since when did you become so profound?" I roll my eyes.

"You know since when." He looks down at his shoes, toying with the hem of his coat. He didn't need to say it. I'm not the only person who's changed since my father died. At least my final moments spent with my dad weren't at the opposite end of a vitriolic tirade in which I was essentially called the family fuck up. I have no doubt Aidan's been replaying the harsh words our father threw at him over and over in his head since. The same way I keep replaying my failures in my own.

"He didn't mean it, Aidan." I've lost track of the number of times I've repeated this phrase to my brother the past few weeks.

Aidan's jaw ticks. "He did. Father got angry and would spew bullshit at times. But this wasn't one of them. This was his wake-up call for me."

"He would have never torn into you like he had if he knew that would be the last time you two spoke—"

"Save it, Dec. I didn't come here to mope about my own issues. I came here to check on you."

My back stiffens. "There's nothing to check in about."

"Really? So that wasn't you bent over a toilet a few minutes ago? Puking your guts out like you just came back from bar hopping?"

"Food poisoning."

"From the restaurant in which you didn't even get a chance to order food?" he presses.

"If that's what I say it is, that's what it is." I cross my arms, not wanting to get into it.

"Wow. You really are just like him, huh?"

"Not nearly as much as I need to be," I admit. It was the truth. My father would have never gotten sick over the fact that one of his closest allies was nearly killed in front of him. He would have never let his emotions keep him from thinking rationally. *I should have kept the waiter for questioning instead of killing him then and there.*

Azula, Zahra's second, had called me earlier to inform me that they were unable to track down the poison and tie it to one of our rivals. The same went for the vulture tattoo. Two dead ends that could have led us somewhere if I had just managed to keep my head on my shoulders for a few minutes. But I couldn't. Not when that man had attempted to come for me. Attempted to come for Zahra. And used my own damn whiskey to do it. The bastard deserved to die.

"Father would've kept his composure. At least long enough to get a real answer out of the man who tried to kill us." I sigh.

"We gave the waiter a chance to divulge, and he didn't," Aidan attempts to comfort me.

"I barely pushed him. I should have brought him back here. Tied him up in our chambers..." I trail off, not needing to explain what I was implying. Staying quiet when you've barely been touched is easy, but over the years, I've found even the strongest man will start squealing when faced with isolation and torture. "That's what father would have done."

Aidan gives my shoulder a reassuring squeeze. "I think you're being too hard on yourself. Father was rarely able to keep collected when one of us was threatened. Or are you forgetting the fact that he literally strangled a man in broad daylight for bumping into Mom when she was pregnant with me?"

"How could I forget? It was the first time I saw him be violent in front of me." It had been the first and one of the few times I had ever been scared of him as a child. Something I knew he sensed, because later that day he sat me down and gave me a piece of advice that has stuck with me forever. *The world is cruel, Declan, and harsh. But it is also beautiful. And the things we find beautiful in this world, the things we love, we must protect at all costs. No matter the cost. Because if we don't, we'll lose the very thing we cherish the most.*

My father was right. The world is cruel. And instead of protecting him from being murdered, I had failed him. I had failed to protect what was good in this world. And I would never make that mistake again.

"I need to speak with Zahra again. Finish our meeting, and discuss how we should proceed following this incident."

The fact that in a span of weeks, not only were both of our fathers killed, but now we were also being targeted made one thing clear. Someone was waging a war against our two families. And if we didn't determine who, it would cost us everything.

———

"Again!" Zahra's voice echoes off the walls of the boxing ring as I watch her take calculated steps toward her opponent. The combination of jabs and kicks she sends flying are as impressive as they are lethal. I wince as I watch her land a solid punch right in the gut of a man towering over her. What she may lack in height, she makes up for in speed and stamina. Her opponent staggers back for a moment, then manages to land a punch that sends her head flying back.

A rush of blood fills my chest as I watch her land on the mat, stopping her fall with her hands. Her head lifts for a moment, locking eyes with me, as she spits blood out of her mouth like it's nothing. She's on her feet a blink after that, and I watch as she grapples her opponent's arm, wraps her legs, followed by her entire body around it, and drags him down to the mat. Try as he might, he can't break free of her grip, and the next thing I know, she's whipped out a knife and has it hovering over his neck. If this had been a real fight, I have no doubts she would have slit his throat. Instead, she leans back and finally releases him. She's magnificent.

How her trainer still manages to find something to critique is beyond me. "Make sure to keep your left arm up at all times. The only reason why I was able to land a punch was because you dropped it for a second."

Zahra gives him a quick nod before turning her attention back to me. The trainer gets the message, grabbing his equipment and leaving. Azula steps in a moment after, her nose scrunching together as she enters the gym. "You couldn't have picked somewhere to meet that didn't smell like sweat and rotten eggs, Z?"

"This was the only time that worked with my schedule, and I wasn't about to miss a session with Malcom. Especially not after what's transpired recently." She shrugs, grabbing her water bottle and chugging.

Her aura of nonchalance is exactly what you would expect from a boss, and the exact opposite of what I had displayed last night. She was born for this role. That much is more than clear. Anyone who questioned her qualifications or ability as a boss was an idiot.

"Shall we begin?" Zahra eyes Aidan and me before nodding toward a bench that I take a seat on. "Azula informed me that you're both updated on the evidence, or lack thereof, we found from the man who tried to kill us."

I nod.

"Cyrus is continuing to run facial recognition software with local surveillance footage, and will update us on any progress he's made. Until then, we continue business as normal." Zahra tosses her water bottle on the ground, opting to sit on the edge of the boxing rink. "Our first outing together confirmed our loyalty to each other...but it didn't quite demonstrate our strength. We'll need to remedy that."

My eyebrows furrow together. "You're concerned about our appearance and not the fact that someone tried to kill us?"

Azula rolls her eyes and clicks her tongue. As if being in the same room together is an insult to her intelligence. I feel Aidan stiffen next to me at the clear disrespect. To Zahra's credit, she does give Azula a small glare, who looks down ever so slightly at the reprimand.

"I'm concerned about *both* things, Mr. McAlister, and how

they influence each other. Someone attempting to murder us in broad daylight indicates we're being underestimated. They don't view us as a real threat. And that is a huge problem, because the second you're not seen as a threat..."

"You're a target that ends up dead," I summarize.

"Precisely." She glances at Aidan to see if he has any additional protests. He doesn't.

"So what are you proposing? Another lunch?" Returning to the same restaurant would be risky given the clear lack of security and ease of our enemies entering without notice, but it would also be a clear way of demonstrating how unfazed we are. Or really how unphased Zahra is. I, on the other hand, am more than fine never eating at The Black Rose again. Their filet mignon was superb; I'd given them that. But nothing worth dying over.

"I was thinking more like dinner. With December around the corner, it's the perfect time to revive my father's charity banquet. We'll invite all the made men as my father did in the past, allies and enemies alike, as well as all the state and local politicians." Zahra's attention is aimed at Azula now, who's typing away at her phone, likely already sending out invitations. A second later, my phone dings, and a save-the-date has landed in my inbox.

Naser's charity gala was an annual spectacle he'd hosted for decades. In many ways, it was another way he and my father had demonstrated their power. Hosting an event where mafia leaders, politicians, and their families were all in attendance, acting civilized would seem impossible to anyone who hadn't had the pleasure of being in the same room with Naser. But his charm, grace, and underlying threatening presence was unmatched. No one wanted to push him far enough and face his wrath.

The respect and fear he elicited from others was something

to aspire to. Something I have no doubts Zahra would easily achieve, and surpass, in her lifetime. "Having everyone who wants you dead in the same room is a bold choice."

"One we can hopefully use to our advantage. I'll contact my staff to ensure additional security precautions are implemented at my father's— at *my* manor." Zahra's matter-of-fact tone is in stark contrast to the slight shake of her hands as she clenches her hands into fists at her side.

Watching her briefly change from a cold-hearted mob boss to a child who had just lost her beloved father is difficult. It feels like looking in a mirror. The pit in my stomach returns full force. There's nothing I could do to erase the pain of losing our fathers, but at the very least, I could be there for her. I could confide my own pain and be a source of refuge for her. There were very few people in the world who fully understood the mix of anxiety, thrill, sorrow, and distrust that comes with being a boss. To be responsible for so many people's lives and well-being, all while yours was constantly being threatened. To never be able to go to sleep fully at peace because you know you could wake up with a barrel pointing at your head or a knife to your throat. If you're lucky enough to wake up at all.

Despite all the lies, backstabbing, and treachery that happened in our line of work, our fathers had still managed to find each other. Two men who were as honest as they could be and were fiercely loyal to those they loved. Though Zahra and I barely know each other, I want her to know that I intend to uphold the same level of loyalty to her as my father did to Naser. How I could get her to trust me was a different story.

Zahra is clearly incredibly intelligent, likely the smartest person in every room she walks into, which means her walls are not only up but likely made of steel and nearly impenetrable. Words alone would not be sufficient to gain her true support. Her true allyship. She would honor any established deals between our two mobs out of loyalty and respect for her father, but I didn't want her to work with me because of duty. I want her to work with me because she knows she can trust me.

"So I finally get to party at Naser's Northshore Mansion? Nice," Aidan cuts through the silence, but the lighthearted comment lands with no one.

"Actually, I was thinking about the Manor in Maine. It's more spacious, and hasn't really been open to strangers before," Zahra says.

The pit in my stomach turns into a sinkhole, and my throat tightens as a rush of guilt and shame fills me. I can't go back to that place. Every single inch of it will serve as a memory of my failure.

"Is that a problem, Declan?" Zahra's deep brown eyes bore into me as if she can read my mind.

I try to force words out of my mouth but all that comes out is a choking noise. To her credit, she doesn't look at me with pity or disgust. Zahra just stands there, patiently, as I take a moment to compose myself. Aidan clears his throat, getting ready to speak for me, but I raise a hand to stop him. I didn't need a mouthpiece. Maybe my openness and slight moment of vulnerability would show Zahra that she could confide in me. Or maybe she would just view me as a weak man unfit for my role. *No. She won't.* I barely knew this woman, yet something in me felt like she would understand me. That she wouldn't judge me for grieving because she likely knew exactly what was going on inside my head right now.

"I was in the Maine Manor, picking up a shipment, when I got a call that our fathers were targeted," I manage to spit out before my throat constricts again and my heart pounds so hard I swear it's about to fall out of my chest.

"You were in Maine?" Zahra's voice has a sharp edge that

makes me flinch. My mind finishes the rest of her question, *'You were in Maine while our fathers were bleeding out?'*

"I drove down as fast as I could to help. We got them into your medical wing immediately but...the damage had already been done."

Zahra's eyes close, her body visibly shaking, and I feel compelled to comfort her. I'm halfway across the floor when she releases a deep breath and opens her eyes. "Azula and I will look into banquet halls in the city. A place where neither of us has any ties to."

I take a step back, wanting to give her some space but also remain close enough in case she decides to take my unspoken offer of comfort. She doesn't.

"I'm late for my next meeting. Azula will show you both out. You can let her know if you need anything else from me," Zahra says tersely, sliding out through the back door of the gym before I can stop her. Before I can tell her I understand. Instead, I just stand there barely paying attention to Aidan and Azula exchanging niceties, wondering if the blood on my hands will ever disappear or continue to stain everyone around me.

7
ZAHRA

"Dammit, c'mon," I groan, staring at the black screen of my laptop while another 'ACCESS DENIED' message pops up on the screen. I'd been at this for hours and somehow couldn't crack through the security system on Declan's phone. All the technology that belonged to the Persian Empire, as well as the Irish mob, had been specially designed by my father to ensure none of our enemies could hack into it. Anyone else's firewalls, I would've been able to bypass in a matter of minutes, an hour tops. But my father's code was very delicate. He had woven extensive threat detections into his code, and I knew that one wrong move from me would trigger an automatic deletion of any and all information stored in Declan's phone. Given I needed that information to prove Declan had lied about being in Maine when our fathers were killed, I couldn't risk losing it.

Which is why I had spent a majority of my day curled up in the dark, dungeon-like room where all our computers and servers were physically stored. Trying, and failing, to remotely connect to his phone and download all the files saved on it, including the geotracker that stored all the locations he had traveled in the past few years. The geotracker that updated every ten seconds and would indicate that he was in the same room as my father when he was killed.

His performance a few days ago in the gym was good, I'd give him that. From the look of emotional turmoil in his eyes to the way his body was slumped over, it was so easy to believe he was nothing more than a devoted son grieving his father. For a moment, he even had me fooled, but I knew better. Declan is a merciless, bloodthirsty, power-hungry killer. That much has been made clear over the past few weeks as I continued my weekly strategy meetings with Cyrus.

Though Azula is my second hand, Cyrus has decades of experience working with my father and his knowledge about all the dirty secrets each mob carried is endless. Secrets are powerful tools that can be used to your advantage or wielded like a lethal weapon against you. While my father had done his best to keep me in the loop about the ins and outs of the family business and provided general warnings to me about our biggest enemies, namely the Italians, Greeks, and British, he never got into the details. From the moment I took over as a boss, I wanted to know everything I possibly could about the men I would be working with, and the monsters I'd have to face. Cyrus was hesitant to help in the beginning, likely due to whatever paternalistic feelings he had toward me, but I had insisted he didn't need to spare my feelings or shield me from the world. And so our meetings began.

Our first few conversations left me unmoved. Our enemies were practically foaming at the mouth to bring us down, and over the past decade, had made us bleed physically, through various bombings and shootings, and financially, setting a few of our shipment facilities on fire. They'd made a small dent in my Empire, but nothing warranted true concern. I would never underestimate my enemies, but their war tactics were par for the course.

It's what our allies are capable of that makes my stomach turn. Or, really, what Declan is capable of. It wasn't his ability to kill men twice his size with his bare hands, or his expertise in torturing captives, that brought a chill down my spine. After all, when it came to torture, Azula's methods would make the devil weep. It's Declan's treatment of the children and wives of his enemies that makes my skin crawl. I'm vehemently against any organizations associated with human trafficking, despite how lucrative the business is. Women and children are not people's property, and I refuse to play any role in the various types of abuse that are associated with the skin trade.

My father felt the same, which is why many Made Men doubted he would ever reach the level of success that he did. As far as I knew, all the McAlister's had worked alongside us to limit trafficking in the greater Boston area. All of the McAlister's except for one. How Cyrus managed to obtain this information, I'm not sure. But he'd heard from an inside source working for the Irish that Declan was looking to expand into different types of business that his father would never approve of once he took over as boss.

My father had instructed Cyrus to gather more information before going to his best friend about his son's betrayal. At first, Cyrus hit a dead end, believing that the families of Declan's victims had simply fled the city and gone into hiding, but he eventually exposed the truth. He was on the way to alert my father of Declan's betrayal when he heard gunshots coming from my father's office. In some ways, I'm glad the truth was never revealed to Declan's father. If the bullet didn't kill him, I'm sure the news about his son would have.

"How you manage to stay in here longer than five minutes is beyond me." Azula makes a disgusted noise as she enters the room. "There's barely any room for a small child to fit in here, and it's so cold I swear I can see my own breath."

"The majority of our servers are in this room. Think of how hot your computer can be when you have like ten browser tabs open. Now imagine hundreds of computers in a room running all of our national and international operations. Without a proper cooling system, all of our technology would overheat, shut down, and we'd be screwed." The thought causes a rush of anxiety to flood my chest.

"Wow, sometimes I forget what a nerd you are about these things." Azula leans against one of our servers and I try not to outwardly cringe.

"Well, I did major and get my masters in Computer Science, so..." A perk of keeping my true identity hidden all these years was growing up and having a fairly normal life. That was what my father wanted for me. And something I would be eternally grateful for.

"Sometimes I forget you know a life beyond all this."

"So do I." The words come out like a soft sigh.

"I don't know how you do it."

"Do what?"

"Continue to live in this world where your life is always threatened and your morals are grey at best. Especially when you've had a taste of the normal world." There's no judgment in her voice. Just curiosity.

"One's life is always fleeting, Azula. Even in the 'normal' world, no day is promised."

"That's true, but haven't you ever wondered if you could do more?"

"All the time. But doing more doesn't mean I have to abandon all I know. Abandon everyone I love."

"Ah, so you're one of those people who wants to have it all?" she snorts.

My eyebrows knit together. "Doesn't everyone want that?"

Azula shakes her head, causing the pin-straight strands of her bob to sway. "Most people are content with what they have. But you, my darling, have never been content. You've always wanted more. Wanted better. Which is why I'm not sure whether this world is for you."

I sit up in my chair, spine stiff. "Are you insinuating that I'm not fit as a boss?" I hissed. Of all the people to doubt me, I never figured Azula would be one of them. She knows how hard I've worked for this. How much it meant to me to be able to carry on my father's legacy.

"Never, Zahra. *Never*," she emphasizes. "You are more than capable of this position. I just don't know if this...lifestyle is worthy of you."

The tension in my shoulders lessens, though the stress is immediately replaced with the thoughts racing around in my head. Thoughts about taking the Persian Empire into a different direction....a less lethal and deceptive direction. Thoughts that I shoved away, as they were simply unrealistic distractions. Nothing worth my time. "Didn't know you had a degree in career counseling. Guess you learn something new every day."

Azula rolls her eyes. "My role as your second is to make sure your head is in the right space, and stay up to date on where we're heading..." She takes a step closer to me as she reads the words on my laptop. "Care to inform me who the rat we need to kill is?"

"I'm sorry?"

"You're trying to hack into someone's tech, right? If it were one of our enemies, you would've broken through their firewall in a matter of seconds at most. But you've hit a dead end. That means the security installed on their device is elite. Likely uses something your father made. So, either you suspect we have a rat within the Empire or...or it's one of the Irish." Her eyes widen.

Dammit. I should have known sooner or later, Azula would realize I'd been on edge more than normal. I don't want her to get involved yet. Not until I've gathered more proof. I don't need her thinking I've gone off the conspiracy theory deep end.

My silence may as well be an admission of guilt.

Her jaw clenches, eyes filled with rage. "Would this have anything to do with the fact that only your glass was poisoned at lunch?"

I give her a nod.

"I guess we have our answer as to why Declan's glass came back clean, but why would one of his henchmen want you dead? Or at the very least, why would they be stupid enough to go behind Declan's back and try to kill one of their strongest allies? Misogyny aside, the Irish would crumble without our tech and protection on the trade routes." Azula rakes her fingers through her hair.

"I don't think they did go behind Declan's back. I think they were following his orders." I feel a weight release from my chest, finally speaking the words out loud.

Azula's jaw drops open. "*What? Why?*"

I search her face for any hints of doubt in me. Any hints that she may think I'm crazy. I find none. "I think he's the one who killed my father, and his own. I have some evidence that points to him and I'm working on collecting more. He knows I'm onto him. Or at least he knows I no longer think it's the Italians. So he's coming for me before I can expose the truth." And I would expose the truth. Even if it killed me.

Azula sits on the floor cross-legged and shuts her eyes. Her body is shaking with what I can assume is rage, and I watch as she takes in deep breath after deep breath in an attempt to collect herself. The whirring of the machines is the only noise that fills the room for minutes until her eyes finally snap back open. "Why didn't you tell me about this from the moment you suspected him? Why the *hell* did you let yourself be alone with him at lunch?"

"I wanted to collect more evidence before I told anyone. I needed to keep the facade that everything was normal so he wouldn't suspect I was coming after him."

"Keeping his suspicions low shouldn't eclipse your safety. I'm your second in command, dammit! Beyond that, I'm your *best friend*. I can't protect you if I don't know you're actively putting yourself in danger."

"No one, not even you, can fully protect me. That's the burden of this job. You'll drive yourself crazy if you think differently," I caution.

Her nostrils flare, likely in irritation that I lied to her and pointed out the fact that she didn't possess magical powers that allowed her to play god. "From now on, you will include me in your decisions."

"Azula—"

"It's not up for discussion. I won't tell Cyrus or any of the inner circle, but you need to include me in your future plans."

A fair compromise that was arguably much more than I had earned.

"So long as you won't try to stop me and the plans I come up with." I wouldn't be restrained. Not even by my loved ones.

She clicks her tongue. "I won't try to stop you, but I may try to improve your plans. I am a strategist after all."

"Deal."

"Deal," she echoes, a dark smirk forming on her face. "So, where do we begin?"

8

DECLAN

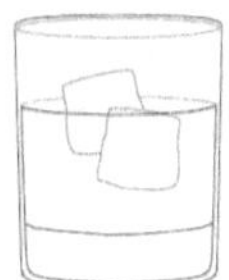

The analog clock on my desk has been taunting me for the past three hours. Nightmares for me are a regular endeavor, but they've worsened since the loss of my father. Usually, I'd be able to roll back to sleep, the dream forgotten by the morning. Tonight is not one of those nights. My nightmare started similarly to the rest. I was having dinner with my father and Naser. The two were joking around as they normally would. In between discussing business updates, they would find the time to tease me about my inability to commit to a woman. This time, the collective sound of booming laughter was higher in pitch. In my dream, Zahra, sitting between her father and me, had an illuminating smile on her face that matched the melodic laugh falling from her lips. Our eyes lock together, and she shoots me a quick wink, as if we'd had a long-standing rapport of her busting my balls. I roll my eyes teasingly, all while pouring her a drink.

My father, Naser, and Zahra clink their glasses together in cheers, each taking a large gulp as the light in the room begins to darken. Almost instantly, everyone turns pale, Zahra clutching at her throat as blood starts to trickle out of her nose and mouth. I rush to help Zahra, laying her on the floor to begin CPR compressions, a feeble attempt to save the woman dying in front of me. Distracted by saving Zahra, I neglect to notice my father and Naser have also begun to bleed. A final faint breath comes from Zahra and the dead look in her eyes makes me sick. I look around to see my father and Naser also dead. A voice starts to fill the room, chanting over and over again.

You did this.

I had jolted awake a few hours ago, my entire body shaking, covered in sweat, and all I could do was rub at my hands. No physical blood is covering them, yet all I can see is red. Nightmares about not being able to save my father and Naser from their killer are bad enough. This new dream, in which I unintentionally cause Zahra's death as well, is its own special type of torture. I had failed Naser already by not being able to protect him. I refuse to fail him again by not protecting his daughter. And yet I'd already managed to let him down.

I want nothing more in this moment than to check in on Zahra to ensure that she is alive and breathing and safe. But I have no doubts she would chew my head off if I try, and not just because it's five am. She would view my desire to protect her as a slight, like I viewed her as some fragile damsel in distress that needed a bodyguard. I can't blame her for thinking that of me. I have no doubts that most men in her life treat her as something weak that needs to be guarded, as opposed to recognizing her strength and letting her reign free.

Watching her spar in the gym, unrestrained and determined, was nothing short of breathtaking. I could have stood there for hours watching her. Rooting for her to burn down her enemies and everything that dared to hold her back. I don't want to dampen her light or temper her rage. I want to ensure she would be able to fight forever. That's the point of having close allies. My father worked diligently not only to ensure our own victory, but also that of the Persians. Our two mobs are so intertwined that if one of us goes down, the other is sure to crumble not long after. Which is why I have to convince Zahra to trust me, convince her to take our support and protection. Not because she desperately needs it, but because our two families need each other. Now more than ever.

The look of disgust mixed with suspicion she had given me in our last meeting clued me into the uphill battle I'm about to face trying to get her on my side. She may continue the ongoing arrangements between our two organizations out of respect for her father's wishes, but she surely doesn't want anything to do with me. I can't fault her for it. She doesn't know me beyond the stories she's heard, and everyone knows how easily stories can be twisted to benefit someone's gain. I've spun several webs of lies in order to seal a deal or obtain an advantage. My family is constantly at war, and wars are seldom won without letting go of some of your morals and values along the way.

Groaning at the faint hint of light from the morning sky starting to peek through my curtains, I throw off my comforter and head straight to my home gym. If I was going to be awake at this ungodly hour, I might as well be doing something useful.

The punching bag groans as I land my first hit. It takes me a few minutes to find my rhythm and truly be able to turn my thoughts off, but eventually I get there. Instead of being tormented by the image of my father, Naser, and Zahra bleeding out on the floor, my mind starts to repeat different boxing combinations over and over again. Admittedly, my hits are a bit sloppier than I would like but I chalk that up to lack of sleep and food this early in the morning.

This workout isn't about being perfect, or even getting my full rage out—I would've knocked the punching bag clear off its hinges if that was the case. No. Today's workout is a desperate search for peace and quiet. A need for something, anything, to distract me from the guilt that had now found a way into my dreams. Sweat starts to drip down my back, and slowly but surely, my mind goes silent.

There's no windows or even a clock in the gym so I lose track of what time it is until a faint scent of sausage, bacon, and eggs hits my nose, making my mouth water. My punches start to slow and eventually I fall to the ground, panting, while the sound of my stomach growling fills the room.

"You know, hitting the gym at five in the morning doesn't make you any cooler than waiting until like, I don't know, nine." Aidan stands above me, a plate full of breakfast in his hand as he brings his fork loaded with egg toward his mouth. "Maybe your punches wouldn't be so sloppy if you weren't sleep-deprived and food-deprived." He shrugs, taking another bite.

"I couldn't sleep even if I wanted to. I figured I may as well do something productive," I groan, laying on the floor, not having the energy to stand up.

"You know, normal people who can't sleep try herbal tea. A bath. Even some melatonin. Not nearly killing themselves at the gym."

"Well, I've never been normal," I point out, taking a piece of toast from his hand and scarfing it down.

"You can say that again," Aidan snorts. "For starters, who actually *likes* whole wheat toast?"

"Of all the things you could harass me about at this moment...you've chosen my favorite *bread?*" I roll my eyes.

"I take my duty as the annoying younger brother very seriously."

"Clearly." I take in a deep breath before finally standing up, ignoring the way my entire body aches in pain.

"Was it a nightmare again?" Aidan's voice drops. Our gym in the basement is incredibly secluded so the risk of having prying ears was low. Still, you could never be too cautious.

I move my head slightly. If he blinked, he would have missed the minuscule nod.

Aidan's eyes are locked on my face. "What was it this time?"

"Same as always. This time, Zahra was added to the mix."

"Damn, Zahra got a cameo in one of your dreams before your *own brother*. What am I, chopped liver?" Aidan scoffs in mock offense.

"Only you would be upset that I didn't dream you were poisoned and murdered."

"I just can't believe someone who's practically a stranger made the cut before I did! I know you're a sucker for a pretty face, Dec, but—"

I sent him a lethal look, nearly growling. "That's the boss of the Persian mafia you're talking about. Show some damn respect."

Aidan's eyes widen as he shuts his mouth and mimes zipping it closed. He trails behind me as I head upstairs into the kitchen.

Maura, our chef and the woman who practically doubled as my grandmother, slams a hefty plate filled to the brim with scrambled eggs, whole wheat toast, and sausage into my chest. "You better lick that plate clean, Declan. You're looking like a skeleton these days. And I know I'm a damn good cook so it's not because my food doesn't taste good."

"Yes, ma'am," I grumble, knowing better than to fight as she slides over a mug of black coffee.

"Can I have some sugar, please?" I ask sheepishly, like a little child asking for an extra dessert. It doesn't matter where I rank in the mob; to Maura, I'm family, which means she could boss me around and treat me like one of her grandchildren. Which includes smacking me over the head whenever she thinks I'm acting stupid.

"Fine. But only because you asked so nicely." She purses her lips, spooning a massive heaping into my mug, just the way I like it

"Oh, c'mon! I get scolded for adding more sugar to my drink, but Declan doesn't. I thought being the youngest meant you were able to get away with shit. This family is rigged against me," Aidan jokingly protests, pouting like a toddler.

Maura grabs a wooden spoon from the counter and wags it in Aidan's face, a warning. "Aidan McAlister, what have I told you about using that kind of language around me? Don't make me get the soap bar."

We both wince at the thought. Unsurprisingly, Aidan and I's preteen years were incredibly angsty and filled with self-important moments where we both thought we could get away with murder (figuratively speaking, of course). Maura was always there to remind us who the *real* adult was. One of her favorite punishments was shoving a bar of soap into our mouths for a few minutes after she caught us swearing. Tattling to our father was no use. He would just laugh and say that he hoped we'd learned our lesson. We seldom did.

"Nope. No. No soap needed here. I can be a good boy going forward. Sorry, Maura." The devilish smirk on Aidan's face, paired with the wink he gives me once Maura has her back turned to him, tells me otherwise, but the simple apology seems to have done its job. She hands him a cup of steaming coffee with two spoons of sugar in it a moment later, before taking a seat next to me at the breakfast table.

Maura gives my hand a gentle squeeze. "If the nightmares are keeping you up again, Dec, maybe it's time you talk to someone..."

"Like who? I'm not sure there's a therapist who specializes in treating mob bosses. Last thing I need is someone blabbing all my issues to my enemies. Voluntarily or otherwise." Information was one of the greatest weapons someone could use against you. Which only makes it harder to talk about your feelings, not like I do that often either.

Society as a whole shuns men who show any sign of emotion that's not anger or confidence. Those messages were only heightened by being raised within a mob. Though my mother and Maura tried their best to be a safe space for me to truly open up and be vulnerable, I could never bring myself to do it. It was too risky. If I revealed how affected I had been by the events of the past few weeks, I'd be viewed as weak. And the second a leader is seen as such, their days and the days of their loved ones are numbered. I refused to have any more of my family's blood on my hands, so I stayed quiet. Silence is safer.

The sympathetic look on Maura's face nearly kills me. I straighten my back and slap a smile on my face in an effort to appear less pathetic.

It falls almost as flat as Aidan's joke that follows. "Would you feel better if I told you Declan was dreaming about a girl?"

Maura snorts. "No. I have no interest in whatever perverted dreams you two have."

"While Declan's dream wasn't PG, it's not for the reasons you think," Aidan presses, waiting for her to take the bait.

"Drop it, Aidan," I warn, though it comes off much less threatening than I hoped it would. Weird. Maybe Maura was right. Maybe I do want to talk to someone about my recurring nightmares and the guilt that's been weighing on me. No. I couldn't. It would be too dangerous.

What I can't manage to force out of my own mouth comes flowing out of Aidan's. "He dreamt he killed Dad and Naser again..." Maura places her small hand on my face, cradling my cheek, as tears start to form in her eyes. "...except he was also responsible for Zahra's death."

Maura's eyebrows draw together. "Zahra?"

"Naser's daughter. The new boss," I answer, the words coming out choked.

A kaleidoscope of emotion rushes over Maura's face. From realization, to sympathy, to something...else. Something I can't entirely read at first. Something that looks an awful lot like curiosity and...excitement. That can't be right. What the hell about me having nightmares could be exciting to her? I'm definitely reading her wrong.

Except her tone does sound lighter. If I didn't know any better, I'd say she almost sounded giddy. "And how often have you been dreaming of Zahra?"

"Just this once. And it wasn't exactly filled with rainbows and butterflies. I dreamed that I accidentally poisoned her. Poisoned all of them." I pinch the bridge of my nose, feeling a headache coming on.

"I see. Have you been spending a lot of time together?" Maura asks, catching me off guard. While she had no misconceptions about what I and my family did for a living, she lived by a strict 'Don't ask, don't tell' policy. She loved me and Aidan, as well as my parents when they were still alive. But she didn't necessarily approve of how we all made a living. I suppose that was the thing about love. It's so complex that it can make it easy to ignore some of the worst parts of a person, because all of their best moments outshine everything else.

"About as much time as two bosses would." I shrug.

"As much as your father and Naser did?"

"No. Definitely not."

Maura gives me her first motherly smile of the day. The one that tells me she's going to give me advice I won't necessarily want to hear, which definitely means she's right. "I don't have to tell you how hard this lifestyle is, Declan. Your father only survived as long as he did because he had a confidant. A friend. Him and Naser relied on each other for more than just business deals. I think it could be worth you and Zahra forming that same relationship."

The thought had crossed my mind more than once. While my brother and Maura were always here for me, they didn't fully understand the complicated emotional and psychological web that was being a mob boss. Especially one who had become boss at the expense of losing someone irreplaceable. Zahra knew that hurt. The hollow look in her eyes is the same one I recognize in myself.

"You know, Maura, I think you're right. I think I could use a friend. And I think she could too."

9
ZAHRA

"Declan is being incredibly persistent." Azula's eyes flicker between her planner, which contains my weekly schedule, and my irritated expression.

"Just because he's throwing a tantrum doesn't mean he's worth my time." I roll my eyes.

"Well, in fairness, I wouldn't say Declan is throwing a tantrum as much as his assistant is. Seems like Declan is adamant he wants to meet with you soon. Not sure about what."

"Probably so he can take another shot at poisoning me."

"He'd be stupid to try that again, less than two weeks after the whole lunch debacle. If he's smart, he'll have someone kill you. Either running you off the road or a sniper so that he can maintain his innocence." Azula nods to herself as if either plan would be foolproof.

"Well, it's a good thing you're on my side and not his. Or else I'd already be six feet under." I bring my attention back to the series of spreadsheets open on my computer.

I'd spent the past two hours backtracking our shipments

for the past six months and one thing was glaringly clear: my numbers weren't adding up. At first, I thought it had to be my own error. A formula being miscalculated or numbers being misentered. But I hadn't made any mistakes. As I meticulously combed through the spreadsheet over a dozen times, one thing was evident. We were in the red. Even though we had no reason to be.

None of our staff had reported any damage to the shipments, which means we had either miscounted how many computer chips and guns we'd had to send off and sell to make a profit or one of our own soldiers had stolen from us. The first option is unlikely given the amount of times myself and Declan's staff crunched all the numbers and projected estimates to be sure everything was in line, which left me with option two. Dammit. As if there isn't enough on my plate, I now have to track down a rat who was stupid enough to cross me.

My eyes shut in defeat and I pinch the bridge of my nose between my fingers. "Tell Declan I'll meet with him tomorrow at noon. And to not be late."

"Wow, I didn't expect you to cave so easily. I guess I'm more intimidating than I thought." A prideful look covers Azula's face.

"You're absolutely terrifying, but my decision to meet with Declan comes out of necessity." I turn my monitor around so she can see it.

Azula cocks her head to the side for a moment, taking in the various columns, numbers, and totals. "Shit...is this saying what I think it is?"

"Someone's stealing from us. Likely someone from the inside, since they were smart enough only to take small enough amounts that it would have gone unnoticed in the moment. But over the course of six months, the stolen supplies have cost us tens of thousands of dollars. If not more. I need to tell Declan about this." The universe trying to bring us together when I'm doing my best to avoid him is incredibly ironic. I suppose that's why the saying goes, 'We make plans and God laughs'. Except this time, it seems like Declan has gotten the last laugh.

"Any chance that this could also be him? Maybe the supplies haven't been stolen, and instead he's just taking a bigger cut of the pie?"

"Unlikely. I received a call from Damon, the Scottish boss, who's been one of our best customers for the past five years. He called me directly, asking when the remaining shipments would arrive since they've been getting some threats from the local street gangs near them. I asked him how many he received in the most recent package we delivered a few days ago and they were clearly ten guns short of what we'd origi-nally sent. I'm having Cyrus hand deliver an extra fifteen, five extra on us, as we speak."

"Dammit."

"My thoughts exactly. I wanted to double-check that we hadn't miscalculated anything, but all the receipts and logs of what we sent confirm that 300 guns left our warehouse and arrived at the delivery center."

"So it was one of our foot soldiers then? Should be easy enough to track them down and remind them who they've crossed." Azula pulls a knife from the holder on her thigh and checks her reflection in it.

"Our distribution center in Los Angeles is one of our biggest. Between our people and the Irish, we have at least a thousand staff working there. It could've been any of them. Given they'd gone undetected for months now, they must know all the blind spots of the building."

"Just send me out there and I'll have the traitor pissing his own pants in a matter of minutes," she seethes.

I don't doubt her words. But I don't want to be the type of boss that leads with fear. I want respect. And respect would come with tracking down the traitor myself, exposing him, and demonstrating not only my physical power but also my mental strength.

"I promise to let you have your fun with him, whoever he ends up being. But I want to take a stab at finding him first. Without having to immediately resort to threats."

"You can take the first stab as long as I get the other twenty that follow." Azula licks her teeth with her tongue.

"That is *not* what I meant."

"Why not? There's few things that give me as much joy as feeling a man bleed under me."

"You're an incredibly deranged individual." I love her regardless, but it has to be said.

Azula places a hand on her chest. "Oh, Zahra, you say the kindest things to me."

"Yeah, yeah. Just get the meeting with Declan set up, will you? The more I think about this mess, the more my blood boils."

"Don't worry, you'll figure it out. You always do." Azula gives me one final reassuring smile before heading out of my office.

Though I appreciate her vote of confidence, I'm not quite sure I deserve it. I just hope I'll live long enough to prove her right. To prove to everyone that I am worthy of taking over for my father. To prove to myself that I can handle being the boss.

—

. . .

Arman knocks on my door, causing my back to stiffen. "Your guest has arrived," he announces.

"Thank you. Send him in." I close all the excess files on my computer screen, leaving only the ones that Declan needs to see. Mainly, the long list of evidence that points to someone stealing from us.

Arman grimaces, his shoulders tensing, while chewing on his lip. I don't think I've ever seen him this nervous before. The head of my father's security had always been a brick wall. Sure, he may have joked around with me as a kid and treated me like a pseudo niece, but anxious was not an expression I'd ever seen on him before.

My hand immediately moves to the holster tucked under my blazer, ensuring it is in place. "What's wrong? Have you been attacked?"

"No. No, nothing like that. It's just, uh..." He tugs at his collar.

"Just say it, Arman. I'm a big girl, you don't have to coddle me. I can handle it," I snap.

Arman winces at my harsh tone, and a small wave of guilt hits me. Arman had been one of the few members of my father's staff who treated me with nothing but respect since the moment I took over. Clearly, I had some of my own insecurities I need to work through. Just because some men doubted my ability to rule doesn't mean that all of them did. And while those who doubted me deserved to be shunned by me, I need to be better at showing grace to those who had put their necks out on the line to support me.

"Forgive me, Arman. The current situation with all the shipments has had me...in a mood."

He gives me a tight smile. "There's nothing to forgive. Declan's here. He just insists on meeting you in the garden."

Declan wants to meet me out in the open air? Damn, maybe Azula was right and he did have a sniper out to get me. Killing me in my own home would be ballsy but I wouldn't put anything past Declan these days. Or maybe it was just a dick measuring contest.

Arman senses my hesitation. "Given Declan has come into our estate twice now, maybe a small compromise with meeting him in the garden would be a kind gesture between allies?"

Dammit, he had a point. I'm still supposed to be pretending that I don't despise Declan. "Has the perimeter been checked?" I ask, hoping I didn't come off as overly suspicious.

"Three times. I wouldn't allow you, or Declan, to remain outside if I had any concerns."

"Thank you, Arman." I give him a small smile before letting out a deep breath and stepping outside.

With spring slowly starting to fade into summer came the suffocating humidity. I debate leaving my blazer inside but that would leave me unarmed, so instead I tolerate the sweat that's already started to form down my back. Declan appears to be equally impacted by the new rise in temperature, though he's smart enough to come in a white cotton t-shirt and black jeans. He looks so...normal. Like any other man I'd pass on the street. Well, any other man who was 6'3, had incredible posture, and biceps that were so defined I'm sure they could be seen from a mile away. Still, there was such a casual undertone to his stance, the way he looked at the tulips in my father's garden with curiosity, and the boyish smile he sent my way as I approached.

"I was beginning to think you forgot about me." Declan

removes his sunglasses, tucking them into his shirt, the color of his eyes a beautiful mix of green and blue.

"Nope. Though I wasn't planning on meeting you outside." I keep my voice cold and distant, like I'd rather be getting a root canal than conversing with him. A fact he clearly doesn't miss as his cheerful expression drops. The twisted part of me relishes seeing the smug expression fall from his face. It's the least he deserves. But the rational part of my brain yelled at me to put on a facade.

I have to get closer to him, both emotionally and physically. With my lack of success in being able to remotely hack into his phone and computer, I'd come up with an alternative. A small bug I designed that could connect to his cellphone and transfer all the files and information stored. The only catch is I haven't tested it out yet. Which means I'm not entirely sure how close I need to be in order for my device to detect Declan's phone...and I also don't know how long the transfer would take. So naturally, this means I have to stall as long as possible, and do the one thing that drew a true shudder from me. Engage in small talk.

"So, any reason in particular you wanted to meet in my father's garden as opposed to the perfectly air-conditioned building a few feet away?" Flashing Declan a genuine smile, I take a step closer to him and feel my phone vibrate. *Perfect, it's working. Now I just needed to keep him occupied here long enough.*

"It's the first warm day of the year. What could be better than taking in the sun and walking around a garden?" He shoves his hands into his pockets almost as if he's...nervous. Like he's waiting for me to scoff at him.

I suppose, in his defense, that is a pretty accurate assumption of what I wanted to do. But no matter how good he is at pretending to be authentic, I can't fall for his charms. Still, I guess there's no harm in letting him *think* I'm softening up to him.

"Well, I can't say I love the fact that I can feel my boobs starting to sweat, but I haven't seen all the flowers that have bloomed yet, so I'll let you win this battle." The words fall out of my mouth before I can stop them. Welp. Can't say I had entirely planned on talking about boob sweat with Declan today, but this is how I normally talk to my friends, so maybe he'll appreciate the clear effort I'm trying to put in. Or maybe he'll think I'm a nutcase. Either works for me.

My face starts to heat and I know for certain I'm blushing. Great. As if he needs another thing to tease me about. He presses his lips together. Hard. No doubt trying to prevent the laugh that is desperately begging to come loose from his mouth.

Gesturing toward the stone path in front of us, I take a step forward and Declan follows. Good. I need him close to me.

Between the sun beating down on me and Declan's cocky-yet-lethal demeanor, I know these next few hours were about to be a nightmare. The only saving grace is the fact that after this, I would have everything I needed to silence Declan for good.

10

DECLAN

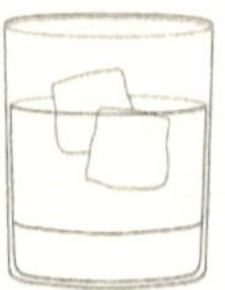

Good news, bad news.

The bad news is that Zahra definitely hates me. Why, I have no idea. The good news is—it's possible that she hates the world right now, not just me per se, which I can't blame her for. The world was a dumpster fire on a normal day, not to mention the fact that she had recently lost Naser... I can't blame her for being angry at everything and everyone.

I try to remind myself of my true intentions for today, to let my guard down in front of her and show her that I'm more than a business ally. I'm a friend. Or, at least, I want to be. Taking a walk in her father's garden was my first attempt at showing her that, to assuage the ongoing guilt and nightmares I'd been experiencing, and instead to remind myself of all the happy moments I'd spent with my father and Naser. Admittedly, I couldn't take credit for this idea. Maura had found me wide awake in the kitchen at three am two nights ago. From the hollow look in her eyes, I suspected she had also been kept up by her own dreams. We both gave each other a sympathetic smile while I made us a warm cup of tea.

Maura rarely divulged the details of her life to us, but that night she let me see a part of her I never knew. She told me about a love so bright and glamorous that it was all she could have ever hoped for as a young girl. Until it wasn't. Until she spent every night wondering whether the blows she received that night would be verbal or physical. With two young kids in tow, she felt trapped. Especially back then, when a woman wasn't even allowed a credit card in her own name. So she stayed. She stayed until a new neighbor moved in next door. A woman who showed her kindness she'd never known before. A woman who helped her escape and remained one of her best friends to this day.

Over the years, Maura had so many good memories that the past faded away like an old photograph. But some nights her memories came back. And in those moments, she poured herself a cup of tea and replayed all the happier days in her head. Over and over again, until she could breathe. So she could feel free again. At the end of our heart-to-heart, Maura had given me a homework assignment—to fight off my guilt by remembering all the good moments. To not let one of the worst days of my life taint the better days to come. I promised her that I would try. And here I was, trying.

"Have the roses bloomed yet?" A neutral question. One that should be safe enough. I brace for impact, but it never comes.

"They have. If we walk a little further, you'll be able to start smelling them." Zahra nods her head forward, encouraging me to take the lead. *Maybe so she can stick a knife in your back.* The cynical voice in my head makes its presence known.

A few feet later, my nose is filled with the sweet and slightly spicy aroma of the expansive array of red, pink, and cream roses covering the bushes in front of me. I nearly jump at the feel of Zahra's arm brushing against mine, not expecting her to come so close to me. The scent of roses is complemented by her perfume, a soft combination of vanilla and cardamom. Absolutely intoxicating. My hand twitches closer to hers, as if there's a magnetic force between us that I can't help but be drawn too. A pull tugging at me so deeply, it almost hurts when I shove my hands back into my pockets.

"Roses were always my father's favorite. He loved their beauty. Their variety. But most of all, he loved their hidden artillery. How something so delicate could also cause an immense amount of pain." Zahra reaches over, carefully inspecting a blood red rose before plucking it from the bush. She adjusts her fingers slightly, ensuring none of the thorns come close to her soft fingers, before extending the flower out to me.

The corners of my lips rise. It isn't exactly an olive branch, but from her, it may as well be. Bringing the flower to my nose, I inhale.

"The water lilies were always my favorite, especially at night when your father would turn the lights in the pond on," I confide. "It felt like something out of a Disney movie....Why are you looking at me like that?" I laugh at her incredulous expression.

Zahra's eyes were naturally large, but now they'd widened so much they looked almost cartoonish. "The big bad mafia boss likes *Disney*?"

Is this...friendly banter? "I mean, I wasn't always a mafia boss. Every kid goes through a Disney phase. You're going to tell me you didn't?"

"Nope. I was more of a Cartoon Network kid." She shrugs.

"Well, that explains it," I tease.

"What's that supposed to mean?" I catch a slight twinge upward in her lips.

"I mean, everyone knows Cartoon Network was for the kids who had issues. Loners. Rebels. Unhinged all around."

"You got all of that from me watching cartoons?" She cocks an eyebrow, placing a hand on her hip, drawing my attention to her lush curves.

Until now, I haven't let myself fully admire how truly stunning she is. From her naturally wide, deep brown eyes, the plump shape of her lips, and the soft curves of her body. My hands twitch in my pockets, wanting to run my fingers through the thick waves of her jet-black hair. *What the hell is wrong with me?* I'm acting like a teenage boy who had never seen a woman before, and not a boss who's used to having models throw themselves at me. It's clear Zahra's beauty, much like her wit, is a weapon she could wield expertly if needed. And if she impacts me this much without even trying, I have no doubts she could easily have me wrapped around her finger if she really tried.

She leans in slightly, cocking her head as she waits for my response. Shit. What had she said? What were we even talking about? Did she notice me ogling her? If she did, I'm sure I would have already had my balls on a stick. Hopefully, she just thinks making a witty comeback is difficult for me.

I clear my throat. "I'm incredibly perceptive. Plus, isn't it part of the job to be able to read people?" Perceptive was certainly one of saying, 'For some reason, I can't seem to get you out of my head.'

"Hmm, I suppose you're right. Well, in that case, given your strong attachment to Disney movies—"

"Hold on, I never said I was *attached*—" I correct.

"I would assume that you spent your childhood living by the rules, well, living by mob rules at least, and doing everything your father asked of you."

Unsurprisingly, she nails me immediately.

"You're telling me you didn't do the same?"

"Nope. I suppose you were right in that I was a little rebel. I nearly cost a three-million-dollar deal between my father and the Portuguese when I was seven." She laughs as if people hadn't been killed for ruining much smaller agreements.

"When you were seven? How did you even manage that?"

"My dad had promised me all week we would get out and grab ice cream after school to celebrate me winning the spelling bee. He canceled on me two days before, promising to make it up to me. I was pissed because I really wanted my triple cookie dough chocolate sundae with hot fudge, so I hacked into his computer, found the contact information of their boss's assistant, and sent a...somewhat aggressive request that we reschedule the meeting to a later date." She pauses, waiting for my response.

My mouth falls open. "Holy shit. Are you being serious?"

"Yup. I thought I'd gotten away with it too. I'd never considered that my father would get a very outraged phone call from Rinaldo, the Portuguese boss at the time, asking why their meeting they'd been trying to set up for weeks got delayed again. Especially since Rinaldo had large suspicions that he had some traitors in his ranks and wanted to use our spyware to confirm. My father was obviously confused, so he checked his calendar and saw that their meeting had been moved...and our ice cream date rescheduled." She gives me a sheepish look. "I guess I wasn't well-versed in covering my tracks back then."

"What did Naser do?" I can count on one hand the times I've seen Zahra's father truly pissed off, and each instance was terrifying.

She snorts, a shameless smile on her face. "I was an awful liar back then, so all he had to do was ask me if I had hacked into his laptop, and he could see my guilt on my face. His face went blank for what felt like an eternity, but the next thing I knew, he threw me into his arms and told me how proud he was of me. He asked me how long it took to crack through his password and firewalls. I told him ten minutes and I swear his eyes filled with tears of joy. He took me out to get ice cream every day the week after. And also enrolled me in a computer science class."

My heart squeezes. Everything about that memory was just so...Naser. The love he had for his family, the pride in his voice that was always present whenever he spoke to me, how brilliant Zahra was. Standing in the garden with her now, I understand fully why Naser went to such great lengths to keep her identity hidden for all these years.

"So that's why your father shipped you away when you were younger? Protecting the child prodigy?" I guess. Every made man knew how crucial it was to keep your best assets protected.

Zahra's eyebrows knit together, vehemently shaking her head. "No. At least not in the way you're thinking. He didn't hide me away like some sort of expensive family heirloom. He kept my identity hidden from others because he wanted me to live a normal life. He wanted to protect my childhood and even my early 20s. I don't think I fully realized it at the time, but it was one of the best gifts he could have given me. The gift of being a normal girl who didn't have to carry the extra burden of being a boss's daughter, the burden of wondering if my friends like me for me, or wondering if someone will try to kidnap, torture, or kill me...or worse. I just got to be Zahra."

"Was it weird being away from your family for most of your life?" I couldn't imagine not living in the same home as my parents and Aidan.

"I was actually home a lot more than most people realized. I went to public schools in Boston. Under high security, of course, but my father figured no one would suspect a man of his stature to send their child to a public school. Most people in our world are elitist assholes who faint at the idea of sending their child anywhere other than some snooty private school. Plus, everyone thought my father's heir was a boy, so..." She shrugs.

"You were hidden in plain sight, with no one the wiser." It was genius. And ballsy. Two words that summed Naser up to a T.

"He did everything he could to ensure I could have the same upbringing as my peers." She looks down and breaks out into soft laughter.

"What's so funny?" I wonder.

"You know my dad never missed any of my recitals or competitions? Whether it was a spelling bee, a debate tournament, or an eighth-grade graduation. You name it, he was there. Except you wouldn't know it was him. He would come in full disguise, including makeup, to make sure no one could spot him, and end up ruining my day. It was incredibly dramatic, though, I can't lie, it meant a lot to me."

"He was an incredible man." Her description of her childhood sounded happy enough, but still I wondered, "You didn't feel lonely at all?"

"I did. In some respects, I was living a double life. For my own security, no one could know who my real parents were so I had to lie a lot to my friends. I couldn't exactly vent to them about my anxieties about becoming a boss one day either."

"Even if you could...it can be hard to understand the full weight of it all." Or at least that's how I had felt ever since I came into power. Knowing my decisions impact not only my own family but also all the people who work for me and their loved ones is a responsibility that is constantly on my mind.

For a second, I catch a slight break in Zahra's armor as she gives me an instinctive nod and her eyes fill with a hint of exhaustion. The moment is gone almost as soon as it had appeared, but it's enough for me to know she was feeling the same immense amount of pressure as I am. Enough for me to know I'm not alone in my inner battle... She knew what it felt like to have your father ripped away from you and not be given a chance to grieve because now you control an empire and tens of thousands of people rely on you.

Her soft voice startles me, grabbing my attention. "That's probably why our fathers were so close." She looks at the rose in my hand. "No one else truly understood them. In our world, feeling lonely is probably the norm, but suffering in silence is also a choice. A choice that they decided against."

"Perhaps it's a choice we can also reject," I boldly declare, holding my breath for her response. She may have opened up to me today, but I have no doubts there are many parts of herself that Zahra is keeping close to her chest.

Zahra picks at her nails, the hem of her blazer, and rubs her neck. None of which signaled that she'll be on board for what I'm proposing. If not for the birds chirping outside or the wind rustling the leaves of the nearby trees, we'd be standing in complete, unnerving silence. My jaw nearly falls down in shock when she says, "I would like that. To have someone to lean on."

I blink, needing an extra moment to process. "Good. Great. Amazing." Dear god. This is rough. I can't remember the last time I'd felt this nervous. Are my hands sweating right now? No, they couldn't be. I pull them out of my pockets and try to nonchalantly wipe them on the front of my pants. "Well, I guess I should probably get going then. I appreciate you cutting my intern some slack and scheduling this meetup."

My feet drag as I start my descent back toward the house. My phone starts to vibrate incessantly, but before I can reach for my pocket, Zahra wraps her hand around my wrist, stopping me.

"Wait, hold up." A panicked expression takes over her face.

I freeze in my tracks. "What's wrong?"

"Um, I also had something I wanted to talk to you about...a potential problem we need to handle." She nods her head back toward the garden. A conversation that needs to be kept private. Shit. This couldn't be good.

"What's going on?" My tone shifts into business.

"I've been running numbers on our shipments and earnings for the past few months and they're not adding up. We've been taking subtle losses that are easy to miss in the moment, but you begin to notice a pattern over time. And I think the pattern is indicative of a major problem."

"How much have we lost so far?"

She purses her lips. "Close to twenty thousand dollars if my estimates are correct. Both in guns and in surveillance devices."

I let out a breath. "Well, at least the financial damage isn't too bad yet."

"It's nothing we can't recover from, currently. But I'm scared of what may happen if this pattern continues. Also, if our thief continues to get braver and braver each month, which, by my predictions, is exactly what's happening."

"Shit."

"My sentiments exactly."

"Any leads so far?" I check.

"Nothing. Except I'm fairly certain it has to be an inside job. None of our shipments were reported missing or damaged. I only started digging because Damon called me demanding an update on the remaining shipments."

My nose flares. Damon was never one to control his temper or his mouth. For his sake, he'd better have watched both when speaking to Zahra, or else I would have to have a long conversation, of sorts, with him.

Zahra continues, not noticing my shift in rage. "…I sent Cyrus to hand deliver him some extra weapons to appease him for now. But if it is an inside job, we have a big problem on our hands."

"Agreed. I can't think of anyone off the top of my head, making me want to head to the warehouses and see them directly. Maybe even plant a fake shipment that we can track," I suggest.

"I like that idea. I'll be in contact about when I can head out west, but the sooner the better. For all of our sakes. I doubt the guns and computers are the only things they're selling. Information is just as lethal a weapon as any." Her grim expression matches the anxiety roiling in my stomach.

"Have you briefed your inner circle yet?" I'll respect whatever boundaries she wants to instate. If this is an inside job, we'd have to be suspicious of any and everyone.

"Just Azula. I'd like it if we kept this information as private as possible for now. I don't want to cause any additional alarm…or let the culprit know we're onto them."

I nod. "Understood. I'll tell Aidan and no one else. You have my number, right? In case you need to update me or reach me at all." Did that come off as desperate? I sure hope not.

Zahra worries her lip between her teeth, uncertain what to say next. "Yes. I have everything I need. It was good seeing you today."

For the first time today, I feel the tension leave my shoulders. "You too. I'm looking forward to future meetings in the garden."

She gives me a smile that doesn't quite meet her eyes as I walk back to the front of the house, where my driver awaits me.

11

ZAHRA

A piercing screech rings through my head as soon as I place the earpiece in my ear.

"Dammit, Azula. If I don't die on this mission, my ears may bleed to death if you keep messing around with the microphone."

"Don't be so dramatic. Plus, I told you we should practice before I used this. Just because you're tech savvy doesn't mean *I* am," she sasses.

"I did offer to practice. *You* were the one who insisted you were fine," I grit through my teeth, adjusting the collar of my trench coat and the scarf around my neck to ensure a majority of my face is covered.

"Mmmm, that's not how I remember it, but we'll agree to disagree. Now let me get a better view of where you're at." Leaning against a cold red brick wall, waiting for her confirmation, I hear Azula typing away furiously.

My meeting with Declan in the garden had proven incredibly fruitful, though at times I found myself unwittingly getting lost in his...aura. I try not to beat myself up about that irritating fact too much. Declan is clearly a mastermind when it comes to deception and manipulation. Using stories about my father, feigning interest in my childhood, playing the role of a mourning son — he truly deserves an Academy Award for the facade he's keeping up. Annoyingly, I had to admit that Declan made for good conversations. I can't remember the last time I felt so...light. The last time I was able to talk about the happier moments of my life without having to deal with looks or words of pity.

With Declan, or at least with the fake-nice Declan, I felt a sense of security and understanding I hadn't felt before. Because under the right circumstances, in a world where he didn't murder my father in cold blood, I could actually see us being friends. Which only manages to irritate me even more. It's hard to find people who understand you in this line of work. Even harder to find someone you can trust. And Declan could have been both of those things if he weren't a massive liar.

The only positive of this situation is gaining sound evidence that confirms all of my suspicions about his deceit, thanks to my bug that worked without a hitch. Immediately after our encounter in the garden, I went straight to work. Combing through years of GPS data was going to take time, so I started with the day that changed my life forever. Declan had sworn he was in Maine when our fathers were shot, but his cell phone placed him right at the scene of the crime. I nearly threw up when I unraveled the truth.

Despite my suspicions, I suppose a part of me hoped I was wrong. A part of me that wants to believe there's no way Declan could have taken my father's life, *taken his own father's life*, and continued on like it was nothing.

Once I exposed that truth, I kept digging. Most of his movements following the murder showed no clear patterns, except for one building he kept visiting. Last week, I had followed him all the way to the site, but was unable to find a secure way to get inside without tipping him off. So, I consulted with Azula, and we decided the best method of action would be to secure the block and nearby streets, and try to speak to the shop owner one on one. From tracking the shop's patterns, they rarely received any visitors prior to ten am, so I made sure to get there right at nine am.

"Do you need me to help you?" I check in with Azula, tapping my foot impatiently. Though I appreciate her diligence, time is definitely of the essence here.

She clicks her tongue in annoyance. "I got it. You're a block across from Dedham and Tremont. Based on our surveillance cameras and the thermal readers we installed outside, only the shop owner should be inside."

"Perfect. And Declan's still occupied?" I confirm. Based on his calendar, he's supposed to have a phone call with his uncle today.

"Yup. His uncle has been talking his ear off for the past twenty minutes. Something about Declan not treating him like his second, and how he'll start waving his dick around to claim his dominance if that doesn't happen," Azula grunts.

"Charming."

"That's certainly a word for it. Regardless, he shouldn't be a problem currently so you're good to go."

I take off immediately, giving a quick glance to my surroundings before crossing the street and opening the large wooden door to the unsuspecting brownstone building. From the surveillance I've gathered, this business, like many in the city, has a front-facing facade. In this instance, I entered an apothecary. The scent of a variety of herbs, supplements, and essential oils hits my nose immediately. Contrary to my expectations, this place has an incredibly cozy atmosphere. To the untrained eye, I could easily see a family shopping here for special oddities, teas, and seasonal candles. But I know better. Given the vast range of natural and synthesized supplements stocked on the shelves, one could easily assume that combining certain chemicals could lead to killing someone just as easily as it could heal another.

"Let me know if I can help you with anything." The old man standing behind the counter shoots me a soft smile that reminds me of my dad. Especially the way both of their eyes would crinkle along with their lips. My hands start to shake slightly as my heart picks up, beating erratically.

Breathe, Zahra, breathe. Remember why you're here. Remember who you're fighting for.

I take a moment to ground myself, noticing the multicolored vials on the cabinets, the extensive array of lavender soaps, and the locally sourced spices.

When I feel my composure return, I approach the man. "There is something you can help me with. A colleague at Savenor's Butchery said you could help me."

Pausing, I send out a silent prayer that the code phrase is correct. Azula and I had tried our best to do our due diligence, but the audio we collected from an outside camera was gargled and difficult to clean, even when running it through our best technology. If my suspicions are correct this building likely contains devices that hinder any planted bugs or recorders from catching full conversations.

The old man's shoulders stiffen, and I swear he grows an

extra six inches in the process. "Lock the entry door. Let's make this quick."

I follow his instructions, turning over the 'We're Open' sign to say 'Sorry We're Closed' and heading closer to the counter.

"So, what is it? Found your lover cheating on you and now you're hoping to keep him on the toilet for the next few days, maybe a week? Or maybe it's the mistress you want payback on? I can give you a tasteless concoction to pour in her drink. All her hair will shed off by next Tuesday." His nonchalant attitude sends a chill down my spine. I suppose I shouldn't be surprised, given he did make a living off this, and I know better than most how exposure to cruelty certainly numbs you over time.

Still, I doubt giving someone the runs or making them bald was something Declan would waste his time with. He has his own means of administering humiliation and torture, which means he must have come here for something more. Something bigger.

It all clicks into place. "What if I'm looking for something more permanent?"

The once soft smile on the man's face turns leery. "Ah, is there a relative who overstayed their welcome on this planet? Perhaps one that has named you in a large share of their will?"

I school my expression, refusing to give anything away, including my repulsion at his assumption, and the fact that he likely has had several customers come to him for that reason. "Are my intentions necessary for your response?"

"No, but they do make for good small talk, don't you think?" He laughs to himself.

"I'll take your deflection as a response that this is a service you offer? Or should I take my business elsewhere?" I threaten, my patience wearing thin.

The old man slams his jaw shut. Clearly, I've struck a nerve.

"How fast do you want it to be? And how much pain do you want them to experience?"

It becomes hard to swallow as my throat dries. "I'm not sure. What options do you have?"

He taps a finger on his grey bushy beard before unlocking various cabinets and removing a series of vials. Laying them all out on the counter, he points to one on the far left. "All of these poisons range in terms of duration, how long they take to kill, and suffering, how much pain they cause. If you're looking for a quick and relatively painless...I'd recommend this one. It's tasteless and relatively odorless when mixed into a drink."

I reach for the tube and bring it up to the light, assessing it as if I have plans to purchase it. "What's it made of?" It's a direct question I doubt he'll actually answer, so I correct myself, "Or rather, how does it...handle the problem?"

"Clever girl, you know I can't give away all my secrets. If I did, I'd be out of business. It's a concoction of different elements, one of which is tetrodotoxin. Enough to kill within a few minutes if not faster, but not so much that it would tip off any toxicology reports."

Tetrodotoxin. The same chemical that was found in the poison I nearly drank. The same poison that killed the waiter, fairly quick and, while I would beg to differ, one could say relatively painless. "Is tetrodotoxin found in all of your poisons?"

He shakes his head. "No. Only this one. Each batch I make has its own special formula."

"And which one of these is your best seller?"

"The one right in your hand. It takes me a while to create, which makes it an even hotter commodity."

"Any recent buyers?" I decide to cut to the chase.

"Now you know an answer to a question like that will cost you. But from your get-up and line of questioning, I can assume you work for the Persian Empire. It was their new boss who was nearly killed recently. Yes?"

My entire body stiffens as he identifies me. So much for trying to keep a low profile. At least he didn't know who I really was.

He flashes his teeth. "Don't worry, your secret's safe with me. I'd much rather we work together than have you as my enemy."

"State your terms," I grumble, irritated that I had somehow fallen into this man's trap.

"A piece of information for the same. A few of my regulars are seeking services elsewhere, but I haven't been able to figure out where. I suspect I wasn't the first herbalist you sought out."

"I'm happy to be of service. Though I must insist you go first." I stand firm.

A glimmer of respect flashes in his eyes. "Very well, my last purchase of the tetrodoxin came from a gentleman a few weeks ago. He was equally tight-lipped as to why he needed such a concoction."

My racing heart feels like it's being ripped out of my chest. "A gentleman? What did he look like?"

"Now, now, my dear. You know I can't tell you that. Even revealing that it was a man in the first place could get me killed. I'll blame the slip-up on being distracted by your beautiful face." He licks his lips, taking me in. Great, now my stomach is also turning.

"I recommend you check Salem. It's easy to hide in plain sight." I huff, completing my end of the bargain. The man strokes his beard, contemplating, as I reach into my purse, I pull out a wad of cash and drop it on the counter. "I'll take the vial. And your discretion."

"At this price, you can have the whole building if you want

it." He gives me a wink as he runs his fingers through the money, and I tuck the vial away into my pocket and head toward the exit. My hand is on the doorknob when the old man sends me his final parting words,

"A word of caution, my dear? Better to believe your own truth than that of others. It makes the killing all the easier."

12

DECLAN

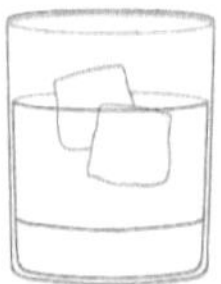

"For fuck's sake, you're not hearing me!" My uncle slams a fist on the table. In his defense, he is right. He'd been throwing a tantrum for the past fifteen minutes, and I had consciously decided to daydream when he stormed my office.

My mind first went through a dozen different scenarios in which we could track down whoever had been stealing from us and the Persian Empire. Unfortunately for me and my uncle, the second the Persians came to mind, all I could think about was Zahra. Her plump lips that matched the softness of her curves and thick thighs. The brutal and cunning way she approached every challenge that came her way. How I had craved being closer to her ever since we met in the gardens. Our last encounter was a few days ago, yet it felt like I hadn't seen her in years. Jesus. What the hell is wrong with me? My father's murder is still out there, I have a rat in my ranks, and my uncle is currently beet red, yelling at me so loud the room is shaking, and all I can think about is...a girl? Except she isn't just a girl. She's so much more.

"May I remind you that I am your *second*. And beyond that, your father gave me additional powers to exert over you. If you continue to exclude me in discussions about the well-being of our mafia—"

"Of our mafia?" I seethe, standing out of my seat and leaning forward. "I don't think so, Uncle. This is my mafia. My men and women. My soldiers, engineers, and doctors. My legacy. Don't forget that for a second." I know I shouldn't poke the bear, but his attitude and insistence on treating me like a child is pissing me off.

"*Your* mafia, that is currently being bankrolled by funds that *I* have absolute power over. Or did you forget?" My uncle flashes his teeth in a harsh sneer. "Keep pushing me, Declan, and I'll cut off your silly little gun supply in the blink of an eye."

What a weak bluff. "Cut off a major income supply? Sure, be my guest."

"Don't worry. I have other plans for replenishing the gap in funds."

My mind immediately goes to the drug trade my uncle used to head for our mafia before my father asked him to end all ties with the drug lords. I debate reaching for the gun tucked in the waistband of my pants. A bullet is all it would take to rid myself of the pest that was my uncle. As tempting as the idea is, I can't do it. I can't bring myself to kill the small amount of family I have left. "You wouldn't dare."

He raises an eyebrow. "Neither you nor the counsel will be able to do anything about it. Your father's will is as it stands, and no one would dare go against his wishes."

Rage ignites in my veins. He's right. My inner circle respected me, but they were first and foremost my father's men. They would want to keep his memory alive as best they could. Even if that memory included a ridiculous clause in his will that my uncle would maintain power over mafia finances and remain my second, until I got married. I loved my father, but if he were alive now, I'd probably shake him. Why he thought including a marriage clause of all things was a smart move, I'll never know. Probably because he was such a hopeless romantic when it came to my mom, and he wanted me to find the same. If only it was that easy. Now I have another problem to solve on top of the pile already on my plate. I need a fucking break.

"Fine," I bite. "The inner circle and I are meeting next week, Monday. At three pm. I'll be sure to save you a seat there."

"And also ensure that I won't be left out of any future meetings," he presses.

I give him a small nod, unable to form words due to my anger.

"Excellent. See lad, that wasn't so hard now, was it?" My uncle taps his fingers on my desk, using his cane to give him balance as he stands and exits my office.

Sitting down, I roughly drag my hands down my face. What a fucking nightmare. The last thing I need is my uncle questioning every decision I make in front of men whose respect I'm trying to gain. And I have no doubt my uncle would be on his absolute worst behavior in all our future meetings.

"Really a charmer that guy is," Aidan says, cutting the tension and startling me as he walks into the office.

"I am so fucked," I groan, leaning my forehead against the cold wood of my desk.

"You don't think he was serious about the drug trade, do you?" Aidan whispers.

I lift my head and see the faint hint of shine in his eyes. Aidan lost his best friends to an overdose a few years back. It had taken a massive toll on him since, understandably so. Our dad had pulled out of the drug trade immediately after that loss, refusing to cause more pain to his son.

"Honestly, I don't know. You know how pissed Uncle was when Dad pulled the plug on that whole operation. Didn't help that most of the connections we used were his, either. Uncle severed many relationships on our father's command. Wouldn't be surprised if he was now looking for his due."

Aidan starts to visibly shake. "Dammit. We have to do something. We can't let him do this. We can't, Declan!"

"I know. I know. I promise you, I will do everything in my power to stop this." And I mean it. I had been the one to continue to piss off my uncle, pushing him so far that he now feels the need to lash out. I'm the boss. And so this responsibility fell on my shoulders. "The charity gala is this weekend, right?"

Aidan cocks his head. "Yeah, why?"

"I need to ensure I have meetings with whoever is eligible and willing to be at my side for the foreseeable future." My skin crawls as the words leave my mouth.

Evidently, I'm not clear enough because the confusion on Aidan's face deepens. "Be at your side? Like a new bodyguard?"

"Like a wife," I growl. "Someone believable who understands I won't be able to give them the emotional depth and attention they're seeking, and is fine with that because they know I'll spoil them otherwise. Someone who would also be willing to sign a prenup, and divorce me in a few years, since they know I'll pay a hefty alimony."

"You're really serious?" Aidan looks at me with his mouth open.

"I am. I will do anything to protect this family from any additional tragedy."

13
ZAHRA

If women had invented heels, they would have found a way to make them significantly more comfortable to wear. Though I absolutely adore the nude red-bottom pumps, I know my feet will be killing me at the end of this night. A small price to pay for the message I'm going to send. Plus, they go perfectly with the tight silk maroon dress hugging my frame. My back is fully exposed, and the deep V at the front of my dress reveals most of my sternum. Everyone's eyes would be on me tonight, regardless of what I was wearing, so I decided to give them another reason to be the topic of conversation.

Hopefully, the bold dress and my schooled expression of indifference would mask my inner turmoil. I knew the day would come where I would have to leave the safe sanctity of my estate and announce my claim to my father's empire in front of all his supporters, but I had always imagined he would be by my side when it happened. A passing of the torch. Now, it feels like I'm heading out to be fed to the wolves. Frankly, if tonight doesn't end well, that's exactly what will happen.

Checking my makeup in the mirror, I curse my father for coming up with the idea of the annual charity gala. On the surface, it doesn't make sense why so many different mafia bosses, politicians, and socialites were willing to come together and participate in an overpriced dinner held in a stuffy hotel banquet hall. At its core, it's a clear message of how much power the made families had on local and state politics. So much so that if my father invited them to a dinner he was hosting, they would do any and everything to ensure they would be there or risk facing his retaliation.

There's also the fact that both Declan and I will be giving a speech tonight to demonstrate our united front. Which meant I have to ensure I don't get lost in his aura. I need to be viewed as boss, and not as the woman by his side. The older generation of mob bosses will likely have reactions similar to his Uncle Lorkan when they hear I am taking over the Persian Empire. I have no doubts they're already writing off the public lunch we had together. As much as I hate it, I need their respect. Without it, the bloodshed aimed at us will never end. Declan's proximity also means I need to have my guards up. I won't put it past him to make another attempt on my life tonight.

"Damn, Z. The attendees are already going to be speechless once they process who you are. With this dress, you may just give them a heart attack too," Samirah, my stylist and one of my closest friends, compliments as she comes up behind me.

"Well, if this dress doesn't kill them, I have something else that will," I tease, moving aside the slit of my dress to reveal the small revolver attached to my stockings.

She stands next to me, looking at me through the full-length mirror in front of us. "It's a charity gala for Christ's sake. Are you sure you need that?"

"A charity gala filled with men who kill people just for

looking at them wrong. Stepping foot inside that hotel without some sort of protection is a mistake I cannot afford. Why do you think I insisted on adding a garter and stockings to this dress?" I ask.

"Honestly, I was hoping you had a secret lover you wanted to impress. Someone you can use to get all that tension and stress you've been harboring for as long as I've known you. That's why I added the bows and made sure the stockings were extra easy to unclip."

Heat comes over my body. "Samirah!"

"Don't worry, I used the strongest silk I could get my hands on to make those, so your little gun is perfectly safe and secure. But if you decide to fraternize in the coat closet with some mysterious, and jacked, gentleman—"

"There will be no fraternizing—" I try to interject with no avail.

"—then I'm sure whatever man gets his hands on you won't be able to resist how good you look both in and out of this dress." A smug look forms on her face as she takes in my irritation.

"If a man gets too close to me tonight, the only thing his hands will feel is the barrel end of my revolver," I deadpan.

Samirah tsks. "You never let me have any fun. How am I supposed to live vicariously through you when you're so serious?"

"You're not. May I remind you that you're the famous fashion designer who gets to travel around the world, while I'm now a mob boss who has to calculate her every move to avoid sudden death or the ruin of a decades-long legacy?"

"And here I thought being a mob boss would be dangerous, sexy, and fun. What a drag."

"Dangerous, definitely. Sexy and fun. Definitely not. Or at least not the way I do it." I shrug, grabbing my jewelry box and pulling out the familiar gold necklace passed down through my family for generations. In size, it would no doubt pale compared to the massive diamond necklaces I would see tonight, but I didn't care about the monetary value of the piece of jewelry on my neck. To me, it was priceless. A simple gold chain that held a Farvahar pendant, a winged figure with a human head, represented centuries of Iranian culture and heritage. Many interpretations of this symbol have been made by historians over the years, but when my father gifted me this necklace as a child, he made his intentions very clear. *May this necklace protect you in this life, my daughter. Every time you wear it, know that I am here with you. Know that your heart will always guide you to the truth and what is right.* If only it were that simple.

Samirah brings me back to reality, giving my shoulder a squeeze. "Well, I'm going to manifest that you won't have to use anything but your sharp wit and lethal smile tonight."

"Knock on wood." I give her a terse smile before beating my knuckles on my jewelry box. The superstitious gene is definitely one my mother passed down to me. My heart twinges at the thought of her. The first person I lost. Where my father's death was violent, my mother's was mundane — a heart attack at a young age. It was something I still struggled to wrap my head around, how one of the strongest people I knew, someone who had inspired me to never dim my own light, could be taken from me in an instant.

Samirah takes one final look at me, dusting off the dress and picking at any minuscule remains of imperfection as Arman enters. "We need to get going, Boss."

Samirah's back stiffens, her tone clipped. "She'll go when I say she can go."

Arman groans. "She looks fine, enough with the fussing. We're going to be late."

"She can't be late to her own event. Nothing starts until she arrives." Samirah brings a tissue to my lips and dabs them lightly before stepping away. "Perfect."

I take a deep breath and release it before walking toward Arman. "We're still entering through the back right?" We wanted to avoid the crowd until after my speech. It not only minimized the security risk of being out in the open Boston streets, but symbolized my power. A boss who can get in and out of a building swarming with enemies and allies alike without anyone the wiser is a boss worthy of fear.

"Yes, Ma'am. The car is waiting for you right outside."

Lifting the skirt of my dress, I follow Arman's lead and do my best to talk myself up. The amount of skin I'm showing tonight is a bit out of my comfort zone, though I can't deny that I do feel especially beautiful. Catching my reflection in the car mirror, my mother's words ring in my head. *Beauty and a sharp mind are weapons that can be wielded just as lethally as a gun.* I hope she was right, but even if she wasn't, I had a gun tucked in my garter that I had no problems using.

———

"Do you want more water?" Azula extends her arm, holding a water bottle in front of my face.

"If I drink any more, I'll probably end up peeing myself."

"Well, that's one way to make this speech memorable." She snickers as we glance back at the security cameras, taking in all the guests that have started arriving.

At least, I hope she's keeping track of the other guests. My attention had remained fixated on only one man this entire time. "Declan's been here for fifteen minutes and he's already flirted with three girls here."

I could only hope his distracted nature tonight meant he

wasn't going to try to poison me again. I suppose to him, getting rid of your enemy comes second to getting your dick wet. Or maybe he thought he could get away with both.

"Hmm, that's interesting." Azula grabs my attention, but when I turn, instead of seeing her stare at the screens, she's looking right at me.

"What is?" I ask, placing my hands on my hips.

"The fact that you're more worried about Declan talking to other women, and not the fact that he's been plotting to kill you." She smirks.

"*Obviously*, I am concerned about what he might have in store for me tonight. I just wanted to point out how blase he's acting right now. It's insulting. He's not taking me seriously as a threat." I click my tongue in irritation at Declan and the fact that I sound like a petulant child.

Azula raises an eyebrow. "Oh, is that what it is? Because for a moment there...you sounded almost jealous that you don't have Declan's full attention."

Is she insane? "Jealous?! Are you serious right now? He tried to kill me."

All I get is a shrug. "Don't act like many of the bosses downstairs didn't get their wives by either kidnapping them or threatening to kill their families. Plus, he's super hot, and it seemed like you two connected in the garden. It wouldn't be entirely out of the question that he changes his mind. Decide to go from your killer to a stalker after your own heart."

Bingo. Now her fantasies made sense. "You're reading dark romances again, aren't you? Are we still into the masked men? Or are they stalkers now?"

"My current read features both. He wears a Jason Voorhees mask, secretly pays her bills, and fucks her brains out. Mask on. A girl can dream." Azula lets out a dreamy sigh and laughs at whatever expression is on my face. "Hey, don't knock it 'till you try it."

"I'm not here to kink shame. Whatever gets you going. I just don't think your romance fantasy applies here." I point between myself and the image of Declan on the screen.

The tall blonde model he's talking to is an absolute bombshell and buying whatever he's selling as she tilts her head back in laughter. No way anything he said was that funny. I'd been around him long enough to know. He gives her a soft smile that reveals a hint of a dimple, and excuses himself before heading in our direction.

"We should clear out. Looks like Aidan and Declan are on their way here." I gather the train of my dress, exiting the security room with Azula in tow as we walk closer to the back of the stage.

Moving the curtain toward the side, I take in the hundreds of people filing in toward their seats at the dining tables, and my throat begins to tighten. Public speaking was never something I particularly enjoyed doing, though I've never felt anxiety quite like this. Giving a presentation in class pales in comparison to convincing some of the cruelest and lethal killers in the world to respect you. My fingers release the curtain and move to the gold necklace around my neck. A reminder that my parents were here with me in spirit, and that they raised me to be strong. They raised me to overcome every obstacle in my way. And that was exactly what I would do tonight. I just wish they would be able to see me do it.

The creaking sound of the stage door opening grabs my attention, bringing me back to the current moment. Aidan walks in first, his hands casually tucked into his pockets matching his tousled hair and the 'too cool for school' smirk he was rocking. He flashes me a wink, before stiffening as he takes in Azula. She waves at him, revealing her elongated and sharpened nails that practically look like claws. Knowing her, she probably could stab someone's eyes out with those if she wanted.

Declan enters a moment later, eyes widening as he nearly stumbles on the flat ground in front of him. He manages to save himself but his eyes remain trained on my body, namely my decently exposed cleavage. A subtle red blush starts to form on his cheeks as he clears his throat and swallows. Hard.

"Zahra, you look incredible. No one will be able to take their eyes off you." His voice comes out hoarse, like he was in desperate need of a drink. Azula hands him a bottle of water, which he chugs in a matter of seconds.

"Well, I figured everyone would be fixated on me regardless. May as well give them something to look at." I attempt to sound lighthearted, but at this moment, all I can feel is a tightness in my stomach as Declan continues to look at me. A tightness combined with a slight heat. Maybe I should wrap one of the curtains around me....

One of the stage managers walks over toward us, frantically whispering into their headset while feverishly checking off the to-do list on their clipboard. "Declan, we're ready for you. The rest of you can also follow me."

The Irishman shoots me a thumbs-up before being dragged through the curtains. Azula, Aidan, and I move into the wings as Declan introduces himself and begins his speech.

"On behalf of the McAlister and Ahzimi families, we would like to thank you all for being in attendance today. Though our families have experienced insurmountable tragedies in the last two months, I can speak for myself when I say I know that Naser Ahzimi would be so incredibly grateful for your generosity and commitment in continuing to attend his annual charity gala. Through your kind donations, we have raised over three million dollars to support mental health services for youth of color in our city. As a token of my appreciation for all the Ahzimi's have done to support our city, my family vows to match any donations made today." Declan pauses to take a breath.

And my ridiculous heart flutters. He can't be serious, can he? This has to all be a part of some long game he was playing to get closer to me before he drove a knife in my back...right?

I turn to Aidan, who leans over to me. "It was both of our ideas. There's not a lot of good we can do in the world. But this was one thing we could do."

The fluttering of my heart now turns into a full-blown pounding. Declan wasn't being duplicitous, and I was wrong in assuming he was. I was wrong. Or maybe Declan was just that cunning. He not only had me fooled, he also had his brother fooled. That's possible, isn't it? My brain feels like it's racing at a thousand miles per hour, going through every single moment of my life leading up to my father's death. All the pieces of evidence I collected afterward pointed to a cover-up. The evidence that pointed at Declan. It had to be him. He had to be the killer. Because if it wasn't him, I just spent two months letting my father's actual assassin run free. It would mean that I had failed my father. And I couldn't fail him.

The applause from the audience dies down, allowing Declan to continue. "In addition to giving the speech, I have the honor and privilege of introducing the new leader of the Persian Tea Enterprise..." His lips form a subtle smirk as he states the cover-up company for my mafia. "Naser Ahzimi's daughter, Zahra Ahzimi."

A wave of startled chatter filled with confusion comes over the room. From backstage, I can't hear anything specific, though I can guess what questions are being asked. *'Daughter?'* *'Declan misspoke, right?'* Lifting my chin up high, I step out onto the stage. The air in the room feels like it gets sucked out immediately, as I look down at the crowd in front of me. To my left, the Ukrainian boss has a tight grip on his drink, his eyes distrusting and also...intrigued. He lifts his glass and tilts it in my direction. My heart skips. I wouldn't dare call him an ally, but his acknowledgment is far from disrespectful. The Italians are staring at me with rage, as if they want nothing more than to rip me apart limb by limb. Typical. In the back, the Colombians look unimpressed, but that's their natural state. Of all the scenarios I had imagined, the banquet hall remaining, for the most part, calm and collected, was not one of them.

I won't fool myself into thinking everything is okay. This is the calm before the storm, and I have to remain alert.

Approaching the podium, I school my expression to one of indifference. It doesn't matter how sweaty my palms are, how breathing feels like a chore, or how fast my heart is racing. No one in this room would know any of that. They would just see my exterior. Collected, unbothered, and calculated. A boss.

"Thank you, Declan, for that introduction and your family's generous donation." The power in my voice echoes through the speakers and surprises even me. "I appreciate your attendance today, in honor of my father and in support of the youth in our city who will greatly benefit from your kind donations. Tonight not only serves as a continuation of my father's legacy, but also as my opportunity to formally stake my claim to my father's empire."

I pause for a moment, eyes flickering from table to table, making a mental note of who was likely already on my side and who I needed to convince. Anger was fine—an indication that they felt threatened by me. What I can't have is patronizing looks or even ones of disregard. Neither of those emotions are close enough to fear, which meant they would be the first to come for me.

"I acknowledge this is the first time most of you in the

room have ever seen me. And that unfamiliarity can be uncomfortable. But rest assured that my father has taught me everything he knows and that my family's business and our partner's will be in great hands. To those who we have partnered with for decades, I look forward to continuing our relations. And for the organizations we have yet to work with, please know that our door is always open." I flash a lethal smile to the Italians, knowing they're reading in between my lines. *Fuck with us, and you'll find out how much hell I can raise.*

A beat of silence is followed by a slow, yet solid wave of claps, starting from the Ukrainians. The tension in my shoulders loosens. I won't delude myself into thinking I've fully won everyone in the room over, but at the very least, I've staked my claim without any major public pushback. The claps slowly make their way around as Declan steps back up to the podium next to me and speaks about our continued allyship.

I keep my gaze aimed forward at the crowd, giving myself something new to focus on so I don't roll my eyes at every other sentence he says. I won't buy into his facade. As I scan the room, I'm hit with a variety of expressions. Jealousy, fear, envy, anger, and hatred. Hatred. My father taught me that expression is lethal.

In a blink, a man jumps to his feet and pulls out a gun, aiming it right at my chest. My hand immediately falls to the garter on my leg, reaching for my own Glock, but I'm too late. A loud pop rings through the hall, and in an instant, I feel the cold wood of the stage pressed against my cheek and a wetness on my skin. Moving my head to the side, I take in the pool of red under me. Blood. I'm covered in blood.

PART TWO
ALLEGIANCE

14
ZAHRA

There are too many sensations around me. Yells and screams from the attendees. The wet, thick blood that is coating my hand, the cool press of the hardwood stage on the side of my face, and the calming scent of cologne that fills my nose, paired with the warmth pressed on my back. Wait what? I whip my neck around and come face to face with Declan, who's currently clutching his left bicep.

"Fucking bastard took a chunk outta me. I'll rip his throat out," Declan groans, a mix of pain and rage in his expression as he increases the pressure on his wound in a feeble attempt to stop the blood. How he even managed to get words out at this moment is beyond me. He attempts to stand and slips immediately on the pool of blood under him.

A pool of *his* blood.

Not mine.

Because he had protected me.

He'd shielded me from the bullet that was aimed right at my chest. Declan McAlister had saved my life, even though he had spent the past few weeks trying to kill me. Or had he? If he truly wanted me dead, he sure as shit wouldn't have just saved me. Dammit, this is all too confusing.

My head is spinning, I can't think straight, and the general chaos unraveling in front of me isn't helping. I need to get control over the situation so I can get some answers. Which means I also have to ensure Declan stays alive long enough for me to get to the bottom of all of this.

Declan groans again as he tries to stand and my patience snaps. I grip his chin and force him to look at me. Not a hint of fear is in his greenish-blue eyes as I hiss, "Stay down. The more you move, the more blood you'll lose. I'll handle it."

Kicking off my heels, I'm on my feet a moment later, taking in the mix of fearful expressions from the politicians and disdain from the mob bosses. I'm losing them. Whatever progress I'd made tonight would be crushed if I don't manage to win them back somehow.

Think Zahra, think. Check your surroundings, all possible exit routes. Where would the shooter go? Who would be the first person to chase after him?

Cyrus. The answer comes to me at the same moment I find him struggling in the back. He has his arms wrapped around the shooter and manages to wrestle him down to the floor. With his knee on the man's back, Cyrus pulls out a knife from his coat and brings it to the man's neck.

"NO!" I order into the microphone left on the podium, causing everyone, including Cyrus, to redirect their attention to me. I point my blood-stained finger at the shooter before curling it inward. "He's mine. Bring him to me."

The room stills and everyone snaps their head to the back, following along as Cyrus slowly brings the shooter closer and closer to me. I can see straight through the aura of indifference he was trying to put on. This man had failed to kill me, and now he would face his own death at my hands. By the time

Cyrus is on stage, the man is fully on his knees begging for forgiveness, though he refused to rat on the person who put him up to this despite my pressing.

With my right hand, I remove my Glock from the garter and aim it at my shooter's head. In my left hand, I bring the microphone up to my mouth and try not to cringe at the blood that drips down my arm. "Let this be a reminder to anyone who dares challenge me, my family, and my allies. When you take aim at the devil, make sure you don't miss. Because if you do, I promise I won't."

I pull the trigger, and a moment later, the man drops in front of my feet, blood and brains leaking out of his skull. To the left, I see the governor faint, his security there to catch him. Somewhere in all the chaos, Aidan had collected a few members of my medical staff and rushed out on stage to help Declan—who was now looking at me like an angel who had come down from heaven to bless him. Clearly, the blood loss had made its way to his head.

"Take him back to the mansion immediately. Dr. Williams will take him into surgery and ensure his wound is treated," I order Cyrus, Aidan, and the paramedics who quickly fall in line, gently lifting Declan onto a stretcher.

Shifting my attention back to the crowd, I feel a slight rush as I realize everyone in the room is locked in to what I have to say next. I no longer feel the apprehension, judgment, or disrespect I felt when I first stepped on stage. Instead, all I feel is power. I lean over the stage and reach for a champagne glass on the Ukrainian's table. Their boss sends me a smirk and a look of approval.

"Please join me in a toast. To my father. To his legacy. And to the Persian Empire." Stating the name of my mafia is risky, given that this event featured many individuals who were not affiliated with an organization...at least not publicly. But given

I've just killed a man in front of a thousand or so witnesses, playing it safe has gone out the window.

From the center of the room, a thick Irish accent echoes my chant, "To the Persian Empire", and slowly I see glass after glass rise. Some do so more reluctantly than others, but I keep my hand raised until everyone has a glass lifted in their hand.

I take a long sip before ending my toast. "To the Persian Empire. And the new legacy I shall bring. Please remain seated as we clean up this mess. Dinner will be served shortly."

Tossing the remains of the drink on the body in front of me, I head backstage, buzzing from the night and desperate to get out of my blood-stained dress.

—

"Are you sure we can't just take the dress to the dry cleaners? I do love it dearly." I pout as Samirah holds a garment bag in her hand.

"Yes, unfortunately, blood doesn't come out of silk easily. And even if it did, do you really want a dress with so much baggage?"

"One woman's baggage is another's symbol of victory," I challenge, drawing out an eye roll from Samirah.

"This is why I stick to fashion. You mafia bosses are so twisted and cooked in the head." She practically manhandles me out of the current dress and forces me into the backup she had on standby.

To her credit, the new dress was much more comfortable, made of a soft sweater-like material, but it was much less flashy than the gown I had donned prior. "Are you sure about this outfit, Samirah? It's not really giving banquet attire."

"That's because I've been ordered to drag your ass into the car. You may have killed one psychopath tonight but we have no idea how many more managed to sneak through security." She tosses a pair of flats on the floor, having already thrown my blood-stained heels in the garbage with minimal protest from me. Getting rid of those torture devices is a bonus of this wild night.

"I think I've more than demonstrated I can handle myself." Am I ignoring the fact that Declan had also played a role in saving me tonight? Perhaps. But that reality is still too confusing for me to come to terms with. I knew I'd drive myself crazy trying to think of why he had taken a bullet for me, so I needed to let it go until I could ask him myself.

"No one is questioning that. But if people wanted you dead before, I imagine the price on your head has increased tenfold now that you've shown what a true threat you are. It's best we not push our luck," Samirah chastises me in a tone similar to one my mom would use, which is likely why I cave.

"Fine. But we better stop on the way to get some takeout. I haven't eaten all day and you know how I get when I'm hangry."

"There's a hot plate of food ready for you at home. Lamb stew."

The promise of my favorite dish has me bolting out of the changing room and toward the back alley, where Cyrus and Arman are waiting for me inside the van.

"I see we swapped out our swankier ride for the one that's armored." I take my seat in the center and let out a gleeful noise when Samirah hands me a bowl of food. The car remains silent until I finish my dinner and set it aside. "Any news about Declan?"

"The doctor said the surgery went smoothly. Bullet came

out without a hitch and he should hopefully be waking up soon," Cyrus answers.

"Good. The moment he comes to, inform me. We have much to discuss." Like the fact that up until now, I was convinced he had been the one who killed my father and tried to take me out as well.

Cyrus shoots me a disapproving look, "Perhaps that can wait until tomorrow? You should really get checked out."

My eyes narrow. "The matter I need to discuss with him is urgent. No need to fuss over me. I'm fine."

"Yes. You're fine, because of Declan," Samirah feels the need to remind me. She practically swoons as she says his name. Since when did she join his fan club?

"Naser is right, even in the afterlife." Arman smiles to himself for a moment before a solemn expression replaces it. Cyrus looks like he's about to bite his head off. Arman slides closer to the door, putting an additional inch of space between him and Cyrus, as if that would save him. "It was a poor joke. I apologize to Zahra."

My body stills at the mention of my father. "What...what do you mean by it?"

Arman's eyebrows knit together. "I was just referencing his final words. About how you could trust Declan."

"I thought my father just kept repeating Declan's name over and over again." My mouth dries as I shift to look at Cyrus. That's what I was told, at least.

"He did. But first, your father told me he wanted you to know you could trust Declan." Arman looks between Cyrus and me, equally confused.

"In all the chaos of that night, I must have misremembered some of the details. My sincerest apologies, Zahra. The death of your father. It rattled me to the core." Cyrus sighs, placing a hand on his heart.

"I know." Despite the uneasy feeling in my stomach, I've never had a reason to doubt him. It's completely reasonable that in the aftermath of my father's death, he had misremembered information he was told. "I want to be brought to Declan the second we get home—

"You should get some rest," Arman protests.

"I will be there when he wakes up. End of discussion." Everyone in the car exchanges looks, but it doesn't matter. My word is final. And if anything was learned tonight, it's the fact that my wrath was not one to be tested.

Unless you want to end up dead.

15
ZAHRA

I hate hospitals. Including the makeshift medical wing we have in the manor. The last time I had been in the waiting room was when Dr. Williams informed me that my father hadn't made it. Everything went black after that. From what Azula told me, I had to be sedated. It was the only way they could get me off the doctor; my grief manifested as rage, and evidently, he was an easy target.

"Promise you won't choke anyone this time," Arman jokes, though there's a hint of seriousness in his voice.

"That was one time, and I think I deserve a pass for it given the circumstances." Clicking my tongue, I start to approach the door currently being guarded by three burly Irishmen. "I'd like to see Declan."

Neither man moves an inch. I commend their dedication to protecting their boss but am not in the mood. "Maybe I remind you that you are in *my* medical wing, with *my staff* who have worked around the clock to ensure your boss is safe and healthy. *Your boss,* who took a bullet for me. Which I would like to thank him for."

Each man inhales sharply as they size me up, but still stands in place.

"May I also remind you that I am a bit trigger-happy at the moment and if you think I'm above shooting three men who get in my way, you are sadly mistaken."

"Zahra!" Arman protests from behind me.

Unsurprisingly, threatening to shoot someone works, each man breaks their stance and finally gives me access to the door.

The fluorescent lights in the room make me squint, along with the incessant beeping of various machines, and the faint scent of chlorine. Aidan laid fast asleep in a chair, his head on Declan's bed, while Declan has a hand on his brother's head as he toys with the various tubes and wires connected with his body. His eyes flicker to mine for a second, giving me a small smile before turning his attention back to Aidan. Looking death in the eye would do that to you, remind you of who you would have lost. Who you would have never been able to speak to again. Who you should have told 'I love you' one last time while you had the chance.

"I didn't realize you'd woken up," I break the silence, keeping my voice down so as not to disturb Aidan's sleep.

"Just happened. Heard you threaten to shoot my guards. Tried to yell to let you in but I couldn't manage to get it out." Declan's usually smooth and silky voice is now hoarse and dry, no doubt a result of coming off the anesthesia. I can't help but wonder if this is what he sounds like every morning when he wakes up. *Of all the things you could be thinking about right now, Zahra, his morning voice should not be one of them.*

I hand him one of the water bottles left on the counter and find myself oddly preoccupied with the thick veins of his neck as he swallows. Maybe Samirah was right, I should have taken some time for myself before coming in to interrogate Declan. Clearly, the adrenaline of the night had been wearing off, and in its place was an overwhelming sense of gratitude that he had saved my life. Gratitude and something else that I refuse to acknowledge. Something I can't even remember the last time I'd felt.

"Much better, thanks." Declan clears his throat, sounding much more like himself. He gives Aidan a good shake, causing him to stir. "C'mon, it's time to wake up."

"Shit, I didn't even realize I'd fallen asleep." Aidan yawns, slightly groggy, before pouncing on his brother and giving him a big hug. "Damn, it's good to see you."

"You saw me this whole time. Including the trip in the back of the car." Declan rolls his eyes, though he returns the hug.

"Don't be an ass, you know what I meant." Aidan leans back in the chair, turning his attention to me. "Tell your Doc I'm sorry. I may have threatened to put a bullet in him if he didn't save my brother."

"Eh, he's been working for us for decades so he's used to it at this point. At least you didn't choke him and have to be sedated because you refused to let go." I shrug, both brothers looking at me with their jaws hanging open. "It was one time. After I found out about my dad, so, I think I'm forgiven."

Declan and Aidan's expressions shift to deep understanding, making me incredibly uncomfortable.

"I was hoping to have a moment alone with you, Declan. Your brother is more than welcome to stay in one of our guest rooms and get some proper sleep," I offer.

Aidan stiffens, adjusting himself so he's in front of his brother. "I'm not going anywhere."

Declan places a hand on his brother's shoulder, gently squeezing. "Aidan, it's fine. She's not going to hurt me. Go get some proper sleep. You need it."

Aidan takes a few more reassurances from his brother to be convinced but eventually he leaves the room, though not before giving me a warning glance that screams 'Don't do anything stupid'. I'd roll my eyes if there wasn't a part of me that understood his sudden protectiveness.

"How are you feeling?" I ask, sitting in the chair next to the bed.

"You mean other than the fact that a bullet just went through me?" he teases.

"Right." I wince. God, I'm bad at this. I never had to comfort anyone through anything. My entire life had been spent learning how to harden myself, so by the time I became boss, nothing could affect me.

"Don't look so concerned," Declan deadpans. "Doctor Williams patched me up quickly. I'm as healthy as a horse."

"Glad to hear it." Though I probably sounded anything but. This is why I never do small talk. "Um, I guess I should say thank you."

He finds my discomfort hilarious, letting out a laugh that shakes the room. "You guess, huh? You'd think I gifted you a fruitcake, not took a whole bullet for you the way you're acting now."

"You're right. I'm sorry. I've just never had to comfort someone before and I'm feeling really out of my element right now."

He fails to school the smirk on his face. "Comfort me? Have you decided to take on a gig as a bedside nurse or?"

"What, no! Definitely not. But I've been warned not to come in guns blazing—"

"Metaphorically speaking, or literally. Because I know there's a risk of both options happening if I piss you off."

"Ah, I forgot you saw that." Perhaps killing a man could have waited until I made sure Declan had been properly cared for.

"I'll never forget it."

"It was quite a scene. Hopefully, it sent a clear enough message."

"It did. There's a lot of things I'm seeing clearer now." The latter part he whispers to himself but I'm still able to catch it.

The words confuse me, but I don't probe more. The list of things I need to ask him about is already extensive; I don't need to add another. At least not tonight.

"I never thought you'd be one to bite your tongue, Zahra. And yet I can tell that's exactly what you've done from the moment you walked in." He groans as he moves to sit up, closing the space between us so our faces are only a few inches apart. "What are you holding back?"

My throat tightens, sweat forming on my palms. "It's always been hard for me to trust people. But with you, it's nearly impossible. I don't know if I can ever do it."

His eyebrows knit together. "And why's that?"

I could lie, but that would only drag out whatever game we'd both been playing with each other even longer. I need answers now. No matter how much they hurt to get. "Because I blame you for the death of my father, and your own. And I hate you for it."

Declan's eyes close, and the machine tracking his pulse starts to beep quicker. His heart is racing. For the first time tonight, Declan looks genuinely uncomfortable, which is saying a lot given that a few hours ago, he had a bullet lodged inside him.

"I don't fault you for hating me." He takes in a few long, deep breaths, slowing his heart rate down slightly, fists clenching the white sheets on his bed. "How could I when you're right? I did kill them."

16

ZAHRA

'*I did kill them.*'

Declan's words ring in my ears over and over again as the room starts to spin. My stomach feels like it's turned inside out and the sterile chlorine smell of the room chokes me. I try to speak but my throat is constricted, refusing to let a sufficient amount of air in.

He killed them. He tried to kill me. And I was sitting alone in a room with him. Defenseless.

In a flash, I'm on my feet, throwing open the closest drawer to me, and grabbing an empty needle. Not my ideal choice of weapon but I'll stab him in the eye if I have to. Whatever it takes to walk out of here alive. Whatever it takes to get my revenge.

Declan's eyes widen as I charge at him. Before I can strike him, he wraps his large hands around my wrists and throws me a bit off balance. His injury has clearly weakened his strength, as he's unable to keep me away. He resorts to begging instead. "Christ love. I didn't mean it like that. It came out wrong."

"Oh no. You don't get to deny it now. Not with all the evidence I have against you. All I needed was your confession, and now I have it," I hiss, though there's a voice in the back of my head yelling at me to listen to him.

Declan cocks his head, voice remaining calm. "It wasn't a confession. Though I would love to hear what you've managed to dig up about me."

"Oh, I'm sure you would. That way, you can spin your web of excuses to try to get out of this." I shift slightly, holding the needle at his neck.

Declan winces. "I didn't kill our fathers. At least not in the literal sense. I couldn't save them. And I should have. I should have been there. But I wasn't. And that is something that will haunt me forever." His eyes begin to turn glassy, causing me to freeze in place. How is he able to do that, come off so genuine and sincere while lying straight to my face?

"LIAR! You *were* there. I tracked your phone's GPS. It had you in the room right when they got shot," I seethe, leaning forward in an attempt to head butt him. He moves just in time.

"No. I wasn't," he hisses back. "Drop the syringe and I'll explain everything. I promise."

"And leave myself defenseless? Never." I refuse to budge.

"Fine, a compromise." He drops one of his hands and reaches under his sheets, pulling out a revolver. "I'll give you this gun. The only thing I have here to keep me safe. If you promise to hear me out and not shoot me the second I give it to you."

With my free hand, I grab the rest of the sheets covering his body and throw them aside, needing proof that he has no other weapon hidden away. Satisfied, I give him a small nod and drop the needle in my hand, replacing it with his gun. I check the cylinder to make sure it's loaded, cock the revolver, and aim it right at his chest. He takes that as his cue to start talking.

"I wasn't lying when I said I was in Maine when our fathers were killed. We had an inner circle meeting earlier that morning that involved a lot of my dad chastising Aidan for not doing enough, which ended with my brother storming off after saying a few choice words that I know will haunt him forever. I ran after him without realizing whose phone I had grabbed. It wasn't until I was already in Maine that I realized I didn't have my own phone. I turned back immediately but at that point it was too late. Cyrus had called me immediately when both of our fathers were shot. But I didn't get the message since I didn't have my phone."

I search his face for a hint of a lie, but all I see is shame. Shame so deep it hurts to look at him without feeling a similar level of guilt and failure. If his story is true, then the geotracker evidence I collected couldn't be trusted.

He rightly takes my silence as distrust. "You can call anyone you want at our Maine headquarters. They'll confirm my arrival. So will my security. And so will Cyrus."

I do just that, calling every single person possible who could confirm Declan's location on that fateful day. Each alibi confirmed his story. One piece of evidence was tossed out, but I still have others in my arsenal. "What about the poison?"

"What *about* the poison?" He raises an eyebrow.

"You visited the old man's apothecary at least five times by my records. The poisons he sells match the same one poured in my drink." I had Azula run a test as soon as I got home. The two samples were a perfect match.

Declan blinks. "I guess I should have figured you've been following me this whole time. How did you manage to put a tracker on me anyway?"

"Don't deflect." I place my finger back on the trigger of the gun.

"Do you really think I was the one who tried to poison you?" He sounds a mix of offended...and hurt. "Did I not just take a fucking bullet for you?"

Rage builds in my stomach at the reminder that the very man I wanted dead up until now had also been the one to save me.

"That *just* happened. Up until a few hours ago, I thought I had evidence that you were in the same room as our fathers when they were killed. A record of you dealing with the old man at the apothecary, and over a dozen stories about how power-hungry and sociopathic you can be. Can you blame me for not trusting some man I just met whose reputation more than precedes him?"

"I visited that morbid poison specialist five times with the hope that I could convince him to fess up to who tried to poison you. Or at least who purchased the poison from him. I tried everything. Flatter, threats, bribery, even breaking in. Came out empty-handed each time."

Oh. He was trying to hunt down the assassin. Because whoever was trying to kill me was likely the same person who had killed our fathers.

"Anything else I did to defend myself about? Given my reputation?" There's a slight edge to his voice as he throws my own words back at me. A part of me wants to retaliate, at least verbally, but I can't blame him for being upset. I would be, too, if someone had falsely accused me of killing my own blood for a seat on the throne.

"Cyrus has tracked down the women and children of your known enemies. Most of them have been trafficked to either the skin trade or for labor. He's tied it back to you." Bile fills my mouth as I get the words out. Even if Declan saved me, I could never forgive a man who treated innocents like property.

"That's impossible. Over my dead fucking body would I *ever* participate in something so atrocious. Whatever information Cyrus found has to be fake. Or doctored." The heart monitor starts to race again, this time tracking Declan's rage.

"Or another thing happening behind your back." I'd never considered the possibility, but between our supplies gone missing and now this...It's just as plausible a theory as any.

"What evidence does Cyrus have?" Declan bites.

"Besides pictures of the trades happening? Receipts tied to your offshore accounts."

"My uncle manages all those accounts. Still does. My dad gave Lorkan power to run the Irish Mafia as my second in his will."

"What? Why?" Everything my father had told me about Declan's father contradicted him ever trusting Lorkan with his legacy.

"Honestly, fuck if I know. A part of me feels like it's a final test my father is putting me through to prove myself. I just wish I knew what message I was supposed to take from it." Declan rolls his eyes. "Regardless, it will all be resolved soon. There's a...clause I can fulfill that will remove Lorkan's power."

I nod. Good. So long as his vile uncle is stopped, the cost doesn't matter. "Do you really think he could do this, though? Traffic innocent victims?"

"I want to say no. My uncle has many issues, and there have been many times when I wanted to strangle him for his vile mouth, but I never thought he'd be capable of something like this. Is he a pompous dickhead? Sure. That's a far stretch from being pure evil..." Declan trails off as if trying to convince himself that he believes the words coming from his mouth.

I'd been there before with countless people I'd once considered allies. Considered friends. Most people manage to disappoint you in the end. If you're lucky, you realize who will fail you while you're still alive to cut them out of your life. "People will do unspeakable things for power."

Greenish-blue eyes snap up to meet mine. "Like involve our family in the drug trade again. That's Lorkan's latest threat for me disrespecting him."

I suck in a breath. "Are you serious?"

All I get is a nod in response. "And if he's willing to destroy my father's legacy by going back to selling drugs, it's not a far reach to assume he'd be willing to tarnish my reputation by getting involved in the skin trade."

"It would also explain how someone had managed to steal our supplies without us knowing. They knew how to avoid all our cameras, only work in the blind spots. Never speak near the audio tracks. Only higher-ranked officials are privy to that information," I summarize.

"Fuck me," Declan groans, dragging his hands down his face. "Killing your own brother though? Lorkan's a monster but I don't know if he's *that* kind of monster."

He looks almost innocent with his hands cradling his face and the loose, tousled strands of his hair covering his eyes. Like a child who just learned their hero had been lying to them the whole time. Or a man realizing not even your own blood can be trusted.

I bite my lip. Hard. My mind is still rattling in a billion different directions with all the events of tonight. Being shot at was one thing, but realizing everything I believed about Declan was wrong threw me off my axis. Now adding on the layer that his own uncle may have killed his father. I'd spare Declan my proclivity to speak what's on my mind even when I know it will crush the recipient.

"What do you think?" Declan asks, though the words come

out more like a plea. *Tell me my uncle didn't kill my father. Tell me, please.*

"I think it's been a long day, and rational decisions are never made with exhausted minds." I shift off the bed, giving Declan a terse smile. "Get some rest. Whatever we decide to do next, you need to be fully healed for."

"We?" he asks, lips slightly curving upward.

"Yes, we. If I wasn't clear, we're a team now."

17
DECLAN

"If you continue to fuss over me like I'm a newborn who can't take care of himself, I will fire you," I grumble at Maura as she wags the shoulder brace in front of me.

Her eyes turn into slits. "Declan. Andrew. McAlister."

My stomach tightens as she punctuates my full legal name. Shit. I fucked up.

"Damn, Dec, you've really fucked up now." Aidan cackles, voicing out loud what I'm thinking.

"Did you really just *threaten* me? The woman who feeds you every night. The woman who nursed you through several hangovers during a rebellious period that well overstayed its welcome? The woman who is on you when you're sick, and who you beg every time to stay longer because you turn into an absolute baby when your stomach hurts?" Her words and the sarcasm laced in them get louder and louder with each question.

"I didn't mean it, I was just being dramatic—"

"Oh no. Don't you try to take it all back. Maybe you're right. Maybe you don't need me. Maybe I'll just quit and have an early retirement. Lord knows I've more than earned my time to relax by the sun, dealing with you two." She wags the wooden spoon in her hands between Aidan and me.

Aidan throws his hands up in surrender. "Hey! What did I do? I'm just an innocent bystander!"

"Innocent my arse. The reason I have so many greys is because of you." Maura rolls her eyes before walking away from the kitchen. "I'll just go ahead and pack my bags now since I'm not needed here."

"Declan. C'mon, man, do something. You know damn well the place would cave in on itself without her." Aidan's panic is as pathetic as it is endearing at this moment.

"She's just bluffing. And trying to make a point." I huff, crossing my arms across my chest and refusing to acknowledge the twinge of pain in my shoulder that follows.

"Well, she can take all my money with that poker face she's rocking. Plus, that doesn't sound like a bluff to me." Aidan nods his head to Maura's room, and the creaking sound of wooden drawers being thrown open, followed by the sharp, aggressive unzipping of her suitcase.

Christ. I had really hurt her feelings this time. Great job, Declan. This is exactly what you needed on top of the never-ending list of problems on your to-do list.

Taking a deep breath, I take a few strides down the hall until I'm standing in the doorway of Maura's room. "What are you doing?"

She clicks her tongue. "What does it look like I'm doing? I'm moving out. Should be done in the next hour. After that, I'm heading straight to Cabo."

"Cabo, huh? It's pretty sunny there," I note.

"I'm well aware. I've packed extra sunscreen," she practically growls as she slams one of her suitcases shut.

"You *hate* the sun. Every time the clouds clear, you practically curse at the sky and do a rain dance for them to return." I smirk.

"Maybe it's not the sun I want to curse at. Maybe it's the arrogant and unappreciative boys that I had to care for like my own. But I suppose that's never how they viewed me. I was just the housekeeper to them," she bites back.

Ah. So that's what this is about. Fuck. I meant my comments about firing her in jest because I wanted to stop worrying about me, but I couldn't fault her for taking it personally. Especially since I know I've been particularly grouchy these past few weeks.

I step into her room and close the door behind us. "You're right. I'm sorry. You do so much for us, and the least I can do is say thank you."

Her back stiffens but she doesn't turn, refusing to look at me. Bile fills my stomach. I hate seeing her this upset. "You don't have to console me. I won't really quit."

"I know." I move forward so I'm standing next to her. "Even if you wanted to, you couldn't. Because you're not the type of person to quit on your family. And that's what we are."

Her eyes shut as a small smile creeps onto her face. "Family."

"So you'll accept my apology?"

"I will. As long as you put this brace on your shoulder and keep it on until I see fit. Don't think I haven't noticed how you wince every time you move your right arm." She smirks, grabbing the fabric laid on her bed and tossing it into my chest.

My jaw falls open as her smirk turns into a grin and she breaks out into a cackle. She fucking played me.

"Conniving woman," I grumble under my breath, adjusting my brace to fit snugly onto my arm.

"What was that?" Maura chides, wooden spoon back in her raised hand like she's ready to smack me with it.

"Nothing, nothing. You know Declan always had a strange habit of talking to himself..." Aidan pauses to twirl his index finger by his temple and side-eyeing me. Great, first I was the asshole older brother, and now I'm crazy.

Maura rolls her eyes and turns on the gas stove, getting to work on whipping up breakfast. My mouth starts to water as the scent of bacon grease, cheese, and eggs fills the kitchen.

"So, when are Zahra and co. arriving?" Aidan steals a slice of bacon from the pan, tossing it in his mouth.

I wince, glancing at my watch. "Shit, I totally lost track of time. Should be in ten minutes. Fifteen tops. Would it be weird if we all met in the living room?"

"Why can't we meet in your office?"

"Because it's a mess," I declare. I had planned on cleaning it up a bit this morning, but Maura's fussing and subsequent successful attempt at getting me to wear my brace threw me off.

"....and?" Aidan cocks his head, confused.

"And what message would it say to our allies if they see my office a mess?"

"That you're a human being who just got shot and maybe didn't have time to throw out his recycling?" Aidan teases.

"Or maybe that I'm a lazy slob who doesn't know how to take care of himself," I correct, irritation growing as my brother looks at me like I'm crazy.

Maura snorts as she turns the stove off. "Nearly thirty years you've been on this planet, Declan, and I don't think I've ever once heard you care this much about your office, or frankly any room of yours, being messy. No matter how much I used to pray for moments like this when you were a teenager."

"Are you saying a man can never change, Maura?" I scoff, pouring myself a cup of coffee. Or, as Aidan liked to tease me, a cup of milk and sugar with a splash of coffee.

She shakes her head, hands on her hips. "No. But the question is, *who* has inspired this change?"

My back stiffens. "What makes you think it's a 'who'?"

"Yeah. Maybe he finally decided to give those self-help podcasts I've been recommending him a shot," Aidan offers.

"You listen to self-help podcasts?" I can't even hide the judgment I know is on my face.

"I've been telling you about them for weeks now! Do you even listen to me?" Aidan clicks his tongue in mock offense.

"I do, but admittedly, our tastes in media preferences are not aligned."

"Don't knock it till you try it, is all I'm saying." Aidan shrugs.

"I don't know, I think I'm on Declan's side on that one," a voice as smooth as silk fills the room.

Turning around slowly, I'm met with the sweet scene of vanilla and cardamom and the sight of Zahra in a long black trench coat, the top half of which somehow manages to grip her curves like a second skin. The dark red lipstick on her plump lips matches the deep maroon of her velvet maroon thigh-high boots. By the time my eyes meet hers, there's a mischievous glint to them. One that tempts me to find out just how lethal she can be.

"Sorry, we're early. I didn't mean to interrupt breakfast." Zahra gives Maura an apologetic smile, no doubt winning her favor. "We can wait in the hallway while you all finish—"

"Nonsense, there's plenty for everyone. Why don't you all take a seat? I'll have the table set in no time."

"We can help," Zahra offers as she walks into the kitchen.

"Oh, there's no need for all that—"

Zahra shakes her head. "I insist. My mother raised me to always contribute, especially when someone invites me over as a guest. It's the least we can do."

I stay frozen in place as I watch Zahra undo her coat, button by button, desperate to see what she had on underneath. Shrugging off her top layer, she reveals a long-sleeved, deep red, fitted dress that falls right above her boots. My hands twitch, practically aching to reach out and caress her soft hips, that sway ever so slightly as she follows Maura into the dining room, plates in hand.

A vision flashes in my head, one where this is our normal, everyday routine. Me waking up to find Maura and Zahra in the kitchen laughing and teasing me about whatever dumb thing I had done earlier in the week. Eventually, I'd pretend to have had enough of the jokes and reach across the island, tugging her closer to me and throwing her over my shoulder back into my room, where I would apologize for all my past mistakes. First with my tongue, and then with my—

"Dude, have some self-respect and get that under control. We're not teenagers anymore." Aidan jabs an elbow into my side, sending a pointed look at the crotch of my pants which had definitely stiffened in the last ten minutes.

"There was a cold breeze. From the window," I snap, hoping he believes the excuse.

"Riiight. A breeze. If I may, I'd like to remind you that she killed a man in cold blood without a second thought in front of like a thousand witnesses," he whispers.

"You can. If I can remind you that man put a bullet in me. And tried to kill her." A rush of heat fills my body as I think back to how utterly tantalizing she was that night. The moment I laid eyes on her and that red silk dress that showed more of her chest and her soft legs than it did cover, I knew I was a goner. I spent that night schmoozing with the Boston elites who would want nothing more than to pawn their daughters off to marry me, and received a few decently promising proposals, and yet all I could think about was the one thing I couldn't have. Zahra.

"God, look at you. Here I am talking about her splattering someone's brains in front of you, and instead of being repulsed, you're actually getting turned on. What the hell is wrong with you?" Aidan scoffs.

"I'm a mafia Don. Blood doesn't make me queasy. I shrug.

"But somehow I'm the weird one for listening to self-help podcasts. This family is cooked in the head."

"Boys, are you coming? Or do you plan on standing there gossiping to yourselves like we can't all see you?" Maura scolds, her voice carrying over from down the hall.

Aidan bolts to the table, likely not wanting to piss off Maura and face her wrath like I had earlier. By the time I enter the dining room, the only seat left is the one next to Zahra, who's deep in conversation with Maura. "I have to say, I'm maybe embarrassingly excited to finally try your famous strawberry scones. My dad would always rave about them."

Maura's eyebrows come together. "I always sent Naser home with extra for you and your mum."

"Oh, I know. They just never made it home. He'd always scarf down the leftovers on the car ride back, and then apologize to me once he realized what he'd done," she snickers before taking a bite of pastry. Her eyes shut close as she savors the bite, and the soft moan she lets out makes me want to drag her into my room and turn my daydream into a reality.

"They're also Declan's favorites. I remember the one time I made blueberry scones instead of strawberry. He didn't talk to me for a whole week." Maura rolls her eyes, taking a big swig from her coffee.

Zahra shakes her head at me. "That's incredibly dramatic, don't you think?"

"I was six!" I protest loudly. I don't know what comes over

me, but I lean closer so only she can hear me. "Plus, let's not pretend like you didn't nearly orgasm a few seconds ago over how good the scones are."

Her deep brown eyes widen, and I feel a sharp sting of pain in my ankle. "Did you just kick me?" I press my lips together, trying not to let the laughter spill over.

"You should just be grateful I went for one of my less aggressive methods to silence you. Next time I won't be so generous."

"Hmm, are you threatening to shoot me? Or just strangle me?" I tease.

"That depends. By the look on your face, my gut is telling me you'd like to be choked. If that's the case, I don't know much of a deterrent it would be for me to strangle you."

The smirk on her face paired with the sultry heat of her voice have me wrapped so tightly around her aura I don't even register someone else speaking to me.

"Declan," Maura raises her voice slightly, "I asked you a question."

Zahra stuffs her face with the rest of the scone in a poor attempt to hide her amusement at me being scolded.

"Sorry about that. I was a bit distracted." I don't even bother to look at the woman next to me. Doing so would only suck me back into whatever magic spell she's put in me to mess with my head. "What do you need?"

"Could you pass the butter, please?"

I reach out to the small dish right in front of me, but before I can grab it, my hand collides with another, much smaller and softer hand. Zahra gasps the moment we make contact, pulling her hand away and clutching it to her chest like I've physically shocked her. And maybe I had. Because the side of her hand she had grazed feels like it's buzzing with electricity. I move quickly, so no one else notices how dumbstruck they are, handing the butter dish to Maura and completely ignoring the way she continues to look back and forth between Zahra and me, only to shrug her shoulders at the end.

"Once breakfast is over, I'd like to brief you all on the intel gathered about the shooter." I shift back into boss mode, locking eyes with each member of Zahra's team.

"Or we can just talk about it now," Azula offers, clearly wanting to get on with her day instead of being here. I can't say I blame her. Up until recently, Zahra assumed I was the one trying to kill her, and I had no doubts her second had been informed of all the evidence stacked against me.

Aidan and I shoot each other a look. "We can't."

"I'm sorry?" Azula blinks.

"We just can't. As soon as breakfast is over—"

"Are you stalling, McAlister? If I were in your shoes and I had information on the man who nearly killed me and tried to kill my ally, I would *run* to update them on what I found. Not sit around waiting to finish my pancakes." Taking a knife into her hand, Azula angles it ever so slightly in my direction that I can feel all of my guards shift their attention to her, ready to protect me.

"He's eating waffles, actually," Aidan cuts in before I can defuse the situation. "And out of respect for my parents, we don't speak about business when we eat meals together. It's something they instilled in us as kids and we continue to live by."

"I see." Azula shifts her attention to Zahra, who offers her a stern smile signaling Azula to back off.

"Corrine and Cillian would be so thrilled to see us all together today." Maura lets out a small sigh. "There are few things your father wanted more than to see you continue to work with Naser's heir side by side."

Zahra extends her hand out to give Maura's a squeeze.

"The same can be said for my father. His friendship with Cillian was one that meant the world to him."

"I know you two are still strangers to each other, but I have no doubt you will learn to lean on each other over time just like your fathers did."

"Funny, this sounds like work-related conversation to me, but what do I know?" Azula rolls her eyes, aggressively stabbing into her omelet.

"Azula," Zahra warns.

"The alliance between our two organizations is more than just business. It's *family*," Maura emphasizes.

Family. There were many moments growing up where that's exactly what I felt, but now I wasn't so sure. How could we be family when Naser kept Zahra hidden from me. Hidden from *us*. I wonder if Zahra feels the same. It's clear her father told her stories about us, but she never got to actually live it herself. I know she's grateful for the sense of normalcy her father was able to give her growing up, but there had to be a part of her that also felt...left out.

Connor, one of my new security details, steps behind me and clears his throat. "Boss, I'm sorry to interrupt, but Mr. Greylock is here to see you and he's being particularly insistent."

Greylock? What the hell did the CEO of one of the largest auto enterprises in the city want from me?

"What do you mean he's *here*?" The man was incredibly private and refused to be featured in any tabloids. No one had even seen him outside of his estate in years.

"He's waiting in the foyer along with his daughter."

As if on cue, a high-pitched voice followed by a loud clicking of heels fills the room. "I know this house is a bit more...vintage than what we're used to, Daddy, but don't worry. I'll spruce it up in no time. Oh! I didn't expect to see so many people here. Our invitation must have gotten lost."

The lanky blonde, wearing a bright pink pantsuit, sends me a massive smile that I can only guess is meant to come off as endearing, but the crazed look in her eye makes me feel more in danger than Azula ever did. Still, I can't shake the fact that I had met her somewhere before. Probably one of a dozen women Aidan had arranged for me to meet the night of the banquet... Oh shit. That's definitely where I knew her from.

I look for Aidan, hoping he'll somehow get me out of this nightmare, but instead he's nearly keeling over in laughter at the disaster that was about to unfold.

"Connor, can you be a doll and grab me and Daddy a chair, please?"

"Absolutely not. This is a private meeting between our two organizations," Azula seethes, freezing Connor in place.

The blonde is undeterred. "Oh, don't you worry, I'm very good at keeping a secret. Plus, I probably should be informed about Declan's business operations, given our relationship."

"Your relationship as his....new assistant?" Azula guesses, shooting me a dirty look. Damn, who spat in her Cheerios this morning?

"No, silly. Declan's my fiancé."

18

ZAHRA

"*...* D*eclan's my fiancé.*"
Fiancé.

Fiancé?

When the hell did that happen? Unless I wildly misinterpreted the situation, I was fairly certain Declan was flirting with me not even ten minutes ago. Granted, he wouldn't be the first man who blatantly tried to get with me when he had someone waiting for him at home. I'd encountered lots of scum in my line of work, and cheaters ranked close to the top in my personal list of men who didn't deserve to breathe.

Declan turns to me, wide-eyed. "I promise it's not what it looks like."

Gross. "Jesus Christ. At least get some new material. It's a bit pathetic how predictable this all is."

"We're *not* engaged—"

The blonde, I believe her name is Natalie, if my memory serves me correctly, interjects, "Well, not yet, but that's why I brought Daddy here so we could work out the details of my alimony."

Ah. Okay. Now I understand. "This is a business arrangement," I summarize.

Declan winces. "Sort of...it's a bit more complicated than that. Do you think we could talk...privately?"

"Sure, but if I was your soon-to-be-fiancé I'd be pretty pissed that you were straight up ignoring me for another girl." I offer him a piece of advice, which he doesn't take and he quickly excuses himself and leads me into his office.

Whether to make us look better or because they can't help being nosy, Azula and Aidan follow behind, refusing to be left out of the conversation.

Declan scratches the back of his neck awkwardly as we all enter his office. "Sorry for the mess. I planned on cleaning up this morning, but I had to deal with a Maura-related issue."

I blink, taking in the nearly immaculate room in front of me, sans a few scattered books on his desk, and a jacket thrown haphazardly on the loveseat close to the bookshelf. If this is what he considered messy, he'd probably have a heart attack if he ever saw my room.

"God, that poor woman. I'm surprised she hasn't quit yet, having to put up with you two," Azula snaps, picking at her nails while glowering at the younger McAlister brother.

"*Hey.* What did I ever do to you to make you so snippy?" Aidan asks.

"The both of you have dragged our meeting on long enough. Throwing frivolous distractions our way—"

"Breakfast is literally the most important meal of the day —" Aidan scoffs.

"And now you've made us a part of a whole circus with Natalie and her father practically preening all over Declan and his money—"

"Natalie...that's her name." Declan sighs with relief.

My head snaps in his direction. "You don't even know the

name of your fucking *fiancé*? Are you insane?" Arranged marriages were certainly still a thing among the various mafias, but at the very least, most organizations had the sense to run a background check on who they were marrying.

"Again, she's not my fiancé—"

"Well, you want her to be, don't you?" I cut him off.

"That's a complicated question. Do I want a fiancé? Yes. Well, really, I would say I need one at this point more than anything. Whether it ends up being her or anyone else... doesn't really matter to me." He shrugs, shoving his hands into his pockets.

Damn. This was the cold and calculated Declan that Cyrus had warned me about. The one that didn't care about anyone else's feelings so long as he got his way. It's what makes him a great boss, I suppose, the ability to turn off enough of his humanity to be able to think about the betterment of his organization.

"What exactly do you need this engagement for? More access to customers? Expanding trade roots?"

"To officially put an end to my uncle's power."

I blink. That doesn't make any sense. "How would getting engaged solve that?" Declan and Aidan exchange pained glances. I am so over this. "If one of you doesn't tell me what the hell is going on instead of continuing to stall—"

"Do you remember a few weeks ago? When I mentioned my father had written in his will for my uncle to be second. There's a timestamp on that clause. The moment I get married is the moment I gain full control of the Irish Mafia, which includes having sole access to our funds and the ability to pick my own second."

"I'm sorry, what? Your dad wrote in a *marriage clause*?" I can't help but let out a laugh. Somehow, the thought of Cillian McAlister, one of the most powerful mob bosses in the world, feeling the need to meddle in his son's love life beyond the grave is just comical to me.

Declan's eyes narrow. "He warned me I had put too much emphasis on work and not enough on finding a partner, so I guess this was his final way of ensuring I didn't dawdle for too long. He knows how much I despise my Uncle Lorkan being in charge of...well, anything."

"Wow, if anyone's dad was going to write a marriage clause in their will, I'm sure most people would've had their bets on it being me. This is oddly refreshing." And perhaps unsurprising. My father didn't think any man was worth my time. I can't say I entirely disagreed with him, given my track record of shitty exes I had in college.

"Yes, I'm glad only one of us has to be bartered off like a prize horse to the highest bidder." Declan's tone is laced with sarcasm.

"I'm counting this as reparations for the patriarchy. Your father always was a solid ally," I tease, which manages to get a very small, blink-and-you-miss-it, smile from Declan.

"So now that we've cleared up the whole fiancé situation—"

As if on cue, Natalie and her father come barreling through the office door, an incredibly distressed security guard trailing behind them. The fact that I don't recognize him informed me that he must be new.

"We're in a meeting, Connor. A private meeting," Declan snaps back into boss mode, and I swear I see a trail of sweat fall from Connor's forehead.

"I-I understand that, Boss. I tried to tell that to Miss Grey-lock, but then she informed me that she was your fiancée and that you would be very upset if you found out that I had prevented her from speaking to you so I thought it was best...." Connor gulps, unable to finish his sentence.

"I see." Declan's expression turns from irritation to pain as he glances at Natalie and her father. It's almost at that moment he finally realizes what the rest of his life will look like and he'd rather do anything or be anyone else. Can't say I could blame the guy. The thought of marrying a complete stranger—one who has made it very clear they only want me for my money—made my stomach turn.

I hated feeling used. It was a feeling that, in our line of work, was unavoidable to an extent. People always assume that bosses are untouchable but years of being trained by my father showed me otherwise. Bosses held all the power, which means someone always wanted something from you and would be willing to do anything or kill anyone to get even the smallest taste of that power. It felt like you were constantly swimming in a pool filled with vipers ready to strike, and Declan was about to gain another viper. Except this would be much worse. Mob wives, by definition, gained a large amount of power and say upon being married into a family. And given Declan has been so hands-off in researching who he was marrying, I'd be willing to bet he hadn't thought far enough to draw up a prenup. Fucking hell, this was bad.

Entirely too much of the Persian Empire's assets are tied up with the Irish. The last thing I want or need is another person I have to run my decisions past. Another person I have to get approval from. I need to fix this situation. Fast.

"We appreciate your diligence, Connor, but Miss Greylock has appeared to have misled you. She is not Declan's fiancé. I am."

19
ZAHRA

The entire room freezes. If not for the grandfather clock ticking in the background, I would have genuinely believed that the earth had stood still. Azula sucks in a deep breath, and Declan's jaw falls open. He shuts it just as fast, but the shocked expression on his face remains.

Unsurprisingly, Natalie is the first to protest. "That *can't* be. He was talking to me all night at the gala. We agreed there's nothing more magical than a spring wedding!"

I raise an eyebrow at Declan while mouthing 'really?' and he just shrugs. Guess he'd forgotten that conversation just as fast as he'd forgotten poor Natalie's name. I gesture for him to say something.

"Natalie, I know this is hard, but Zahra and I...Well, we just make sense." The words fall so easily off his tongue that I could almost believe he truly means them.

Natalie's eyes start to water and her bottom lip trembles. "But...but...Daddy, say something!"

Mr. Greylock looks straight at me as I turn my expression

from sympathetic to cold and calculated. He takes a long, hard swallow before consoling his daughter. "Sweetheart, there's nothing I can do. It appears Mr. McAlister is already spoken for—"

"No! That's not fair! I want *him*." Natalie points at Declan while stomping her foot like a toddler.

Wow. I have no intentions to fight over a man. Now or ever. I'm almost tempted to tell her if she wants him this badly, she can have him, but that would jeopardize both my and the Irish's mafia. So instead I say, "I understand this is really upsetting, Natalie. Trust me, I'd be pissed too if I was led on like you were. I heard the Ukrainian boss is looking for a lady. And he's not known for his...wandering eyes." I nod my head toward Declan, who scoffs.

Natalie lets out a final sob before leaning closer to me and whispering, "Really? Do you think he would be okay with my expensive tastes?"

"More than okay. Azula, remind me to send Mr. Ivanov's contact information to Natalie. Now, if you don't mind, we need to continue our meeting." I nod to Declan, Aidan, and Azula.

"Of course! Of course. I appreciate you helping a girl out. These dating apps, even the more elite ones, are such a drag." Natalie scoffs in disgust. "C'mon, Daddy, I have a Pilates class at two. I'd hate to be late."

Natalie's heels clacking in the distance momentarily fills the awkward silence in the office. Shoving my hands in my pockets, I look at Declan. "So, we should have a contract made soon. While I know our two families are allies, I think it's a good idea to clearly list out what additional power you get as my husband and I as your wife. We can also include personal finances in that contract so we don't have to file a separate prenup."

Declan's eyebrows knit together as he crosses his arms over his chest. Or at least he tries to. The movement is immediately followed by a wince as he rubs the top of his shoulder. The same shoulder that stopped a bullet aimed to kill me. "You're actually serious about this? I thought you just said that to get rid of Natalie."

"Wow, you finally learned her name. Too bad things didn't work out between you two."

His green eyes narrow at me. "We can't get engaged."

"And why not? That clause your father put in his will isn't going away on its own. We can get married long enough for you to send your uncle packing and then we'll get divorced. Easy."

Declan shakes his head. "Except it's not that easy. The clause says I have to get married and stay married for at least a year. Likely because my father figured I would do something like this just to one-up my uncle. If I get divorced any sooner than that, my uncle regains his power. Permanently."

Shit, okay. I guess this wouldn't be as quick a fix as I had imagined. "Well, your uncle is a psychopath who needs to be stopped sooner rather than later. A year will go by much quicker than you think. Plus, it's clear to me that you haven't even thought much about the consequences of marrying a complete stranger beyond the fact that it will free you of any ties with your uncle—"

"And how is marrying you not the same thing as marrying a stranger?" Declan sounds exhausted, but not just from lack of sleep. This is the type of exhaustion that's buried deep in your bones and is hard to get rid of. It's the exhaustion that comes with knowing every move you take could not only be the end of you, but the end of your loved ones and your legacy. It's a type of exhaustion I knew well. Which is why I soften my tone and speak to him not as a boss, but as a regular man.

"I'm not going to deny that we've only recently gotten to know each other, but at least I know this lifestyle. Which means I'm also well aware of the fact that any wife of a boss gains power. Look at how Connor just treated her, thinking she was your *fiancée*. Given how entwined our two families are, any person you bring into your organization can and likely will impact my family. So to me it seems entirely too risky to bring in someone you barely knew...especially given our current circumstances." I allude to the thief in our ranks whose identity we have yet to discover.

Declan nods slowly. "You're right. I shouldn't have been so rash in trying to solve the problem that is my uncle without thinking about the other consequences."

"So then what do you think of my proposal?"

"Figuratively speaking or literally?" His attempt to make light of the situation falls flat. The energy of everyone in the room is nothing somber.

"Both, I suppose." My throat tightens knowing that the next words that come out of his mouth will likely change our lives forever.

"I accept Zahra. I accept."

Azula sucks in a breath, reality likely sinking in for her. "Zahra. As your second, I think both parties involved should take a moment to think this through before we do anything we'll regret."

My eyes narrow. I don't like her insinuating that I hadn't thought this through. Everything I do is calculated, and she knows that. "Your opinion on the matter has been noted."

Azula's undeterred. "It's going to take a few days for your lawyers to write up a contract. And I'm sure Declan's would like to review as well?" she asks Declan, who gives her a quick nod. "Then, how about we reconvene in a week. Should be more than enough time for all the documents to be prepared and negotiations to be handled."

It's a fair request. One that will result in the same decisions made here today. "Fine. I'll have the contract sent over as soon as I can. If there's anything that immediately comes to mind that you would like to be included, please let me know." I glance at my watch, realizing how much time we've lost. "Unfortunately, I can't stay any longer to discuss more details of the shooter. Perhaps we can schedule another meeting in a few days. To discuss our marriage contract and other business-related things?"

Declan gives me a curt nod before I walk out of his office. The longer I stayed there, the more the rational part of me would overthink this. But I can't. Declan's uncle needs his power taken from him immediately, and I can't help but revel in the fact that I'll be responsible for his demise. While I'm not wary about seeking revenge against Lorkan, the idea of getting married to Declan puts me on edge. The more I interact with Declan, the more I find myself pulled toward his palpable energy. And the more I notice parts of myself in him. Parts I had long buried under the surface.

20

DECLAN

"Are you out of your fucking mind?" Aidan exclaims the second our security confirms Zahra has left the mansion. "You can't accept Zahra's proposal."

"I already did." I shrug, walking over to my desk and groaning as I sink into my office chair.

"No, you still have time to back out. No contract has been signed. Vows haven't been exchanged. You're still a free man as far as I'm concerned."

"Aidan, you and I know that I never have been, and never will be a free man." I won't disillusion myself into believing anything else. I'm not even sure I've really ever wanted another life. The mafia is all I know. It's more than just a business, it's family to me. And every family has their own rules to follow, their own expectations. Sacrifices that have to be made. At least marrying Zahra meant marrying into a family that has been allied with us for decades now. Marrying someone who knows what it means to make hard decisions, to prioritize everyone else's needs above their own. Natalie, or any other heiress that Aidan threw my way, would never truly understand the life I lead. Would never truly understand me. Zahra would. Which is why we are a perfect match.

"Declan, you're not thinking clearly about this. This woman nearly got you killed—"

"Don't be so dramatic. She didn't force me to take a bullet for her. I chose to."

"That's exactly my point! You barely even know Zahra and you're risking your life for her. What happens when you *do* get to know her? What happens if you fall in love with her?" he spits, as if falling in love is one of the worst things that can happen to a person.

"I didn't think I would have to remind you of all people that I'm more than capable of keeping my head on straight. Especially when it comes to business."

Aidan lets out a frustrated breath. "Of course I know that it's just... Listen, this is uncharted territory for me. For all of us. Marrying someone like Natalie is simple. You hand over your credit card every time she starts to stick her nose where it doesn't belong and she'll look the other way. Zahra is different. She's a boss. Born and raised to play the game and do whatever it takes to maintain her power. There's no placating her and there's certainly no controlling her—"

"Good," I deadpan. "I don't want a wife that can be easily swayed by money or status or any other frivolous means. She's cunning, and strong, and determined. Exactly what I need as my partner. She's someone who can stand beside me and be equally as threatening. Equally as feared. Equally as respected. Zahra is perfect. So she'll be my wife."

"For a year." Aidan's words freeze me in place. "She'll be your wife for a year, Declan. Don't think she won't end this arrangement as soon as she's able to. Which is the entire reason why I'm cautioning you against this. You're already speaking like this marriage is permanent and not a means to an end. You need to protect yourself, Declan. Not just physically, but also mentally. You cannot fall for Zahra. At least not any more than you already hav—"

"I won't," I snap, wanting an end to this conversation. I don't need a reminder of the fact that I had clearly found myself becoming increasingly infatuated with Zahra. I thought the feeling was mutual, with all the stolen glances she'd aimed at me when we were together. Instead, she'd been convinced that I was the one who had killed her father. Clearly, we'd been on completely separate pages the entire time.

Aidan is right. I can't delude myself into thinking this marriage will be anything more than a business arrangement.

"I appreciate your concern, both as my brother and as my second. But I have the situation under control. I promise."

———

Maybe Zahra: Hi, it's Zahra. Lawyers are working on our marriage contract, any non-negotiables?

I blink at least a dozen times before responding

Declan: How did you get my private cell number?

Zahra: Is that serious question?

Zahra: You do recall I'm a trained hacker, right? :P

I—Was that a tongue out emoji? Is this the most relaxed conversation we've had? What emoji was I supposed to send in response?

Declan: Righhhttt obviously

Zahra: So the contract?

The only thing that came to mind was including a clause that prevented any man from coming within a ten-foot radius of her. For her safety. Obviously. Not because I was jealous of every red-blooded male with a pulse. Though I doubt she'd go along with it, so instead I say,

Declan: Let me think on it and get back to you

Declan: What are you up to today?

I hit send before I can talk myself out of it. Double texts were a known sign of desperation, weren't they? Dammit.

Zahra: My trainer's putting me to work

Her text is followed by a video of her deadlifting weights in the gym, and damn if that didn't turn me on. Watching her lift my weight with ease was probably meant to intimidate me, but instead it just made my cock incredibly hard.

Declan: Practicing so you can throw me around?

Zahra: Obviously…need to make sure I can keep you in line ;)

If only she knew how tightly she had me wrapped around her finger already.

———

"We have a problem. A big one."

I slam my father's will on the desk, wishing I could bring him back to life just to strangle him. Two days after Zahra's proposal, her lawyer called me asking if I had taken the time to read all the stipulations of my father's will surrounding the marriage. I'd started shifting through this morning, and I still had five pages to go through. The sun was starting to set.

"Leave it to dad to refuse to give up any control even from the grave," Aidan grumbles, legs draped across the armrest of the couch in front of me as he jots down key takeaways from each page. "He really did everything in his power to make sure you couldn't fake your way out of this."

"Living in the cottage house with my wife, having dinner together at least five times a week, no international trips longer than a week apart from each other...Is this man crazy?!" I rest my head against my desk, exhausted.

"Sounds like all the things he did with mom. Sans living in the cottage. You know that would've been too small for her." Aidan smirks. Our mother certainly had expensive tastes, not that it bothered my father one bit. He lived to spoil her.

"Yeah, but they were married because they loved each other, not because they were trying to stop Uncle Lorkan from ruining our legacy." Yanking the bottom drawer of my desk open, I grab the bottle of whiskey, unscrew the top, and take a large gulp.

"He probably figured you would try to cheat your way out of this clause. This is his way of holding you accountable." Aidan walks over and grabs the bottle from my hand, also taking a drink. "Dad did shit like this to me all the time. Only difference is my punishments included being cut off financially or kicked out of the house, not sleeping with a super hot, though admittedly super scary, woman."

"There's nothing in the will about sleeping with Zahra," I

scoff, then groan at the stack of papers in front of me, "...right? Or did I miss that? God, I swear if he wrote something in here about an heir—"

"Relax, I'm just busting your balls. Did Zahra's lawyer give you a sense of how she's feeling?" Aidan asks, looking at me with pity.

"I think she assumed I had kept all these clauses hidden from her, which her lawyer talked her down from. Probably told her I hadn't bothered to comb through Dad's will, which is true. From our texts, I get the sense she's pissed, but less at me and more at the whole situation." I shrug.

"Wait. Wait. You two have been *texting*?" Aidan gasps as if that's the most shocking thing we've been discussing.

"Uh, yes? Why is that so surprising?"

"What do you two even talk about?"

"Oh, ya know, about whether we want burgundy-colored drapes in the master bedroom or cream...what the hell do you think we're talking about?" My question is laced in sarcasm.

"Alright, I get it. You got jokes." He rolls his eyes, plopping himself back on the couch.

I guess I can't fully blame him for being surprised. The text exchange I had with Zahra earlier also caught me off guard. The video of her at the gym resulted in me spending an embarrassingly long time taking care of myself, coming at the thought of her soft lips wrapped around me...

"Boss, Ms. Ahzhimi is here." Connor's voice snaps me back into the moment. He still hasn't been able to look me in the eye since I talked to him after the whole Natalie debacle. I ripped into him a bit, but not as hard as I normally would, knowing he was still green in this position.

Aidan's the first to speak. "Why? We agreed to start contract negotiations on Friday."

"I invited her. We never got to talk about the banquet shooter after Natalie stormed in," I remind him.

Aidan clicks his tongue. "Right, I forgot about that. Alright, Connor, you can send her in."

"Actually, I was planning on meeting with her alone. Over dinner. You can stay here and keep reading though." I toss him the remaining stack of documents to sift through.

"So, it'll be just you two alone?

"Correct."

"Is that a good idea?"

"It's the one I'm going with so..."

"But I'm also hungry," he protests.

"I'll have Maura bring you something to eat." I walk out of my office before he continues to list reasons why I shouldn't have dinner with my soon-to-be fiancé. *Soon to a fiancé who's counting down the days until she can divorce you,* I remind myself.

"She's waiting in the wing." Connor gestures to the hallway across from my office. "The delivery was made right before she arrived."

I give him a nod before walking down the hallway. Zahra's intoxicating scent hits me before the sight of her. And god, what a sight it is. Her long, wavy hair falls loose on her fully exposed shoulders and collar. Her long-sleeve cream shirt hugs every delicious curve of her breasts, and her long, loose pants barely hide the incredible ass I know is underneath. My hands twitch, desperate to touch her.

"I can take that for you." I gesture to the coat draped over her hands.

"Thank you." She smiles softly, extending her arm out. Our hands brush as I take her jacket, and a rush of electricity runs down my spine. Zahra must have felt the same, as she lets out a small gasp and her pupils dilate. Fuck, I need to get that reaction out of her again.

Placing her coat in the closet, I take a second to compose myself. *You're about to talk about the man who almost killed both of you, Declan.* Definitely not the time to get a hard-on over barely touching a girl. *Get a grip.*

"The dining room's this way." I start walking toward the room where we had breakfast a few days ago.

"Take out? I'm surprised Maura allows that in her house." Zahra raises an eyebrow, taking a seat and opening the first container in front of her. "*Oh*, Pad Thai, yum."

"What Maura doesn't know won't kill her. I'll just toss the empty containers in the garbage before she spots them." I stand frozen for a second, debating how close I should sit to her. Zahra makes the decision for me, setting a plate down in the seat next to hers while digging through the other contents of the plastic bag.

"There's also dumplings, Thai fried rice, and Pad Woon Sen."

"Pad Woon Sen is my favorite...Although I do have a confession to make." Her expression turns serious.

"Oh?"

She leans closer, and I do my best to keep my eyes locked on her face and not the slight hint of cleavage that's practically screaming for my attention. Zahra lowers her voice so it's barely a whisper, "I have no idea how to use chopsticks."

A snort leaves my nose before I can stop it. "You're so dramatic. Here I thought you were going to tell me something serious."

"It is serious. Azula makes fun of me for it all the time." She laughs and I realize this is the first time I've ever seen her so relaxed. It's a refreshing look for her.

"Well, we can't have that now, can we. Let me show you." I pull apart two chopsticks and take her right hand into mine.

"How'd you know I'm right-handed?"

"It's the hand you used when you took down that assassin at the banquet," I comment, taking in how small her hand looks cradled in my palm. "So, you want to place one stick in the space between your thumb and your index. This one is going to be stationary and there for support. Now, this other chopstick you want to hold like a pencil and use it to grab your food. Just take a second to get used to how that feels."

I pull back and relish the deep concentration of her face as she laser focuses on her hand. A minute later, she pulls out a dumpling from the take-out container and places it on her plate. "Damn, I can't believe that actually worked. You're a pretty good teacher," she teases.

"Well, I benefited from having a student who's a quick learner, so." I wink, dumping a heap of Pad Thai onto my plate. We eat in a comfortable silence for a few minutes before I decide to shift the conversation to the main reason we're having dinner tonight. "Are you okay to talk about the banquet shooter?"

She nods.

"We were able to find out more information about his past than his present. He worked as a paid guard for a few years, then for the federal government, handling the deportation of immigrants. Seems like he got some sadistic joy out of separating families—"

"I should have put an extra bullet or two in his head just for that," Zahra growls, and I have the sudden urge to find everyone who's ever crossed her just so I can watch her get revenge.

"He quit his government job over a year ago and there's no record of what he does now. We would've written him off as any other enemy to our mafia, or even an incel who wanted to brag about killing a powerful woman to his friends...if it weren't for the vulture tattoo on his chest."

Zahra stills. "A vulture? Like the man who tried to poison me at The Black Rose?"

"The tattoos were identical. Even the ink was manufactured by the same company. We had our coroner run a bunch of tests once we saw the similarities."

Her expression turns blank as she purses her lips. "So someone is incredibly hell bent on trying to kill me."

"It would appear so. Has Cyrus had any luck tracking down the original assassin?"

"Still nothing. But maybe we can add this additional man into our facial recognition system and see if anything comes up." She runs her hands through her hair. "You're likely a target now too, if you weren't before. Especially considering you took the bullet that was meant for me."

She places her hand gently on my shoulder, and I swear some of the lingering pain alleviates.

"Not to mention the fact that we're getting married." My tone is light, but I can tell that's weighing down on her too. "I can always find another way…"

Zahra shakes her head. "No. This is the best path forward. We can pool all our guards and resources, and hopefully track down not only whoever is trying to kill me, but also whoever is stealing from us."

"We're safer together," I summarize. Between her sniffing out the poison during our first meeting and me spotting the shooter during the banquet, we'd both managed to help each other escape death.

"We are," she admits, though it comes out begrudgingly. Likely because, as a boss, she knew relying on others always came with a risk. The same hand offering to feed you could strike you down on a moment's notice in our world.

"I've had my staff start to clean the cottage for our arrival.

You can include any interior design instructions in your contract."

"I'm fine with whatever is there already. From what your lawyer has said, the house is right on a hill overlooking the shoreline so I can't imagine I'll be spending much time inside." She shakes her head, laughing under her breath. "I can't believe we're doing this. Can't believe I'm actually getting married."

"I know the feeling. We'll keep it very small. Get married at the courthouse—"

"We can't. Your father specified he wanted an extravagant event in his will. Demanded we spend at least ten million dollars on it."

"You're joking."

"I wish I was. It's on the last page. If Cillian was still alive and decided to go into wedding planning, he'd make a fortune."

"Of all the things he would spend his time on, I never thought it would be this. My father, the matchmaker," I groan.

"Definitely unexpected, although a bit endearing. He wanted to be sure you were happy and taken care of. I can't fault him for that."

"So you're going to take care of me, Zahra?" I give her a wicked smirk, which she meets with an eye roll.

"I'm not the mother goose type, so don't expect me to cook you dinner or clean your laundry. But I do promise to have your back. And to defend our legacy."

Our legacy. I suppose that's what it is now. I like the sound of that.

Taking her hand back into mine, I give it a hard squeeze. "I promise you the same. Until my dying breath."

21

ZAHRA

"Hmm, that looks a little off. Do you mind if I adjust it?" I reach my hand up, pausing right before I reach Declan's face, and brace myself for the rush that will come with our skin finally making contact. The fact that my body always had some kind of response whenever I came into contact with Declan is an incredibly irritating development. Especially given the fact that very soon we'll be living together.

"Go for it." He leans his head to the side, giving me full access to the small speaker slightly falling from his ear.

With our height difference, I have to stand up on my toes to correctly place the earpiece. "Okay, you should be all set. Let's test it out."

I walk away, putting a few yards between us and whispering into the mic embedded in my watch, "Declan? Can you hear me?"

"Loud and clear." His thick accent fills my ear. "Do you want to come back so we can go over the plan one more time?"

That would be sensible, though it did make my personal

plan to put some physical distance between us a bit harder to achieve. I debated telling him we're all set, but our mission is too valuable to have it go wrong. I'm embarrassed to admit that I keep feeling this magnetic pull toward him.

I walk up to Declan, leaving no less than six feet between us. "Alright. So we'll scan the perimeter first, checking for any unknown vehicles or workers. Once we're sure that's set, Azula and Aidan will do a final check of all security cameras in the building. Then we'll go in."

I had contacted my Uncle Fergal, who's been overseeing various trade routes for us, but he denied hearing or seeing anything suspicious. Once we hit another dead end, we decided to finally clue Aidan into the rat problem. He had refused to stay home, which is good, given that we shouldn't barge into our warehouse without some sort of backup. If one of our own has chosen to betray us, odds are high that they're not working alone.

Azula's voice comes through both of our speakers. "For the record, I still think I should be the one on the ground while you two are miles away in the surveillance van."

"They won't push back on two bosses coming in to check on their shipments. They will try to stall our seconds, though, in the hopes of covering their asses. We've discussed this."

"Just because we've discussed this doesn't mean I have to like it," Azula retorts before going back to being silent.

My eyes lock with Declan's and we give each other a nod before heading toward the warehouse. One thing we agreed on is to stay as close to each other as possible during this time. We'd only split up once we were inside, once he ensured all our staff were located in the main level, allowing me time to install additional high-camouflage security cameras in the loading dock.

We take thirty minutes to check the outside of the warehouse and install a set of cameras that would cover any blind spots the preinstalled cameras were missing. From what we could tell, nothing on the outside was worth our attention. Every vehicle and loading pod is set in place, which means whoever was stealing was smart enough not to leave any traces behind.

Walking side by side, we approach the two security guards at the front door, who immediately let us enter.

Declan's voice booms through the warehouse a moment later. "LISTEN UP, I need everyone in this building front and center in the next five minutes."

Few things were funnier than seeing a bunch of six-foot, two-hundred-plus-pound men scramble like headless chickens in front of us.

Marky, an Irishman who's the acting leader of this group, is the one to greet us a moment later. "Boss, Boss." He nods to me and Declan. "What's going on? We didn't receive a call that you were dropping by."

"Nothing you need to be worried about. We've started doing surprise drop-ins at all our sites. Just to ensure quality control," I lie. They didn't need to know the real reason we were here. "I'm counting nineteen workers, but there's twenty assigned here. Right, Marky?"

"That's right, Boss."

"Any idea where our missing soldier is?"

"No, Boss."

My eyes lock with Declan. "Alright, nobody move until I find who's missing."

I pull out my Glock and turn off the safety as I enter the first storage room—empty. Rooms two and three are the same and I'm starting to believe that whoever our rat is long gone.

The final room I enter looks pristine. A little too pristine. As if someone has tried their best to scrub any evidence of them being here. Throwing the storage lockers open, I come up dry. Wherever the final soldier is hiding, I will find him and make him regret crossing me.

I walk to the first shipment box in the center of the room that appears untouched. Sifting through the materials, I realize dozens of computer chips and a handful of guns are missing.

"Motherfucker." The curse is out of my mouth when a sharp stinging pain hits the back of my skull and I fall to my knees.

My gun is kicked across the room before I can regain my composure. Two large hands wrap around my neck and squeeze. Even if I wanted to scream, I can't. Instead, I preserve as much oxygen as I can, digging my nails into my attacker's arms and rolling our bodies forward in an attempt to gain the upper hand. Now on top of my assailant, I'm able to take in his face. His expression is a mix of anger...and fear. As if he knows he has to kill me if he wants to live.

His hands squeeze my neck tighter and black spots form in my vision, followed by a painful burning in my chest from the lack of oxygen. The grunts of the man strangling me start to sound distant. *Think, Zahra, think.* A final rush of adrenaline hits me as I release one of my hands and reach for my knife that's tucked away in my pocket. With my last bit of strength, I unleash it and stab my assailant right in the thigh. I feel a rush of warm, sticky blood leak from his leg.

Sweet, sweet, oxygen floods my lungs a second later as a loud howl leaves his lips. What an amateur. Any soldier worth his salt would never have given up so easily. I pull my knife out of his leg and he manages to kick me off. Reaching out immediately, my nails dig into his shirt, partially ripping it, but refusing to let go. The room door slams open but I have my eyes fixated on the man—or should I say boy—in front of me.

My knife stabs into his other thigh, and I relish in the

sound of his flesh ripping, effectively incapacitating the traitor. I plan on leaving it in initially, not wanting him to bleed out before I can get answers from him, but with his shirt ripped, my eyes immediately go to the tattoo of a vulture on his chest. Not again.

All I see is red as I yank my knife from his thigh and aim it at his heart.

"Who are you working for? Tell me, NOW!" I demand.

He says nothing.

"Tell me or I swear I'll do everything in my power to ensure you live, just so I can spend the everyday of the foreseeable future torturing the information out of you. I'll break bone after bone, and stick you back together, just so I can do it again," I spit, grabbing his head and banging it against the concrete floor.

That manages to enrage him. "A woman could never break me."

"A woman has already broken you," I seethe, applying pressure to one of the stab wounds, drawing another screech from him. "At least this way you get to choose how you are broken. You still have some pieces of you left. I promise that won't be the case in a few months."

"I choose THE KING. A princess will die, and THE KING WILL RISE," he screams, wrapping his hand around my wrist and shoving my knife into his heart before I can stop him. The color drains from his face immediately, his limp body falling to the ground in a thud.

"NO!" I slam my hands down on his bleeding chest. "TELL ME WHO SENT YOU. TELL ME. TELL ME." I pull the knife out of his chest and continue to slam my fists into his lifeless frame, screaming as I realize once again I've gotten closer to the truth, only for the rug to be pulled out from under me.

"Zahra, breathe, I need you to breathe." Declan's face

hovers a few inches from mine, as I realize he's kneeling right next to me. His voice softens as he adds, "I'm going to pull you off him, will you let me do that?"

My fists relax at my side and I give him a small nod. He lifts me with ease and pulls me into his lap.

"I had him, Declan. I had him right in my hands. I just saw the tattoo and I lost it. I just lost it," I groan, adrenaline fading as my head starts to pound.

"I know you did. I promise you we're going to figure this out, but right now we need to get you cleaned up and have your head checked out." He reaches out and tucks a loose strand of hair behind my ear. "Can you walk or do you need me to carry you?"

My body screams for him to carry me, but I can't let my men see me like that. They need to see me strong. Undefeated. Unbroken. I pick my words carefully. "I need to walk out."

Declan's eyes harden as he understands my unspoken reasoning. He gives me a nod before grabbing the arm of my assailant and dragging his body along with us.

The soldiers standing in the center of the room part as I walk through. I say nothing, opting instead to look them all in the eye and let the bloodied corpse speak for itself.

22

DECLAN

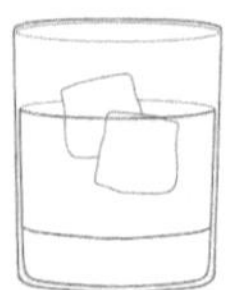

"You don't need to hover over me. And you can wipe that guilty look off your face. I'm fine and your doctor is just being dramatic," Zahra groans as I replace the ice pack on her forehead with a new one.

"My doctor said you have a concussion and need lots of rest for your symptoms to go away."

"I don't have a concussion, I'm completely fine," she huffs, standing up from the coach and taking a few wobbly steps forward. "See. Fine. You can take me home now."

"I'm sorry, love, but I'm going to have to take the word of my doctor. You know, the one who went through years of extensive training, over a stubborn mob boss who will never admit to being hurt." I gently guide her back onto the couch, refusing to acknowledge the fact that the term of endearment had rolled so easily off my tongue.

She looks up at me and blinks. "Wow. I really must be concussed, because I swear you just called me 'love'."

"Hmm, you must have misheard me." I adjust the pillow

behind Zahra so it props her up more, before taking a seat next to her.

"You sure? Because I don't think concussions mess with your hearing."

"They can actually. It's a fairly common side effect." Blame it on her concussion, nice one, Declan.

"I can't say I believe you but I'm willing to ignore it, so long as you stop looking at me like you're the reason I have this giant lump on the back of my head." Zahra winces as she moves the ice pack to the back of her skull.

Her words are meant to comfort me, but I don't deserve them. "I should have been there. Shouldn't have let you go into that room alone."

"You didn't *let* me do anything. We agreed on the plan ahead of time, and you did exactly what you were supposed to do. In case I need to remind you, the traitor is dead, whereas I am very much *alive*." Zahra leans back and closes her eyes. I'd dimmed all the lights in the room, but her injury was still very fresh, and she'd declined to take any of the stronger pain meds my doctor offered.

"You still got hurt," I huff, as if I wasn't talking to a literal boss. As if I wasn't a Made man myself.

"I run a fucking mafia, Declan. Getting hurt is part of the job description. So is being unable to fully protect the people you care about, no matter how much you want to. You and I know that better than anyone," she whispers.

"That used to be easier for me to accept," I admit.

"What changed?"

"What do you think?" I pick at my fingernails, wanting nothing more than to end this conversation, but refusing to walk away from Zahra.

"Our fathers being murdered," she guesses correctly. She

takes a long, hard swallow, eyebrows pinching together, and I can tell she's trying to hold in tears. "Damn concussion is making me emotional."

"I thought you said you weren't concussed."

Her lips lift up slightly. "You're right. I'm not. Must just be my allergies then."

"That makes sense, the room is quite dusty."

Zahra snorts. "If Maura heard you say that, she'd whack you upside the head with a feather duster."

"Probably. Who knows, maybe she'd swing so hard we'd both be concussed," I tease.

"Ha-ha." A full-on smile breaks out on Zahra's face for a moment before her expression turns serious. "Blaming yourself for their deaths is an unfair burden to carry."

I shake my head. "I should have been there."

"You had another job to take care of," she argues.

"That doesn't matter. I should've been there. If I had taken a second before I left to make sure I had my phone with me, I *would've* been there," I seethe, repeating the same words I've been saying to myself every day.

"Then you would have been dead. There's no way their killer would have let you walk out alive."

"Maybe that would've been for the best," I snap. The immediate shame that hits my stomach is too much. Pinching the bridge of my nose, I shut my eyes as if that will somehow allow me to disappear.

I feel a soft caress on my cheeks and my eyes snap open.

Zahra's delicate hands are placed on either side of my face, and she looks a mix of concerned and empathetic, as if she had read my mind. "Just because they're dead doesn't mean you should be too. Survivor's guilt is one of the deadliest poisons you can consume, Declan. It seeps into your bloodstream and consumes you bit by bit until there's nothing left. You have to fight it. Every minute of every day. Promise me you'll fight." She searches my eyes, desperate for me to agree.

"I've been fighting. It's just exhausting." I wait for the judgment to come. Zahra excelled at keeping her composure and demonstrating how lethal she is even after her life had just been threatened. Admitting weakness is not something a boss should ever do, and I had done just that.

I mentally prepare myself for a berating, to just suck it up and get over it. Instead, Zahra surprises me—giving me a glimpse of the person hidden behind all the armor. "I know it is. It drains me every day too. There are so many days when I just want to crawl into a ball and let it all consume me, but I can't. *We* can't. Too many people are counting on us. All we can do is take it day by day, and hope that tomorrow feels a bit lighter than yesterday."

I place my hands on top of hers, letting the contact ground me. "Day by day. I can do that."

"Good. I'm going to hold you to that." She lets out a sigh of relief before gently removing her hands from my face and sinking back into the couch.

We sit in comfortable silence, long enough for me to think she's fallen asleep, until Zahra speaks. "A princess will die, and the King will rise. How many times do you think he practiced that line in front of a mirror?" she snorts, though a deep frown consumes her face.

"At least fifty. Probably part of whatever initiation he went through to join his league of misfits. Along with that awful vulture tattoo."

"His league of misfits nearly killed me three times."

"*Nearly* being the operative word," I remind her.

"I knew my rise into power would be controversial. I anticipated a few old heads getting up in arms about it. A couple of threats to pull out of old deals. Jokes about marrying me off to their younger sons so I could join their family. I never anticipated a whole coup against me though." She drags a hand down her face.

"A coup is a bit dramatic, don't you think?"

"What would you call three men coming together to kill me because they're upset I'm in charge?"

"Sexism?" I shrug, pride filling my chest as I draw out a soft chuckle from Zahra.

"Fair enough." She clicks her tongue, though she looks partially defeated.

"What is it?"

She angles her head toward me, opening and closing her mouth as if speaking would somehow be her demise.

"You've already heard some of my darkest thoughts, Zahra. I promise I won't scare easily from yours."

"It's not that, it's just... Sometimes I wonder if I should just step down. Let Cyrus take over. It would be easier for him. He wouldn't have to prove his worth every time he stepped into a room. He would just garner the respect. Isn't that what every mob boss should have? Immediate respect."

I shake my head vehemently. "He only has that respect because of your father. Without Naser, he's nothing."

"That makes two of us, I guess."

"No. No, it doesn't. Your father was an incredible man, don't get me wrong, but I have no doubts your legacy will supersede his tenfold." Between her hacking skills, ability to sniff out a rat, and the absolute dominance she maintains in the most dangerous situations, she's more than a force to be reckoned with. "I made you a promise to fight. Can you make a promise to me?"

Her eyebrows furrow together. "Depends on what you're asking me."

"To never let anyone steal your light, or take your fight from you."

Her jaw hardens as my words settle. The shield she let down for me, only for me, is put back in place as she looks me dead in the eye and says, "I promise."

23
ZAHRA

“I ordered twenty yards of silk in mulberry, not periwinkle. I'm going to murder someone!” Samirah screams, tossing the pastel purple fabric on the floor.

“Mmm, maybe it's time to take some deep breaths. Killing people is more of my forte.” I take in her disheveled appearance, from the loose bun on her head, to the lopsided way her glasses sit on her face and the way she keeps frantically sketching in her notepad. I don't think I've ever seen Samirah so frazzled.

“Don't you start! The whole reason why I'm like this is because of you.” She points her pencil at me, and for a moment, I really think she might stab me.

“What the hell did I do?” I shrug.

“*What did you do?* How about the fact that you gave me less than two weeks' notice that you were going to get married, and that it was going to be one of the largest events this side of the country has ever seen? A million-dollar budget—"

“Technically, our budget is ten million dollars,” I tease.

“Jesus Christ. Ten million dollars and you had initially told me to just order cotton. You should be ashamed of yourself." Samirah tsks.

"A dress is a dress." I shrug.

Samariah shoots daggers at me. "I'm going to pretend you didn't just say that to me of all people. Especially given that I still have to make your wedding dress. I'd consider staying on my good side, or else I'll have you walking down the aisle looking like a pom-pom."

"Well, she'd be the most beautiful pom-pom on this side of the Charles River so I guess she has that going for her." Declan's deep voice fills the room, sending an electric trickle down my spine.

I turn around and look up, meeting his gaze. "What are you doing here?"

It's been just over a week since the warehouse incident, which was followed by my concussed impromptu therapy session with Declan. He continued to insist on nursing me back to health, though he did compromise by letting me heal in the comfort of my own home. Declan had finally returned to his manor a few days ago once my doctor gave me the all-clear, and I'd figured he'd want to spend as much time alone as possible, given we'd be living together very soon.

"Samirah called me in for my tux fitting." He smiles, giving Samirah a small wave. "How's your head?"

"Well, I haven't had any complaints yet, so."

Declan's eyes widened. "I, uh... That's good to know."

"That's it? No laugh. Or even a small smile. Life's too short not to enjoy a little sexual innuendo." I place my hands on my hips.

Declan raises an eyebrow at me. "Sorry, I guess I didn't realize we had moved into the 'dick-jokes' stage of our relationship."

"Well, we are getting married soon, so what better time

than now to show you I have the same humor as a prepubescent twelve-year-old boy."

Samirah struts back into the room, garment bag in tow. "She's being serious too. Her sense of humor ranges from something that would make a middle schooler pee his pants to incredibly unfunny dad jokes. I recommend not entertaining her. It only makes it worse."

I throw my hands up in mock offense. "That's rude! Maybe Declan was looking forward to hearing my stand-up comedian bit."

Samirah raises an eyebrow. "Declan, on a scale of one to ten, how much do you want to hear another *hilarious* joke from your fiancée?"

"Mmm, I think if I want her to stay my fiancée, I should just shut my mouth and go try on my tux."

"Hey!"

Declan gives me a wink before taking the garment bag from Samirah and walking into the bathroom to change.

Samirah leans closer to me while we wait for him to return. "Just so you know, I also ordered some lace lingerie that should arrive right in time for your wedding. They're couture, so for my own sanity, try to stop him from tearing them up. It would be such a waste of craftsmanship."

My palms start to sweat. "Um, there will be no need to worry about lingerie being ripped apart because there is a zero percent chance that Declan will be seeing me in my underwear soon."

"Well, that's just a waste. What good is marrying a man that is attractive if you don't get to enjoy some of the benefits?"

"I'm marrying him so we can get the benefit of removing his deranged uncle from power."

"So you're telling me there's not even a small part of you

that wants to get some…additional benefits that come with being with Declan?"

"Well, I have my own money and my vibrator works just fine, so…plus we need to keep this professional. That way, none of our feelings are hurt once we evidently get divorced."

"Gah. I think you're strong enough to separate feelings from sex. You've done it before."

Normally, I'd agree with her, but after the night we spent together where we let our guards down around each other, I'm so sure. I'd like to blame uncharacteristic vulnerability on being concussed, but the truth of the matter is, I felt pulled to Declan. That's the only explanation I'd manage to come up with for why I found myself looking forward to his texts asking how my day was, or why I asked to schedule several impromptu meetings to 'strategize', only for us to spend most of the time decompressing about the weight of it all. The past few weeks, I've learned to lean on Declan in a way I never thought I'd lean on someone. And that reality comforts me as much as it scares me.

Our families would always be allied, and frankly, we needed this relationship to maintain its strength for both of our organizations. Friendships were fine but complicating that relationship by making it something more is a risk I can't and won't take. Everything I've ever done is to ensure that my legacy and my family's legacy would be maintained. I wouldn't jeopardize that by crossing the line with Declan.

"Declan and I are allies. I'm willing to say we've evolved into friends, but that's it. Sure, I may have grown to recently enjoy his company, but our business relationship is entirely too important for me to jeopardize it." I cross my arms on my chest, standing firm.

"Well, you're much better than I am because if my fiancé looked *that* good in a suit, nothing would stop me from claiming him forever." Samirah nods her head to the topic of our conversation, and my mouth goes dry.

The white sleeves of Declan's shirt are rolled up to his elbows, showing off the intricate knotted tattoo on his forearm and the prominent veins and muscles underneath. He's opted to leave the top of his shirt unbuttoned, enough for me to see a hint of his collarbone. I'd always thought men wearing suspenders looked overly pretentious, but on him they're nothing short of perfection. My palms start to sweat at the thought of me using those suspenders to tug him closer and closer to me. The way I'd undo the rest of the buttons of his shirt as he rips off my dress. How I'd beg him to use the same suspenders to tie me up, leaving me at his mercy to do whatever he wanted....

"So how do I look?" Declan's deep voice brings me back to reality, smirking as he catches me staring. He brings his hands up to his collar and flexes it slightly, practically putting on a show for me. "Do you approve?"

I not-so-subtly drag my palms down my pants, struggling to maintain my composure as if I didn't just have one of the filthiest daydreams about this man, who is also my fiancé. *Your fiancé, for business purposes only, Zahra.* "Yeah, it looks fine to me." I shrug, hoping it comes off as casual.

"Don't insult my work." Samirah clicks her tongue, waving me off. "Declan, you look incredible. How does the fit feel?"

"Pretty good. The pants might be a little tight though?" He spins around to give her the full view, and I try my best not to look at the bulge in the center of his pants.

"You're right. I think I can add a little bit more to the waist to give you some breathing room. We can always use a belt to adjust." Samirah takes the measuring tape wrapped around her neck and places it around his waist.

"Are you free now for lunch?" Declan asks me.

"She sure is," Samirah responds, shifting Declan around as she diligently marks the changes she needs to make to his suit.

I give her a quick glare before redirecting my attention to Declan. "I should have some time if you don't mind me updating you on some progress with the vultures."

His expression tightens as he nods and heads back into the changing room to switch into his day clothes.

"Might I recommend you meet somewhere private in case the tension decides to snap?" Samirah teases.

"No tension will be snapping. We're adults who can handle being alone in a room together. I'll have lunch sent to my office. Can you tell him to meet me there?"

She rolls her eyes and waves me off. "God, you're no fun. Mark my words, Zahra, you can't keep depriving yourself of your needs forever. One day, you're going to take what you want. Not because it's for the good of your family or the good of the Persian Empire, but because it's what *you* need and I can't wait to see it."

24
DECLAN

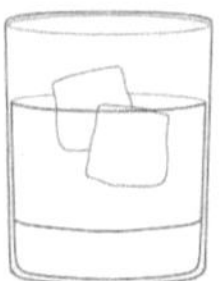

The last time I was in Zahra's office, I'd be willing to bet she wanted me dead. Now, we're sitting together on the couch, with her curled up in a ball under a blanket while she uses chopsticks to eat dumplings. A weird sense of pride fills my chest, knowing I taught her how to do something she'd always wanted to try. I know I have no right to claim parts of her, but I found myself desperate to learn more about the Zahra hidden underneath.

"So, it sounds like we could have some promising leads soon?" I nod to her laptop set on the table.

"I think so. I have an algorithm set up that will populate photos of anyone with tattoos similar to the vulture ones we've seen. There's probably going to be a lot of false positives but at least it's a start. We didn't have much luck with the Boston cams, so I decided to expand the search to all the cities where we have big warehouses for trades. It took a bit longer than I wanted to hack into all the city cameras in New York, Chicago, and Seattle—"

"It took you like a week to do all that," I exclaim. "I can

barely figure out how to use Bluetooth to connect my phone to my smart TV."

Zahra snorts. "Well, you're not known for being a hacker. I am. And while a week isn't too long, I know if my head was in a better space, I would've been faster."

"Are you still experiencing symptoms from your concussion?" My eyebrows knit together as my hand twitches to touch her, but I control the impulse.

"No. I wasn't referring to that. My mind's just been all over the place. Thinking about the group that's set out to kill me. Your uncle. The wedding...." She leans her head on the back of the couch and closes her eyes. "Life felt so much simpler when our fathers were still alive. Now nothing makes sense anymore."

My lips turn into a frown, knowing that some of her current distress is caused by me and my family, and I can't do anything about it. Or, really, I'm too selfish to do anything. I could probably convince her to break off the engagement, plot to find another way to stop my uncle...but I don't want to. I like having her around me. I like how she always managed to understand me and the struggles I was going through. How the more time we spent together, the more our conversations shifted from going over business details to recalling stories of our childhood and laughing about the dumb shit we used to get into. Every hour we spend together feels entirely too short, and I find myself relishing the idea of us living together soon. Of getting to spend even more time together.

I don't know what it means to feel this way. Or maybe I do but I don't want to speak it into existence. The moment that I do, it could change things forever. So instead, I take the small bits of her she's willing to give me. Lunches, dinners, and pretending to be a happy, engaged couple in public. While my uncle knows his power is temporary, he isn't aware of the marriage stipulation that will put an end to his reign. Both of our lawyers have discussed how it's in our best interests for everyone to think this relationship is real, though a few of our loved ones know better.

"I know the feeling. A year ago, I thought I knew everything; now it feels like I know nothing." I reach over and take her hand into mine, squeezing it.

"Glad to know I'm not the only one who feels like a headless chicken." She smiles, keeping our hands entwined. "I'm glad I can talk to you about this."

"Even though a few months ago you wanted me dead?" I tease. Admittedly, that fact should upset me more than it does, but I suppose you become desensitized to that sort of thing when you grow up in the mafia. Everyone either wants to kill you or take something from you.

She winces. "Yes. Even though a few months ago, I jumped the gun and blamed you for something that wasn't your fault. Sorry you had to take a bullet for me to realize how wrong I was."

"No apologies needed. I'd take a bullet for you any day. Without hesitation." The weight of my promise shifts the temperature of the room, and suddenly sitting a few feet away on the couch feels like we are practically on top of each other. I clear that thought from my head, knowing better than to go there. Reaching over for my jacket, I think of a distraction. "I actually have something for you."

"For me?" She leans closer, intrigued.

"I was hoping these would be ready for you sooner, but the jeweler took a while to ensure they were all in your size." I place the box in front of her, lifting the lid to reveal five different engagement rings. "Things have been moving so fast, we haven't really had a chance to talk about what you may like so I figured I'd give you a range of options."

Her jaw drops open. "Declan, these are stunning. I-I don't know what to say."

"Just take your time. If you don't like any of these, I can also have some more shipped over for you to try on." Though there was one ring in the batch I secretly hoped she would be drawn to.

Zahra's fingers brush against mine as she takes the box from my hand, trying on ring after ring. She starts with the most expensive of the bunch, an emerald cut twenty-carat diamond worth just over five million, and ends with the one that is no doubt the least flashy of the bunch but carries the most meaning to me. She raises the final ring, taking in the intricate design of leaves on the band that come together into the shape of a flower, where a round diamond sits.

Her eyes glisten as she shuts the box and holds the floral ring in her hand. "This one. This one's mine."

"That was my mother's." I have no doubt I probably look insane with how wide I'm smiling.

Zahra shakes her head, placing the ring into my hand immediately. "Declan, it's stunning. But I can't take this from you, it's too much—"

"No. It's not..."

"Declan..." she protests.

"If I wanted to keep this ring for myself, I would have. I chose to include it in the box, just like you chose the ring. It's yours," I insist, taking her hand into mine, slowly sliding the ring onto her finger, and admiring how perfectly it fits.

She clutches her hand close to her chest. "I'll protect it with my whole heart. I promise."

My throat tightens as I struggle to find a response. "Well, now my parents will be there at our wedding. Not exactly how I expected but..."

Her eyes meet mine, carrying the same pain. "I can't say

I've thought much about what my wedding would look like until recently, but one thing I did always think about was my father walking me down the aisle. I guess now I'll be walking alone, since I have no one left—"

"You have me." I reach over, gently bringing her into my arms. "You have me. And together we'll get through this. Through anything."

To my surprise, instead of pushing back, she tucks her head into my chest and lets me run my fingers through her hair. Her grip on my waist tightens as she whispers, "Together."

25

ZAHRA

"Am I making a mistake?" I gasp, hands shaking as I take in my reflection in the mirror. I'd opted for simple makeup topped up with a burgundy lipstick. The loose waves of my hair fall down my back as I grip my white silk robe so tight my knuckles turn white.

"Wow. Are you having cold feet? This might be the first normal reaction you've had about getting married." Samirah smirks, placing the garment bag containing my dress on the couch. She walks up behind me and looks at me in the mirror. "You wouldn't be the first runaway bride in history, so you say the word and I'll sneak you out."

Her tone is light but I can tell she's serious. Samirah has always been there for me, and I know my wedding day will be no exception.

I shake my head, dragging my sweaty hands down my thighs. "I won't run away. I don't want to."

She cocks her head to the side. "You don't? Then what's wrong?"

"I don't know. I just know that my heart's racing, I can

barely breathe, and my hands are so damn sweaty." I groan. "I'm not having a panic attack though. I know what those feel like, and this is not it. I just feel on edge."

Samirah eyes me up and down, tapping a finger on her chin when a mischievous glint comes over her eyes. "Dare I say this could be butterflies?"

"What? No. Absolutely not." That would be insane. Had Declan and I gotten closer over the past few weeks? Sure. With how much time we'd been spending together, it was practically inevitable that we'd become friends, but that's where it ended.

"Hmm, you're being a little defensive here..."

"No. I'm not. I'm being honest. Any feelings I have for Declan are strictly platonic. And they need to stay that way. Friendships are risky enough in our line of work. Loving someone gets you a one-way ticket to the execution block." I shrug, picking at a loose thread on my sleeve.

Samirah winces. "Harsh."

"Harsh, but true. It's why my father sent me away when I was a kid. Kept my identity hidden. He loved me so much, he knew that the second any of his enemies found me, I'd be either killed on the spot or used as a bartering tool. His love for me made him weak. And you can't be weak as a boss." I swallow the lump in my throat as I remember my dad wouldn't be here to see me today, wouldn't be standing by my side.

Samirah vehemently shakes her head. "You're wrong. Your father's love for you wasn't a weakness. It was his greatest strength, and probably the only thing that kept him grounded. Being a boss is grueling. The danger you're put in, the tough decisions you have to make, the lives you have to take. All of those are enough to make a person numb to it all, but your father never did. He stayed grounded. Tried to live life as honestly as he could, despite who he was. And he did that because of you. He did that because he loved you and wanted better for you. Love isn't weakness. It's the only thing that has the power to heal all the pain the world hurls at us."

My vision starts to blur as tears fill my eyes. Dammit. I can't even remember the last time I cried. Probably my father's funeral. "You're turning me into a pile of mush. I'm going to ruin my makeup." I laugh, deflecting from the heaviness that's filled the room.

"You better not. I spent so long making sure you look perfect, not that you don't already. Declan won't know what hit him." She beams, tucking a loose wave behind my ear.

"I doubt it. He's used to being around pretty women." I shrug.

"So loud and so wrong. You haven't seen the way he looks at you. I'm willing to bet the second Declan sees you, he's going to drag you into a closet and beg you to let him have his way."

"*'Have his way?'* What century are we in?" I snort.

"You can make fun of me all you want, but I know deep down you hope I'm right." She doesn't wait for me to respond. Instead, Samirah unzips the garment bag and reveals my dress: A lace ball gown that cinches at my waist, with off-the-shoulder sleeves, and embroidered with the most delicate and intricate flower design I'd ever seen.

"Samirah," I breathe out in awe, chills running down my spine.

"I take it, you approve?" She places a hand on her hip, proud.

"Approve? This is so incredibly stunning, any words I say won't do it justice. Thank you. Thank you so much." I take in the dress again, tracing my fingers along the delicate lace.

"It's what you deserve. Every bride deserves to feel special on her wedding day, but you? You deserve to feel like you're a queen. Because you are." Samirah reaches into her bag, pulling out a large square velvet case. She holds the lip open for me to see the delicate headpiece inside. "And every queen needs a crown."

———

"Of all the people in the world I had to be paired with, why did it have to be *him*?" Azula growls, tapping her nude heel.

"You're my maid of honor, and the maid of honor has to walk down the aisle with the best man. You can't be surprised that Declan chose his brother for that role."

"Speak of the devil and he shall appear." Aidan's voice comes from behind me, causing Azula to stiffen. He takes a few steps forward so he's right in front of me, eyes softening as he takes me in. "Zahra, you look absolutely stunning. My brother won't know what hit him. If Declan stumbles during his vows, it's not because he hasn't been practicing. It's because he'll be too distracted by you."

My throat tightens. This all feels too real. Up until the moment I put on my dress, I'd been able to keep my feelings in check and remind myself this was a business arrangement between two friends. Once I saw my reflection in the mirror, the walls I'd put up had come crumbling down, and for a moment all I could feel was...excitement. I'd forgotten about the reality of who I was. Forgotten the true reason for getting married today. Instead, I twirled around in my ball gown and let myself pretend I was a normal girl, in the dress of her dreams, about to marry a man who understood her better than anyone else.

I'd never resented being the heir to a mafia. Never wanted to be anything but a boss. That is still true, but I couldn't deny that a part of me wondered how differently my life would look if I put my own needs first for once.

"Flirting with your brother's fiancée is pretty low. Even for you, Aidan." Azula rolls her eyes at him.

"I was merely complimenting my future sister, 'Zula, no need to get jealous." He smirks as he moves to stand next to her.

Even with her heels on, he towers over Azula, not that she's phased. "One, don't ever call me that again or I'll feed your balls to our guard dogs. And two, I will not now nor will I ever be jealous of any woman forced to deal with you. The only thing I'll feel for her is pity."

Aidan mock gasps, placing a hand on his chest. "You wound me, dear Azula. How will I ever recover?"

"Here's hoping you never do." She crosses her arms. "If Declan doesn't show up in the next five minutes, I'm barging into his dressing room and dragging him out myself. The sooner this ceremony is over, the faster I'll be able to put as much distance between us as possible."

"And here I thought you were just playing hard to get," Aidan snickers.

Azula's expression shifts from irritated to blank, emotionless, and cold, a façade that's typically only reserved for the enemies we've captured and assigned her to torture.

For all of Aidan's mouthing off, he suddenly turns white as a ghost, as if he's realized he's been poking a grizzly bear for the past five minutes and not a koala. He puts at least six feet of distance between them and tucks his hand behind his jacket, no doubt confirming his gun is in place. Azula snorts; her smug look tells me how much fun she's having toying with Aidan like he's her prey.

"Sorry for the delay, Samirah wasn't satisfied with my collar and decided to hem it." Declan's smooth voice fills the room and sends chills down my spine. Fuck. He has entirely too much of an effect on me.

"I should have guessed it was her. Samirah has always been a perfectionist." I grab the sides of my gown, turning so I'm face-to-face with him. My heart races, heat filling me, as Declan's eyes widen and trail down my body. I can't stop the smile on my face as I realize his own mouth is slightly gaped open.

"*Zahra*… You look angelic. God, I swear you'll be the death of me." His gruff voice is in stark comparison to the way he places his palm on the small of my back, closing the distance between us so our chests are flush against each other. I ignore all the voices in my head yelling that this is too close—too much for two people who are meant to keep this marriage strictly professional. Instead, I dive right back into my fantasy, where for tonight I'm not Zahra Ahzimi, head of the Persian Mafia. I'm just Zahra. A girl marrying a man who's currently looking at her like she's the answer to all his prayers.

"Declan…" I whisper, fully aware that we're not alone in this room, but wanting nothing more for a moment where it can be just us. As if he can read my mind, he pulls us toward the back of the hallway. Azula and Aiden take the hint and try their best to distract themselves and give us some privacy.

"We don't have much time, love." He clicks his tongue in frustration, the heat of his palm holding me steady.

"I know. I just wanted to ask if you could promise me something. If we could promise each other something," I correct.

"Anything," he states, without hesitation.

"Can we pretend tonight is real?" I ask breathlessly.

His grip on my waist tightens, as if he needs me to keep him grounded. If only he knew the feeling is mutual. I grip his forearm, holding him in place. Declan takes a deep breath.

Then another. He cups my face with his free hand, tracing my bottom lip with his thumb. "This is real," he practically pants.

My mouth waters, wanting nothing more than for him to close the distance. How does he manage to have such an effect on me with the slightest touch? I'm playing a dangerous game. One that's going to wreck me when all is said and done, but none of that matters tonight.

"Shall we?" he asks, shifting so that he's standing by my side—never lifting his hand that, at this rate, may as well be permanently attached to my back.

We'd decided to walk together down the aisle, a suggestion he had made after I confessed how much I hated the idea of walking alone. To everyone else, this would symbolize that our families may have experienced great tragedy, but we still stand strong. To me, it would symbolize how much Declan understood me, and how he didn't even hesitate to comfort me. I nod, bracing my shoulders, as we walk toward the giant wooden doors separating us from the altar.

26

DECLAN

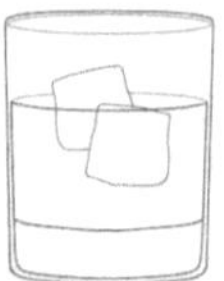

The rest of the world doesn't exist to me at that moment. It doesn't matter that this cathedral is filled with thousands of our friends, family, and enemies praying for our demise. The only thing that matters is the stunning woman standing next to me who's about to become my wife. *Wife.* And not just a marriage of convenience, but a real marriage. At least for tonight. That's what she had asked of me. To treat this night as if we were really getting married. As if we were really in love. I'd accepted her proposal before I'd even had the opportunity to give it a second thought. She may think this is only for tonight, but she doesn't realize that I'm now determined to make this permanent.

I'd gotten to know Zahra incredibly well these past few weeks, and one thing that was immediately clear to me was that she never wanted anything for herself. Or, rather, she never voiced it. Everything she does is for the betterment of her Empire and those employed under her. It's beyond admirable. For as much as I would like to think I'd do the same, my early twenties were filled with selfish moments. Even now, I'm pulled to make her fall for me, pulled to make Zahra mine. And not because it'd be beneficial for the alliance between our two mafias, but because I want her. All of her.

She wants me to. She may not have fully admitted that to herself, but the look in her eye when she asked me if we could pretend told me all I needed to know. Zahra wants me. Wants us. She's just too scared to take it. Luckily for her, I'm a stubborn bastard who refuses to go down without a fight. Especially if that fight now includes a battle for her heart.

We reach the end of the aisle, my hand still on her waist as I support her walking up the stairs onto the altar. A faint gasp leaves her lips as she takes in the traditional Iranian wedding table in front of her. "Declan, did you do this?"

Leaning down, I press my lips to the shell of her ear. "We're in an Irish Cathedral. I figured it would only be fair for your culture to be represented as well."

She reaches out and entwines our fingers, giving my hand a hard squeeze. "Thank you. I love it. Truly."

For all their bickering earlier, Azula and Aidan are able to put on a united front as they address the crowd. Aidan starts, "Thank you all for joining us in the union between Zahra Ahzimi and Declan McAlister. Please take your seats. The alliance between the Ahzimi and McAlister families has gone on for decades, but today is not about the relationship between their two families and instead is about the love they have for each other."

My brother eyes me and while he's putting on a show, I know there's some truth to his words. He hands Azula the microphone.

"In celebration of their love for each other, we have here the traditional *Sofreh Aghd*, or Iranian wedding table. Each item on the table represents an element of Zahra and Declan's new life together. The mirror stands for reflection and introspection, honey for sweetness, wild rue to ward off any negative energy, and flowers for growth and beauty."

"Warding off negative energy is definitely needed here," I tease, earning a small snort from Zahra.

"The couple will now exchange their vows." Azula gestures to us.

I move my palm off the small of Zahra's back so she can turn to face me, not missing the slight frown on her lips as we break contact. Her grip on our entwined hands tightens, a sign she isn't willing to fully let me go.

She lets out a deep breath. "Declan, to many people here, this may come off as sudden, but that just shows how little they know about us."

Zahra and I had agreed on the public-facing story that we'd been together for years now in secret. While arranged marriages between allied mobs are common, we want to show a stronger united front than a business agreement. Two mob bosses allied for their own individual benefit is to be expected. As is the reality that one boss would turn on the other. Two bosses getting married because they love each other is unheard of. And that makes us all the more lethal.

Zahra's thumb draws idle circles on the back of my hand as she continues. "But I don't want to spend this moment thinking about everyone else. I want to spend it focused on us. I never in a million years thought I would be here today. Growing up, I watched my father love my mom inside and out. There was never a moment when I doubted his adoration of her. My parents' relationship was one in a million, so much so that I had accepted the fact that I would never be able to achieve what they have. Never be able to have a love as strong and safe as theirs. But I was wrong. Few people have made me feel as seen and understood as you have. And in a world that constantly feels like things are being taken from me, I can't put into words how much it means to be given your heart."

My vision blurs for a moment as I take in her words. Naser and Farah's love filled the room whenever they were with you. My own father would say it was contagious and inspired him to be a better man. The cynic in me screams that Zahra's words are just an act put on for everyone watching us, but deep down, I know better. I know there's honesty in her words. Know it because I myself feel the same about her.

Without giving it a second thought, I cup her cheek and press a kiss on her forehead. A wave of joy fills my chest as she melts into me. Aidan clears his throat, reminding me that as much as I wish this moment between Zahra and me could be private, it's anything but.

"My lovely Zahra. You are the strongest, smartest, most stunningly beautiful person I have ever laid my eyes on. From the moment we met, I knew you were going to change my life forever. I didn't even try to deny the pull you had on me, because I knew our love would be inevitable. I was never one to believe in the universe or fate, but falling in love with you has shown me what it means to believe. To believe in love, to believe in hope. To believe that someone can be there for you through it all.

I've never been nervous about public speaking, but preparing my vows, I found myself second-guessing every-thing. How do you sufficiently manage to tell someone who has managed to become your entire world how much you love them in just a few words? The task seems impossible. Still, I'm going to try my best with the caveat that you deserve so much more than a small speech, and I promise to spend every day of our lives together telling you how special you are. Zahra, I love your heart, your determination, the way you care for others. I love the way your eyebrows crease together when you're thinking hard. I love your wit, and most of all, I love that you chose me to spend the rest of your life with." I exhale immediately, aware of how sweaty my palms are, and the slight gleam in Zahra's eyes.

Aidan clasps his hand on my shoulder, giving it a squeeze. "Declan, do you take Zahra, to love and protect, to support and defend, from now until your final breath?"

"I do." It's the easiest promise I've ever made. Reaching into my pocket, I take out her wedding band and slide it on her finger.

"And do you, Zahra, take Declan, to love and protect, to support and defend, from now until your final breath?"

"I do." She nods, giving me a soft smile as she slides my ring into place on my finger.

"I now pronounce you husband and wife, you may now kiss the bri—"

My hands cradle Zahra's face before Aidan finishes his sentence. I finally, *finally*, get to taste her. Zahra throws her arms around my neck, locking her fingers in my hair, and pulling my head down so our lips are a mere inch apart. A moan leaves my body when our mouths finally connect. My tongue traces her bottom lip, begging for entrance, which she immediately gives me, and God, she tastes so damn good. Our bodies press closer until we're flush against each other. With all the layers of her gown between us, it's easy to hide my grinding my hard cock against her, and the gasp that falls from her lips is music to my ears. It takes every ounce of my self-control to break us apart, but not before I nip her bottom lip—a promise of what's to come.

Aidan coughs, awkwardly clearing his throat. "Please gather your belongings and follow security. They'll guide you to the cars waiting to take you to the reception hall..."

"You're coming with me," I whisper to Zahra, placing a kiss on her cheek, as we run down the aisle hand in hand.

"Where are we going?" She laughs.

"Before I have to share you with the world, I want you all to myself."

27
DECLAN

I kick the door to my dressing room shut, pressing Zahra up against the wall as my fingers claw at the back of her dress.

"Careful, Samirah went days without sleep to make this dress. You'll have to deal with her wrath if even a stitch is out of place." Her teasing laugh turns into a soft moan as I turn her around and start undoing the corset. Desperate. I am fucking desperate for her.

"Noted," I groan as her entire back is exposed to me. "No bra?" I growl, trailing hot kisses down her spine.

"Samirah built one into the dress." She shudders, letting her gown fall to the ground, leaving her in nothing but the faintest hint of a lace thong.

My hands shake with the need to devour her as I trail them up her arms, watching goosebumps form all over her body. Slow, Declan. Take it slow. *You have no idea what she's into or how far she's willing to take this.* "Turn around and let me see you, love."

She listens immediately, and fuck if that doesn't make my

cock twitch. Zahra's confidence doesn't sway a bit as she tosses the loose waves of her hair back, allowing me to take in the sight of her luscious tits and soft curves. Her nipples are peaking, ready for my mouth, and I can tell her heart is racing from the quick breaths she's taking.

"You can touch me, you know. I'll only bite if you tell me too."

I raise an eyebrow. "Is that a promise?" All I get is a smirk in response. "Careful, angel. I have to admit my tolerance for letting you take control in the bedroom is much lower than in real life."

My stomach squeezes at the confession. I won't ask her to do anything she doesn't want to do, but as a boss, I know how impossible it is to let go of control. So much so that the desire for control had also bled into my sex life. It hasn't been a problem for any of my one-night stands, and I hope it won't be a problem for Zahra, but I know better than most how hard it can be for a boss to give up any inkling of power.

Her eyebrows draw together. "What does that mean? Are you a Dom?"

There's no judgment in her voice, just open curiosity. God, this woman is perfect. *My wife*, I remind myself, is perfect.

"Yes. A pleasure Dom specifically," I state, not missing the way Zahra's thighs squeeze together in response. My sweet girl is turned on.

"What does that mean?" Whether she noticed it or not, she's taken a few steps closer to me. There it is again. The pull of our energies that always brings us closer.

"It can look different depending on the Dom. For me, it typically means that I use your orgasms as a tool of my domination. Making you come over and over again. Deciding what to do and how to do it, to make you come repeatedly. That's not to say I don't get off as well, but it's almost always after

I've turned my partner into a screaming mess. You would be in a submissive role in that you'd give me full control over your body, but everything we do is consensual. We'd have a safe word you could use, in case I ever pushed you too hard." I shove my hands into my pockets, wanting nothing more than to wrap them around her soft waist and close the distance between us, but I can't. Not until she tells me what she wants. What she's okay with doing.

Zahra's pupils dilate, and she licks her lips. Contemplating. "That...sounds amazing. Honestly. But I'm not sure if I can do that. It's hard enough for me to orgasm once, especially if toys aren't involved. Multiple times is asking for a miracle."

Holy shit. She has no idea what she's just fueled in me. "Would you be willing to try?"

She shrugs. "Sure, as long as you're okay with being disappointed."

A growl escapes my lips. "First of all, you could never, *ever* disappoint me. Second of all, you need to pick a safe word right now. Because I don't know how much longer I can go without touching you."

Zahra grabs my suspenders, tugging me closer, and whispers, "Rose."

"Rose," I groan as she nods in confirmation. "You're mine."

Her expression turns serious. "For tonight."

Ah. Right. The pesky promise we made to "pretend." Little does she know I have every intention of breaking that promise and making her mine forever. I lock our lips in a desperate, harsh kiss, tugging her bottom lip between mine, before lowering my head and latching my mouth onto her breast, sucking hard on one of her nipples while my hand toys with the other. Her head falls back with pure ecstasy as I rotate between tracing my tongue around her peaked nipple and sucking.

"Fuck, Declan, that feels incredible."

I groan, pulling away to discard my shirt and pants. "How wet are you?"

"Hmm, I'm not really sure. Maybe you can tell me?" She gives me a coy smile, reaching for her thong and slowly shimmying out of it until it drops to the ground.

Any self-control I have snaps. In an instant, I grab her and move us to the leather coach in the dressing room, adjusting her so she's seated on my lap. My hands grip the tops of her thighs. "Look up, love."

She gasps as she finally notices the full-length mirror right in front of us. Her skin is flushed bright red, her hair is already a wild mess, and the skin around her nipple is starting to bruise, forming a hickey. She leans her head back into my chest and places a hard kiss on my neck.

"Good girl," I praise, drawing out a sweet moan from her. I move her thighs apart slowly, so she's on full display. My heart beats so fast, it makes my head spin. "Now, look at the mirror and tell me how wet your pussy is."

Our eyes lock in the mirror as she bites her lip. For a moment, I think she's going to call this off, but instead, she trails her eyes down her body. "I'm soaked, Declan. Absolutely soaked."

"Damn straight. And what about my wife's sweet clit?" I groan as her wetness starts to leak onto my lap.

"Your wife's sweet clit is swollen and begging to be touched." She giggles, reaching back and gripping my hair.

"Is that so? Well then, maybe it's time I finally take care of you." One of my hands stays firm on her chest, holding her in place, while the other trails all the way down to her core. My index finger dips into her pussy, gathering her wetness, and using it to coat her clit. Fucking, hell. Soaked. She was already soaked, and I've barely touched her. Pride fills my chest. Zahra bucks her hips, trying to sink herself deeper onto my fingers when I pull away completely, bringing my fingers to my mouth and tasting her sweetness. "Fuck, you taste so good."

"D-Declan. I need more," she begs.

"Do you now?" This time, I add two extra fingers, teasing her pussy more and more. My thumb finally makes contact with her clit, and I watch her in the mirror, trying to figure out how exactly she likes it. Circles don't seem to do much for her, neither does moving too fast, but a hard and slow up and down motion has her writhing on top of me—moans filling the room.

"Oh fuck, baby. Just like that. Yes, Declan, yes." She grabs my thighs, propping herself up so she can grind her hips on my hand. Her eyes fall shut, to my immediate irritation, and I pull my hand away.

Zahra groans in frustration, glaring at me through the mirror. "Why the hell did you stop?"

"Because you weren't watching me. Watching *us*," I correct, moving my hand from her chest and cupping her chin. "This mirror is here for a reason, love. I want your eyes on us the whole time. I want you to watch the way I'm playing with your cunt while you ride my fingers. Is that understood?" My tone shifts, demanding, as I let my full Dom side out. Dammit. I hope I haven't pushed her too far. My stomach twists as I wait for her to call this off, but she doesn't.

Instead, she just looks at me in the mirror and says, "I'm sorry. I'm still learning. Can we try again?"

I slide my fingers deep inside her in an instant, searching for that one spot that will make her scream, hot blood rushing through my body when I find it. My thumb moves to her clit as I rub against her G-spot, and she grabs my hand, holding it in place. Her wedding ring shines in the mirror, and seeing my claim on her drives me completely feral. "Look at my sweet wife fucking my fingers. You're so damn wet, love. This pussy was made for me. Made for my fingers. My tongue. My cock. God, I can't wait to feel you squeezed around me."

"Yes, Declan, yes," she moans, leaning her head back into my shoulder...and shutting her eyes.

I halt all of my movements again, though I leave my fingers buried inside her.

"Dammit, not again," Zahra whispers to herself.

"You know the rules," I scold, "or do I need to remind you?"

She shakes her head, eyes glossy and wide. "No. I was supposed to look at us in the mirror and I closed my eyes. It was my fault. I deserve to be denied," Zahra pants, desperate.

I feel the precum leaking from my cock. Dammit. She really is the most perfect human in the whole world, and somehow she's all mine. I press a kiss to her forehead. "Are you sure you're okay? I know you haven't used your safe word yet, but we've also never done this before. We can stop whenever you want. I promise I'll make you come no matter what."

The smile on her face makes my heart stop. "I'm alright. Better than alright. I've been on the verge of an orgasm at least three times now, which feels nothing short of a miracle. We could stop here and I'd be fully content."

A rush of rage fills my chest toward every past man she's been with. Not only because they got to touch what's mine, but because they were so incompetent that the action of me *almost* making her come was worthy of praise. "I thought I made myself clear. I'm not stopping until I've made you come. Over and over again."

Angling her head back toward the mirror, my fingers start toying with her again. The pants and moans coming from her are so obscene, I know they'll be playing in my head forever. I can't stop the praise falling from my lips as her eyes lock with mine in the mirror. "That's it, Zahra, that's it, my good girl.

Keep bucking your hips just like that. God, you're so damn wet. Look at you drenching my fingers. You want to, come, don't you? I can see it in your eyes. My sweet angel. Use my fingers. Use me. And come. Come right now. Do you hear me? Come *now*," I growl as I feel her pussy tighten around my fingers, signaling her orgasm. "Fuck *yes,* baby, that's right."

Her grip on the back of my head turns painful as she rides out the waves of her after shock. My fingers are back on her clit in an instant, making her squirm against me. "Declan, I can't. I can't do it again. It's too much."

I refuse to let up. "If you want me to stop, you know what word to use."

My eyes search hers, waiting for a sign that she really does want me to stop. Instead, she brings my head down to hers and kisses me. Hard. I feel a bolt of electricity shoot down my spine.

The intensity of my strokes pick up in pace, and before I know it, she digs her nails into my forearm as another orgasm hits her again. By the time I build to the third orgasm, tears start to fall from her eyes alongside her words— "Please don't stop, Declan. Never stop. I need more...more. Fuck that feels good... I don't think I've ever felt this good," she moans.

I grip my cock through my pants and stroke it hard as she writhes under me. It's only when I'm on the edge of coming myself that I stroke her clit just the way that she likes it and let us both fall over into bliss.

We both take a second to compose ourselves. I grab the blanket draped on the back of the couch and wrap it around her like a cocoon, cradling her into my chest. She's quiet, but I'm surprised given how much energy we just spent. "Are you alright, my love?"

She gives me a small smile. "Yes. Just exhausted. Thank you."

"No need to thank me for the orgasms," I tease, giving her a wink.

Zahra shakes her head. "I wasn't thanking you for that. Or at least not just that. Thank you for agreeing to pretend. For giving me one night of normalcy."

My throat dries instantly. Right. Pretend. She's still deluding herself into thinking that's all that's happening between us. A part of me wants to set the record straight, but the rational side of me knows this isn't the time. She's already had her fair share of vulnerable moments tonight. If I push her too hard, she'll shut me out forever. So instead, I let it be, choosing to savor the rest of the night.

PART THREE
SYNERGY

28

DECLAN

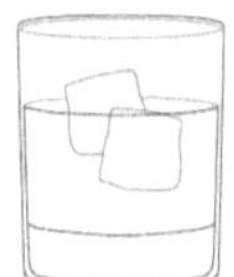

Zahra's determination to pretend nothing happened between us on our wedding night is as commendable as it is frustrating. I can't say I know much about Disney princesses, but she may as well be Cinderella. Except instead of turning back into a maid when the clock struck midnight, she immediately shifted into treating our relationship as a strictly platonic arrangement between our allied families. I'd mentally prepared myself for some of her defenses to go back up following the reception, but I refuse to let us go back to square one.

Immediately following the wedding, we both spent days packing up our essentials in preparation for today—move-in day. My father's cabin house has officially been renovated with our selected changes and alterations. The only thing that's left is us. I was determined that living under the same roof would allow us to get back on the same page. Now that I've seen what we can be together, been able to taste her, feel her tight cunt wrapped around my fingers, I would never let her go. She was my *wife*, and she could try and deny it all she wanted, but we were inevitable.

One thing's for certain—her body definitely likes me. That much was clear by the way she kept coming on my fingers. Now I just needed to help her realize that she could have all of me too. That we weren't doomed to some painful fate. That our love for each other could handle any threat.

Connor clears his throat. "Boss, Mrs. McAlister and her movers are here."

"It's Mrs. Ahzimi. It's customary to keep your last name after marriage in Iranian culture," I correct him. My heart begins to race as I pace toward the front door and throw it open.

In true form, Zahra is currently bossing around about a half a dozen men twice her size, telling them which boxes to handle with extra care and remove first from the van.

"If this is you moving light, I'd hate to see how many trucks you'd need to bring over all your stuff," I tease, propping the entry door open and stepping aside so the movers can enter.

"You're one to talk. How did you decide which five sports cars out of thirty you wanted to bring?" she jests.

"The same way any normal person would. I put all my keys in a hat and let fate decide."

"Hmm, not sure that same strategy will have worked for me, especially when it comes to deciding what clothes to bring over, but I appreciate the suggestion."

"You're right, maybe you should have just let me choose what stays and what goes. I may have given Samirah a run for her money." Or picked only the skimpiest outfits from Zahra's closet, because I'm a selfish man who loves to ogle his wife.

"Mmm, from that plotting look in your eye, I have a feeling letting you near my closet is asking for nefarious behavior to occur. And we can't have that." She nails me with a serious look, but there's a twinkle in her eye. One that makes my blood rush to my heart.

"Nothing nefarious. Just an additional hand to help speed up the move-in." I wink.

Zahra's eyebrows pinch together. "Ugh, that's on me. Cody was having a really tough time adjusting to the move. I knew it was going to be a problem, I just didn't realize how upset he would be."

Cody? Who the *fuck* is Cody? Our entire time together, she never once mentioned a lover. Sure, most bosses were known for having a side piece, but I never really pegged Zahra as being the type. My chest heats, filling with rage, as violent images of me tracking down this loser and putting a bullet in him fill my head. Killing her boytoy won't win me any brownie points, but given she admitted how she hadn't orgasmed with a partner in a while, I doubt she would miss him that much.

"Eventually, I was able to get Cody to cooperate. I really appreciate you opening your house to him. I really don't know what I would've done if he wasn't allowed to live with us." She gives me such a sweet smile that I almost forget what we were even talking about.

Almost. "What do you mean, move in with us?!" If she thinks I'll be okay with her boyfriend playing house, she has another thing coming. There's no way I was going to share my wife. Because that's what she is. *My* wife.

Zahra worries her lips together. I don't think I've ever seen her so nervous before. Fuck me. Who is the guy? How does he have so much control over her? And how come this is the first I've ever heard of him? Did no one else catch this?

She sucks in a sharp breath. "I spoke with your lawyers and your staff...They all reassured me it wouldn't be a problem."

Fired. Everyone on my payroll is about to be fired. Either that or this must be some long-winded prank Zahra is pulling on me, because there's no way that anyone in my employment would even for a second think that I would be fine with—

Zahra reaches for the straps of her backpack, readjusting it so the front of the pack is facing me. I'm immediately met with a glass dome and an incredibly skittish-looking spotted cat. "I promise Cody won't be a bother. He really just sleeps for most of the day, wakes up to eat, and then goes back to sleep. He'll probably run away from you for a while, but once he gets used to you, he'll turn into a big snuggle bug."

Oh. *Oh.* "Cody is a cat?" I clarify.

"Yes. The best cat in the whole world." She wraps her hands around her backpack, as if to give it a hug. The look of sweet innocence on her face makes me forget how lethal she is. "Why, what were you expecting?"

A real human man that you were in love with. One that I had already planned on dismembering limb by limb. "Nothing. My staff just didn't inform me you were moving in with a cat."

"Oh. Well, you don't have to worry about taking care of him. I fully accept Cody is my responsibility. That was the only way I got my father to agree to letting me keep little fluff after I found him on the street."

I peer into the bag again. The cat, who's giving me a pretty lethal side eye, looks neither little nor fluffy, but I'm not going to correct her. Not when she looks so damn...adorable sharing this part of her life with me.

"I'm surprised your dad used the word 'no' around you. I always assumed you had him wrapped around your finger," I tease.

Zahra rolls her eyes. "I can't exactly deny that he spoiled me, but he wasn't exactly fond of the idea of me taking in a stray kitten that was covered in fleas. He tried to bribe me with purchasing a big, fancy, purebred cat in exchange for him taking Cody to the pound. I told him that if he dropped Cody off at the shelter, I would never speak to him again, and I meant it at the time. I was quite stubborn and angsty when I was fourteen."

"So nothing has changed since?" I quip.

"Don't be rude," she deadpans, while fighting off a smile, "or I'll ask Aidan to tell me all the juicy gossip on what you were like as a teenager. Oooh, or even better, I'll ask Maura."

I groan, "God, please don't. It took me a while to get my shit together, and I'd rather keep my past in the past."

"Well, now I'm even more intrigued. You're telling me you weren't always the perfect heir?"

"Definitely not. I thought that maybe if I acted out, it would convince my father to just pick someone else for the job. Did a lot of stupid shit in my teens and early twenties. A lot I'm not proud of, but I guess I needed to learn my lesson on how to grow up and be an adult the hard way." I shove my hands into my pockets,

"What made you change?"

"One day I woke up, hungover as shit, and joined my dad and Naser for their weekly meeting. They were talking about the Italians. How they had just trafficked over a thousand women and children. And how our two organizations were going to put an end to their vile business for good. The next week, we led the police to their storage facilities and watched them rescue everyone. I nearly threw up at the sight of the victims. The pain in their eyes. The conditions they were kept in. I think growing up, I had judged my dad for the lifestyle he chose. But at that moment, I no longer saw life in black and white. Things were gray. So gray that a man can both take lives and save them at the same time. After that, I took things seriously and caught up fast. But a part of me still feels guilty for rejecting my fate for a while."

Her eyes soften. "It's normal to push back on things you

feel are forced on you. Especially something as dangerous as being a boss."

"You never rejected it though." A truth she had told me already.

"No, but my dad…gave me space to rebel. Kept my identity hidden, sent me away so I could live my life as normal as possible. If I'd been raised in the traditional way an heir is, I probably would've done the same thing as you."

Her words bring me a level of comfort I didn't realize I needed. "I appreciate that. Now, should I show you our new home?" She doesn't protest me emphasizing the 'our', instead, she just takes my extended hand and follows me inside.

29
ZAHRA

"Well, my love, I guess it'll just be the two of us in here."

I try not to sound too disappointed as I let Cody out of my backpack. He immediately hides under the bed, leaving me to wallow alone. Not that I have any right to wallow. Except for the fact that when Declan led me to my bedroom—*my* bedroom, not *ours*—I felt my stomach pinch. Which is utterly ridiculous. I'm the one who asked Declan for one night of pretending. I'm the one who was too cowardly to face him after our wedding. I even used packing as an excuse for why I wasn't talking to him as much anymore. Of course, he was going to go back to us being just friends. And friends don't sleep in the same bed.

Declan's cabin house, which I suppose is also now my house, is the perfect mix of cozy and modern—everything a girl could ever dream of. My bedroom is just as perfect, with a massive bed that allows me to sleep like a starfish with ease, covered in silk sheets. There's a walk-in closet that's the same size as my room, a massive desk that would store all my computers and equipment.

In front of the bed is a stunning antique full-length mirror that looks similar to the one in Declan's dressing room on our wedding day. My cheeks heat as I think of the last time Declan and I were together. How he had spread my legs and made me watch him finger me until I came over and over again. I can't stop thinking about how good he made me feel, how hot it was for him to be so dedicated to my pleasure.

Up until Declan, the only time a man was able to make me orgasm was when they used one of my toys on me. *If* they agreed to it. I'd never understand why, but evidently, lots of men found using sex toys in the bedroom as an affront to their ability. I'm willing to bet Declan isn't one of them. My eyes move back to the mirror, and for a second, I swear I see the image of Declan and me tangled together in the glass.... God, this was going to be a long year living together.

If his uncle doesn't kill us first. Declan's lawyers filed our marriage license immediately, but apparently, neither of our mafias had ties with the office processing our documents. By the end of the week, our license should be officially filed, immediately cutting Declan's uncle off from any power he has. Thus far, his uncle has left us alone, sans a glaring look here and there at our ceremony. He probably figured we did this to strengthen our alliance, or, knowing him, that I had seduced Declan into getting married. Little does he know what's coming for him...

I groan as I look at all my suitcases, unzipping the first one in front of me. I may as well get started unpacking. My laptops and devices are the first thing I take out. I have too much anxiety about packing them into a box, so I opted for bubble wrap in a carry-on instead. I chicken out on asking Declan for the WiFi password, not wanting to come off as too needy. Plus, what good is being a hacker if I can't crack someone's password with ease? I manage to connect to the internet in a matter of minutes and also make a mental note to talk to Declan about improving his security system.

I shift to unpacking my clothes when I catch my laptop flashing from the corner of my eye. Shit. When I connected to the WiFi, one of my malware software automatically installed onto his servers, allowing me to dig through the entire security system of the cabin house. Thankfully, I've coded this software so that it's extremely hard to detect and likely won't trigger any alerts. I'm unsure if Declan would believe that I'd accidentally managed to hack into his system, and I don't want him to think that the trust that's slowly been building between us these past few weeks is nothing but a farce.

Quickly, I close out the various tabs that have popped up on my screen, trying my best not to be tempted by all the things that would normally catch my eye. I'm almost in the clear when I notice the final screen includes a series of various security cameras. One of which appears to be pointed right at me. "What the fuck..." I whisper-yell in rage.

Lifting the laptop in my hand, I move across the room slowly, trying to decipher what angle is showing up on the camera. Step by step, my eyes flicker from the screen to my surroundings, moving ever so slightly until I freeze. A very zoomed-in image of my face pops up on my laptop screen, and I lean into the mirror. It takes me a few seconds to scan the wooden frame until I see it. Embedded within one of the grooves is a small camera, barely detectable to the eye. From the way the mirror is angled, it misses the majority of the bed, allowing me and whatever guests who stayed here in the past a modicum of privacy. Well, as much privacy as one can get when there's a camera in their room.

Typing away ferociously on my laptop, I search for a way to

turn the camera off. The code doesn't seem unbreakable...but it does seem a bit more complex and will likely require a few hours for me to crack. I contemplate taking the old school way out—breaking the camera and bringing it to Declan so I can chew him out for spying on me. I tap aggressively through the recording history, noticing this camera was rarely used. In fact, the only reason it's turned on in this moment is because Declan's security did a system-wide reboot a week ago, which likely triggered all dormant cameras to be reactivated.

Fine. Maybe I wouldn't pound Declan's face in for something he was likely unaware of. For now. I'd give him a chance to rectify the mistake. Not having the mental energy to hack into the camera, I decided to easily edit the configurations instead and have it play hours of B-roll footage, leaving no one the wiser. I should have just left it there, but now that I knew a camera was hidden in my room, I needed to know what other rooms were bugged and what corners of the cabin house were safe for me to speak and move freely.

One of the first things my father taught me was to always assume you are being watched. Especially in spaces where you think you're safe—those are often the ones that are most lethal to let your guard down. Flipping through the different live security streams, I make note of all the cameras in the kitchen, living and dining rooms, garage, and perimeter of the cabin. All cameras are in standard form, and mercifully, none are in the bathrooms. Some paranoid bosses opted to leave no room uncovered, but even I was against watching people do their business.

I'm nearly finished when my body freezes, throat tightening, at the final security footage of Declan's office. He's sitting at his desk, eyes closed, head leaning back against the chair as he bites down hard on his bottom lip. The image in itself is enough to send a rush of heat down my body, but it's the sight of Declan's hand wrapped around his massive cock that has my legs start to feel like Jell-O. His very massive and very *pierced* cock. Wetness starts to pool between my thighs as I imagine how good he would feel inside me. How much he would stretch me. How the piercing at the tip of his cock would feel pressed against my G-spot. Declan lets out a low moan, as if he can read my thoughts. As if he's aware that I'm watching. Except he's not.

He's currently enjoying a very private moment. Watching him makes me a hypocrite, given that I'm annoyed that there's a camera in my room.

I'm about to close the video when Declan lets out a feral groan and pants, "That's right, Zahra, slide that sweet tongue of yours over my cock. Show your husband how hungry you are for him."

A soft gasp leaves my lips. He's thinking of me. Imagining me taking him into my mouth—

"*Fuck*, baby. That's right, lick up all the precum that's leaking from my tip. So good. You're my sweet little wife, aren't you?" He hums in approval, dragging his thumb over his very swollen head over and over again. I make a mental note of how exactly he likes to be played with as I feel my nipples tighten.

Declan continues to pump and squeeze his cock over and over again, letting out a mix of curses, groans, and pants of my name. Any rational part of my brain is long gone, and in its place is the strong need that consumed me on our wedding night. I leave my laptop on the center of the bed and prop myself up against the headboard, pulling my travel vibrator out of the suitcase.

"I bet you're soaking wet right now, aren't you? Your pussy is waiting to be filled by me, isn't it, Zahra?"

Though he can't see me, I nod vehemently, turning the vibrator on and placing it on my clit, moaning at the content.

"Ah, ah, ah. Did I give you permission to touch yourself yet? You haven't earned that right yet, love." He clicks his tongue and I begrudgingly move the vibe off me. For a moment, I swear he must know I'm watching. Except I have no doubt in my mind that if he knew I was just a few rooms away, equally as turned on as he is, he'd immediately barge in and make a whimpering mess of me. A chill runs down my body as I realize how well he knows my body. How even though he's fantasizing about me giving him a blow job, he knows in real life I'd be so turned on I'd be touching myself.

"Don't pout, Zahra. You know I'll always give you what you want. Now spread those legs of yours and use two of your fingers to play with your pussy the way I did the night of our wedding." He lets out a wicked laugh, followed by a groan as he continues to work his cock in his hands. From the pace of his breathing, I can tell he's getting closer and closer to coming and that thought has me bucking my hips for more.

I adjust my vibe to the perfect setting and place it on my clit while using my other hand to slide two fingers inside me. To my utter shock, my legs are already starting to shake as my orgasm builds. I don't think I've ever been able to come this fast but I wanted nothing more than to fall over the edge with Declan.

"That's it. That's my good girl. Fucking herself while she lets her husband fuck her mouth. You're mine, Zahra. All. Fucking. Mine," he growls, giving himself one final squeeze before rope after rope of come shoots out of his cock. "Swallow it all, love. I know you can handle it." Declan moans, and the noise sends me into my own orgasm, and a wave of pleasure hits me over and over again.

I bite down on the closest pillow in a feeble attempt to dampen the loud screams of pleasure coming from me. We both lay still, panting in complete ecstasy for a few minutes, until, much to my disappointment, he tucks his cock back into his pants and leaves his office.

Slamming my laptop shut, I know two things for certain. The first was that Declan still wants me. The second is that, as much as he may want me, I can't let myself give in to him. Mixing love with the harsh reality of running a mafia would be a foolish decision. Falling for Declan is an unnecessary additional complication—no matter how much of a challenge it may be to deny him. I needed to keep my wits about me, especially now that I'm in his orbit, constantly being tempted by the pull between us.

30
DECLAN

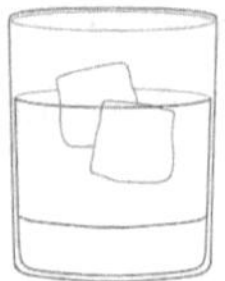

Most mobsters fall into one of two categories—either not being religious because they view themselves as God, or somehow still being able to believe in a divine power, despite knowing that said divine power exists, they're going straight to hell. The Irish fall into the latter, which is why my mom always prayed for us before she went to bed, and dragged our asses to Mass at least twice a month. Evidently, I should've gone more as a child because I was now living in my own personal hell.

Being so close to Zahra but not being able to claim her as my own is driving me fucking crazy. The amount of times I've found myself jacking off to the thought of her is beyond embarrassing. Even teenage Declan would think I needed to get a grip, and that's saying something. It doesn't help that she manages to consume the whole house, in the best way possible.

The scent of her perfume fills nearly every room, and her adorable fluff ball of a cat has taken a liking to me, dropping its toys in front of my room. Best of all, her normal prim and proper attire has been replaced by loungewear that hugs every inch of her curves and makes me want nothing more but to bury my head into her plump breasts.

"Whatever you're making, it smells absolutely divine," she groans, settling into the barstool next to the island in the kitchen.

"Just a classic Irish breakfast. Should be ready soon." I smile, handing her a mug filled with black coffee while I prep mine, adding a hint of cream and five scoops of sugar. "Surprised you're not making comments about how it's offensive to call this sugary monstrosity a coffee?"

Her lips twinge up. "You said it, not me. So long as you're aware."

I roll my eyes and turn off the stove and loading her plate with pork sausage, bacon, eggs, mushrooms, hash browns, and sourdough.

"This is your regular breakfast? No wonder you're so large. You have the appetite of a bear." She snickers, diving in.

"My breakfast comes with a side of beans, and white and black pudding, but I made sure to leave those off your plate, given I know you Americans find that offensive." I take a seat next to her, feeling a rush of electricity run down my spine as our legs brush against each other. "Plus, you have a martial arts session with Arman in a few hours. The extra protein will give you an energy boost."

How I'd come to memorize her schedule is beyond me, but somehow it seemed my brain was only aware of two different timelines: moments where I was able to spend time with Zahra, and moments where I waited until it was finally time to be with Zahra.

"Yeah, well, I'm going to need more than a session to burn all this off." Her light tone has a slight edge as she winks at me and pokes a finger at her soft stomach.

The slight dig at her body sends a rush of anger through me. "What are you talking about?"

She waves me off. "Not all of us have the gift of a fast metabolism, or the ability to eat whatever we want and still have washboard abs—"

Without thinking, I cup her jaw in my palm so she's looking right at me. "You don't need to change a damn thing about your body. It's fucking incredible." I nearly growl at the thought of her thinking differently.

Zahra's pupils dilate as she leans into my touch, and she swallows hard. "I didn't mean to sound like I was fishing for a compliment—"

On instinct, my thumb traces her bottom lip, followed by her jaw. "I know you weren't. But in case I haven't made myself clear, every inch of your body is *perfection*."

I don't voice the rest of the thoughts in my head. How I want nothing more than to punish her for even thinking for a second that there was anything wrong with her body. I want nothing more than to strip her bare in this kitchen and show her just how much I've been dying to get my hands on her lush ass and thighs. I'd spread her on this table, and use my tongue, fingers, and cock to bring her to the edge, over and over again, until she was nothing but a writhing mess begging me to let her come. I'd deny her at first until she realizes how utterly stunning she is, and how she has me so tightly wrapped around her finger.

My hardening cock brings me back to the present, forcing me to readjust myself in my chair. Fuck. I hope she doesn't notice.

Mercifully, her eyes are still trained on my face. "Thank you. Sorry for my little insecure moment."

"No need to apologize. Just make sure it doesn't happen again." My voice deepens, betraying my inner fight.

Her back straightens—the smirk on her face is a clear challenge. "Is that a threat, *Boss?*"

"What if it is?"

Her tongue darts out, tracing her bottom lip. Taunting me. "I don't do well with threats. Even if they're empty."

I tilt my head. "What makes you think my threats are empty?"

Zahra sucks in a breath, but fear is nowhere to be found in her eyes. Instead, it's filled with...intrigue. Like she wants nothing more than to see how far she can push me until I fully lose it. I drag my hands down my slacks, in a feeble attempt to ground myself. To say she's thrown me completely off my axis would be an understatement and from the look on her face, she's more than aware.

"Finish your plate," I bite, nodding my head to her plate.

Her smirk turns into a shit-eating grin. "Yes, sir."

Jesus Christ. I give her a dark chuckle. "You're playing a dangerous game, love."

All I get is a shrug and a wink in return. The epitome of nonchalance. Though I don't miss the way she crosses her legs and squeezes her thighs together.

Game on.

———

"Alright, give me a 2-3-2 next," Arman shouts.

Zahra responds by using her first to throw a devastating right hook, followed by a left jab, and another right punch. The precision of her hits has rattled Arman's large frame, as he stumbles back into the corner of the rink.

"Nice, Zahra!" I yell from across the rink, slapping my hand on the mat.

Her only response is a small smirk as she closes in on

Arman and berates him with a series of jabs and kicks to the stomach. His fate seems like a done deal, Zahra clearly having the upper hand, when he grabs her foot mid-kick and pushes her back, launching her across the boxing rink. She lands with a loud thud.

Despite knowing this is all practice, I jump to my feet to help her, but she doesn't need it. On her back, she presses her palms behind her and kicks up in one fluid movement. Though Arman is significantly larger than Zahra, he lacks stealth and speed. Arman charges straight at her, but she's faster— managing to move out of the way and jump onto his back, wrapping her arms around him. She tightens her grip around his neck and torso until he slowly stumbles down to the mat and eventually taps out.

Zahra lets out a howl of cheer as she unwinds herself and stands up, pumping her fist into the air like she just won a heavyweight title.

"Don't be such a brat," Arman groans, coming to, rubbing the back of his neck.

"C'mon, you gotta admit that body hold was solid, *and* you didn't see it coming." Zahra catches me staring at her and winks. Her entire body is flushed and covered in sweat, and I swear she adds an additional sway to her hips as she walks toward me. Leaning over the ring ropes, she points to the bench. "Can you toss me my water bottle, love?"

She snickers, using my regular term of endearment for her. I don't trust what may come out of my mouth so instead I choose to give her the bottle without a word. Zahra holds the bottle above her head, opens her mouth wide, and lets the water pour into her mouth and down her chest. The entire scene is so damn sensual, I can't control the rush of heat that fills my chest. My hands curl into fists, desperate to touch her, and judging from the look on her face, she knows exactly what she's doing to me.

"Enough with the games. None of this is going to help you in the middle of a war," a loud voice barks from the entryway. Cyrus. He slides into the rink with the poise of a killer, waving Arman away while scolding Zahra. "Or do I need to remind you how many recent attempts on your life there have been? And how we've made no progress to figure out who is coming for us?"

She winces in response, making me want to slam Cyrus' head into the mat.

"Get in position, Zahra," Cyrus commands. The entire energy of the room shifts, a harsh chill running down my spine.

She does as she's told, standing in the center of the rink and bringing her hands up to cover her face. Cyrus lunges at her immediately. The two lock arms, grappling for the upper edge. Cyrus wins, slowly pushing Zahra closer and closer to the back right corner of the ring. She lets go of her grip on his arms, ramming her elbows into his head and neck, forcing Cyrus to take a step back. With the small space between them, Zahra can duck out of the corner and bring the fight back to the center of the ring. They exchange blow after blow and one thing is made incredibly clear. Whether Arman realized it or not, he was holding back. Cyrus has a completely different agenda.

Zahra sends a right hook flying and nails him right in the nose. Cyrus stumbles back, spitting blood on the mat, and swings his arm at Zahra's face. She manages to block the hit with her arms, but the impact stumps her and sends her stumbling backward. Her cocky demeanor falters for a second, short enough that if I wasn't hyper fixated on her, I would have missed it, but it's enough to rattle me.

I lunge to enter the rink, but Arman holds me back. "No. She'll be pissed at you for stepping in, *and* there's a very high possibility that she'll find herself in this situation one day with all the enemies you two have. She needs to see that she can overcome it. Or learn from her mistakes."

An irritated growl forms in my chest, but I take a step back. As much as I hate it, he's right. Zahra can hold her own. I've seen it firsthand time and time again. There isn't a single part of me that questions her strength...though that does little to assuage the very large part of me that hates seeing her get hurt.

I wince as Zahra and Cyrus continue to exchange blows. Her previous sparring with Arman has clearly drained her, and each jab she lands not only takes a toll on Cyrus but also on herself. She dodges a punch but loses her footing, enough for Cyrus to drag her down onto the mat. He wraps one of her legs in a triangle hold and pulls on it hard. She lets out a guttural scream—a mix of pain and rage—as she uses her free leg to kick Cyrus over and over again. Zahra lands a kick right in Cyrus' shoulder, causing him to loosen his grip. She nails him again, right in the nose this time, sending his head flying back into the mat, delivering the final blow.

Except this time, she's not shouting in celebration. She's whimpering in pain, clutching the ankle that Cyrus had gripped. "Fuck. I think it's sprained."

I'm in the rink in a matter of seconds, wrapping her arm around my neck. "Lean into me, and I'll help you stand up."

She listens, allowing me to wrap my hand around her waist and lift her gently. Even with me stabilizing her, I can tell she's in pain. Sliding her into my arms, I carry her over to the bench and take a closer look at her foot. "It's starting to swell. We should have a doctor look at it—"

"I'm fine," she groans, gritting her teeth as she forces herself to stand up.

"*Zahra.*" I struggle to hide the irritation in my voice. I understand her stubbornness better than anyone. A boss is never allowed to show weakness. "We need a doctor to take a look at you."

She shakes her head. "It's nothing I can't handle."

Except when she goes to take a step forward, she nearly stumbles onto the floor.

That's it.

I throw her over my shoulder, ignoring all her protests to put her down. She even tries one of her fighting moves against me, in an attempt to get me to break, but with how spent she is, it barely impacts me. Instead, I readjust her so I'm carrying her bridal style and can easily look at her face. "Zahra, please. Do this for me," I beg.

Whether it's the shock from hearing me say please, or the injury she sustained, her eyes soften and she curls into my chest, giving me a small nod.

31
ZAHRA

I'd always convinced myself that I hated being fussed over, but I have to admit that having Declan as my temporary nurse has me rethinking my stance on the matter. Declan had called over Dr. Williams to our cabin, who immediately concluded that I have a grade 1 ankle sprain and should hopefully be fully healed in the next week or two. His assessment had convinced me I would get up on my feet in no time, but he may as well have told Declan I'd shattered every bone in my body the way he was acting.

He ordered me to rest on the couch, icing and wrapping up my ankle tightly in a bandaid and elevating it with a few pillows. When I insisted I needed to get up to clean Cody's litter box, he sent me the dirtiest look, nearly barking at me to stay seated while he took care of everything. And Cody, the little traitor, has fully taken to Declan. My cat follows Declan around the house and occasionally meows for a treat, which Declan is more than happy to oblige.

The tabby cat took months to even allow me to pet him and I saved him from the streets. Meanwhile, Cody constantly purrs up a storm whenever Declan sits down next to him on the couch, and he rubs himself against Declan all the time. The two are so obnoxiously adorable together, I swear it's fucking with my head. Declan is hard to resist as a tough, broody mob boss, but as a softie who takes care of me and my cat—there's no way I'd be able to keep things professional between us for long.

"Alright, it's time for some ice." Declan enters the living room with a large ice pack in hand and takes a seat next to me on the massive couch. His warmth immediately envelopes me and all I want to do is bury my head in the crook of his neck and fall asleep.

"I can do it myself," I offer, extending my hand to take the ice from him.

Declan just shakes his head. "I know you can, but I like helping you. It makes me feel useful." He lifts up the blanket that's covering my swollen foot and gently undoes the bandage. Purple and blue bruises have started to form around my ankle, but they should hopefully start to fade soon. Declan places the ice pack directly on the injury, and the sudden sensation makes me hiss.

"Sorry." He gives me a soft smile, one that makes my insides feel like they're nothing but goop, and lifts the ice pack off my foot.

"It's fine. Always stings at first but then it feels better." I place my hand on top of his, guiding it back toward my ankle. Leaning my head against the backrest of the sofa, I groan. "I can't believe I twisted my ankle."

"Cyrus was coming at you quite aggressively." Declan's shoulders stiffen and I watch his jaw pinch.

"He's just doing his job. He's right that I need to be prepared for anything. Going easy on me in the rink doesn't help me out in the long term," I reassure him.

Declan bites his lip, contemplating what to say next. "It was hard just standing there. Being unable to help."

With anyone else, I'd roll my eyes and scoff. I prided myself on being able to get by in life without relying on anyone else around me. My dad warned me at a young age that many would think of me as a spoiled mafia princess—a damsel in distress—and I vowed to him to be anything but that. Which I had succeeded in. Still, I know there are many men who view women as docile and weak, unable to fend for themselves or run a mafia. Declan isn't like that though. He never doubted me, my strength, or my capabilities. His concern for my well-being and safety came from a place of caring, not dismissal.

"I appreciate that, but the only person who can fully protect myself is me. And even then, there's no guarantees." I sit up straight and place my hand on his shoulders. "I don't want to come off as ungrateful for how concerned you are. Or for your work, helping me to get back on my feet. If I'm being honest, I can't truly remember the last time someone made me feel so special, so cared for a lo—"

I stop myself, knowing once I crossed that line, I'd never be able to take it back.

Declan raises an eyebrow, challenging me. "Don't stop now. Finish that sentence, Zahra."

"I can't. You *know* I can't. You know why."

He releases an exacerbated sigh. "No, I don't know why, so you better tell me why you keep denying yourself. Why you keep denying us. Denying the inevitable. Before I lose my mind."

"Love makes us fragile. And we can't afford to be fragile when we're on the brink of a war and we don't even know who we're fighting."

Declan shakes his head feverishly. "No. You don't really believe that. I see you, Zahra. Really see you. I see how big your heart is. How much you care for your friends, the members of your empire. Your parents. You're telling me you didn't love them?"

"Of course I did," I bite, "but that just proves my point. When my mom died of a heart attack, I lost a part of myself. I was finally getting to feel normal again after nearly a decade of mourning her when I lost my dad. Now I'm back to feeling empty. I try to mask the pain. Mask the hole that's left in my heart from their deaths but I *can't*. It's still there, and I know it always will be. Which is why I can't allow myself to love again. I can't weaken myself any more than I already am." My voice shakes, demonstrating my exhaustion.

"You. Are. Not. Weak," he growls, cradling my face in his hands, forcing me to look at him. "You suffered great losses, and you're hurt. But that does not make you weak."

I place my hand on his chest, using the beat of his racing heart to ground me. "You may not think that, because you're also going through the same thing. You've felt it. A loss so great it rips you into pieces. But you know the other bosses see it differently. They view even the slightest indication of sorrow as evidence that we're wounded prey that they can slaughter at the right time. Which is why no one can see how much we're hurting. No one can know the truth."

Declan's thumb draws idle circles on my cheek as he looks at me, confused. "I'm not disagreeing with you there, but what I don't understand is why you would deny yourself happiness, the chance to feel something beyond pain and grief."

"Because love is dangerous. It's lethal. Not only do the people we care about become an even bigger target to our enemies, but once they're taken from us...We also feel it all. I deny myself because the next loss I experience might kill me. The grief of losing my father has suffocated me, and I am terrified of what may happen if another person I love is ripped away from me. There's a lot I can handle in this world. Experiencing physical pain and torture has never bothered me. But the mental anguish of being alone? I can't handle it." I squeeze my eyes shut, unable to look him in the eyes as I whisper, "Everyone I love dies. Loving me may as well be a curse."

"Zahra..." Declan's eyes soften as the emotions on his face shift between confusion to...pity.

Fuck, I hate that. "I don't need you to feel sorry for me—"

He reels back. "What are you talking about?"

"I see pity on your face. You're probably thinking, *'Poor little Zahra. A mafia boss who can't even handle a few deaths.'*" My voice cracks, eyes starting to sting as my stomach turns. Dammit, what the hell is wrong with me? I will not cry. *I will not cry.*

His grip on my face tightens slightly, not enough to cause me any pain, but it does force me to look at him. Or at least it would if I didn't squeeze my eyes shut. "Look at me, love."

I shake my head.

"Please. Zahra. Don't make me beg." His voice is rough. Desperate. His thumb moves from tracing my cheek to my jawline.

After a few centering deep breaths, I give in, losing myself in the blueish-green of his irises.

"There you are." The warmth in his smile settles my racing heartbeat ever so slightly. "You're wrong, Zahra. I don't pity you. I *understand* you. I know exactly what you mean about carrying the weight of losing someone. The lingering fear that another person you love can be taken from you at any moment. The harsh reality that no matter how hard you try, you can't shield anyone from death. I always thought my father was some untouchable, unbeatable force. And for the most part, he was...until the end. Losing my father turned my whole world upside down. Made me question everything. My power, my safety, the future of my mafia. My ability to take care of those I love."

Leaning my forehead against his, I whisper, "How did you get past it?"

"I haven't yet. It still haunts me every day."

"Do you think it will go away? The pain? The fear?" I search his eyes for any answer.

"I think it'll get quieter. And over time, we'll barely realize it's there. But I don't know if it can ever fully leave us." His gaze falls to my lips. "Which is why we shouldn't deny ourselves what we want. Just because loss and pain are inevitable doesn't mean we have to stop ourselves from feeling joy. Stop ourselves from experiencing love."

He sounds so sure. And though I can admit his reasoning was sound, the voice in the back of my head telling me to keep my guard up is screaming at me in full force. "I hear you. But it feels too risky..."

"Everything we do in this life is a risk. Some just pay off more than others," Declan counters, as if he can sense I'm on the verge of breaking. On the verge of giving in to all the tension that has been building up since the moment we first met. "Why if we try?"

"Try?" I ask breathlessly.

"Try having a real relationship. A real marriage. One where we stop denying our feelings for each other, and just live."

"*Just live,*" I repeat, the words sounding practically foreign to me. Even when my identity had been hidden from the world, and I had pretended to be a normal kid, in the back of my mind I always knew who I was. What my future would entail.

"So, what do you say?" Declan's tongue peeks out of his mouth, wetting his bottom lip as his thumb traces mine.

"I say y—"

I'm cut off by the loud BANG of our front door being thrown open and slammed against the wall, followed by shouting coming from our security. I move onto my feet, ignoring the searing pain from my injured ankle. Declan whips his Glock out immediately and stands up in front of me, blocking me from anyone who may come in. I reach for the one I tucked away behind one of the couch pillows in case of emergencies. Both of us aim our guns at the entryway as frantic footsteps approach.

Connor's voice is the first I can make out. "SIR, STOP. You cannot go any closer—"

"I'LL DO WHAT I DAMN WELL PLEASE. I'M THE SECOND IN COMMAND OF THE GODDAMN MAFIA. NO MATTER WHAT SOME STUFFY LAWYER TELLS ME!" Declan's uncle shouts back in return, the walls shaking with his anger.

He stalks into the room a moment later, revolver dangling from his hand, and rage filling his eyes as he glances between Declan and me.

"What the *fuck* have you two done?"

32
DECLAN

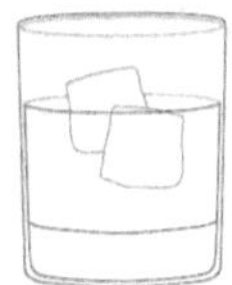

"Judging by your dramatic entrance, I'd say you know exactly what we've done." Zahra adjusts her position on the couch so she's no longer hidden behind me and holds her chin up high.

Her unrelenting defiance is one of my favorite things about her, but I don't miss the way my Uncle Lorkan's hand twitches, moving his finger on the trigger.

"Make another move, and I'll put a bullet in you. And this time it will be somewhere that won't heal as easily as your knee," I sneer.

"You think you and this little girl scare me, boy?" Lorkan bares his teeth.

Closing the distance between us, I stalk straight up to him and press my Glock to his temple. "Insult my wife one more time, and I swear on everything in this world, good and evil, I will have your brains splattered all over my rug in an instant."

Lorkan's undeterred. "Do it. Given the damage you've caused, death would be a mercy instead of being forced to watch you ruin our family's legacy."

My finger goes to the trigger. "The only one who's ruining our legacy is *you*. Thankfully, we put an end to that."

"You stupid, insolent *boy*. So blinded by love, you're living in your own reality, aren't you?"

I feel Zahra stiffen behind me, and my stomach turns. Before my uncle barged in, we'd bared our own insecurities to each other, and I finally felt like she was willing to let down her walls and give us a genuine chance. I won't let my uncle's bitterness and resentment cost us the hope of happiness. "What's done is done. My father's will stated clearly that once I got married, all remaining power you had would be handed over to me."

"I knew my time was limited. I never for a second believed Cillian would leave me his empire for an extended period of time, but of all the people to replace me, you chose *Aidan*," my uncle spits as if he isn't talking about his own nephew.

"You can't be surprised that, as Don, I chose Aidan as my second. He is my brother after all."

"He's a spoiled brat who was handed everything in life and still found reason to complain. He's weak. A mockery to the McAlister name—"

"THAT'S ENOUGH!" I growl, grabbing my uncle by the collar of his shirt and shaking him so hard he loses his footing and drops his gun. I kick it across the room, leaving him defenseless. "You, of all people, have no right talking about the McAlister name, given your recent involvement with drug lords and traffickers. I don't know how you sleep at night."

Lorkan thrashes against me, shoving at my chest until I finally let him go. "What the fuck are you on about? Those are some bold accusations without any proof."

"We have proof. Photo evidence, and a lengthy track record of receipts and transactions from the various accounts you had control over." Zahra winces as she stands up on her feet.

I move instantly, extending my arm for her to use to stabilize herself. My uncle rolls his eyes in response, and I nearly throttle him again.

"Evidence can be easily doctored," Lorkan scoffs.

"So, at the end of the day, all we have is your word. Forgive me if that isn't enough to sway me." I click my tongue.

"This arrogance is unbecoming of you, Declan."

"You're one to talk. Now, if you're done making a scene, you can either walk out on your own accord, or Connor can throw you in our holding cell. To be clear, this will be your one and only chance to walk out of this house. If you threaten me or my wife again, I will make sure that never happens again." The threat lingers in the air. Connor has grabbed my uncle's gun from the ground and seems excited at the prospect of finally shutting Lorkan up.

Lorkan's face turns red. "How dare you speak to me like that! Have you forgotten who I am?"

"Not for a second. But it's clear you've forgotten who *I* am." I grab Lorkan's throat and squeeze, restricting his air flow. "All of your access to our main accounts has been stopped. You will have an extremely limited line of credit that you can use for food and shelter. We will be heavily monitoring your spending. *All* our allies have been informed to update us on any suspicious activity you partake in. Make no mistake, you may be my uncle by blood, but as of today, you are nothing to the Irish Mafia." I spit, hot blood pulsing through my veins.

My uncle claws at my hand for release but he finds none as his face turns from bright red to a purplish blue. A rush of power fills me as I watch his stance falter as he flounders for oxygen, knees buckling under him. My uncle's grip on my hands loosens, a sign of how close he is to losing consciousness, when I feel a small warm hand wrap around my wrist.

"Declan, I think the message is received. Let him go."

Zahra's soothing voice causes some of the tension in my shoulders to release, but my grip remains. She uses her other hand to grip my jaw, turning my head so I'm looking at her. "Let him go, Declan."

I drop Lorkan, leaving him a panting mess on the floor until Connor lifts him up with ease and drags him out of the room.

Zahra's grip on me hasn't faltered a second, not a hint of fear in her eyes. Instead, she's looking at me with a sense of pride and longing. A soft gasp falls from her lips as I wrap my arm around her waist, closing the distance between us until she's pressed against my chest. "Remind me what we were talking about before we were so rudely interrupted?"

She gulps. "I, um. Don't remember."

"Alright, before you two start with the kissy face, I just want to make it known that I'm here," Azula speaks up, grabbing out attention.

Zahra's head snaps to the corner. "When did you sneak in?"

"Around the time Declan decided to turn his uncle into a human stress ball. Which I must admit was quite entertaining."

"Glad I could be of service." I smirk, coming fully back to reality. I frown as I realize Zahra's been on her injured ankle this whole time. I slide my arms under her legs and lift her up, ignoring the twinge in my shoulder from where I was shot. "No more standing, you need to rest to heal properly."

I place Zahra on the coach before sitting down next to her, turning to face Azula, whose eyebrows are raised so high they practically reach her hairline.

"I didn't realize you two had gotten so...cozy." Azula grins, winking at Zahra, who doesn't move a muscle.

Instead, Zahra gets straight to business. "What brings you in?"

"Aleksander Ivanov, the Ukrainian boss, wants a meeting with you. He claims he has some crucial information that you need to hear surrounding a potential assassin." Azula's hands twitch at her sides, like she's dying to get revenge. Dying to skin someone alive. Knowing her reputation, she probably is.

"What does he want in return?" Zahra asks.

Smart girl. No one in our line of work offers favors. Everything came at a cost. Often one that isn't worth what you get in return.

Azula tenses, and I already know I'm going to hate whatever Aleksander has asked for. "His only request was that he get to meet with you. Alone."

It takes me a second to realize what she means. "Absolutely not. Zahra and I are partners. Not just in allyship between our two families, but in marriage. Wherever she goes, I go and vice versa."

Zahra snorts in response. "Ignore my husband. Aleksander's request is reasonable so long as he's fine meeting us here. My desire to eat out has dramatically decreased since the incident at The Black Rose. A girl only gets so many close calls on poisoning attacks before she dies."

My hands curl into fists at my sides and the only reason why I'm not immediately freaking out is because my mind is entirely too distracted by the fact that Zahra just called me her husband. *Her* husband. Still, the idea of her being in the same room as a man as lethal and callous as Aleksander Ivanov made my stomach churn. "You will have security in the room with you even if I'm not allowed."

"Do you really think that little of me?" Zahra's eyes narrow. The harshness in her voice covers up the subtle hint of hurt.

Shit. That is not at all how I intended to come off, but by

replaying the words in my head, I can see how she got there. I take one of her hands and cradle it in between my palms. "*No. I'm not saying I want you to have protection because you can't handle yourself. I have not one single doubt in my mind that if you wanted to rip Aleksander limb from limb, you could do it. There is not one single thing I think you can't do.*" *Including healing my frozen, shattered heart.* "I just can't stand the idea of anything bad happening to you and knowing I did nothing to help. If I can't be there, I at least want some extension of me with you. And if that includes my security team, then so be it."

"Declan, we just talked about this. You can't protect me from the world. No matter how much you want to." Her eyes are trained on me, as if she's hoping something will click and I'll finally accept the truth from her lips.

For now, I chose to live in denial. "Just humor me. Please."

Zahra shifts her attention back to Azula, and the two somehow manage to have a full conversation without saying a word. It's as scary as it is impressive.

"Give me your gun." Zahra lifts her free hand out in front of me.

"Why? You have your own." And probably a dozen or so other ones hidden in her belongings.

"Because, my dear husband, you said you wanted me to have a piece of you with me when I meet with Aleksander, and what better security than your own gun?"

She said it again. *My dear husband.* The words may as well be a siren song because the next thing I know, I'm placing my Glock in her hand, as she and Azula plot out the logistics of the meeting and how they'll sneak the gun into the room. Aleksander's men will no doubt request to search her and the room ahead of time. We rattle off ideas back and forth until we land on a solution we're all satisfied with, Azula giving us a quick wave goodbye before making her exit.

Zahra and I sit in the comfortable silence of the room until she falls asleep in my arms, the exhausting day finally catching up to her. I debate carrying her into her room so she's more comfortable, but that would mean sleeping alone tonight instead of pressing up against her warm body. So instead, I shift us slightly on the couch so I can lay down with her on my side and let the steady rhythm of her breathing lull me to sleep.

33
DECLAN

"I can't believe I actually agreed to this," I grumble, pacing back and forth in my office while Azula picks at her nails and Aidan awkwardly sits next to her on the couch. At my signal, Connor's standing by the door, primed and ready to run across the hall to the meeting room, where Zahra and Aleksander are currently sitting.

"She'll be fine. The table has a secret compartment underneath it. Once she sits, she'll be able to get her gun. I all but strip-searched Aleksander and his cronies. Plus, we have a video and audio livestream setup." Azula turns her cell phone so I can see the footage of Zahra as she gestures for Aleksander to sit across from her.

From the angle of the camera, I can see her reach under the table and slide my small revolver out from the compartment, tucking it into the sleeve of her coat. Some of the tension in my shoulders drops. "When did you install a camera?"

Azula's eyebrows knit together. "I didn't."

Now it's my turn to be confused. "I know where all our

main security cameras are set up inside. This room, to my knowledge, doesn't have one."

"Zahra informed me that there's some dormant cameras throughout the cottage. From what she could tell, they hadn't been used in years, so likely forgotten about. She configured my phone so I could access it too."

I curse myself for not being more diligent. I had combed through the cottage myself with security over a dozen times to ensure our home was safe for Zahra. And still I missed these cameras.

Azula smirks at me. "I'll take your non-response as an indication you didn't know she had hacked into the security system? I wouldn't take it personally. Knowing her, she probably installed additional firewalls afterward to ensure no one else could hack in."

Grabbing my laptop, I shove it into Connor's chest. "Load the security footage of the room now."

He fiddles with my computer for a few seconds, remotely connecting to all the cameras in the house and pulling up the footage of the meeting room.

Turning the volume up so everyone else in the room can hear, I take a seat at my desk.

"I appreciate your flexibility in meeting me in my home." Zahra's soothing voice flows through the speakers.

"How could I turn down such hospitality?" Aleksander gives her a flirty smile as he takes in the plate in front of him. *"What's for lunch?"*

"One of my favorites, Kalam Polow. It's an Iranian dish. Rice, cabbage, spices, and mini meatballs." Zahra settles in her chair, reaching for her cutlery.

Aleksander watches Zahra as she takes the first bite and swallows.

"No poison. I promise." Zahra's tone is light, and she

gestures for him to join her, which he does enthusiastically, chuckling to himself at Zahra's brashness.

My fists tighten around the arms of the desk chair, causing it to groan.

"Relax, man." Aiden's tone is teasing as he shakes his head. "He's nothing to warrant that reaction yet."

"He's alone in a room with my wife and is flirting with her," I grumble.

"He's said all of like, five words to her," Aiden presses me, like when we were both kids and he had to be right.

"Well, he's spoken to them flirtatiously, and that pisses me off," I snap.

"Jesus. You two are a bunch of toddlers. And it looks like they're about to start talking again, so maybe you can table the bickering for now, so we can actually listen in?" Azula rolls her eyes as she focuses her attention back on her phone.

"I have to admit that I was a bit surprised you reached out to my staff to request a private meeting. Especially given our families have never been allied before." Zahra cuts straight to the point.

"Well, I was quite enamored by you at the charity banquet. I've met a lot of lethal and imposing men in my life, and yet none of them made as strong an impression on me as you did that night." Aleksander rolls his sleeves up to his elbows as he leans in closer. Given the camera angle, I couldn't say for certain, but I wouldn't be surprised if his eyes quickly trailed down Zahra's body, checking out her figure.

The chair underneath me groans again.

"I appreciate that. With my father's legacy, I knew I had a lot to live up to, and that the current Dons have their apprehensions about me—"

"They can shove their apprehensions up their ass. None of them have the balls you do. Metaphorically speaking." He smirks, laying

down the charm. Zahra, to no one's surprise, doesn't move a muscle.

"I can't say I disagree with you. Which is why I'll cut straight to it. What makes you think you have information that I would care about?" Whatever game Aleksander is playing, Zahra is clearly ten steps ahead of him, not revealing the fact that we have been spinning our wheels trying to find out who is behind the various attempts on her life.

"Between the near-fatal poisoning of the shooter at your banquet and the rat at one of your warehouses, I'm sure you've pieced together that this is much bigger than a few disgruntled voices. Someone really wants you dead. No matter the cost." How the hell did Aleksander know about the warehouse attack? If I was in the room with him, I'd immediately demand he tell me everything he knows.

Zahra, however, keeps her calm. *"I handled the banquet shooter with ease. Everything else is just a rumor. An attempt to tarnish my name and make me seem weak."*

My heart twinges as I think back to our recent conversations. If only she could see herself how everyone else does.

"On the contrary. I think it shows what a threat you really are. Everyone sees it. Which is why they're so hellbent on killing you," Aleksander counters.

Zahra remains silent.

"Would you feel more enticed by what I have to offer if I talk more about the vulture tattoo? I've heard all your failed assassins carried that mark."

I watch as Zahra toys with the cuffs of her blazer under the table. One of her subtle tells is that she's nervous and trying to calculate her next move. She clicks her tongue. *"Is that what you've heard?"*

"Yes. Along with the fact that you can't seem to tie it to anyone who could be a potential threat. You've scrubbed every security

system you could hack into—which I have no doubt is vast—and yet you've come out dry. If anyone would have been able to put the puzzle pieces together at this point, it would have been you." Aleksander's tone is a mix of matter-of-fact and the subtle hint of being impressed.

"And yet you've managed to outsmart me? Which is why I'm in desperate need of your assistance? Is that what you've come here to boast about?"

"On the contrary. The only thing I've benefited from is luck. And timing." Aleksander reaches into the coat of his jacket, and Zahra immediately tightens her grip on my gun, aiming it right at his knee underneath the table. *"I was cleaning out our family heirlooms. You may recall that decades ago, our families were much more aligned. Evidently well enough allied that the Irish and Persian inner circle would visit my father's house in Mykonos."*

Confusion covers Zahra's face, and I'm sure mine. Whatever allyship we must have had with Ukrainians ended long before I was born. Neither my father nor Naser had mentioned anything to me.

"I see the surprise on your face. I wouldn't have believed it myself if not for this." He places an old, tattered photo on the table and slides it toward Zahra.

Zahra scans the photo diligently but it's hard to make out the contents of the image from the security cameras. Her hand starts to shake and I want nothing more than to see what she's seeing. She sucks in a gasp. *"Oh my god..."*

"They say a picture's worth a thousand words and I suppose this one is worth a million. My father's the man sitting next to yours as they lounge by the pool. Declan is truly a spitting image of his father, Cillian, who's standing inside the pool, and next to Cillian is—"

"Lorkan," Zahra spits his name. *"T-This photo can't be real. You've doctored it."*

Aleksander shakes his head vehemently. *"No. You're more than welcome to run it through any software you need, but that photo hasn't been touched. Your eyes do not deceive you."*

Dammit. What's in the image? What does she see that's causing her so much distress?

"The tattoo on Lorkan's chest—"

"Is identical to the ones worn by the men who tried to kill you," Aleksander finishes her sentence.

Aidan chokes on air, while Azula practically growls. The room starts to feel like it's spinning as I squeeze the arms of my chair, looking for something to ground me. Lies. 1``

It had to be an altered image. I know all the tattoos my uncle has and not one of them bears resemblance to the Vulture that's been haunting us.

"It c-can't be. Declan would have seen it growing up... He would have warned me."

My heart aches at the pure agony in her voice. I nearly barrel out of the room, stopped only by Aidan grabbing my arm and calming me down. I need to be there with her.

"From what I can tell, he covered it up a year later. It's hard to tell in this photo with the Celtic knots he added in." Aleksander removes another photo from his pocket for Zahra to assess.

Zahra swallows hard, pinching the bridge of her nose between her fingers. *"I assume this is why you requested to meet one-on-one."*

Aleksander nods. *"While I know Declan isn't Lorkan's biggest fan...I wasn't entirely sure how he would handle the fact that this uncle has tried to kill his new bride."*

Zahra winces at the same time I do. We both know my Uncle Lorkan has done some heinous things, but until recently, I was certain he never wanted the full responsibility of being a boss. He had always boasted about being able to enjoy the power of being high up in the mob without bearing the full weight of being the final decision maker. Maybe his tune has changed. Or maybe he'd been lying this entire time. My stomach turns at the thought.

"I appreciate you bringing this to my attention." Zahra braces her shoulders.

"Of course. I hope it serves as a gesture of good faith. And an expression of my desire to restore what was once a strong bond between our families."

Aleksander extends a hand out for Zahra, which she shakes. The initial exchange is nothing to bat an eye at—until he refuses to let go. Instead, he leans in and presses a kiss to the back of Zahra's hand. In an instant, I'm shoving my brother and Connor aside, barreling out of the office and heading straight down the hall.

By the time I throw the door to the dining room open, Aleksander is fully back on his side of the table. He greets me with a smirk like he didn't just have his grimy lips all over my wife. Speaking of the angel, Zahra turns her chair so she can look right at me, her eyebrow is raised at my sudden interruption. "Is it time for my next meeting, *husband?*"

I blink. Husband was more of an adjective than a term of endearment, yet it reduces some of the tension in my jaw. God, the hold she had on me is as impressive as her quick wit. I didn't think twice about barging in, but it would certainly blow our cover if I revealed why I came barreling in.

"Yes. I tried to ask Azula to wait, but you know how impatient she can be." The lie leaves my lips with ease, though I have a feeling my wife's second will make me pay for it one day.

Zahra lets out a small chuckle that manages to ignite every inch of my body. She stands from her chair and turns her attention back to Aleksander. "If you'll, excuse me."

"Of course. Please don't hesitate to give me a call if you

need me." He casually shoves his hands in his pockets, licking his bottom lip as his eyes flicker to Zahra and then me.

I take a step forward, ready to ring his neck with my bare hands, but Zahra steps right in front of me, blocking me from his path, and distracts me with the sweet warmth of her body as she leans her back into my chest.

"I'll be sure to be in touch. My staff will escort you out." Zahra gives him a soft smile before taking my hand into hers and leading us out of the room and back into the never-ending hellscape that was our reality.

34
ZAHRA

Declan's grunts and groans of frustration and the thump of his fist slamming into the punching bag fill the room. Again. And again. And again. The last words he uttered came out as a growl as he instructed Aidan— *'Find Lorkan and bring him to me.'* His brother had left, Azula and Connor in tow, before Declan had even finished the sentence. Instead of waiting in the office until we got word that the traitor was captured, Declan had barged straight to the basement of our home.

He'd thrown the gym door open and slammed it against the wall with such ferocity I'm surprised the door didn't fall from its hinges. Declan didn't bother changing into his workout gear as he ripped open his dress shirt, tossing it on the floor, and started his barrage against the punching bag. The first punch he threw sent the bag flying, which I knew was no small feat. Ten minutes into his barrage, his entire body is dripping in sweat, and the temperature in the room has increased at least ten degrees from the heat radiating from Declan's body.

Once he started his punches, he never let up. Hit after hit, every time I thought he would pause to take a breath or shake his hands out, he did the opposite, adding more heat to every punch he threw, as if it wasn't just a punching bag in front of him. Initially, I figured he was imagining it was Lorkan in front of him. Lorkan, his uncle. The man who tried to kill me. The man who killed my father. And Declan's.

The longer this goes on, the more I'm convinced there are bigger demons Declan is fighting.

Declan lets out a loud hiss as his knuckles finally burst open, blood dripping down his hand and onto the cushioned floor of the gym. He haphazardly wipes the blood off on his dress pants, wipes the sweat off his forehead with the back of his arm, and spits on the ground. My throat dries at how utterly obscene he looks right now. *Are you serious, Zahra? Stop ogling the man when he's clearly on the brink of a mental breakdown.*

The rational part of me is right. Now is not the time to focus on how Declan is standing right in front of me, looking straight out of one of my fantasies. He needs a friend. Needs to know that just because the world is cruel doesn't mean he's alone.

His fist connects with the punching bag again, except this time, before he can pull back, I wrap my hand around his wrist and hold him in place. "That's enough."

Declan freezes, but his eyes are feral. As if he lost himself so much in the violence that he doesn't even realize where he is now. I imagine it's a lot like how I looked when I killed the man at the warehouse. He had been able to calm me down then. Had been able to stop me from fully snapping. And I would do the same for him.

Keeping one of my hands on his wrist, I move the other to his face, brushing away the sweaty strands of hair that have fallen into his eyes. "Declan. I need you to take a few steps back and sit down."

He blinks, standing in place before speaking. "I'm getting my blood on you."

My heart squeezes at the sound of his voice—gruff and defeated. "That's okay. I don't mind it. What I do mind is you hurting yourself for no reason."

Declan's eyes fall to the ground.

"Let's get you cleaned up."

He begrudgingly lets me bring him into the small trainer's room attached to the gym. I shove him onto the bench, leaving a water bottle next to him, while I rummage through the different medical supply cabinets.

Declan chugs the water in a matter of seconds, but protests as I open some alcohol wipes. "This really isn't necessary."

"It is," I insist, and begin cleaning his wound.

He tries, and fails, to pull his hand back. "I don't think I need to remind you that I've had much worse injuries. I just survived a bullet to the shoulder; a few cracked knuckles is nothing."

"Just because you've survived worse doesn't mean I can't take care of you now," I insist, grabbing another alcohol wipe.

"Zahra—"

"Declan, whatever excuse you're going to say, I'm not going to listen. You were incredibly stubborn when it came to taking care of me after I sprained my ankle. I'd also been hurt much worse in the past but that didn't stop you from dotting over me like a mother hen."

His eyebrows narrow, tension forming on his face. "So I took care of you, and now you're returning the favor?"

My heart feels like it's been punctured. It's more than that, more than me just wanting to call it even. I want to be the one who helped heal him. I shake my head vehemently.

"No. This isn't transactional. Our relationship isn't trans-actional."

Declan looks at me like I'm a puzzle he can't quite solve. "It's not?" he asks.

I can't blame him for asking. Up until this point, the only explicit conversations we've had about our relationship included laying out the very specific details about how our relationship is only transactional. But the more we got to know each other, the more the lines started to blur. Maybe those lines were never even there to begin with. I just kept fooling myself with the idea that we could keep things strictly business. Strictly professional.

"I'm your...friend," I state, wincing at how simple that sounded. 'Friend' doesn't seem to quite scratch the surface of what we are to each other. But at the same time, saying I'm his wife feels like rubbing salt into the wound, a reminder of our business arrangement, as opposed to what it should be—a declaration of love.

Declan stays quiet. Contemplative. He continues to study me in a way that makes me want to squirm, so I try to distract myself instead. "Do you want to tell me what you were thinking about when you were hitting that punching bag like it owed you millions of dollars?"

He shuts his eyes, and for a few minutes, I'm convinced he won't open them until I leave. Eventually, he whispers, "Every time I think I'm finally treading water, a tidal wave slams me back down and I'm drowning. I thought I was ready for this. Ready to be a boss. And yet all I've done so far is allow traitors to enter our ranks right under my nose. My whole life, I've underestimated my uncle. And it got my father killed."

"Declan, you can't blame yourself for that—"

"Except I can. My uncle was always reckless, with an uncontrollable temper. I don't think he has a rational bone in his body, which is why I know my grandfather counted his blessings that my father was born first. My entire life, I watched as people disregarded my Uncle Lorkan. Sure, he inherited some wealth and say in the business, but at the end of the day, my father held all the power. Lorkan was at his beck and call. People would harass him all the time about it. On a good day, he would curse those people out, and on a bad day, he would pick fights. Using their disrespect as an invitation to get his anger out.

"Despite his outbursts, my father would always tell me Lorkan was harmless— *'A hot head with no real desire to be boss.'* When I was a kid, I was skeptical. I saw the jealous look in Lorkan's eye when he was in the same room as my father. The harsh glares he would send mine and Aidan's way. But the older I grew, the more I chose to believe my father. Lorkan was hostile and violent, but he was also a recluse. He hated schmoozing at charity events or having to attend meetings with allies, which is why I never would have imagined he'd want to overthrow my father. Until now. Maybe all the years of being told he was second best finally got to him and he snapped. He killed his own brother. Killed Naser. He almost killed *you*. And I've done nothing to stop him," Declan spits out, his hands curling into fists. I have a feeling that if he could aim fists at himself right now, he would.

"We still don't know for certain your uncle killed our fathers." It pains me to say it but it's true. Aleksander's evidence is compelling, but we need more than a few photos, especially since this would tear a hole into a family already hanging by a thread.

"We'll find out soon. Once Aidan brings him to me." Declan opens his eyes, a faint sheen covering them.

I grab the liquid band-aid next to him and dab it onto his knuckles, blowing on them slightly to help the glue dry faster.

"You're good at that," Declan notes.

"At using a bandaid?" I ask, confused.

A hint of a smile forms on his lips as he shakes his head. "At taking care of people. And their wounds."

"Using alcohol wipes and some bandages isn't exactly rocket science." I shrug.

"That's not what I meant," he presses. His gaze pours into mine as if he'll be able to find the solution to all his problems.

Suddenly, all the oxygen feels like it's being sucked out of the room. My lips move, but no words come out. I stand frozen and unable to put together a coherent sentence while my mind races in a hundred different directions.

"There you go again." Declan sighs, shoulders slouching, as he lifts one of his injured hands and strokes my cheek, sending a thousand goosebumps down my body.

My eyebrows scrunch together. "What do you mean?"

"Every time I think you're finally going to admit what's happening between us, finally give in to the inevitable, you put your walls up and pull back," he tsks, biting his bottom lip as he leans his head closer, his forehead nearly touching mine.

His woodsy cologne mixed with the smell of his sweat fills my nose, and the combination of the two are so intoxicating, I want to bury my nose into his neck. I don't trust myself to speak, so instead I place the palms of my hands on his chest and push gently, hoping to put some space between us. Declan wraps his large hands around my wrists, keeping me in place. He adjusts one of my hands—the one with my wedding ring on it—so it sits directly on top of his heart. The gesture breaks me.

"D-Declan," I whisper, feeling the steady pulse of his heart.

"Say the words Zahra, and I'm yours. Say you want me. Say you *need* me. And I promise you, I'll spend every second of every day worshiping you." His voice has dropped as a heated look fills his eyes. My core clenches immediately as our wedding night replays in my mind. Back when we pretended the world outside us didn't exist. Pretended that everything was normal. God, I would give anything to relive that night again.

You can, the devilish voice inside my head whispers. *You can have it again.*

I can't. It's too risky. Too painful. As much as I want to deny it, Declan has already sneaked his way into my very being. The thought of losing him makes my stomach turn now. I know with absolute certainty that fully giving into him, giving into my desire to claim him as mine, will end in nothing but shattered hearts and broken dreams.

I jut my chin out in stubbornness. "You don't get to be a mob boss and have a happy ending. It's one or the other. And I refuse to give up everything I've ever worked for."

I wait for Declan's irritation, or rage. Wait for him to finally give up on me. "You don't have to give up either. You also can't deprive yourself of joy because you're scared of feeling pain. That's no way to live your life."

"I can handle pain just fine," I scoff.

"Physical pain, absolutely. But you refuse to let yourself feel any *emotional* pain. You try to shove it down and pretend it doesn't exist. You have to feel it. The pain, the sorrow, the grief. I tried to ignore it in the beginning, tried to ignore how much losing my father broke me. But it only made it worse."

His words repeat in my head. Over and over again. I know he's right, know that denying myself the time and space to *truly* grieve my father has only hardened me over time. But I'm scared... "I'm scared that if I let myself feel it, feel the grief, it will consume me. That I'll lose myself forever," I admit.

"I had the same fear. And I can't deny that in the beginning, it does feel all-consuming. But over time, the constant searing pain of losing someone turns more into an occasional throb. It doesn't go away, but it does feel less debilitating." Declan places a hand gently, but firmly, on the small of my back. Grounding me.

"How did you get it to hurt less?" I ask breathlessly, desperate for an answer.

Declan's eyes start to shine. "By allowing myself to feel it all, and remembering all the happy moments that I spent with my father. Remembering how much I loved him."

My throat constricts and the room feels like it's spinning as my vision blurs. I lose track of where I am in space and time, and I try my best to ground myself in the different sensations around me. My lips taste salty, and my wet cheeks are pressed against something warm and firm. Declan's scent fills my nose, and I feel him squeeze my waist with his arms. There's an incredibly irritating panting noise coming from the room, like someone is hyperventilating, and I flush when I realize *I'm* the one making those noises. I want nothing more than to crawl into my room and hide forever, but Declan keeps me firmly in place. With nowhere to go, I let myself think back to all my favorite moments with my father.

How we could code together for hours on the couch while my mom watched her soap operas. The way he always cried when I performed, rather poorly, at one of my elementary school musicals. The way he always told me he loved me before I went to bed—even when I was an angsty teenager and responded to these goodnight texts with a thumbs up. How much we used to laugh together. The way he adored my mother like she hung the moon herself. Is it possible for your heart to feel like it's being ripped into a hundred different pieces and stitched back together at the same time? That's how mine feels right now. And as much as it hurt...it's also the best I've felt in a long, long time.

35
DECLAN

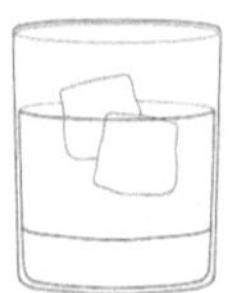

I lose track of how long Zahra falls apart in my arms. Her tears come thick and fast, not letting up once since she started. I temper down the impulse to say or do something other than just hold onto her. I would give her my words of comfort once her tears started to slow, but for now, she needs to feel it. Needs to get it all out. Her sobs are filled with pain, agony, and sadness. Each cry she lets out is followed by a deep breath. One that I can tell centers her, over and over again. Eventually, the sobs turn into sniffles, and I press my cheek to the top of her head.

"How are you feeling, love?"

"Like a complete mess." She laughs, wiping her cheeks with the back of her hand. "But also like the hole in my heart isn't as deep as it has been."

"Good. That's good." I curse myself for not being able to come up with anything beyond those small words, but Zahra doesn't seem to mind. "Can I ask what made you feel better?"

Her bottom lip trembles. "Thinking about my dad. All the

happy memories I had with him. I hate that he's not here with me now…"

"I know. No one can ever replace him." The same way nothing could ever replace my father.

"That's true. Though I have a strong feeling he would agree with you on one thing." Her lips twitch up, only the hint of a smile.

"Which is?"

"That I deserve to be happy. Even though he's no longer here to see it." She sniffles, putting on a brave face.

"You do. You deserve that and more. And when you forget it, I'm more than happy to remind you." I cup her face in my hands, relishing in the way she leans into my touch…and bracing myself for the inevitable moment she pulls back.

While Zahra has finally let some of her guards down, I know most of her walls are still in place. Still, I can't help but celebrate this win. She's finally let herself *feel*. Finally, she accepted that she doesn't have to be in a perpetual state of mourning and that she's not selfish for wanting to experience some joy in her life. Now all she has to do is act on it. Until she does, I will be here waiting. I'll only take what she offers. For as much as she says she's ready to live, she hasn't said the words I want to hear the most. That she wants to *live* with *me*.

Zahra stays in my embrace, and I'm convinced I could stand here forever. I have no idea whether it's been minutes or hours in our quiet bubble but eventually I hear a mix of voices yelling at each other outside the trainer's room. We separate immediately, a frown taking over my face, as we head back inside the gym.

Zahra and I freeze as we watch Azula grad Aidan by the neck and slam him against the mirror of the gym.

"Don't you *dare*, get started with me, Aidan. I'm not the

one who fucked up and let your shithead of an uncle get away," she spits, digging her sharpened nails into his skin.

"How many times do I have to tell you? He was already gone by the time I got there. *Now, let go of me,*" he growls the last bit through gritted teeth.

Zahra's eyes narrow, and in an instant, she turns back into a boss. "If you're trying to scare Azula, you have another thing coming. There's not a single thing in the world that throws Azula off a hunt. And that is exactly what she's doing now. Hunting down the man who tried to kill me, and anyone who gets in the way."

Aidan opens his mouth, but nothing comes out beyond a struggled gasp for air.

"Azula. Let him go," Zahra demands. Azula's lips peel back in a snarl as she releases Aidan, but not before giving him one final squeeze with the tips of her nails. Neither of us misses the way he winces in response.

"Have you ever considered putting a leash on your guard dog?" Aidan snaps uncharacteristically. Azula always manages to bring out his snarky side.

"Careful, Aidan, Azula's bite is much worse than her bark," Zahra warns. "So Lorkan was gone by the time you arrived?"

Aidan gives her a quick nod. "His entire estate was a ghost town. None of his groundskeepers or staff were around. I imagine someone tipped him off. The good news is that an empty estate means I was able to rummage through his office. His passports and emergency cash were all gone. I was able to find his phone though. I'm surprised he left it."

Aidan reaches into his pocket and pulls out Lorkan's phone, handing it to me so I can inspect it. "That seems like an incredibly reckless move. One that I doubt he would make, especially if he made sure his entire staff was also gone by the time you got there."

"Maybe it wasn't reckless. Maybe it was intentional," Zahra muses, taking the phone from me. "He probably figured I'd be able to hack into his phone and track him. Which would be a correct assumption. But maybe he still left something of value on this."

"You don't think he scrubbed it?" I ask.

"It's possible. But if he left in a rush, the odds are he did a sloppy job. So there may be some things I can salvage." Her eyebrows knit together as she stares at the phone with intense determination, like hacking into the phone will solve all our problems. I don't want to trample on any lingering hope she still has, but the news of my uncle's betrayal has rocked me to my core. Everything I knew was a lie. Except for Zahra. She has made it more than clear how she'll always be by my side.

"How long will it take you to crack it?" Azula asks.

"I don't know. Either way, we're still behind. Lorkan's gone and we have no idea where he is, who he's talking to, or who could be protecting him," Zahra groans, dragging a hand through her hair.

Instinctively, I place a hand on the small of her back and bring her closer to me. "We'll find him. Dead or alive. I promise you."

Zahra gives me a quick nod, but the tension in her body remains.

"Alive would be ideal. A quick death isn't a mercy he deserves. And I'll make sure that he pays for it." Azula sneers, voice laced with venom and rage.

Aidan's gaze flicks to mine and we exchange knowing looks. Whatever hell we were imagining Azula would bring down on our uncle likely pales into comparison to what she was thinking of now.

"Start with all of Lorkan's allies who would rather see him in charge than Declan. I wouldn't be surprised if he agreed to collaborate with the Italians or Russians in their trafficking routes in exchange for their help to put him in power," I order Azula and Aidan. The former looks at me skeptically but eventually agrees to my demand.

"Let's go, pretty boy. It's time to make up for your mistake of letting your uncle get away," Azula growls, not waiting to see if Aidan listens to her before exiting the room.

Aidan looks at me, incredulous.

I nod my head in the direction of the door. "Do as she says. And maybe try actually working with her instead of going at each other's throats. I have a feeling that if you two put aside whatever bullshit is going on between you, you'd find Lorkan in a matter of days. If not hours."

Aidan scoffs and rolls his eyes, but eventually he gives in, giving my shoulder a hard squeeze and Zahra a quick look of sorrow before following Azula. Not that my wife notices.

From the moment I handed Zahra my uncle's phone, she'd been inspecting it. I'm no hacker, but I doubt whatever she's really looking for will just magically appear on the surface of the phone. Still, she refuses to move. Refuses to have her eyes on anything else but the target in front of her, like a cheetah staying crouched behind blades of grass before finally going in for the kill.

I adjust my hand so it now sits on her hip instead of the small of her back, and give it a gentle but firm squeeze. My intentions are to snap her out of her trance, but I also can't help but notice how soft she is or how her breath hitches in response to my touch.

Zahra's eyes snap up to meet mine as her tongue peeks out and traces her pouty lips. She drops the hand that's holding the phone to her side and places her free hand on my chest, right on top of my heart. "I'm going to need time to hack into this phone."

"I know."

"We don't have time," Zahra says, exasperated. Desperate.

The urge to make her feel better overwhelms me. I tilt her chin up with my index finger, forcing her to look at me. "Zahra. So long as you are in this house, with me here, I promise you are safe. No one, not my uncle or his allegiance of vulture-doting morons, will lay a single finger on you. I will stand guard outside your door every second of the day, handcuff myself to you, or do whatever it is you need me to do so you'll feel safe."

Zahra's lips quirk up as her expression softens. "Handcuffs sound complicated, but I can't deny that I'm intrigued."

The flirtatious shift in her tone would have caught me off guard if not for the intimate moments we'd shared just a mere hour ago. I have no doubts that if Aidan and Azula hadn't burst our safe little bubble when they did, I would have confessed all my feelings to Zahra. How I wanted her to know that every-thing between us had been real for me. That I knew deep down, it'd been real for her too.

She leans into my touch for a moment, but nowhere near as long as I need. Cupping her chin in my palm, I bring her face closer until my lips brush against hers.

A soft whimper leaves her lips, and my desire to taste her is palpable. As is my frustration as she gives her head a shake, and pulls back from me. "I have to start working on cracking Lorkan's cellphone. My mind won't stop racing until I've made some progress."

The rational part of my mind is in agreement, but my cock is painfully strained against my pants, begging me not to listen. In the end, Zahra's look of determination is enough to call to my practical side. I sever any touch between us, knowing that the longer we stay close to each other, the less I'll be able to control myself I don't miss the lust in Zahra's eyes as she looks at me, or the clear quickening of her pulse as I lean in and whisper, "Soon, my sweet wife, you're going to lose all that control you have and let yourself take what you want. And when you do, I'll be more than ready to give it to you."

I walk away before I lose what small amount of composure I have left, relishing in the gasp that falls from her lips and the step she takes toward me as I leave.

36
DECLAN

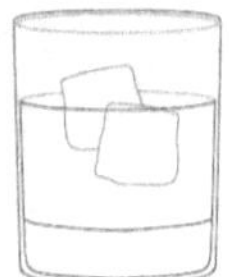

I knew Zahra's determination was boundless, but I didn't expect to only see her for a few minutes over the past three days despite living in the same house. If it wasn't for me bringing her meals and making sure she was drinking enough water, I likely wouldn't have seen her at all. The only good news is that Zahra was right—my uncle hadn't had time to wipe his phone as he frantically packed up his life and fucked off to who knows where.

The terminology and mechanics of what Zahra is doing are way beyond me, but from what I gathered, she was able to see that his phone was filled with various folders, notes, and text messages. The only problem is that everything on his phone is protected by a strong encryption that even Zahra is unfamiliar with. Which means one wrong attempt at cracking the code of my uncle's phone will likely trigger a series of protections that would delete everything we've been trying to get access to. Zahra has spent the past few days trying to identify any signatures from other hackers she'd encountered in the past, with the hopes that it would clue her into weaknesses. She hasn't had any success yet.

Just like I haven't had much success in convincing her not to stay up super late every night. Instead I always stopped by her office, wished her goodnight, and relished in the small moment she would set down her computer and smile up at me.

While I enjoy that Zahra has been accepting my help and letting me take care of her, the fact that I've only seen small glimpses of her the past few days is driving me crazy. Especially given the last time we talked, we were mere moments away from letting go of all our inhibitions and giving into our desires.

And after months of push and pull between us, I'm not sure how much longer I can remain patient before I snap and beg her to let me have my way. Because if it comes down to it, I will get on my knees and beg. Beg for her to let me in. Beg for her to let me taste her. Beg her to treat the union between us as a real marriage, because as far as I'm concerned it is.

Dragging my feet, I head to my bedroom and glare at the cold, empty bed that should be filled with Zahra's warmth. Every night that we've lived together, I've found myself having to ignore the devilish voice inside my head that yells at me to grab my wife and have her sleep beside me. Taking off my clothes, leaving only my boxers, I climb into bed and groan, knowing tonight will end the same as any other. With me sleeping alone.

———

I startle awake at the loud whooshing sound of the wind outside, as it causes a large tree branch to slam against my window. New England winters are notorious for being long and brutal and this year is no different. Still, I can't recall the last time I'd actually been woken up by some of the chaos outside. Perfect. I've always struggled to fall asleep once woken, so I have no doubts tonight will be long.

I flop back in fourth in my bed, trying—and failing—to find a spot that's so comfortable it will magically put me back to sleep. Fucking perfect. I'm barely sleeping as it is with the entire world imploding around me. This is the last thing I need.

I'm not typically one to self-medicate with alcohol, but at this rate, I'll try anything if it helps me get back to sleep.

Standing outside my office, I begin to type in the password on the keypad so I can enter, when I realize the doors are already unlocked. My guard goes up in an instant and my hand instinctively goes to the gun that I tucked away in the back of my boxers when I left my room. My mother used to always say my father was being paranoid when he refused to be anywhere, including his own bedroom, without at least some protection, but I always thought it was smart. You never know who will come for you. Or when. Best to have your guards up at all times.

Using the barrel of my gun to push the door open, I step inside my office. From what I can see, everything is still in place, and for a moment, I swear I hear my mother's voice now calling me paranoid. And maybe I am. Maybe I had forgotten to lock my office door. That would be an uncharacteristic move, but I can't say I've been acting much like myself lately, regardless.

Still, something feels off, so I head straight for my computer, logging on to the livestream of security cameras around the perimeter of the cottage house. All of our staff are in place and ready for anything, easing some of the tension in my stomach.

Shifting my attention to the various cameras inside the house, I flip through the different rooms. My eyes start to feel heavy and I'm about to call it quits until I land on the final livestream footage. One that gives me a full view of Zahra's bedroom.

My throat dries and any hope I have of talking myself out of looking away and giving her some privacy goes out the window as I'm graced with a sight that makes my cock turn rock solid. Zahra's laying in the center of her bed in nothing but a silk robe parted down the middle. But that's not all. My sweet wife's legs are spread wide open as she works her glistening pussy with a vibrator, taking turns sliding it inside and toying with her clit.

Before I can even think twice, I move the mouse to the audio and turn it up as loud as it will go. In an instant, her hot pants and moans fill the room, and I feel like precum leaking out of my dick.

"Yes, yes. Just like that. Fuck me just like that," she moans and a hot wave of jealousy comes over me. Who the fuck is she thinking about while getting herself off? She better pray I never find out because if I do, I'll kill them with my bare hands.

"Declan," she moans, and time stands still. I'm convinced I imagined the whole thing as I watch her increase the intensity of her vibrator and draw torturous circles on her clit when she pants, "Declan, please. Let me come. I need to come. I need you."

I need you. The words I'd been so desperate to hear from her lips. The words that confirmed everything I know deep down —she is mine. And now I get to show her exactly how well I take care of what is mine.

Pacing down the hall, I head straight for her room, knowing that nothing and no one can stop me from what I've set my mind on. Tonight will end with me feeling her slick cunt squeeze every last drop of my come from my cock while she begs for more, and I give it to her.

My hand wraps around her doorknob, and an instant later, I'm met with Zahra's wide eyes and panting breath. I pause in the middle of the doorway, waiting for her to freeze in shock or yell at me to leave.

Instead, she spreads her legs wider and moans, "What took you so long?"

37
ZAHRA

"What took you so long?" I moan, moving the vibrator slightly off my clit so I don't come without Declan's permission. Although a part of me wants to, just to see if he'd punish me for it.

His eyebrows knit together, definitely confused by my calm demeanor to him walking in on me getting myself off.

I turn the vibrator off so I can form a full sentence. "I hacked into your private security account a few nights ago to ensure you had the best view of my bedroom. Though I had hoped you'd be more neurotic about checking security cameras. I figured either you weren't watching or you weren't interested—"

Declan lets out a growl and gestures to his hard cock. "Does this look like I'm not interested?"

My core clenches in response and I can't stop the moan that falls from my lips. He's still standing in my doorway, entirely too far for me to be able to touch him, and yet somehow he's managed to light up my whole body.

"You said you needed me," Declan states, his voice at least two octaves lower than usual.

"I did."

"Did you mean it?" he asks, a hint of vulnerability in his voice.

"I did. I do. I need you, Declan. Your body, your heart. Need it like I need my next breath." I swallow hard as I let myself have something for once.

"You have me. All of me. I'm yours," Declan declares, stepping fully into my room and locking the door behind him. "And you have no idea how desperate I am to show you how much you own me."

Declan moves so he's kneeling on my bed, as his eyes trail down my body and his hands search through the sheets for my vibrator. "Do you remember our safe word, love?"

Goosebumps cover my whole body. "It's 'rose.'"

Declan's pupils dilate. "Good girl."

My back arches as he turns on my vibrator and hovers it mere inches from my core. "D-Declan, please," I beg.

"Please, what, Zahra? I won't lay a single finger on you until I have your consent." His voice is firm, and it grounds me. It's clear that even though Declan's a Dom, I still have power in this situation.

"Use me, Declan. Make me come so many times I lose count. Show me what it means to be yours."

A deep shudder runs through his body, and I can see his restraint dwindling by the second.

The temperature of the room shifts as he asks me, "Pick a number five through twenty."

I blink. Of all the things he could have said... "What?"

"Since it's our first time together, I've decided to let you pick how many times I make you orgasm tonight. Anything less than five is unacceptable to me. And I have a feeling we need to build your stamina up, so twenty seems like a fair cut off."

He can't be serious. Can he? There's no way I can come that many times. The fact that he made me come twice on our wedding night felt nothing short of a miracle. The rational part of my brain says I should play it safe, but the heat building inside me wants to please Declan. To show him I'm not afraid.

"Let's start with ten. If you can even get me there." I'm poking the bear and I know it.

"Don't be a brat." Declan's eyes turn into slits, and I gasp as he slaps my pussy. The slight sting to my core is followed by a blossoming heat all over my body.

His hands move to my hips, and he moves me up the bed until my head is resting on the pillow. He crushes his lips to mine, and my mouth opens for him instinctively, desperate to taste him.

Declan hums in approval as I drag my nails down his back and claw him closer to me. His hands trail down my hips, to my thighs, until he cups the back of my knees and spreads them wide. "Don't move," he orders before sliding off the bed and disappearing into my closet.

"Where are you going?" I pant, feeling my arousal drip down my thighs. The only response I get in return is the sound of dresser doors opening and closing.

I debate reaching for my vibrator and getting myself off, but before I make up my mind, Declan returns holding a bunch of different scarves in his hand.

"Yes," I state.

"I haven't even asked a question yet." He smirks.

"I trust you. With my whole heart." The words fall from my lips with ease.

Declan swallows hard as he blinks away the watery sheen in his eyes. "You are an angel on earth. Sent down just for me."

He slides onto the bed, kneeling above me as he grabs my ankle and wraps the smooth silk around it, tying me to the side of the bed frame. My other ankle gets the same treatment, and before I know it, my legs are fully stuck in place.

"Fuck, Zahra, look at your swollen cunt. It's practically begging for me to taste it," Declan moans, palming his hard cock through his boxers, and he looks at me with such...devotion in his eyes.

"You'd be the first to try," I confess.

Declan's jaw drops open, the look in his eyes is feral. "No one's ever eaten you out before?"

I shake my head.

"Good. Less men I have to worry about hunting down and killing." He kneels down in front of my core and places a rough kiss right onto my clit.

My hips buck, desperate to increase the pressure, but the restraints keep me locked in place. I'm completely at Declan's mercy.

"Don't stop," I beg.

"Don't worry, love, I promise you'll come on my tongue tonight, but first we need to finish what you started." Declan smirks, grabbing my small bullet vibrator I had abandoned the moment he walked through the door.

Pressing the toy to clit, he turns it on and my body lights up with pleasure. "Jesus, love, look at how soaked this little thing gets you. You're coating my fingers and we haven't even hit your favorite setting yet."

I open my mouth, ready to ask him how he would even know that when he clicks the button on the side, a rough moan leaving my lips.

"Ah, there she is. My sweet wife is so close to coming, isn't she?" Declan asks, using his free hand to toy with my nipples, adding the perfect blend of pleasure and pain.

The pressure building in my core has me seeing stars and tears start to form in my eyes. "Declan, I need to come. Can I? Please?" I moan, reaching for his hand that's so expertly moving the toy along my pussy.

"Such a good girl, asking for my permission. Let go, my sweet wife. Let go," he hums. My vision starts to blur, and I swear I see stars. Declan increases the pressure on my core as my muscles tense and my back arches, bliss rocking through my entire body as his words send me fully over the edge, no doubt soaking his hand even more. Just when I think I've come down, the tension builds again, and I realize that Declan hasn't moved the vibe off me. Before I can muster up the energy to say something, I fall apart for a second time.

My bedroom is filled with the sound of my pants, while Declan caresses my face and praises me for coming twice.

He unties me from the bed and cradles me into his arms, gently massaging the small of my back. "Two down. Eight more to go," he pauses to press a kiss to my shoulder, "but only if you're up for it. Remember, you can use your safe word whenever you want. I won't be upset if you do."

I lift my cheek up from his shoulder and lock eyes with him. "I want to keep going. Especially if the orgasms come with a side of cuddling."

Declan cups my chin, using his thumb to draw idle circles on my cheek. "I'll give you a bath after as well. And anything else you need to come back down. Last thing I want is for you to think I'm only here to be with you physically. Making you come has been nothing short of a dream, but it's more than that for me."

His hand slides down my neck, to my bare chest, and rests on top of my heart.

I place my hand on his. "I know, Declan. It's more than that for me too."

"Good. Now that we've got that settled, do you want my fingers, cock, or another one of your toys inside you next?" He adjusts me slightly in his lap so the tip of his very pierced cock brushes against my clit.

My mouth waters and I moan before I can even think to stop myself.

"That wasn't an answer, Zahra. Use your words, my love." Declan snickers, clearly enjoying his effect on me.

"Your cock, Declan. I want it buried so deep inside me I'll feel you for days. And when you're done, I want you to fill me up with your come until it drips out of me," I confess one of my deepest desires. My heart races, waiting for his judgment or his refusal.

Instead, his jaw falls open, hands twitching at his sides like he's fighting himself for whatever small bit of control he has left. "Are you sure you know what you're asking for? Because once I come inside you, I don't think I can have you any other way again."

His words are a promise. One I plan on making sure he keeps. "I'm sure. I have an IUD, and tested negative recently."

"I'm also negative. I haven't thought of anyone since the day we met. You've consumed every single inch of my mind and my heart." Declan presses his forehead against mine.

"You're mine, Declan McAlister. Even when I denied myself, deep down I knew the truth. You are mine."

"You own me. Now it's time for me to show you how grateful I am to be yours."

38
DECLAN

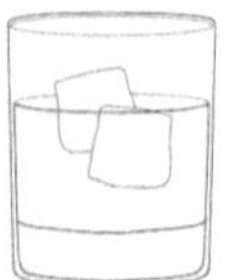

I grip Zahra's hips, relishing how perfectly soft she feels in my hands. Her body molds into mine instantly as I bring us flush against each other. An electric pulse that trickles down my spine lifting her onto me, as I use the wetness of her pussy to coat my cock until it's perfectly lubed and ready for her. I'd dreamed about this very moment nearly every night since we first met, and none of those dreams compared to the sensation of teasing her cunt with the tip of my cock.

Her nails dig into my shoulders, hips bucking and begging for more. Begging for *me*. "Declan, stop denying me," she pants, eyes filled with desire.

"Why should I? You've been denying me, denying *us*, from the moment we met. I think it's only fair I pay back some of the torture you've put me through." I jolt my hips forward so I'm halfway buried inside her, and groan as I feel her hot core grip me hard. Jesus. I was at complete odds with myself. Part of me wanted to drag this out as long as I could. Teasing and punishing her. Another part of my brain screamed at me for dragging this on longer. In the end, I give in to the magnetic pull between us, lifting her hips slightly off me, before fully sinking inside her.

Zarha's back arches immediately, her screams of pleasure filling the room. Despite her moans and pants for more, her eyebrows knit together in frustration.

"What is it, angel?" I ask, following with a harsh kiss on her neck.

"It feels *so* good, but I can't get myself fully there. It's so annoying," she groans, dragging a hand across her face.

I slow down my movements, leaving my cock buried inside her. "You came twice a few minutes ago. What was different then?"

Whatever she needed from me, I would do it.

"I...don't know. My mind felt clear. Empty. I wasn't thinking about anything beyond how good you were making me feel. But now my mind's racing. About whether you're enjoying this, whether I can make you happy by coming again." She gasps as I instinctually buck my hips into her.

"You are so. Fucking. Perfect," I growl, unable to contain myself. "I want you to focus on all the sensations you're feeling right now, and let go of whatever's holding you back. Let me take care of you, Zahra. It's all I want to do."

I start toying with her clit, relishing how she writhes in ecstasy. Keeping my eyes locked on her, I see the exact moment she decides to give in. The exact moment she descends into submission. She squeezes the hell out of my cock, and lets another orgasm wash over her. The shocked look in her eyes nearly results in my own release. Worrying her lip between her teeth, she moans, "Dear God."

"You might be an angel, love, but I promise I'm no God. So, if you're going to scream anything while your sweet pussy milks my cock, I'll let you pick between 'Declan' or 'my husband'."

I jerk my hip slightly, letting my dick get used to how fucking good she feels around me, how much she feels like *mine*, and giving her a second to catch her breath.

"Husband," she purrs, lips curving into a smile.

"Your husband," I emphasize, shifting us so she's laid out on the bed, moving carefully so I remain inside her. She gasps as I slide in and out of her at a torturously slow rate. "Your husband, who needs you to keep count of how many times I make you come. Out loud. Or else I'll stop."

She shakes her head while lacing her legs around my hips and locking her ankles to keep me in place. "Don't stop, please, please, don't stop, Declan."

Fuck, it's hot seeing her beg like this. My cock pulses inside her as she bucks her hips in an attempt to get some extra friction. My hands go to her waist, holding her in place. "Count Zahra, or I won't give you what you want."

"Three. You've made me come three times so far," she pants, trailing a hand down her chest and a wicked idea pops into my head.

"Good girl, now why don't we keep going?" I ask, adjusting the angle of my hips and increasing my tempo as I continue to thrust in and out. Zahra's back arches off the bed as my piercing scrapes over her G-spot, and the pants falling from her lips clue me in to how close she is to falling over the edge.

I break apart from her just as she's about to come, and slide off the bed.

Zahra's eyes are locked on me, mouth wide open. "Where are you going?"

"I need something," I state, eyes shifting around the room. Where would she hide—

"The only thing you need is to bring your ass back to bed and take care of me," she whines, tugging at my wrist.

"So impatient," I tsk, reaching for the drawer of her nightstand, pulling it open, and unveiling various vibrators and dildos. "My naughty little wife," I hum in approval, shuffling through her sex toys until I find one that meets my standards. "I should punish you for not letting me watch while you use these," I warn.

"I'm sure there's some footage I can dig up if you're interested." She juts her chin toward the hidden camera in her mirror.

Possession fills my chest. "You better make sure those videos are beyond secure. Or else I'll have to go around gouging people's eyes out for seeing you that way."

A rush of chills run down her body, and her nipples peak. So, she likes it when I get possessive? I'll keep that in mind for the future.

I continue rummaging through her drawers, when I finally make up my mind and pull out the rose-shaped toy with an extended bud in the middle resembling a tongue.

Zahra swallows hard, eyes filled with lust, as I climb back on the bed and gently push her knees to her chest. I guide my cock to her center, dragging my pierced tip up and down her clit.

"*Fuck*, Declan, that feels so good," Zahra groans, hands clawing into the sheets as her eyes close.

"Look at me, Zahra," I order, waiting patiently until her eyes meet mine. "Give me one of your hands, love."

She listens immediately, holding out her left hand. I take a second to admire the wedding band on her finger. *Mine.*

"I want you to hold this toy on your clit while I fuck you. Can you do that for me?"

Zahra nods, taking the toy from me, turning it on, and placing it directly on her sensitive bud. Her eyes flutter close, but she manages to open them again, as if she already knew I was going to ask her to look at me.

"You're so perfect," I moan, sliding the tip of my cock into her entrance. Sinking myself in fully, I grip her chin. "You don't come until I tell you too. Do you understand?"

I feel her wetness drip onto the bed as she nods. "Yes, Declan, yes. Now, can you please fuck me already?" she whines.

Her wish is my command. I grind my hips, letting my cock find her sweet g-spot, and when I hear the familiar gasp leave her mouth, my mind goes laser-focused. Any restraint snaps as I buck my hips like a madman, thrusting in and out of her hard. Zahra matches the pace of my cock with the toy in her hand as she tortures her own clit.

I lean down until my lips are hovering over her ear. "You are taking me so fucking well. My sweet wife playing with her clit while I fuck her pussy. Such a good girl, letting me decide when she comes," I praise, quickening my pace.

"Declan, I don't think I can hold on much longer," Zahra whimpers, using her free hand to dig her nails into my back.

"Oh, you will, love. I haven't given you permission to come yet," I moan, taking one of her nipples into my mouth, feeling her body hum underneath me.

"Please, Declan, please," she begs, tears starting to form in her eyes as she denies herself.

"I know how incredibly strong you are, Zahra. You can do anything you set your mind to," my words make her beam with pride, "which is exactly why I want to test your limits."

I pull my cock out of her in an instant, immediately missing the sensation and warmth of having her fully wrapped around me. Zahra's expression is a mix of dumbstruck and livid, as she glares at me in frustration. She opens her mouth, likely to yell at me, but I silence her with a scorching kiss, letting our tongues collide as I slowly guide her down onto the bed so she's on top of me.

"Sneaky little devil," I chide as she attempts to slide herself down on my cock. "Did I tell you to ride me?" I smack her ass hard, causing her to gasp and jolt.

"N-No. But I need you, Declan," she pants, clawing her nails into my chest in desperation.

"And you'll have me. Exactly how I want you too," I warn, letting my Dom come out.

Her eyes widen as she nods. "Yes, sir."

My entire body hums with satisfaction. "Turn around and place that hot pussy on my tongue."

Zahra swallows hard, chills running down her body. "W-what?"

"Did I stutter?" I grip her lush hips, lifting her off me.

"No."

"No, what?" I press.

"No, sir. You didn't stutter," Zahra breathes, sitting up and exposing her hard nipples.

"Then why is my tongue not buried in your sweet cunt yet?" I click my tongue in disapproval.

Zahra responds by *finally* getting into position. Her thighs hover above both sides of my face until I extend my tongue and lick her entrance. She loses all her restraint, sitting fully on my tongue, while moaning, "*Declan*, fuck."

I lift her for a moment so I can say, "Take my cock into your mouth while I eat your delicious cunt. And don't come until I give you permission."

Her sweet mouth is around me in an instant. She uses her tongue to play with my piercing, and I swear I see stars. I need to contain myself before I come too quickly. Thankfully, I had the perfect thing to distract myself. I suckle Zahra's swollen clit between my lips, drawing a loud moan that sends vibrations up my cock.

Zahra and I moan together as my precum leaks and she

licks it up with her tongue, and I reward her by sliding my tongue inside her again, lapping up every last drop. I brush against her G-spot and mercilessly stroke it, all while pinching her clit between my fingers. Her wetness trickles down my chin, and I know she's close. Dangerously close. "You want to come, Zahra?"

She practically sobs, mouth still wrapped around me.

"Then let go. Let go." I suck harshly on her clit, feeling her dip her nails into my thighs, marking me.

Her scream fills the room and no doubt makes it down the hallway. I can't bring myself to even care. In case there was any doubt before now, everyone would know Zahra was mine.

"That's four, Declan." She smiles for a second before closing her eyes. I adjust us so she's under me, and I can suck on her breasts. A few minutes later, I feel her nails dig into my neck. She groans. "No...no."

I halt all of my movements. She hasn't said her safe word, but I need to make sure I'm not pushing her too far. "Do you want me to stop, Zahra?"

Zahra shakes her head vehemently. "No. That's not what I meant. Don't stop."

I make no move to continue. "Are you sure?"

"I was saying 'no' because I didn't want to come again without you filling me with your cum. I need you, Declan. I need all of you."

Electricity runs down my spine, and I thrust fully inside her before I take my next breath. She's so damn wet, and pliant, and *mine*. "Mine," I growl, grinding my cock inside her, desperate to feel her squeeze me again. Driving myself harder, harder, and harder against her until—

"Fuck, I'm coming again. Declan, please come with me, please, oh, baby, pleaaase..." Zahra moans so deep I feel it in my bones, and I finally let go. All I see is stars as I let rope after rope of cum fill up her tight cunt.

"That's right, my love. Take it, take all of it," I moan, cradling her into my arms, as I slowly grind into her. I needed every last drop to be buried deep inside her. Needed her to know how much she belonged to me.

"Five," Zahra hums in sweet content, nuzzling her cheek against my chest, until I finally come to my senses and realize I'm probably crushing her.

I gently press my lips to her forehead and roll us so we're both on our sides. The movement causes my cock to slide out and I'm fixated on the way my cum leaks out of her. On instinct, I reach down between her thighs and slide it back inside her, cupping her pussy with my hand so it remains.

"Mmm, is it bad that I find that super hot?" Zahra exhales, tucking her head under my chin.

"Nope. It just shows how perfect we are together, because the thought of you being filled with my cum is making me hard again."

"You're insatiable." She laughs, drawing idle patterns on my chest.

"When it comes to you? Absolutely."

"Well, I suppose I'm no better. I can't feel my legs anymore and I'm so hungry I could eat a large pizza by myself, and yet I still want more of you." Zahra does her best to stifle her yawn but I can see how exhausted she is.

"Maybe demanding I give you ten orgasms was a bit ambitious. I know you haven't been getting much sleep lately."

"Backing down from a challenge, are we? That doesn't sound like you," she teases, trailing her hand down to my abdomen, stopping right above my crotch. Tempting me.

"First of all, I should punish you for even suggesting I'm giving up—"

"How would you punish me?"

"By not letting you come for a week."

Her pouty lips fall open. "That's cruel."

"You are excellent for my ego, sweet wife." I snicker as she rolls her eyes. "Second of all, I just want to make sure you're okay. I know you didn't use your safe word, but this is all new...and I hate the idea that I'd scare you away," I confess.

"I appreciate you wanting to look out for me, but I'm a big girl who can handle myself. I'll give you a pass this time since you're being so sweet." She leans forward and nips my bottom lip with her teeth.

"Understood. Now, why don't I get us something to snack on and we finish what we started?" I offer, sliding off the bed and taking a sheet to wrap around my waist.

Zahra stretches her arms, flashing me her perfect, full tits. "Don't take too long, or else I'll have to get started again on my own." She winks, letting out a sexy little chuckle as I run out of her bedroom toward the kitchen.

39
ZAHRA

"Would you stop shooting daggers at me, Maura? I told you I have no idea who broke your favorite bowl. I just came in to inspect it once I heard a crash downstairs." Connor throws his hands up in defense.

"You're going to have to learn how to lie better working for the mafia, Son. I caught you red-handed," she spits, dumping a burnt piece of toast on his plate and storming back into the kitchen.

"Damn, the last time I pissed Maura off that bad, she gave me burned food for weeks. You better start sneaking in some takeout," Aidan warns, diving into his immaculate breakfast.

"I swear on my life it wasn't me!" Connor exhausts.

"I believe you, Connor," Declan has the nerve to speak up, knowing the truth of what happened.

After Declan had left last night to get us a snack in the middle of my journey of having ten orgasms in one night, I had lasted all of two minutes before I decided he was taking way too long. Before I had time to think, I threw on a robe and followed him downstairs.

To my absolute delight, I actually managed to startle him, causing Declan to jump nearly a foot in the air. I laughed so hard, it came out as an incredibly horrendous-sounding snort. Declan warned me that if I didn't stop laughing, he'd make me pay for it.

Naturally, that only made me laugh harder, and the next thing I knew, he had me bent over the kitchen island, using one hand to support my hip as he thrust his cock into me and the other hand to cover my mouth as I moaned and pleaded for more. Somewhere between my seventh and eighth orgasm, I reached for something to grab onto and instead managed to knock over Maura's favorite bowl.

Declan immediately threw me over his shoulder and carried me back to our room before we were caught. The rest is history. I've tried to speak every time Maura started on her tirade this morning, but each time Declan would give my knee a squeeze and whisper in my ear, "She can't know the reason why one of her prized possessions is lost is because I couldn't control my hormones around my wife. I would never live it down."

And so here I am acting none the wiser while poor Connor gets the cold shoulder from Maura.

I'm on the verge of confessing when Azula speaks up about more important matters. "We may not have been able to catch Lorkan, but we did get some good intel. One of our troops out in Turkey claimed to see Lorkan sauntering around Istanbul."

My eyebrows shoot up. "That feels especially reckless given our close ties with the Turkish mafia. Don Demir always supported my father growing up. Though I admittedly haven't heard much from him since I came into power."

I try not to sound bitter, but my father assured me Don Demir would come to my aid if I ever needed it. *'When the time comes, he'll be on our side. The side of progress. I know it.'*

"I suppose I can't be too surprised that the Turkish haven't contacted us. It's not like we've made our hit on Lorkan public while we search for him," Declan reassures me.

Neither of us wanted one of our over-zealous allies to kill him before we could get some answers, or risk our enemies teaming up with him against us.

"Even if you did, I'm not sure how much of a difference it would make." Aidan pinches the bridge of his nose.

"And why's that?" I ask.

"Lorkan is under Don Demir's protection." Azula sends a tense look to Aidan, whose gaze has fallen to his brother.

"So, we'll call Demir and tell him to make sure Lorkan stays put until we get there. Then we collect him," Declan states, looking eager to enact the plan he just laid out.

"I don't think that will be possible," Azula says, pulling up a photo on her phone and sliding the device over to me.

My heart stills as I process what's in front of me. An image of Lorkan and Demir sparring in the gym, shirtless.

A vulture covers Demir's chest.

"Motherfucker," Declan growls, slamming his fist on the table.

My heart sinks to my stomach, throat tightening and making it difficult to breathe. Clenching my hands into fists, the sharp edges of my nails digging into the flesh of my palm, grounds me. Pain I was used to feeling. Pain I knew how to handle. Betrayal is still a new emotion, one that made me feel like my organs were being ripped out of my chest. An emotion that I need to channel into rage and vengeance.

"I knew my reign as boss would be hard for some to swallow, but it appears we have deeply underestimated how many people would turn their backs on us, simply because they're afraid of working with me." The sharpness of my voice could cut through stone.

Azula protests, "No one has tried to denounce you after the statement you made at the charity banquet—"

"Yet. No one has tried to denounce me *yet*. We assumed it was because they had accepted me after I showed how fit I am for this role. And maybe for some Dons, like Aleksander, that is true. But for others, it appears their quietness is not due to their support but because they're plotting against me," I summarize, feeling Declan shake with rage next to me. I'm sure he also came to a similar conclusion once he saw the photo of Demir and Lorkan.

"The time for being discreet has passed. We must act now," Declan seethes.

"I understand your rage at this moment, but maybe we should all take a deep breath before we make any hasty decisions. The last thing we need is a war between all the major Mafia families in the world." Aidan, surprisingly, serves as a voice of reason.

"I refuse to hide and cower while my wife continues to be attacked. Her safety is my number one concern," Declan growls, wrapping a large hand around my thigh.

Whatever rational thinking Aidan had goes out the window when he says, "Maybe it would be best for Zahra's own safety if she takes a back seat for a while and lets us handle it. You can run the Irish and the Persians until some of the heat on us cools off—"

"Over my dead fucking body!" I grit through my teeth.

At the same time, Declan reaches over the table and grabs his brother by the collar. In this moment, it's not Declan facing his younger brother; it's Declan McAlister, the boss of the Irish mafia, reprimanding his second in command. "If you ever speak of such treason again, I will remove you from your post and exile you to the barracks back in Cork."

"I didn't mean any disrespect—"

"Stop talking, Aidan. I will not ask you again." Declan tightens his grip on Aidan's shirt.

I wrap my arm around Declan's bicep and squeeze. "Let him go, Declan. I'm sure by now, Aidan has realized he misspoke and is remorseful." I eye Aidan, hoping for his sake he goes along with it. Declan loves his brother more than anything but he still has a reputation and expectations he has to follow as a boss. The last thing I wanted to see was Declan hating himself for the punishment he'd have to deal out to his brother.

Azula sneers. "You're lucky your brother and my boss are kind and considerate rulers. If it was up to me, I'd slit your throat right now for even suggesting Zahra step down from her rightful position."

"Are you always this bloodthirsty? I can't believe Zahra lets you loose without anyone to monitor you," Aidan clips in response.

Azula's grip tightens around her fork, eyes narrowing on Aidan's neck before she drops it on the table dramatically. A warning.

I refocus our attention. "We need to move quick. Declan, how fast can all your core members come together for an emergency family meeting?"

"Everyone we need is here in the city." Declan looks to Aidan, then Connor.

"Then we'll all convene tonight at the main mansion."

Aidan swallows hard, tersely scratching his neck. "You're calling in both of our inner circles?"

"My life has nearly been taken more times than I want to admit in the past few months. Our fathers' lives were taken before that. If anything, it was idiotic not to include them sooner. Idiotic to underestimate how big a threat Lorkan truly is."

It was also idiotic to believe my father's allies would be more inclined to side with me. Our family has always been a powerful threat, and with me at the helm, I represent something equally as impactful as fear. Progress.

"Azula, can you contact Aleksander? See if he can be in attendance somehow," I order, wondering how long it will take until Declan protests the idea.

He lasts less than ten seconds. "Why the hell do you want him involved in all of this?"

Declan casts a possessive look over me, and I have no doubt his logical side is being clouded by a mix of jealousy and whatever alpha male instincts he has that are screaming at him to protect me.

I place my hand on top of his, the one he's had wrapped around my thigh for the entirety of this meal, and give it a gentle squeeze. "Because there's something bigger that I still think we're missing. And Aleksander has been the first person to give us a lead that wasn't a dead end. He's not as attached to what's at stake, so maybe he can tell us what we're missing and look at things with fresh eyes."

Leaning forward, I press my forehead against his. "I love you, but we're both in over our heads now. Aleksander has proven himself to be useful so far. Let's see how much more he can give us."

Declan's eyes shut as he inhales deeply. "Fine. I'll do whatever it takes to protect you."

"As will I."

40
DECLAN

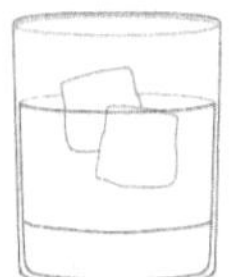

The last time I was in this room, I put a bullet through my uncle's knee for insulting Zahra. Now, I'm sitting next to the entirety of the Irish and Persian inner circle as we plot how to end Lorkan once and for all.

"I just don't understand why you didn't tell us sooner. We could have had thousands of men across the world scouring for Lorkan. His head would have been on a pike in minutes." Cyrus slams his hand on the table in frustration.

Zahra does her best to hide her flinch, but I still catch it. My hand immediately grabs the Glock tucked into my pants. That would be the first and last time he made her upset.

"I'm sure you would have loved to be the one to catch him and put an end to things, Cyrus," Aidan snarls, shooting daggers across the table.

Aidan had started having a lot of uncharacteristic outbursts lately especially where Cyrus was involved. The two were never fond of each other, Cyrus would also complain about my brother being a bratty kid, resulting in Aidan receiving even more lectures from my disappointed father. The tension between them appears to worsen over time.

My brother put on a front of being carefree and that nothing bothered him, but I knew the truth. For as much evil Lorkan has done, he always tried to shield Aidan from our father's disappointment. When I first declared Lorkan had been exiled from our mafia, Aidan hadn't fully processed the reality. Now that I was calling for our uncle to be brought to us for his execution...I'm sure reality has started to sink in for Aidan.

"We did send a soldier to keep an eye on Lorkan—" I defend.

"A low-level soldier who was compromised. Zahra informed me that you received a package containing his severed head yesterday," Cyrus spits.

"Arguing among ourselves isn't going to help our cause. We need a united front. Everyone needs to be on the same page," Arman warns, eyeing Cyrus.

"If your family meetings are always this lively, I hope to be invited to more. You can't write a family drama this good." Aleksander snickers from his corner of the room.

To my immense displeasure, Aleksander not only agreed to attend this meeting but also flew in from New York to attend it in person. The only reason why I haven't choked him with my bare hands yet is because Zahra has had entwined our fingers this entire time.

"If you'd like to make it through this meeting, I recommend keeping your comments to a minimum. While we appreciate your allyship, Aleksander, you are here to provide the intel you have gathered thus far about Lorkan's ongoing travels. And nothing more," Zahra warns.

He responds by putting his hands up in mock surrender.

"So, what's our plan of attack?" Cyrus asks, eyeing Zahra.

"We take a plane to Turkey. At least a hundred soldiers with us, and our generals. There's a thousand already waiting for us in Istanbul. We demand to speak to Don Demir and don't take no for an answer. I'm tired of taking the timid approach to being a boss. If blood needs to be shed, then so be it."

"You're talking about bringing war to one of your biggest allies," Aidan protests.

"I'm talking about bringing war to one of *my father's* biggest allies. An ally who has chosen to harbor a man who has tried to kill me multiple times, and nearly killed his own nephew in the process." Zahra gives him a look so lethal that I can see him visibly shake.

Azula speaks in Zahra's defense. "Once we show Don Demir the evidence we've collected against Lorkan, he will either have to hand him over or enter a war with us, which I doubt his inner circle will support. We control nearly all of their trade routes."

"Doesn't Don Demir have the same tattoo as Lorkan? Which means he's probably on his side? What makes you think the two won't come up with some bogus story on how they got matching tattoos in Vegas to cover up their betrayal?" Aidan brings up a good point.

"Zahra's continued to make progress on Lorkan's phone. Once she hacks into his phone, there will be an endless pile of evidence that indicates his guilt. Demir will be forced to submit to us, or risk a fight with our mafias." I challenge.

"Phone?" Cyrus inquires, raising an eyebrow at Zahra. "You have Lorkan's phone? Why didn't you mention this?"

She sighs, pinching the bridge of her nose between her fingers. "Because, despite my best efforts, I still haven't been able to crack it, so it's practically useless. I've wasted enough time already, hoping the phone would provide me with some sort of miracle. But we can't wait any longer. We need to act."

Cyrus looks at me, assessing, as if he's waiting for me to talk Zahra down, waiting for me to speak over her. I do neither. "Zahra has my full support. And the support of my men."

"Then we go to war," Azula states bluntly.

Cyrus shifts his focus to Zahra. "We go to war."

41
ZAHRA

"For the record, I hate this plan," Declan protests for the hundredth time.

"You're going to be following behind us the whole time. It's like we'll be together." I place a hand on his chest, knowing my words will do little to assuage him.

"But we will be separated, which is a giant problem in my book." He juts his lip out in a pout. Because even mafia Dons get pouty when they don't get their way. "Remind me why I can't be the one who comes with you?"

"Because after all of your brother's protests, I realized he was right. We should at least give Don Demir some sort of benefit of the doubt before we go in guns blazing and ruin our alliance with the Turkish. Cyrus was by my father's side when he initially signed a contract indicating the terms of our alliance, and has continued negotiations with them since, so he'll hopefully be able to butter Demir up and convince him to hand Lorkan over. "

"And if he doesn't..." Declan brings me flush to his chest and uses a hand to toy with the chain of my necklace.

"And if he doesn't, you'll be right there, listening to the conversation so you know when exactly to send backup. If we have to go through with Plan B, then we'll hold everyone in his inner circle captive until he gives in. Which he will."

"There's nothing I can do to change your mind, is there?" Declan sighs, placing his large hand on top of mine and holding it to his heart.

I shake my head. "No, but I'm pretty sure my stubbornness is one of your favorite things about me," I tease.

He rolls his eyes while Cyrus approaches us. "Zahra, our plane is ready. Declan, yours is also set and awaiting your boarding."

We decided it would be best for Cyrus and me to travel in a smaller private plane to eliminate any suspicions of our ill intent. Declan, Azula, Aidan, Connor, and the rest of our soldiers will travel in our classic jet, flying a slightly different route so it doesn't look like Cyrus and I are flying in with a militia. They'd land an hour or so after us, and hopefully by the time they do, Lorkan will be in our clutches and ready to be transported back home, where he'll get the punishment he deserves.

Standing up on my tiptoes, I place a harsh kiss on Declan's lips, relishing in the way he immediately wraps me in his arms and lifts me closer into his embrace. He tugs on my lip as I pull away. "We'll be reunited soon. I promise."

Declan sets me down as I tuck away a loose strand of his hair that's fallen in front of his eyes. "Don't be a martyr, Zahra. And don't be afraid to ask for help," he warns.

My heart swells at his gentle but stern tone. The passion in his eyes. The way he's fighting his instincts as a boss to take over. Because he trusts me and my capabilities. There's another emotion in Declan's eyes that I can't bring myself to fully think about right now or I'd never leave.

Cyrus clears his throat in the background. " We really need to leave if we want to land in time."

"Go, before Cyrus drags you onto the plane." Declan gives me a quick kiss before running toward the other side of the tarmac.

"You really have that boy wrapped around your finger," Cyrus notes, causing me to bristle.

Cyrus never really had a knack for being warm and fuzzy. Blunt is his specialty. I shake it off. "Are you ready for what's to come? Demir is one of your oldest friends."

"I'm ready. Everything that happens next is necessary. You remember that, Zahra." His words send a chill down my spine as I settle into our seats and hear the pilot come over the intercom, instructing us to buckle in and prepare for the ride.

"I want you to know that I'm not above begging. Especially given the fact that I'm currently talking to an inanimate object while being propelled tens of thousands of miles in the air," I groan at the monitor in front of me, currently projecting the encryption code on Lorkan's phone.

If I ever met the person who protected his device, I don't know if I'd stab them in the neck or beg them to teach me their ways because this code...is absolutely brilliant. Every time I thought I had it cracked, I realized there was another part I had completely overlooked that would no doubt trigger a full deletion of whatever is stored on here.

The code haunted me, and not only because of the fact that it has been my hardest challenge to date, but also because I can't shake the feeling that I've seen it before. There were parts of the code I could've sworn I'd created myself, and the other parts felt as if someone had taken my code and combined it with...my father's.

Holy shit. Could that be it?

I scrub my tired eyes harshly, taking a long, deep breath before finally looking back at the screen. Line by line, I ask myself, "What would this code be telling me if it wasn't just speaking one language but two?" The first few translations in my head are rough and nonsensical until I realize that this code is supposed to read from right to left.

While I'd been fluent in speaking Farsi my whole life, I always struggled with reading and writing. I largely attributed this to my American brain struggling to adapt to having to read words in the opposite direction of what I'm used to. Reading the code properly was a bit of a slog, but finally, fucking finally, I understood it.

"Please, please, please work." I send a quick prayer out to the universe and my dad as I type a few commands on my laptop, suck in a breath, and press enter.

A spiral forms on my screen, spinning for an excruciatingly long period of time before it finally stops. Then, the home screen of Lorkan's phone flashes in front of me.

The lingering tension in my shoulders finally dissipates after weeks, but my hands are shaking as I click through his phone. Most of it is standard, protected contacts, tracker apps, notes from various trade meetings, but one thing catches my eye - a folder titled 'For Zahra.'

I click it without giving it a second thought; whatever patience I have is long gone. My stomach starts to turn when the folder opens, and by the time I've rummaged through its contents, I'm convinced I'm going to vomit on the floor.

At first, I don't believe it. But the documents, pictures, and videos can't be argued with. Especially not the final video, the one of my and Declan's father being struck by a round of bullets, while their murderer sneers with joy.

I jolt as a sharp pain strikes my neck, and when I look up, I see Cyrus with a tight grip on a syringe.

"My sweet Zahra, I'm sorry no one ever taught you to let the men handle business."

I scream, thrusting and thrashing my body...or at least I *try* to. But instead, my entire body falls limp, and the last thing I see is the rough brown carpet of the plane, followed by a never-ending fortress of darkness.

42
DECLAN

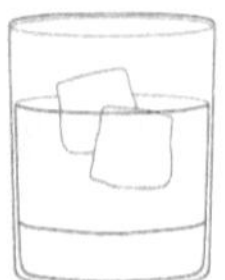

From the moment our plane took off, a chill buried itself in my spine.

Everything about this feels wrong. I've never been one to ignore my instincts but everyone keeps assuring me that everything's fine.

About ten minutes into my assurance seeking, my brother pulls out a laptop and brings up a flight tracker for Zahra's plane. I stare at it for the majority of the flight, even after the cabin lights turn off and Azula chastises me for not resting in case we're heading into a battle. The only thing that makes me crack is Aidan promising to stay up and keep watch, vowing to wake me if anything suspicious comes up.

Sleep is even more unpleasant than being awake. Tossing and turning in my reclined chair, I'm overcome by nightmare after nightmare, all of which end the same—with Zahra dead. In the first nightmare, Lorkan shoots her in the head. In the second nightmare, she's poisoned by Don Demir. By the third nightmare, she gets strangled by one of the Italians. I do nothing to save her in any of those cursed dreams; instead, I stood there frozen, as death overcame her.

My eyes fling open after the fourth and final nightmare. One that's entirely too familiar - me showing up late to save my father, Naser, and Zahra from their doom. Mercifully, my timing works out well, as a minute later the pilot announces our landing.

The instant the tires hit the ground, everyone jumps into action. I take the laptop from Aidan's hands. "Looks like they landed in Istanbul an hour ago, according to the tracker. But I haven't gotten any messages from Zahra or Cyrus." I double-check my phone as the pit in my stomach grows.

Azula mimics my actions, lips turning down into a frown. "Things are also silent on my end. That's not like Zahra at all..."

"Let's not immediately jump to the worst possible scenario. Don Demir is a smooth talker and it's very possible he's just been schmoozing the whole time, and Zahra's silence is an indication that nothing of much excitement—good or bad—has happened," Arman speaks up as the voice of reason.

As much as I'd like to believe him, I know I won't relax until I have my eyes and hands on Zahra.

"Boss, it looks like we have company," Connor calls out as he peers through one of the windows. Following his gaze, I see a bunch of large black SUVs, flying flags with symbols of the Turkish mafia, roll up and surround the plane.

"No one leaves this plane without being armed," I bark, heading toward the exit door and throwing it open. "Keep your hands on your weapons the whole time and don't be afraid to shoot."

It takes endless restraint not to draw my Glock as I walk down the stairs of the private jet onto the tarmac. Demir's soldiers stand at attention, hands on their own guns. At first glance, they had us outnumbered, but they had no idea we had the private airport surrounded with our own soldiers camouflaged in the desert bushes, waiting for my cue.

Once myself, Aidan, Azula, Connor, and Arman have fully settled, the Turkish mafia soldiers part down the middle to reveal Demir...standing shoulder to shoulder with Lorkan.

I scan the field quickly, noticing my wife's absence, as well as a missing Cyrus. My heart pounds as I do a double-take, coming up empty again. Finally, I lock eyes with the waste of human flesh I was so unfortunate to call my uncle.

He conducts his own assessment of the circumstances, likely realizing this will be the end of him one way or another, until he locks eyes with me.

"Where's Zahra?!" The question is so loud it reverberates across the tarmac, but that's not what surprises me the most. It's the fact that the first words out of my uncle's mouth are to ask me about where my wife is. As if he doesn't know....

Nothing about this is right.

"What the fuck do you mean, where is she? She landed here an hour ago to talk to Demir about handing your sorry excuse to us so you can pay for what you did," I seethe.

Demir's expression is one of genuine confusion. "No one else has landed here but you all. We've been waiting here for hours after one of our surveillance teams spotted your plane on an international tracker."

"You're lying!" I shout. "Bring me my wife right now or I swear on every fiber of my being I will burn your city down brick by brick until I find her," I snarl, baring my teeth.

"Look around the tarmac, Declan, do you see any other planes here? Even if we had Zahra hidden somewhere else, there's no way we would have been able to hide an entire plane in this tiny airport. Especially if she was supposed to land right before you did," Demir tries to reason with me.

My body starts to shake as I search the empty stretch of asphalt in front of me.

From behind, I feel Connor approach me. He lowers his voice so only I can hear. "I just heard from our men hiding along the perimeter since last night. We're the only plane they've spotted."

What. The. Fuck?

I snap my head toward Aidan. "You told me Zahra and Cyrus had safely landed an hour ago without any issues."

"Cyrus?!" my uncle seethes. "You left her alone with fucking Cyrus?"

"Of course she's with Cyrus. Who else was going to protect her when she faced off with you and Demir?" I shout while my head spins in a thousand different directions.

Lorkan ignores me, continuing his tirade. "You stupid, insolent boy. She will never be safe so long as Cyrus is alive. Though I suppose I shouldn't be surprised he's managed to fool you, given you can't even sniff out the traitor in your midst."

I try and fail to make sense of what Lorkan was saying, but none of it is adding up. "You're just trying to deceive me. Like you've deceived everyone else in your life," I protest.

"If that's the case, why is your brother looking at the ground like he's hoping it will swallow him whole? Zahra is clearly not here, but I have a strong suspicion Aidan knows where she is." Lorkan dangles an accusatory finger at my brother.

"You're fucking delusional." I laugh, though it comes out broken. Especially as I look at Aidan and see deep guilt in his eyes. The last time I had witnessed such a haunted look in his eyes was during his final encounter with our father. When he said he wished our father would just die and leave me in charge.

No.

No.

Aidan's entire body is trembling as he looks at me. "Declan, I'm so sorry I promise I can explain."

My hands are gripping his shoulders in an instant, shaking him. "What did you do, Aidan? What the fuck did you do?"

"I had no choice. I owed Cyrus a debt. A massive one. And he promised me he wouldn't harm you," Aidan pants out his confession.

"Any harm that comes to Zahra will harm me. It will rip my heart and soul into pieces. Do you not understand that?" I growl, pulling my gun out of the holster.

"I made the deal with him before you two had become so infatuated with each other. Once his plan was in motion, I couldn't stop him. The only thing I could do was bargain for your safety. For your life." The more he speaks, the more I feel like ripping his tongue out of his mouth.

"Where. Is. She?" I grit through my teeth, bringing the gun to his temple.

"I don't know where he took her."

My finger is seconds away from pulling the trigger but Azula slaps my hand away before I can put a bullet in my brother's brain. "If you kill him, we may never be able to find her. He may not know where Zahra is but might have contact with Cyrus. We need him alive."

Aidan swallows hard, guilt draining the color from his face. "I don't know where he took her, but I do know he won't release her until he gets exactly what he wants."

"Which is what?" I was so tired of the games. The betrayal, the deceit. A bitter cold runs through my body, as my heart starts to twinge in pain.

"He wants full control of the Persian Empire."

43
ZAHRA

All I can taste is metal. No doubt from the blood that came after Cyrus slapped me in the face and told me to be quiet while he dumped my body in some dingy basement. Every muscle in my body is screaming at me in agony, and I'm shaking from how frigid the room is.

I have no idea where I am, or if anyone even knows I'm gone. What I do know is that I'll either be killed soon or used as a bargaining chip and then killed. Neither option sounds appealing, but for once in my life, I can't think myself out of this.

The longer I'm trapped in this dark room, the more my eyes adjust until I can finally see my surroundings. The room is nothing more than a cinder block cellar with a metal door on the left wall, the faintest hint of light peering from under it. A potential escape?

I groan as I shift and the chain wrapped around my ankles weighs me down. That is definitely going to make things more complicated. Although they seem to have a great bit of slack to them, perhaps enough that I'd be able to lift the excess chain and use it as a weapon. My hands are bound by a rope, chaffing my wrists. Sharp. I needed something sharp to cut the rope. From there, I would figure out the chains. Figure out how I can defend myself. A loud creak freezes me in place as a silhouette fills the door frame, light pouring in behind the figure like a halo.

Except the figure is anything but an angel coming to save me—it's the man who's been plotting my demise behind my back for months. And I hadn't even realized it.

He presses a button on his phone that triggers the lights to turn on. I blink rapidly at the sudden change, eyes blurring as he carries two chairs over.

"Sit," he orders.

Defiance fills my bones, but it's not enough to overpower my need for the explanation I have a feeling he's about to give. How did I end up here? And why? Sitting down, hands tied behind my back, I subtly assess the chair's frame and, finding a loose screw, I start to toy with.

"Sweet, courageous, little Zahra. I knew you were going to be nothing but trouble from the moment you were born. Of course, back then, I was still convinced I could change your father's mind. Get him to see that his plan for the future was nothing but a fool's wish." Cyrus sighs, reaching down to grab the water bottle he brought in.

My throat clenches at the sight, reminding me how dehydrated I am. I press my lips together. I refuse to beg for anything. He would not get that from me.

"Oh, where are my manners? You probably want some water, don't you?" he chuckles. I gasp as water splashes all over my face and the top of my shirt. Being soaked only makes the chill in my bones worse.

"Bastard," I growl, spitting at his feet.

"Now, now, little Zahra. I won't answer any of your questions if you disrespect me."

My lips curl back in a sneer as he calls me *little Zahra*. What was once a term of endearment, my father called me as a child, has now been sullied by Cyrus.

"I suppose it's best to start at the beginning. As you know, your father and I immigrated to this country together, with hopes and dreams of starting a new life. We experienced many highs and lows the first few years. The start of our new tea and coffee business, a market crash that rendered that shop futile, and the rise of a new endeavor - surveillance and hacking." Cyrus' tone is oddly fond, especially for a man who killed his best friend.

"Once your father aligned with Cillian, we were golden. With the protection of the Irish mafia and the eventual rise of our own, we were untouchable. And everything was worth it. The ridicule of our parents saying we would never make it in America. The sneers from our so-called neighbors who would cross the street whenever they saw us, or yell at us to go back to our home country. None of that mattered anymore because we ruled the city. But, as you know, once you're at the top of the mountain, everyone else wants to push you off it."

Cyrus pauses, running his hands through his salt and pepper hair, and rolling up his sleeves. "The Italians were the first to take a hit at us—"

"For thwarting their drug routes," I guess.

Cyrus smirks. "For talking to their biggest supplier about adding our own routes. Though I can see Naser never told you the full truth on where our decades-long feud with the Italians started."

"You're lying, my father asked Cillian to pull out of the drug trade. He would never get involved in it on his own accord!"

"Your father," Cyrus laughs, "was a very, very different man before you came along. Everything changed after that. Even though he'd deny it at first, I saw the look in his eyes the first time he held you. Nothing else mattered to him but you. He would give up anything—his power, his expansive wealth, the organization he had built with me from the ground up—all of it. He would give it up for *you*."

Tears prick my eyes, and my heart physically aches as I think of my father and how he was ripped from me. I can't process what Cyrus is saying. "My father loved everyone who worked for him, he would never abandon his mafia."

"Naser was an idealist who thought he could have it all. The second you were born, he became infatuated with the idea of turning the Persian Empire into an organization that only engages in more...legal operations. I entertained his dreams early on. What did I care if he restarted his tea business and marginally increased our income by trading various spices and goods? But then he started to talk about slowly phasing out the gun trade and living a simple life. Once your mother was killed, he was dead set on his plan to abandon any mafia ties. No matter the cost."

Killed? What the hell is Cyrus on about? "My mother wasn't killed...she died of a heart attack."

Cyrus clicks his tongue. "A half-truth Naser told to protect his little Zahra. She did indeed die of a heart attack, one that was caused by an unspecified poison they found in her drink at a restaurant your father burned to the ground after her death. Whether he was the true intended target or not remains unknown. But as far as he was concerned, he was the one who killed her. Him and his position as Don."

My entire body starts to shake. It was hard enough to wrap my brain around Cyrus betraying me; now, everything I knew about my mother was a lie, too? My head spins and my stomach turns, nausea rolling through me. *Focus, Zahra. Focus.*

With all of Cyrus' monologuing, I'd been able to remove the loose screw from my chair and start to chip away at the rope binding my hands. I just hoped by the time I was free, Cyrus would still be in the room so I could choke him with my own bare hands. I wanted to be the one who saw the life drain from his eyes. Slowly. Painfully.

Cyrus continues, "Once his obsession with abandoning the crime life formed, he couldn't be swayed. I had hoped everyone would look at him like a madman, riddled with delusion, but instead...he was met with support. Cillian was a little skeptical at first, but he could see how much this lifestyle was weighing down on Aidan, even from a young age. Lorkan took minimal convincing as well. This lifestyle had taken a lot from him."

A week ago, I would have laughed if anyone had told me Lorkan was anything but bloodthirsty for power, but given I'd just been kidnapped and chained by a man whom I had once considered to be a second father, I was willing to accept that everything else I thought I knew was a lie.

"Your father had it all figured out. The day he died—"

"You mean the day you killed him!" I screech, thrashing in my chains with rage.

He waves his hand. "Semantics. The day he died, he was meeting with Cillian to discuss an official shift in organization priorities. You and Declan would be brought in soon to hear about their three-year plan for phasing out the gun trade and any other mafia-related endeavors. At the end of the three years, you and Declan would be phased in as the new bosses or, I guess, CEOs. Whatever is more palatable for civilians. Your rise was supposed to be a beacon for prosperity and happiness. Like that of the Homa, a native vulture to Iran."

"A vulture?" My eyes widen. "Like the one all the men who have tried to kill me had tattooed on their chest?"

The sinister smile on Cyrus' face doubles in size. He's enjoying this.

"The vulture tattoos you know are near replicas of the images they were inspired by." Cyrus reaches into his pocket and pulls out a series of images.

The first one I'd seen already from Aleksander—Lorkan with his chest emblazoned with a black vulture. Cyrus tosses the image to the floor to reveal one of Cillian sitting inside a tattoo parlor, a fresh vulture tattoo on the skull of his head. One that would be easily hidden, once his hair grew out. The final picture has tears streaming down my face. My father, sitting on the floor playing with me when I was likely no bigger than a year old. At first, I don't even notice what Cyrus wanted me to look at, too caught up in seeing my dad so happy, until I scan the entire image. Tattooed on my father's right foot is a vulture identical to Lorkan and Cillian's.

"The men who tried to kill me...they had the same tattoo. One screamed that a queen would die at the end of this." My voice is so scratchy I barely recognize it as my own.

"Your father and his two idiot best friends acted like school girls getting those matching tattoos. *'A physical symbol for the progress they would make in the future.'*" Cyrus rolls his eyes, mocking my father's voice. "When I formed our rebel group, it was my idea to reclaim the vulture tattoo as a symbol of strength, honor, and tradition. Plus, I knew the truth would be revealed to you one day. And you would view the one symbol your father intended to use to guide you, as the one you feared most."

Cyrus hadn't laid a finger on me since he entered the room, but every word he spoke felt like it was slicing through my skin. A never-ending torture.

"The men who tried to kill me. At the restaurant, the

banquet, the rat at our main warehouse. They were all your soldiers. *Your* soldiers who wanted me dead…so you could come into power."

"Precisely."

"You killed my father, your best friend, all because he wanted to protect his family? Because he wanted better for me?" I scoff, shaking my head in disbelief.

"I killed your father because he turned his back on me. Everything we had built together, the loss, the pain, the bloodshed. We had finally gotten to reap the benefits of what we sowed and he was going to throw it all away! Make us nothing more but lowly paupers again. All because after decades of being a lion running his pack, he decided it was time to cut off his own claws. What kind of honorable man does that?" he shouts, voice echoing off the walls.

"Once he was dead, you knew I would seek vengeance. Though you probably never accounted for the fact that I would notice it was a setup. Despite all the bad blood, I knew that the Italians never killed my father or Cillian." It's hard to be smug when you're chained in front of the man who's going to kill you but I refuse to let him see any more chinks in my armor. As if I willed it, the rope binding my hands finally breaks. I keep my hands behind my back, leaving Cyrus none the wiser.

"You impressed me with how quickly you discovered the truth, or at least a piece of it. I debated whether I could still manipulate you into thinking it was another rival, but the risk was too high. Plus, I figured once you and your father were dead, it would be way too easy to convince your underlings that we needed to exact revenge and sharpen our forces." Cyrus shrugs.

"You were going to start a war? Are you out of your mind? Do you remember how many soldiers we lost in the last one?"

Cyrus drags his chair closer to me, his hot breath wafting over my face. "Don't lecture me, little girl. I was alive and *fought* in the last war. And while it was bloody, it was also incredibly profitable. Wars build revenue. And loyalty."

I channel every ounce of rage that has been building for the last thirty minutes and thrust my arms out and around, using the remainder of the cut through rope that was wrapped around my wrists to strangle his neck. Tugging as hard as I can. I may die today, but I will do everything in my power to ensure he dies with me.

We crash to the floor and I use my legs as leverage, tying them around his waist in an attempt to further restrict his air flow. I'd clearly caught him off guard, which I need to use to my advantage. Cyrus chokes and claws at me, and in my weakened state, I don't know how much fight I have left in me. Still, I yell at myself to hold on, feeling every muscle in my body ache with pain.

Behind me, the entry door to the room flies open and soldiers rush in, ripping me off Cyrus. He's rising to all fours, panting for oxygen, and raises a shaking hand to point at me.

"You'll pay for that. I was going to kill you first, but now I think I'll wait for your husband and friends to arrive and kill them one by one as you watch."

No. No. Declan can't find me. I refuse to let him or Azula or Arman die because of me. They deserved to live, deserved to carry out the dream my father had planned for us. "He won't come. He knows it's too risky."

"He will. I saw the look in his eyes when you boarded the plane. *Love.* The most lethal thing on this planet."

Love. That was the emotion I'd seen in Declan's eyes. The thing I'd felt in my gut the past few days. He loved me, I loved him. And I would never get to tell him that.

Cyrus finally stands and kicks me as hard as he can in the gut. Pain sends me crumbling to the floor. My head smacks off the concrete, and black swallows my vision, the world slowly fading away until all I see is Declan's face.

44
DECLAN

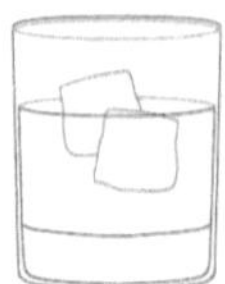

"We can't just sit here on our assess and do nothing!" I scream in frustration, throwing my whiskey glass across the room and watching it shatter.

It's been twenty-four hours since I made the biggest mistake of my life and let Zahra board that plane. Twenty-four hours since I last saw her. Last held her. Last told her I loved her. And I'm unraveling at the seams.

Arman places a hand on my shoulder in an attempt to calm me down. "We're doing everything in our power to find her, but all of her electronic devices are turned off so we have no way of tracking her. Your brother already told us everything he knows—"

"Unless he's lying! He's been doing a lot of that lately," I snap, clenching my fists together.

Demir sends me a pitiful look that makes me want to punch a hole in the wall. "Maybe you should talk to him. Hear out his side of the story. It's possible he may remember more when he sees you."

"I can't be alone in a room with him right now. I don't trust myself." It's the truth. Any logical or rational part of me disappeared when I realized that my wife, the only woman I had ever loved, had not only been kidnapped but that my own brother played a role in it.

"It may be the only way we find Zahra. Do it for her. We'll deal with the traitor later."

Traitor. That's what my brother is now. Aidan had always been reckless and beat to the rhythm of his own drum, but I never would have guessed he'd turn his back on our whole family. Turned his back on *me*. For all the issues he had with our father and the expectations of being a mafia prince, our love for each other never wavered. Never faltered. Or at least, that's what I thought.

Bile rises in my stomach, and I don't move a muscle.

"Declan, as much as I want to strangle the boy, the smart decision right now would be to talk to him," Lorkan speaks, making my hands curl into fists instinctively.

"Don't think I haven't forgotten about you. Or that heinous vulture tattoo," I hiss. He's lucky my main priority is getting Zahra back. Or else he'd already be dead.

Lorkan straightens his back. "There is so much of your own history you don't know. So much Cyrus has spun against you." He reaches into his coat pocket and places an envelope filled with photos on my lap.

My throat closes as I see separate photos of my father, Naser, and Lorkan—all with their own vulture tattoos. "W-What is this?"

"Three men who had experienced enough loss in their lives, hoping to start a new one. Give their families, or what was left of their families, a better future. Naser and Cillian had been slowly plotting over the past decades how to remove our ties to any mafia business and switch to a more legal and less violent way of life. Which is why your father put me in charge of the finances once he passed. So I could ensure I continued his vision, once you were ready to hear it." Lorkan's shoulders sink, like he's been carrying the weight of this secret for too long.

"Why didn't you tell me?" I barely manage to get out, still shocked by the news.

"You were still grieving. You had enough on your plate to handle."

"And the vulture tattoo?" He still hadn't provided an explanation for that.

"The vulture in Iranian culture is meant to represent hope. Cyrus and his sadistic mind chose to bastardize the vulture for him and his cronies," Lorkan growls. "Another 'fuck you' to Cillian and Naser because he viewed the desire to leave the crime business as a slight. He feared the financial losses he would experience. Which is why he killed them."

Jesus Christ. The more I learned, the more I felt like everything I knew was a lie.

Lorkan places a hand on my shoulder, "Aidan may be our only way of getting closer to her and Cyrus. Talk to him."

Pinching the bridge of my nose between my fingers, I comply, turning to Demir. "Take me to him. But be sure to have a camera streaming in that room. If I lose it...someone needs to come in and stop me."

"As you wish." Demir gestures for me to follow him as we start our descent down the stairs to the main foyer. Demir had insisted on locking Aidan up in one of the guest rooms as opposed to the holding cells in the basement out of respect for my late father.

I rub my chest, feeling an aching pain, as I open the door and come face to face with my brother. Immediately, I feel an urge to free him from the chains locked around his wrists, but then I remind myself that Zahra is likely much worse off wherever she is. And if she couldn't be comfortable, then he definitely doesn't deserve to be either.

The door shuts behind us and Aidan immediately starts talking. "Declan, I'm so sorry. I never meant for you to get hurt by all this."

"Never meant for me to get hurt in all this? What about Zahra? Or Lorkan? Or anyone else in our family. Do you realize how many lives you nearly ruined? How many people nearly died because of you. I swear if she's dead—" I can't even finish the sentence without my throat constricting.

"She's not. He won't kill her without using her to bargain for something. He'd view it as a waste of resources," Aidan states bluntly.

I blink and then my fist breaks his nose. To his credit, he just takes it. Aidan shakes his head, spitting blood onto the carpet. "I didn't mean it like that. I was just trying to explain how Cyrus thinks. We're going to need to get inside his head if we even have a chance of getting Zahra back and making it out of this alive."

He's right. Still, it felt good to punch him in the face.

"How did you even end up getting caught up in all of this, Aidan? You never once showed interest in learning the business side of things, and suddenly you're doing Cyrus' bidding. What could he possibly have on you?"

"I made a deal with the devil. One I regret to this day, but at least he's kept good on his promise to spare you." Aidan swallows hard as I gesture for him to continue. "You remember Max's death?" Aidan asks me.

I can't recall the last time he said his best friend's name out loud. But I do remember the look in his eyes when he found Max's cold blue body on the floor of their apartment. Max had been struggling with misusing substances for about a year at that point. Aidan had finally been able to get Max to agree to get help. I'd gone over to the apartment that morning to help Max pack and assist Aidan in taking him to the best hospital in the city. Except by the time we had both arrived, Max had overdosed. His pills had been laced with fentanyl and no one had been there to save him.

"I remember." I nod, thinking of how broken and lost Aidan had been after that.

"I lost a part of myself that day. One I don't think I'll ever get back. It wasn't just the loss that affected me, it was the feeling that I had done nothing to help him. That I waited too long to act. I've blacked out most of that day, but the one thing I can never let go is seeing the paramedics haul Max's body away, while Dad's voice played over and over in my head, *'You never take anything seriously, Aidan, and one day you're going to regret all the time you've wasted.'"*

For the first time since we flew to Turkey, I took a long hard look at my brother, or really the shell he had become over the past few years. My stomach turns seeing how lost he is. I wait for him to continue.

"I wallowed for a few days until a plan popped into my head. I may not have been able to save Max, but I could at least avenge him. I remembered Cyrus mentioning in passing that he still had intel on the various drug rings in the city. He tracked down Max's dealer for me, and I arranged a meet-up at our old apartment."

"Jesus Christ, Aidan." I shake my head.

"I know I was reckless as always, but meeting in my apartment allowed me to confirm he was Max's dealer. Though the idiot must not have realized he had given Max a bad batch. When I let the scum inside our apartment, he made a joke, asking where his best customer was, and I saw red. I punched him in the gut as hard as I could, wrestled him to the ground, and just kept hitting him over and over again. He was unrecognizable by the time I snapped out of my haze."

I have no room to judge him. I've committed equally gruesome murders in my life.

"When I finally came to and started to clean up the mess...I realized he had a familiar tattoo on his neck. A crown, with a centerpiece detailed the Greek mafia's family sigil."

"Holy shit. The Don's son...he died around the same time as Max. Their funerals were a few weeks apart," I recall.

"Aye. Once I realized who I had killed, the heir to the Greek mafia, I called Cyrus in a panic. He assured me he would handle everything. Make it look like a drug deal gone bad to avoid an all-out war between our two organizations. So long as I was willing to help him in the future. His words may have been thinly veiled in empathy but I saw the look in his eyes. He was thrilled to find me in such a compromising position. Thrilled that I would be at his beck and call. To this day, I'm convinced he knew what I would do once I crossed paths with the man who was responsible for Max's murder. I played right into his hand." Aidan hangs his head in shame.

Dear God. A war with the Greeks. Few mafias had the resources to annihilate us, but they were one of them. "He played us all."

"And he continues to. I swear on my life, Declan, I had no idea that he was the one who killed Naser and our father. Dad and I may not have always seen eye to eye, but I loved him," Aidan pleads with me to believe him.

And I do. I may want to rip his head off for the damage he's caused, but his explanation sounded more like the Aidan I knew. One who loved with such ferocity that sometimes it consumed him and led to idiotic choices.

"What was the favor he asked of you?"

"To keep him updated on Zahra's whereabouts at all times.

And who she was talking to. At first, I figured he was just being protective of his new boss...but over time, I couldn't shake the feeling that something bigger was going on. I didn't ask any questions though. I just kept my head down and did what I was told, like a good soldier." He rolls his eyes. "He always acted jumpy whenever Uncle Lorkan came around. I assumed they hated each other, but it seems like Lorkan was onto him this whole time."

"Fucking Lorkan," I sigh.

"This past day has been an absolute mindfuck," I groan, dragging my hands across my face. I understand my brother better now, but I don't think I'd be able to see him as anything other than a traitor. At least not until I Zahra was safely back in my arms. "How do we get her back?" I plead, desperation in my voice.

Aidan's response is deeply unsatisfying. "We wait for him to reach out."

"What if he doesn't?" My tongue is as dry as the desert.

"He will. We're all a part of his circus now. And there's nothing he loves more than getting to act as a ringmaster."

45
ZAHRA

Sensory deprivation is already getting to me. I tried my best to keep track of time, counting seconds in my head, but it's easy to convince yourself you're wrong. How long have I been inside this room? Hours? Days? Weeks?

Cyrus' men sporadically open the door to throw in some stale bread or a small bowl of water. The bucket in the corner serves as my bathroom. Despite how miserable I am, I'd stay here a thousand years if it meant keeping Declan safe.

He can't find me. He *won't* find me. I'm determined to make it so. I refuse to let Cyrus use me as a pawn in his game, refused to be the reason why Declan gets murdered. My nightmares are filled with images of his cold, dead face. Every time I would discover his limp body, I'd jolt awake, finding myself shaking and covered in sweat. The last time I woke, I swear I heard a deep chuckle come from the connecting room, as if they were watching me fall apart. I stopped crying because I refused to give them the satisfaction.

The screeching sound of the door scraping across the barren concrete floor sends a chill down my spine, and the bright light coming in from the room beyond nearly blinds me. Cyrus walks in first and sneers down at me as I sit chained to the floor. "It's time to be reunited with your husband."

Declan? Is he here? No. I refuse to believe it. I squash down the feeling of hope that fills my chest. Cyrus will kill Declan the second he lays eyes on him. I need to keep Declan as far away as possible, no matter how much I miss him. No matter how badly I want to tell him I love him. I should have said it before I left. Now I may never get the chance.

"Pick her up, and make sure there's no slack on those chains," Cyrus orders his men, refusing to do his own dirty work.

With the light filling the room, I could now see the large purple bruises around his neck. "Are you scared to get close to me, Cyrus? I promise I won't choke you as hard this time," I snort, relishing in how red his face turned.

Cyrus' eyes nearly pop out of his head in rage. His hand flies across my mouth, and I taste copper. "That is your first and last warning, girl." He pulls a gun out from the holster and aims it at my temple. "No more funny business, or I'll splatter your brains out in front of your husband and the rest of your inner circle."

I slam my mouth shut, not for my own sake but for that of my family. I need to be strong and unwavering because that is what they need from me.

The two massive guards remove the long chains that keep me trapped in the room, leaving me with only handcuffs around my wrists and shackles on my feet. Cyrus leads me into the security room where they've been watching me, keeping his gun aimed at my temple.

A rush of relief comes over my whole body when I realize Declan isn't physically here. Instead, he's being broadcast on a large screen. To his left and right are Azula and Arman, respectively. Declan's eyes meet mine and I can see them start to fill with tears as he takes in my expression.

"I look that bad, huh?" I attempt to keep my tone light, but my voice is riddled with pain.

"There's not a single moment that I've ever thought you were anything less than stunning, love. I just miss you is all." Declan's smooth, silky voice comes through the speakers, and immediately, I feel more settled and ready to brace whatever comes next.

"Ah, young love, so silly and impractical." Cyrus snickers.

Declan reels as he finally takes in the barrel of the gun aimed at my head and the man who's responsible for causing us so much pain. "I swear on my entire being and soul, Cyrus, if you harm even another hair on her head, I will—"

"You will do nothing!" Cyrus snarls, grabbing the back of my head and yanking my hair hard enough to draw a wince from me. Declan's face turns white in horror. "You have no power here, Declan. You don't get to make demands. I do. And if you ever forget that, I'll put a bullet through her head faster than you can blink. Do. Not. Test. Me."

Cyrus uses his gun to whip my head, and I hiss in pain.

"You're right. I'm sorry. You're in charge. Just tell me what I need to do to keep her safe. That's all I care about." Declan's jaw is tense, and I know it's taking everything he has to follow Cyrus' orders.

"The first thing you're going to do is tell Arman to stop trying to find our location. He's not nearly as good a hacker as he thinks he is. From the moment you logged on to the video chat, we could tell he was trying to track us. Tell him to stop now, or the next time I hit her, I'll make sure to break a bone."

Declan grits his teeth before nodding. One of Cyrus's men gives him a thumbs-up. Good. Without Arman, Declan will never find me. Which means he'll get to live.

"What I want is simple. I want the legacy of the Persian Empire to continue. I want us to uphold our status as the most lethal mafia in the entire world, alongside our Irish allies. But in order to do that, we need a leadership that isn't afraid to take risks. A leadership that isn't going to abandon everything they built for the hopes of a 'normal' life. I have been cultivating support for my vision of the future. Enough support that will carry us forth for decades. All that has to be done is for you and Zahra to renounce your claims to the mafia and instate me as Don. You do that, and I promise to let you and all your loved ones live. I'll help you create new identities and ensure you stay hidden and protected." Cyrus puffs out his chest like an animal marking his territory.

"The Irish won't take well to a leader who isn't from their home country," Declan grits, though it isn't a full denial of the proposal. No. He can't actually be considered this? Can he?

"Which is why I've already enlisted your father's cousin, Fergal, to serve as the new head of the Irish mafia. His values are aligned with my vision, and he would be a fit ruler." Cyrus drops another bomb on us. Fergal had been overseeing various shipment routes and warehouses for us.

He's the rat who had infiltrated our ranks.

Declan has also come to the same conclusion. "Fergal. I never would have guessed he had it in him." Declan's eyes lock with mine through the screen, and I give him a small shake of my head, all while I scream inside for him not to give in.

"You will hand her over first, and then we will resign our positions," Declan attempts to bargain.

"You and I both know that will never happen. We'll schedule a meeting that will be broadcast with both of you signing away your power. Once the meeting ends, you two will be free to leave," Cyrus states his terms.

Declan grits his teeth, eyes narrowing as he hisses, "Fine. As you wish. The sooner we get this done, the better."

I lose all sense of reality. "Declan, no! You can't let him take over. I'd rather die than see him ruin our father's legacy. Let me go, let me die, and you live. Live for the both of us—" I scream in pain as I feel an electric current run down my body. Collapsing on the floor, I lift my head to see one of Cyrus' bodyguards standing above me with his taser in hand.

"ZAHRA, NO. YOU FUCKING BASTARD!" Declan screams.

"THAT. IS. ENOUGH," Cyrus commands. "Declan, you either accept my proposal now, or I'll spatter her brains all over the floor and track you down next. I am offering you an out. And I suggest you take it." Cyrus loads the bullet into place, aiming the gun at my stomach.

"I accept, I accept. Just let her live, and I'll do whatever you ask of me." Declan's voice is riddled with exhaustion.

"See, was that so hard?" Cyrus chuckles, turning the safety of his gun back on. "We'll be in touch." Cyrus gestures to his guards to cut the livestream, while I moan for Declan to fight back.

"You can try to get rid of us all you want but we have thousands of loyal soldiers in our corner. They will never turn their back on us," I seethe.

"Oh, I count on that. You see, once I have Declan and your precious inner circles in my possession, I plan on staging your deaths as an act of retaliation from the Italians. From there, it will be easy to convince any loyalists to stand with me and Fergal as we 'avenge' you. I'll have your entire staff eating out of the palm of my hand and defeat the Italians at the same time."

A guttural scream leaves me. How could I have been this naive? How could I not have known what kind of monster was lurking in my ranks?

"Tantrums won't help you, Zahra. Nothing will. This battle started long before you, and now it's time for me to finally get my justice." Cyrus turns to a guard. "Take her back into the room. The longer she stays here, the greater the odds are that I'll put a bullet in her head just to shut her up."

Cyrus' men laugh as they throw me back into the room, and for once, I welcome the darkness and hope it consumes me so I don't have to face the pain that's to come.

46
DECLAN

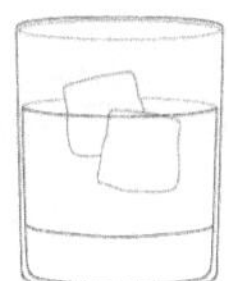

"Are you out of your fucking mind?! If you think I'm going to let you and Zahra even consider a deal with that viper, you have no idea how I operate," Demir grits out through his teeth.

It's funny how he thinks he has a say in the matter. Like I didn't just watch my wife get beaten and held at gunpoint. Like I didn't see the resignation in her eyes. She had already come to terms with the fact that she was a dead woman, and that is unacceptable to me. Seeing her starved and physically assaulted was unacceptable. No rhyme or reason could console me now. The only thing I'll consider justice is watching Zahra torture Cyrus slowly while he begs for his death.

"You cannot stop me from being with my wife, Demir. Not ever, and especially not after I've seen what they've done to her. I recommend telling your soldiers to back off. I can see them ready to pounce on me. I'm sure of your misguided orders to keep me safe. I promise I will put a bullet in every single one of their heads before they even get within two feet of me." My hand is already wrapped around my Glock tucked away behind my back, ready.

Demir growls but waves at his soldiers to back off from me. Smart man. "I understand how devastated you must feel right now, but you heard what Zahra said. She was practically begging you not to consider the offer. If you love your wife as much as you say you do, why not respect her wishes and let her go?" he asks.

I don't even blink before I lunge at Demir, Azula holding me back before I can reach him, "Do not attempt to use my wife's life and the words she said under duress as a means to manipulate me, Demir."

Azula squeezes my shoulder hard. "Declan, I am as enraged as you are, but if Zahra has any chance of surviving, we're going to need you alive. And right now, your odds of staying alive are quite slim." She nods her head to Demir's guards, who all have their guns drawn and aimed at my head.

"You are a madman." Demir shakes his head.

I shrug. "You kept pushing me, next time I won't let anyone stop me from what I do next."

Arman remains hyperfixated on his laptop, typing away like an absolute madman. I pull a chair closer to him and hear him mumbling under his breath, "I will not let her down. This has to be an in..."

I refuse to feel hope, especially after Cyrus immediately noticed we were trying to hack into his system and find his location. He's likely already moving himself and Zahra to another location to ensure we won't reach them. My only hope is that Cyrus's arrogance continues to build, leading him to make a careless mistake that would lead me to Zahra.

Arman continues to mutter over and over again, and eventually, I crack. "Are you going to tell us what you're working on so we can try to help?"

He lets out an exhausted breath. The dark black circles under his eyes inform me that he's gotten as little sleep as I have the past few days—none. Of all the words to come from him, I never expected, "Zahra was wearing a necklace."

It's official, we've all lost our sanity without Zahra. Why the hell does he care about a damn necklace?

Azula snarks. "She was also wearing a shirt and pants, but I don't see how discussing her outfit choices at a time like this is helpful—"

"Her necklace may have a tracker in it. When she was born, Farah, her mother, had a farvahar necklace made just for her and asked me to include a small tracker embedded inside the gold. No one besides myself and her parents knew about it. They didn't want it to be used for nefarious means or have her refuse to wear it in a rebellious phase. I recognized it the second I saw it on her neck. The question is whether I can hack Naser's code and pinpoint her location."

"Holy shit," Azula exclaims. "Arman, are you serious?"

Arman grunts as he continues to type on the computer. From the expression on his face, he isn't convinced this is anything other than another glimmer of light that would be crushed out by a midnight of darkness.

Every second that goes by feels like a year. We're all crowded around Arman, looking over his shoulder and holding our breaths, and he tries again and again to remotely access the tracker in Zahra's necklace. My mind is racing with thoughts I'm dying to ask him, but I know it will only slow him down. So instead, I let the questions run in my mind. Is the tracker even still working? What if the battery is dead? How would we attack if we did get her location?

Eventually, our hovering gets to Arman and he snaps at us to give him space so he can focus. Demir and his cronies call it a night, leaving the rest of us in his living room.

By one in the morning, only Arman and I remain awake. His typing speed has dramatically decreased, and every now and then, I swear I catch him falling asleep only to startle back awake.

He never stops for more than a minute. As much as I appreciate his tenacity, I'm starting to wonder if this will be another dead end. I refuse to let Zahra remain in Cyrus' clutches for another day. She already looked dehydrated and beaten, and I can't imagine what other level of hell they're putting her through. I'd give Arman until the morning to try to find Zahra, and if he isn't successful, I'll contact Cyrus and tell him I plan to renounce my position immediately in exchange for her return.

Zahra would eventually understand why I'd given up everything for her. Even though she begged me not to. Even though the mafia life is all we know. She would understand because I saw the love in her eyes when we were reunited. She would do anything for the people she loved. Which is why she would understand the sacrifice I chose to make—

"Declan. I think I may have something." Arman swallows, exhaustion written all over his face.

I snap to attention, rushing to look at the computer screen, sucking in a breath, "Are you sure about this?"

"Not completely, but it's the only lead we have."

I nod, banging my fist on the table to stir everyone awake. "We're going to need all hands on deck for this retrieval. Zahra is our number one priority but I also want Cyrus captured. He will suffer as we have before he dies."

"And you'll be the one to ensure his suffering?" Arman asks.

"No. I'll leave that honor to my wife."

47
ZAHRA

The cool concrete of the room has started to give me a strange sense of comfort. If nothing else, the dark bareness of this room allows my mind to wander occasionally to better moments and better days.

My eyes flutter shut as I let the exhaustion come over me. I send out a silent prayer, asking for a night where my dreams don't come so I can sink into the empty darkness. Because that is better than my countless dreams of death.

Someone is in the room with me. I don't hear the door creak over, or a flush of light from the security room door, but I can't shake the instinct that someone is here. My eyes flutter open slowly, vision so blurry at first I'm convinced that I must be hallucinating. I rub my eyes once, twice, and finally a third time, but the face of the man sitting next to me doesn't change—my father's face.

"Baba?" I whisper, as if saying his name louder will make him disappear.

The wrinkles around his eyes form as he smiles at me. "My sweet Zahra, I can't tell you how happy I am to see you again."

Tears of joy fill my eyes. It's really him. He's here. But if I could see him...

"Am I dead?" I ask, a sudden rush of sorrow filling me. I must be dead. I never got to say goodbye to Azula or Samirah. Never got to thank Arman for all he's done. Never realized that my last moment with Declan would be our final time together.

My chest squeezes with grief.

My father reaches out to take my hands into his. Real. Everything feels so real. My family was never super religious, but I did have hopes that one day I'd be reunited with all the people I'd lost. Maybe one day I'd eventually be reunited with everyone who is left. Everyone who gets to live, while I remain...as a spirit? Is that what I am? "Am I a ghost?" I ask my father, realizing he never answered my first question.

He lifts our entangled hands and presses a kiss to mine. "You are not dead. Nor are you a spirit."

"So, I'm hallucinating? Great. That's exactly what I need right now," I deadpan.

He snorts so endearingly, I let myself believe this is real. "You're not hallucinating, but you are dreaming. I can't stay long but I am here to tell you that help is on the way. So, you need to get ready, Zahra. You need to fight. Just keep fighting... so you can live. Don't forget to live."

His voice starts to fade, as does the image of him. My father's skin starts to glow brighter and brighter until I'm nearly blinded by the light. The sound of an explosion has me up on my feet, and the next thing I know, I'm being pulled out of the darkness.

48
DECLAN

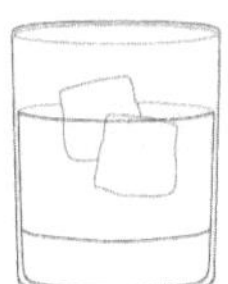

"There it is, Boss." Connor points at the container ship two hundred feet away from us on the dock. "It's not as guarded as I thought it would be."

"Likely because they want to blend in with the other ships," I grunt, ready to cut down anyone and anything that gets in my way.

Arman had been right. Cyrus is hiding away in a docked ship just off the coast of the Persian Gulf. We'd taken a quick flight to Bandar Abbas, the closest port city, overnight while our retrieval plan. My uncle Lorkan informed me that this was one of Naser's favorite cities in Iran. My uncle, father, and Naser would take a boat out to Hormuz Island, hike along the rainbow mountains, and discuss a better future for us. I have no doubts that Cyrus chose to dock here as a sick way of mocking Naser. Another thing he'd pay for.

"Mind if I do the honors, pretty boy?" Azula licks her lips, gently pushing Connor out of the way. She positions her gun, and a breath later, I watch as body after body drops into the harbor.

We all pull out our binoculars and check for any stray guards we may have left alive. Connor gives the all clear and we start barreling toward the ship. Connor uses an industrial grade laser to cut through a large metal door on the side of the ship, allowing us to enter.

"The main security unit is in that room, according to the map Arman found." Connor nods his chin toward the farthest back corner of the ship.

"Kill any soldier who gets in our way. I have no room in my cells for traitors," I growl at the group of men and women behind me. We'd enlisted all the elite members of my firing squad for this mission.

One by one, members of our unit stalk down the hall, killing anyone and anything we see.

My heart feels like it stops when we reach the end of the murky hall. All that's left between me and Zahra is this thick metal door.

Connor reaches into his pocket and pulls out a small grenade, waiting for us all to tighten our masks before letting it fly.

The detonation rocks the boat, and we all brace ourselves as the metal wall in front of us slowly disintegrates.

"MOVE, MOVE, MOVE!" Connor shouts to all the soldiers behind me, gesturing toward Cyrus' soldiers who come flying out of the room.

The sound of bullets flying fills the ship. Azula, Lorkan, Aidan, and I head inside. I had debated whether or not to bring Aidan with me. Frankly, I wanted to leave him back in Istanbul, but Arman claimed we may be able to use him to our advantage. Aidan knows the real Cyrus better than any of us does.

"BOSS, THEY'RE IN HERE!" Connor calls out from the control room.

I push through everyone and everything in my way, not

stopping for a second until my eyes lock onto her. Zahra. My sweet, strong, courageous wife is laid out on the floor, while one of the medic soldiers inspects her.

"Her pulse is steady, and breathing is fine, but it looks like she's been drugged with something because her motor skills are definitely off." The medic informs me as Azula and Aidan run in behind me. Azula scans the room and snarls as she sees Cyrus sitting in the corner, handcuffed and shackled. We had done it. We had won.

Zahra groans, struggling to stand up on her feet. I move to give her support, but she keeps shoving me away, which feels like a knife to the heart. I try to remind myself that she's drugged right now and probably doesn't realize what she's doing. Or who I am. The last thing I want is to make her feel even more traumatized than she already is by forcing her.

She uses a chair nearby to prop herself up. "It's...a...trap..." she mumbles, moving away from me. "It's a trap..."

"No, it's not a trap, Zahra, it's me. I'm here to help—"

"You should really listen to your wife, Declan." Cyrus smirks, tossing his handcuffs to the side, aiming his gun at Zahra's chest, and pulling the trigger.

"NO!" I scream as Azula rushes to tackle him to the ground, but it's too late. The pop of the gun hits my ears seconds before Azula wrestles Cyrus to the floor. I watch in horror as Zahra falls to the ground...with Aidan on top of her.

He flips onto the floor, clutching his abdomen, as blood leaks through his fingers. His blood. Zahra crawls toward him —unscathed. "You saved me," she whispers, tears falling from her eyes. She moves her shaky hands on top of his and presses down in a feeble attempt to help stop the bleeding.

"You brought my brother back to life. It's the least I could do." Aidan smiles before wheezing and groaning in pain.

Aidan's eyes start to shut, a telltale sign that the end is near. I nearly vomit at the thought.

I fall to my knees next to Aidan, but my body feels like it's frozen in time. "WE NEED A MEDIC STAT," I scream so loud my throat aches in pain. I feel like I'm watching in slow motion as our entire medical team rolls in, gently shoving myself and Zahra away so they can get to work.

"We need to get him to a hospital," one of the nurses shouts, as they lift him onto a makeshift gurney.

I search the room for Cyrus, but he's already been knocked unconscious and chained up by Azula.

"You should also get her fully checked out," another nurse states, pointing to Zahra. "Why don't you ride with us to the hospital?"

I nod, lifting her into my arms and relishing in the way she immediately curls into me. "Declan?"

"Yes, angel?"

"I love you. I wasn't sure if I'd be able to say that to you ever, so I need to say it now."

My throat constricts. I had dreamed of hearing those words from her so many times. None of those dreams compared to this moment now. "I love you too, Zahra. You and me, we were always inevitable."

She hums in agreement, holding me closer as we step outside into the sunlight, leaving behind the cold, damp darkness of the ship.

49
ZAHRA

One week later.

"I'm not sure what I love more—seeing you covered in weapons from head to toe, or seeing you completely naked underneath me," Declan groans, helping me adjust my utility vest so all my various knives are on display.

"You're insatiable." I roll my eyes, pulling him closer by wrapping my fingers in the belt loops of his pants.

"For you? Always." He presses a soft kiss to my forehead. "You sure you want to do this?"

"I need to. Cyrus killed my father, and yours. He tried to shatter my legacy. Our future. And so he will die by my hands." I lift my chin, determined. Torture was more of Azula's forte but killing Cyrus was my destiny. I did make sure to get a few pointers from her.

"Okay, let's go." Declan moves so he's beside me and entwines our fingers together. Azula and Connor are waiting for us outside of my father's office, the place where he and Cillian were murdered, as we descend to the holding cells.

The temperature drops the moment we reach the basement, and none of us makes a sound. The sound of water dripping in one of the cells fills the hallway. Except I'm certain it's not water. From the coppery scent that fills the air, I know it's blood. My throat constricts with every step we take down the hallway filled with the scent of death. I can feel Azula practically hum with content. This was her safe space, and knowing she was by my side grounded me.

We stop in front of a padlocked door, which looks eerily similar to the one inside my own holding cell on Cyrus' ship. I raise an eyebrow at Declan, who smirks. "I have a flair for the dramatics, what can I say?"

I place my hand on the sensor on the wall, waiting as it scans my palm and unlocks the door. Declan gives my hip one final squeeze before I shove the metal door with all my strength, causing it to slam against the walls of the holding cell.

Cyrus doesn't even have the decency to lift his head as I enter. His two arms are extended and chained to the walls; feet also chained to the ground beneath him. From his lethargic appearance and the rotten tray of food in the corner, I can tell he hasn't eaten anything. Not that I cared. This would all be over for him soon. After I've had my fun. "Put a chain around his neck. I want him to be forced to look at me."

Azula immediately enters the cell, chain in hand, expertly wrapping it per my instructions.

Cyrus' shuts his eyes in petulant defiance, trying to gain control of the situation like always.

"Don't make me tape your eyes open, Cyrus, I swear I'll do it," I hiss, pulling out a knife and toying with it in my hand, "Or better yet, I'll slide off your eyelids. Wouldn't that be nice?" I guide the sharp edge of the knife over his eyebrows.

Cyrus growls and finally looks me in the eyes, "Well, well. Look who finally decided to act like a boss."

I don't even flinch at the putrid smell coming from his mouth, "I always had this in me. You were the one who doubted me. Who thought he could do better. Now look at you." I laugh, relishing the way his eyes fill with rage.

"Naïve little girl," he spits, trying and failing to move his chains so he can get closer to me. "You may kill me today, but my legacy lives on. Or need I remind you, I was able to create a whole army of your own men and allies against you? You may live today, but I promise your time will come soon. My men will make sure of it."

I feel Declan stiffen behind me at the threat. I hold out a hand, telling him to stay back, as I move my knife under Cyrus's chin. His may speak with confidence, but his eyes told a different story. "You can threaten me all you want, Cyrus, but I can see the fear in your eyes."

He writhes again, causing his metal chains to clink against the concrete floor, "YOU SEE NOTHING. YOU MAY KILL ME TODAY, BUT I PROMISE I WILL ALWAYS I WILL ALWAYS HAUNT YOU. DAY AND NIGHT. I WILL ALWAYS BE APART OF YOU."

I grip his tattered shirt, ripping what remains of it off his body. Bile fills my mouth as I see a vulture tattoo on his chest. A symbol of the mockery he's made of me and my father, a symbol I planned on reclaiming today.

I replace the classic hunting knife in my hand with a curved blade, pressing the tip into Cyrus' chest. "Let me make myself clear, Cyrus, your lies, your army, your memories, your legacy, and your name will all disappear with time. Until nothing is left, but remains of your bones buried so deep in the ground no one can find you."

I give him no time to respond, cutting into his skin slowly, just as Azula had shown me. Fighting and killing, I knew like the back of my hand, but this special type of torture was her expertise. For as much as Cyrus boasted a few seconds ago, he was screeching in agony as I traced around his tattoo. Slowly, I angle the sharp edge of my curved knife inward, causing sticky blood to pool onto my fingers. More screams and curses fall from Cyrus' lips, but I refuse to let the sounds deter me. I make my final cut and watch Cyrus's tattooed skin fall to the ground.

Blood continues to leak from his chest, and eventually Cyrus' screams turn into whimpers as he falls to the floor of his cell, spasming slightly. Azula removed the chain around Cyrus' neck so I can check his pulse. "He's not dead yet, but he will be soon," I note.

I toss my knife to the ground now that it's tainted with his blood, and step closer to Declan, who is beaming at me with pride, and pulls me into his chest. "My strong, violent wife."

Declan holds onto me, arms wrapped around my waist, as we stand silently watching the life drain from Cyrus' eyes. As he takes his final breath, exhaustion finally hits me. Exhaustion and a deep lightness in my chest. One that I hadn't felt since my father's death.

"We'll handle the body." Azula breaks the silence, nodding to Connor.

I nod as Declan guides us out of the cell. "Let's get you cleaned up."

"I thought you liked me bloody and violent?" I tease.

"I do. But Cyrus' blood isn't worthy of staining your hands," he insists.

"Declan?"

"Yes, love?"

"You make me feel hopeful," I confess, feeling goosebumps up and down my arms as he holds me again.

His warm lips brush my temple. "And you make me feel like everything in the world is right. Because so long as I have you in my arms, it is."

50
ZAHRA

T wo weeks later.

"You're going to have to talk to him eventually, you know," I chastise, as Declan draws idle circles on my back while we lay in bed.

"I've literally talked to him every day since we got back," Declan counters.

"You've spent five minutes each day asking if he's healing okay from the bullet wound and whether he wants Maura to send over any more casseroles. When that's done, you head straight home, play with Cody for an hour, and then distract yourself with sex," I summarize.

Declan narrows his eyes. "Making love to my wife is anything but a distraction. And if I remember correctly, you were the one who begged me to 'fuck you so hard you'd feel me for a month.'"

I shrug. I'd never be ashamed of anything Declan and I do or say to each other. And he loved it. "All I'm saying is you haven't had any hard conversations with Aidan yet, and you can't keep avoiding it forever."

"I know. I just get so mad every time I'm alone with him. And then I feel guilty for getting upset because he did save your life. I don't know what to do. I want to forgive him, but he's also why your life and his were endangered in the first place." He buries his head into my chest, as I stroke his hair.

"I can't tell you what to do when it comes to forgiveness. But what I can say is, it's okay if it takes time. Or if you're never able to forget what he's done. I just want you to be honest with yourself about it. And know that I'm here for you." I sigh as he drags his stubble across my bare breasts. He brings one of my nipples to his mouth and sucks on it hard. I moan in response to his touch, then push him off me, laughing at the pouty expression on his face. "Did you even hear me?"

"Of course I did, I just get easily distracted by how beautiful you are." He smirks as I roll my eyes and slide out of bed. "Where are you going?"

"We have a meeting we're already running late to," I remind him. One that would potentially change the course of our lives.

He knows how nervous I've been about this, so instead of begging me to come back to bed, he stands up, places a kiss on my forehead, and gives me a reassuring hug. "Everything will work itself out. I promise."

———

Instead of meeting in the dining room at my father's mansion, we called our inner circles to the living room of our cottage. If we were going to start a new era of the Persian and Irish empires, we needed to build new traditions. My only hope is that everyone else will be on board.

Declan and I walk into the room hand in hand. He stiffens slightly at seeing his brother on the couch, sitting next to Lorkan, but keeps his expression calm. I'm the one who asked for Aidan to be here. If Lorkan's brash ways could be over-looked, given that his morals were actually aligned with my father and Cillian. I think it's fair to give Aidan a second chance, given that he was being blackmailed by the man who had manipulated all of us. I'm not sure Declan fully agrees with my perspective but he supported me nonetheless.

"Thank you all for coming. As you all know by now, my father and Cillian had a plan for both of our families. A plan where we would be less exposed to violence and treachery by removing ourselves from any illegal trades. We would shift to our main products being tea, whiskey, and surveillance tech-nology designed for the average family, maybe larger corpora-tions that align with our new goals, but no more gun trades. No more hacking into our enemies' databases and exposing their weaknesses. We would live a normal life. Or at least we would try to return to normal business. But only if we all agree," I state, locking eyes with each person in the room.

Azula's eyebrows knit together. "What?"

"While my father and Cillian's plans were well-intended, they failed to consider those working for them and what they may feel. This would be a big shift, one we want to make, but only if our inner circles are in agreement. The transition won't be easy; we'll likely have to change our spending patterns. And neither of us is naive enough to think the other mafia will just leave us alone, so security will have to remain tight, if not even higher than before. But we plan on keeping everyone who wants to remain working for us. We have enough funds in our bank accounts to support all our employees for the foreseeable future." I lay out all the logistics before finally taking a deep breath.

"You're really serious about this?" Azula looks like she's going into shock.

"I am. We are." I correct, squeezing Declan's hand. "But only if everyone else is on board. If not, we'll just continue to keep business as usual. Or as usual as it can be."

Before I killed Cyrus, we'd tortured everything we could have out of him—the names of all the people in our ranks who had betrayed us, what other mafias had supported his attempt at usurping me and Declan, and all the other lies he's told us. While things still didn't feel fully settled, we at least felt comfortable enough knowing everyone who betrayed us was either dead or would be soon.

Azula stands. "Can I talk to you for a moment? Privately."

I follow her out into the hall and wait for her to start. "Why are you doing this, Z? This is going to change everything."

"I know, but I feel it in my heart that this is what we should do. It's what my dad would have wanted. I only wish he was alive to see it." Though there was a strong part of me that feels he's looking over me now, that he's proud of what I'm trying to do.

Azula looks like she's...nervous. An expression that doesn't belong on her face.

"What is it, Azula? Tell me."

"Your new life... I don't fit in. All I know is destruction. All I am is a killer," she grits through her teeth, head hanging down in shame.

My heart aches for my best friend. Is that really how she sees herself? I bring her into my arms, squeezing her into a hug. "Azula, you are fierce, and strong, and so freaking brilliant. There is no version of my life where you don't fit perfectly in it. We'll just have to adjust. Learn how to fix our problems with words and not knives," I tease.

"Lame," she retorts, returning my hug. "Thanks, Zahra. I needed that."

"Anytime."

We return to the room, Azula is the first to speak. "Zahra has my full support. No questions asked. Always and forever." She smiles at me, though I can still see a hint of hesitation in her eyes. Change takes time to adjust to. But we would have each other.

Lorkan swallows hard, toying anxiously with the cuffs of his sleeve, "This is all your fathers wanted. All the three of us wanted. And yet...I can't say I ever believed for certain it *would* happen. Or that I would be alive to see it carried out." Lorkan smiles at me, though it doesn't quite meet the pain in his eyes, "I'm in favor of working toward this new future. I just wish Naser and Cillian were here to see it."

My throat tightens, and I nod at Lorkan, knowing if I speak, my voice would crack and reveal my lingering grief. Declan grabs my elbow as a subtle reminder that he's here. A reminder that we're in this together.

Arman is the next to speak. "You and your family have always had my unwavering support."

"You *are* my family, Arman," I correct, placing a hand on his shoulder.

I turn to Connor, who was recently promoted to Declan's head of security, given how valuable he was in rescuing me.

He blinks, "I get a vote?"

"You're a part of our inner circle now," Declan confirms.

"Then I vote yes." Connor smiles awkwardly, clearly not expecting any of this.

The final person left is Aidan, who is still recovering from his injury. Declan looks down at his shoes as Aidan addresses me, "First, I want to apologize to you, Zahra. And to my brother. For all the pain I've caused you both. I will do whatever I can to make up for it. Second, I am fully on board to start a new life. I think we all agree the mafia world has taken enough from us."

"Yes, it certainly has. I accept your apology, Aidan. The second you took the bullet for me, I considered us even." Which was true. Declan's forgiveness was a separate case. One I couldn't force.

Aidan's face falls as he realizes the same.

"Alright then, let's end here. We can our various financial officers join us for a meeting soon where we can plot out making this transition as smoothly as possible."

I lean my head against Declan's shoulder as everyone leaves. He gives my waist a quick squeeze before standing up from the couch. "I have something I want to show you. I've been working on it for a while."

He leads me outside, then has me cover my eyes with my hands, keeping a hand on my waist to guide me through our backyard.

"Alright, you can open your eyes," he hums, standing behind me, arms wrapped around me.

My eyes take a second to adjust to the light before I take in the scenery in front of me—a cobblestone walkway that leads to an adorable stone bench at the end. The next thing I notice are the rows of rose bushes that frame the path, a mix of mine and my father's favorites. "I know this probably pales in comparison to the rose garden you grew up with but I figured we could start here and make it your own over time."

"It's perfect. Everything about this is perfect." Tears start to form in my eyes as I take in the sheer beauty of the garden. Take in what Declan has made for me. We walk hand in hand down the aisle, stopping every now and then to smell the blossoming roses, until we sit on the bench, Declan pulling me onto his lap.

"This must have taken so long to put together. When did you start?" I ask.

"Right after our meeting in your father's rose garden." He blushes.

"I hated you then. I was still convinced you'd killed my father," I groan, embarrassed at myself.

"I know, but I couldn't get you out of my head. Couldn't shake the feeling that we always belonged to each other." He presses his warm lips to my cheek.

"We brought each other out of the darkness and into the light. What greater life is there than one filled with love?" I ask, cupping his face in my hands.

"To living life. And choosing love," he declares, locking our lips together. I relish his touch, the scent of the roses around us, and the warm, gentle glow of the sun, which shines nearly as bright as the love we have for each other.

EPILOGUE
ZAHRA

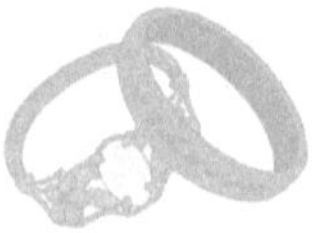

"I can't believe we already have to head back," I groan, looking at the calendar. It's our final day of the honeymoon, which Declan insisted we take. I initially reassured him I didn't need it, largely because I was afraid of leaving this new era unmonitored back home. But now I was the one whining about our incredible trip coming to an end.

Declan had given me the grand tour of Ireland, castles, hikes, and small towns that looked like they belonged in a snow globe. The best part was how normal I felt on the whole trip. While our security team was present, they'd done an excellent job keeping themselves hidden and out of sight. Our escape from reality was much needed and I couldn't help but be bummed that things were coming to an end.

"Are you sure you don't want to do any more sightseeing today? We have time to squeeze something in," Declan checks.

"I'm sure. As much as I loved how much we've done these past few days, I need a day to just rot by the pool." The villa Declan brought us to not only has an incredible view of the coast but also a lovely heated pool I've been dying to take advantage of. "Care to join me?" I toss my cover-up to the side, revealing my bikini that shows way more skin than it covers.

Declan's jaw falls open and I give him a little spin. He looks ready to pounce on me when his phone rings. He shoves it aside, but I shake my head, excited about getting to tease him.

"Arman is calling. You should definitely get that. I'll be waiting for you by the pool." I wink, hearing him grumble, and pick up the phone as I head outside.

Another plus of this villa? It's incredibly secluded. I'd never felt comfortable enough to be naked at home, but out here I know no one will see me. I slide off my swimsuit and lay down on the pool chair. The warm sun feels incredible on my body. I lose track of how long I lay there, falling in and out of sleep until the sun goes away, causing my nipples to peak at the change in temperature.

My eyes open and I realize it isn't the clouds that had covered the sun, it's Declan. "How long have you been laying here naked, Zahra?" Declan growls, crawling on top of my body and immediately toying with my hard nipple.

"Since you've been on the phone. What took you so long?" I moan, arching my back into his touch as he takes my breast into his hand and squeezes it gently.

"Azula and Aidan got in a fight again. He wanted to let me know how I should handle it, and you know, he's terrified of her, so any solution that involved confronting Azula was a no-go for him. I should have just let the damn call go to voicemail or better yet tossed my phone in the fucking pool."

"That sounds like a waste—oh yes, Declan, please." I grip his shoulders hard as he uses his thumb to toy with my clit.

"Does that feel good, love?" He slides two fingers inside me, drawing a loud moan in response from my lips. "Fuck we should move this inside, someone might see."

Despite his words, Declan continues to work his fingers inside me at a torturous pace. He angles his fingers so they rub against my G-spot with each stroke, all while he gives my clit the perfect amount of pressure and attention it needs.

"No one else lives out here," I remind him, wrapping my hand around his wrist. "Now fuck me like you mean it," I beg, tired of his slow, methodical pace.

"We don't have any neighbors, but the security we hired may hear us." Declan speeds up his pace. The warning should encourage me to stop, but instead, more wetness pools down my thighs at the thought of someone watching us come together. "Jesus, Zahra, you're soaking my hand even more now. Is that what you're into, love? Having someone watch us while I turn you into a sobbing mess filled with my cum?" Declan asks, sounding proud of me.

The more time we're together, the more I feel confident in my sexuality and in speaking up for what I need. I never thought I'd be a kinky person but Declan makes me feel so safe and respected, which draws out so many different sides of me. "I've never really thought I'd be into being watched, but now that I'm thinking of it...It makes me really, really hot," I confess, bucking my hips to match Declan's relentless pace. He pinches my clit just how I like it, and before I know it, my core clenches, and I come all over his fingers.

"My beautiful wife, you look so good coming on my fingers," he moans, licking my wetness off his skin. He moves his hands up and down my legs, massaging my thighs. "I could take you to a club if you're interested. Completely anonymous," he offers.

"A club?" I ask, having a strong feeling he didn't mean the normal clubs you can go to.

"A sex club. We could fuck each other while everyone else watches. If that sounds like something you would want to do?"

My nipples hardening and wetness pooling from between my legs serve as my initial response, but I have questions. "I don't want anyone else touching me. Or you."

Declan's jaw clenches at the thought. "Hard agree. We may be trying to live a new life, but I have no problems killing anyone who touches what is mine. We'd go into a section of the club where it's clear we only want to be watched. Nothing more. But only if you want to."

"I want to. That sounds incredible," I moan, rubbing my thighs together. "But not nearly as incredible as the thought of you sliding your cock inside me now," I beg, spreading my legs.

Declan's eyes lock on me, mesmerized, but he shakes his head. "Only good girls get to come on my cock. And you were very naughty, stripping naked when I wasn't around. Which means you need to be punished."

He slides off the chair and extends a hand, which I gleefully take. All of Declan's punishments involve me having multiple orgasms and him continuously checking in about my safe word so I felt in full control. He pulls us into the room, depositing me on our bed

"We'll have to head out to dinner soon, so I'll leave you to get ready in a second. But first, why don't you bend that cute ass over my dresser?" Declan orders before walking into his closet.

I follow his orders, feeling exposed but also excited. When he returns to our bedroom, he has a wicked smile on his face, and a small metal ball and a pair of my panties in his hand. He drags the ball up and down my core before sliding it inside and helping me step into my underwear.

"Stand up, Zahra," he instructs and I do as I'm told, expecting to struggle, but feeling pretty normal. "You're going to keep that inside you the entire time we're in the restaurant until we get back home. You can always use your safe word, though, understood?"

I nod, taking a few steps around the room as I adjust to the feeling. "Is this it? Seems pretty tame."

He raises an eyebrow. "Let's see if you'll be saying that by the end of the night, my wife."

———

I'm not sure if Declan was lying in hopes that the anticipation would be enough to get me aroused or if he highly overestimated how much I would like this toy, but so far, I've essentially forgotten it's there.

We'd just been seated in a secluded booth, its round shape allowing for additional privacy, in the Michelin-star restaurant. This place apparently has served a lot of big-name clientele that appreciate anonymity, so orders are all placed on a tablet. Each table is connected to the kitchen downstairs and the food basically takes its own elevator ride up to our table that opens in the middle for us to take our plates. The idea is futuristic and overly pretentious, but Declan insisted the food was some of the best he's had.

I'm scrolling through the menu when I freeze. The ball buried deep inside my core starts to vibrate, making me squeeze my thighs together. The movement causes the toy inside of me to brush up against my G-spot, and I moan so loud that Declan clamps a hand around my mouth. "Quiet love, just because these booths obscure us from any wandering eyes doesn't mean they don't have ears."

The vibrator inside me must have a mind of its own

because it quickens in pace, causing my core to clench, and my hips to buck under the table. I can feel my wetness pool down my thighs and I send out a silent thank you to the universe that I decided to wear a long dress that ends right above my ankles.

My eyes shut close as my pussy continues to be tormented and I feel Declan's lips at my ear. "You can come, sweet wife, you just have to promise to keep quiet, alright? I can't have all these people here know what a dirty little thing you are."

Whether it's Declan's words or the reminder that we're in a room filled with people that sets me over the edge, I can't be sure. I lean my head against the soft velvet of the booth, locking eyes with Declan, his large hand still covering my mouth as I come so hard I feel the aftershock building immediately after it, and I fall over twice in less than a minute.

The buzzing stops immediately and Declan lifts his hand so he can bring a glass of ice water to my lips. "I don't think a toy has ever made you come that hard before. Or maybe it wasn't the toy. Maybe it's the fact that we're in public."

I'm too spent to respond so instead I drink the water and rest my cheek on his chest as he orders some food for us. "Does it have a timer?" I ask, leaning into his touch as he strokes my scalp.

Declan shakes his head. "No. It's remote-operated." He removes his hand from his pocket to reveal a small remote inside.

I swallow hard. "I'm in for a long night, aren't I?"

The wicked look in his eyes is all I need in response. Declan leaves my question verbally unanswered, choosing to use his actions instead, always when I least expect it. He makes me come right as the food arrives, claiming he didn't want me to burn my tongue on the hot meal. I orgasm again when we send our plates back after finishing, and a third time, a few bites into dessert. Following each orgasm, Declan always takes the time to check in on me, making sure I'm hydrated and praised with his words of affection.

I stare at the half-eaten chocolate cake in front of me, a mix of satiated and desperate for more. "Do you not like the cake? I can have them send something else." Declan brushes a loose strand of my hair out of my face.

"The cake is delicious, but there's something else that I want."

"The sundae? Let me put the order in—Zahra. What are you doing?" Declan reaches for my hands that are currently undoing the button of his dress pants.

"I need you buried inside me, dear husband," I whisper, filling with satisfaction as he drops my hands. Declan may know all my weaknesses, but I also know his. All I had to do was call him husband and he'd let me do whatever I wanted.

"Are you sure? If someone sees us, we could get in a lot of trouble." His words say one thing, but his actions say another as he pulls me in between his legs and lifts my dress out of the way.

"The booth has an additional curtain you can adjust. I saw the setting on the tablet," I state, messing around with the buttons on the screen until a curtain covers the small entrance of the booth.

"You knew about this the whole time, and still let me play with you out in the open," Declan tsks but his tone is filled with pride. "My naughty wife," he chastises before lifting my hips, removing the toy inside me, and sinking me onto his rigid cock.

"Oh fuck, Declan," I moan into his shoulder, doing my best to keep my voice down. I lean my forehead against his and we both watch as he thrusts in and out of me over and over again.

"Be sure to keep that mouth of yours quiet. I know you like to be loud, but you can't be right now. When we get home, though, I want your screams to fill the villa." He removes his hand from my waist for a second to give me a small smack on the ass. It's enough to send me jolting forward, g-spot rubbing against his piercing.

I can't come up with anything intelligible, so instead I moan, "Home?" into his ear.

"We'll go home soon, my love, I promise. I know you want to let loose. But first, I need to feel this tight pussy squeeze my cock and take every drop of cum I have to give. Can you do that for me?" he asks, settling his cock back inside me, this time rubbing it against my G-spot.

"Yes. Yes. Right there, Declan, right there...oh fuck, fuck I'm coming. I'm—" Declan grabs my face, silencing me with a kiss as I feel his hot cum fill me. I don't think I'll ever get used to this feeling, the sensation of him owning every part of my body while also prioritizing my own pleasure. He's perfect.

Declan lets out a satisfied hum as he comes down from his orgasm. He pulls out and tugs my panties into place so the fabric can hold his cum inside me. "Finish your cake, love, and then we'll go home."

I do what he says, unable to control my giggles as he tosses the curtain aside and lifts me into his arms bridal style. Most of the patrons in the restaurant ignore us, and the ones that do look send us sweet smiles, clearly unaware of what we had just done.

Declan keeps his promise of making me a screaming pile of want and need when we return home, taking me to the bathroom, eating me out in the kitchen (*'his dessert'*), and making love to me one last time in the villa. The next morning, I wake up deliciously sore as we head to our jet.

As the plane takes off, I'm gripping the armrest. Hard. Flying has never been an issue for me before, but after being kidnapped by Cyrus, being in a plane set me on edge.

Declan places his warm hand on top of mine, and I slowly start to relax. "It's alright, Zahra, you're safe."

"It's funny how small the world looks from here. Instead of how vast it truly is. If I didn't have the tracker on me, who knows how long it would have taken for you to find me."

"It doesn't matter how big or small the world is. There's not a single corner of this universe I wouldn't turn over to get to you."

"That does remind me though. I got this for you." I pull the necklace with the dog tag attached out of my pocket. "I figured since you can track me now, it's only fair I can do the same."

Declan beams, tracing the Farsi inscription over with his thumb. "What does it say?"

"One of the few things I can actually read in Farsi. A poem by Hafiz. It says, *'Your heart and my heart are very old friends.'*" I place a hand over Declan's heart.

He does the same to me. "Always," he declares.

"Always," I promise.

THE END.

BEHIND THE BOOK

A rough vision of the opening scene of this book one random night in my head when I 17-18 years old. From the moment I envisioned a strong woman being underestimated and in plain sight, and one man who from the beginning knew she was the real threat in the room, I knew one day I would write that scene, and more importantly write this book. The Devil and Her Details, is thus not only a long term passion project for me, but also a book where I was able to let go and have so much fun. I love my hockey/contemporary romance books, but there's something about the mafia/dark romance space that makes me feel an additional layer of freedom. I knew that I could have my characters act out in rage and violence and have it be more understood. I think this was particularly healing for me, because a majority of this book was written when I was (probably still am), very angry at the world.

Unlike Zahra and Declan who can fix their problems with fists and bullets, I, like many others in our current political situation in the U.S., have to force ourselves to move on day by day while we watch so many of our loved ones, friends, and community members be attacked for the color of their skin, their immigration status, their sexuality, their gender, etc. The real world is messy and justice doesn't always prevail. The Devil and Her Details is also filled with a world that is messy, and characters like Zahra and Declan who don't always do the right thing. But they still have hope that they can do better. That they can be better. Some of my personal anger definitely spilled through the pages of the dark nature of this book, but I also hope that my desire for a better life. A desire for a world that is accepting and just also comes through. Zahra and Declan end knowing that their future will likely be stressful, unpredictable, and hard... but also that it's a future worth fighting for. Because they deserve better. I hope this book can be an outlet for my readers who are also angry or frustrated, but most importantly, I hope this book can also inspire. Channel the anger into action and change. That's what I try to do. That's what brings me hope for the future.

ACKNOWLEDGMENTS

This section truly could (and maybe should) be a book in itself. Every time I go to write an acknowledgement page I feel like I can never do anyone justice. A 'thank you' simply doesn't feel like enough, but I hope it at least shows how much you mean to me!

To Kelly my ride or die, thank you for driving me around for my first book tour, and for always being there for me. Love you always.

To Alexa for always jumping to read my messy and typo-filled drafts even when you're in the middle of a reading slump.

To Ellie, Emma, and Sierra Si., thank you for helping me manage my social media and scream about my books so I can have more time to write. Also thanks for talking me off a ledge whenever I'm in full panic mode.

To Emilia for tolerating all my texts when I'm stressed about being an author/therapist/flopping at pottery. Your insights about bookish things and playing with dirt are always so helpful!

To Elizianna for making this INCREDIBLE cover that I will cherish forever.

To all the incredible folks at Heartbond Bookshop for being the first bookstore to stock my books and host my first ever signing.

To A and J for being the first readers to ever show up to my signings, and always having my back. And M for always screaming in my DMs and checking up on me. I feel so special to have you some of the best readers ever supporting me.

To Willow for being the cutest cat ever and always snuggling me whenever I am stressed (which is often).

To Erin for somehow tolerating me (and all my nightly rants) as a roommate.

And last, but certainly not least, thank YOU for reading this book and supporting me. I couldn't do any of this without you!

With Love,
    Mina Myles

ABOUT THE AUTHOR

Mina Myles is a romance author by night and PhD student by day. Her home base is Southern California, but if you've read one of Mina's books then you know her heart is still in Boston.

Mina's characters will have you kicking your feet, but don't move the tissue box too far because pain and angst are never too far behind. After all, what's the sweet without a dash of salt and a little spice?

To be the first to know about future releases sign up to her newsletter: minamylesbooks.com/newsletter

You can also find her on
Instgram: @minamylesbooks
TikTok: @minamylesauthor

ALSO BY MINA MYLES

Stay tuned for more Dark Romances from me!

For readers who also enjoy contemporary (while still angsty and spicy) romances you can check out:

Outplayed (Westchester U Book 1)

The Ice Out (Castle Harbor Book 1)

Troped (By Mina Myles & Sierra Spencer)

www.ingramcontent.com/pod-product-compliance
Lightning Source LLC
Chambersburg PA
CBHW031202310726

48969CB00001B/186